T0198812

NO PAIN, NO GAIN

Memoirs of a Muscle-Head

TOBY LEWIS

authorHOUSE®

AuthorHouse™
1663 Liberty Drive
Bloomington, IN 47403
www.authorhouse.com
Phone: 1 (800) 839-8640

Published by AuthorHouse 05/17/2018

ISBN: 978-1-5462-4090-7 (sc)
ISBN: 978-1-5462-4089-1 (e)

Library of Congress Control Number: 2018905380

Print information available on the last page.

MY BROTHER-IN-LAW WOULD more than one time say to me, "Dude, if you tell this story to a person that don't know you, no way will anyone ever believe it's true.

My name is Mike Dunn, and I'm just a bartender with an incredible story to tell. Every man has a story to tell, mine is just unbelievably incredible. I graduated from high school in the top ten percent of my class, and one of the most highly recruited defensive tackles in the state of Texas. My life before high school I owe to the saving grace of Jesus Christ and the parents of my childhood best friend Paul Maples. Paul is white, I am black, we met in the year of nineteen sixty-six, two years after the equal rights amendment was signed by President Lyndon B. Johnson, who we were all proud to say was a Texan. Though the laws were signed, this was still Texas and Jim Crow was not going quietly into the night, but people like Paul and his parents excepted the progress society was making and went with it. The initial breech of the color barrier was not made in the classrooms of the south, but the sports fields of the south. Though Paul and I went to separate segregated schools in the small Texas town of Angleton, we'd met a year prior to the signing of the Civil Rights Act, playing in the county pee-wee football league. The kids from the black neighborhoods played in the same league as the kids from the white side of town, so even before they were schooled together most of the players knew each other from Saturday football games. Paul's father coached his team, the Brazoria Blue Devils, and no matter the outcome of the game, Coach Louis Maples saw to it that the kids shook hands with the opposition and afterwards joined him and his kids at the local Dairy King for ice cream treats. The tension was always there because up to now, these kids rarely had personal contact with people of a different color, but Coach Maples just seemed to know what he was doing would be impactful. Most of the players avoided any contact with the kids of another race other than was required by the coaches, a handshake, a pat on the back, or a good game gesture. Everyone ate their ice cream and burgers in their separate segregated groups, making for a good public picture on the surface. An occasional fight would break out between the boys who cared little for racial harmony, with the fights quickly being squashed by the coaches and parents.

1

Paul Maples, on the other hand, was much like his father and never allowed himself to get involved in racial squabbles. I could never tell if his reluctance was due to his father's presence, or if he was really a good person.

The following year, the pee-wee league charter was amended, and the administrators voted to integrate the ten-team conference, creating quite a ruckus from some of the sterner white parents. The Federal Government had driven home its message to integrate all the public schools despite the sometimes violent resistance from the whites in the south. Though I wasn't aware of it, Coach Maples saw me as one of the exceptional players, so when the coaches assembled all the players for try-outs the next season, he picked me as his first black player, to my utter surprise. Each team had to have at the minimum five negro players. I just accepted it as the luck of the draw, and my mind was set to make the best of it. Football and boy scouts were my escape from what most would consider a terrible home life by today's standards. My mother was what the other mothers in the Black community referred to as the "village bicycle", meaning every man in town had taken a ride on her, in other words, she was the town tramp. Sometimes forgetting that I was in the next room playing with their own kids, I often heard the other mothers commenting on something ungodly my own mother had done. I carried this shame around like a bale of wet hay, and my only solace was to lose myself in my sports which put me emotionally in another world. My mother had six children, me being the second youngest, all six being sired by a different man. There were other kids in town born out of wedlock, so this was not a distinction I carried alone. The difference was the other kids knew who their fathers were. My mother either did not know or chose not to tell me only to keep some ungodly secret hidden, which ever, she took it to her grave with her. One of the rumors around town was she slept with the husband of her older sister out of pure meanness, and the burden of her sin was mine to carry. The many stepfathers I had always seemed to be more preoccupied with abusing me than being her man. My release from the abuse was to spend as much time away from home during the day as possible. I participated in every school activity possible to keep from having to go home until late in the evening. During the summer months, I would haul hay or tend to the hogs of one of my mother's former lovers, who was a pig farmer, to earn a dollar. All of which I held on to, to cover the cost of pee-wee football registration and things I needed to be in the boy scouts.

My mother was an awful person, but like all little boys, I sought the love of a mother, and refused to believe she would always be that terrible human being, I could not have been more wrong.

The Reverend Martin Luther King Jr. was assassinated the second year I played in the integrated pee-wee football program, being children, understanding the impact of the murder was not as tragic as it was to the adults. I felt the sadness of the grown-ups, but the personal hell my own world was in did not allow me to mourn Dr. King the way everyone else did. The shock I felt the day Paul Maples walked over to me at school to tell me how sorry he and his family were about Kings death was mind blowing to say the least. I thanked him for showing that he cared, but at the same time I was dealing with my mother's most recent boyfriend who was coming into my room at night and doing awful things to me. I pleaded with my mother to save me from the things the monster was doing to me, but if sacrificing me was the cost to keep her man, then so be it. She called me a liar and told me if it were true, I would get over it. This was the point in my life my love for my mother began to dissipate, and I sunk deep into sports and school activities. Paul's mother, a saint of a woman, headed an organization that set up activities for the mentally retarded citizens in the county and she needed help from some of the local youth. I volunteered my time, not just to be helpful, but to have a reason to spend more time away from my own hell. Me, and Paul along with his older brother and sister grew to be friends in the program. They were the first white people I actually knew other than the rednecks I went out of my way to avoid. Race relations in the schools had not gotten past the point of human civility, Dr. King's death had broken through many social barriers, but America still had a long way to go, especially in the southern states. Me and Paul grew to be not only team mates on the junior high football team, but real friends, causing a stir from his white friends and my black friends. The summer program called "the Brazoria County Teens aid to the Retarded" turned the kids in the program into a cohesive group despite color or race, we spent entire summers assisting in functions for the mentally challenged all over the state. The Shriver family, an extension of the Kennedy's, were heavily involved in forming events aimed at helping the mentally challenged so the Brazoria County TAR's were suddenly something bigger than a group of teenagers spending quality time with the mentally retarded people.

My mother met another man, which she married, and we moved across town to a mobile home park that rented trailer space to families of color if there was someone white to vouch for the negro family. The man my mother married worked for the man who was part owner of the trailer park which to my surprise resulted in me becoming a pawn in my new stepfather's game of bullshit.

The trailer park was at the outskirts of town just outside the city limits, and anyone living beyond this line was not eligible for city trash pick up. Mother's new husband, as part of allowing him to park his trailer and new family in the park, signed on to become the community garbage man, which meant I was his only employee. The new husband was a cruel degenerative man from the start. He cheated on my mother with other women in this small town where there were no secrets. She seemed to stick her head in the ground like an ostrich like nothing was happening. I once mentioned it to her thinking she would see the light, and take us away from this uncaring person, instead, she silenced me and immediately informed the man of what I said. The next day, I came in from school to find him waiting for me with clenched fists and in a rage over what he considered a betrayal by me. At the age of twelve, I took a beating that would have maimed a full-grown man, as my mother stood there and watched uncaring. My sister, a year younger still living with us attempted to intervene but was restrained by our own mother as the man continued to pummel me with blows to the face and upper torso. What I did not know, at the time, was that same sibling was being violated sexually by this same man who was mercilessly beating me right before our mother's eyes, my mother never lifted a finger to save either of us from this monster. Eventually the punches ceased, and then came the verbal assault, as I sat on the floor watching my mother through swollen, teary eyes waiting still for her to do something, anything to show some sign of caring. All was in vain, the man screaming in my face as if I were a man myself forbidding me to participate in any more after school sporting activities. I was to come home immediately after school to be his helper picking up the trailer park garbage and the household refuse from two subdivisions down the road from where we lived. One of those subdivisions was where the Maples family lived, and the first day we turned onto Meadowview Lane, all the Maples kids were out in the street playing kick ball. Paul looked up to see me on top of the trash filled dump truck emptying the garbage cans as my stepfather was tossing them up, and he walked over to ask why I hadn't been at school the past few days. My face was so badly beaten and distorted, my dear mother would not allow me to attend school. Under the glare of my stepfather's eyes, I concocted a quick lie,

"I fell off the back of the truck and hurt my head the other day I told Paul."

This lie would also explain the battered condition of my face and head, I should be okay to come back to school in a couple of days. Say hi to your folks for me, I said as the truck pulled away to the next house."

On the way home from the county dump that same evening, the stepfather turned off the highway onto a dirt road with three or four houses and pulled into the drive of the third house. After shutting the engine down, the man gave me a steely glare.

"You stay here until I get back, I got some business to take care of that don't concern you or your momma," the man growled at me.

I'd fallen asleep after a while to be awakened by the sound of a woman's voice. I opened my eyes to see through the haze of the front porch lamps, my stepfather hugging and giving a kiss on the mouth to the fattest, most disgusting white woman I had ever seen.

"The man got into the truck and before even touching the ignition key, turned to me and said in a threatening tone, your mother catch wind of this and you going to get more of what you got the other day boy, you hear me?" I said nothing in response and just kept looking through the front windshield unmoving and uncaring about him or my mother. I lived with the shame and humiliation of picking up the garbage of my school mates and friends along with the beatings for the rest of the year and on through the summer. My sister, at the age of thirteen, ran off with a man some eight years older than she was and, my mother made no attempt to bring her back home. I occasionally would run into her around town, and she would say how

4

sorry she was about having to leave me behind, but she'd taken all the raping and watching me being beaten up that she could. She and the man she took off with were married now and expecting their first child. My sister seemed happy and I had no hard feelings, I was happy for her.

Me and Paul had I guess become true friends, on the days I didn't have to work for my stepfather, I'd walk the mile from the trailer park over to the subdivision to his house to play with he and his brothers and sisters.

One day he just up and said, "Mike, my parents are concerned that you always got bruises on your face and the only time we ever see you is when you and that stepdaddy of yours come through here to pick up the garbage. You quit the track squad and you didn't even make it to the baseball tryouts this summer. Daddy's even worried that you won't be playing football this year. You know he thinks you're the best player in town, that's why he always picked you to play on the Blue Devils pee-wee team."

I thought for a minute before answering.

"I'll be coming out for the seventh-grade team this year Paul I said, my stepfather is a mean one and he makes me work almost everyday and I don't even get paid."

"Momma and Daddy said if you need help Mike, all you got to do is say so, they said the law won't allow them to interfere unless you say you're in some kind of danger". Not wanting to make trouble for my mother, I remained silent about the abuse.

"I'll be alright Paul, and you can tell your Daddy, me and you will be the two best Wampuscats on that Jr. High squad this year". My mind was made up though, no matter what the price, I was going to be on that seventh-grade football team.

Right near the end of the summer, Paul's mother, Pat, unexpectedly showed up at the trailer house. Paul had asked me earlier that week if I would like to go on a camping trip with his family before the end of the summer.

"Sure, I said, but I'd have to okay it with my mother first".

For fear of what her husband might have to say about it, I never breached the subject, so Paul never got my answer to his invite. His mom pulled into our driveway one evening and tooted the car horn to get my attention. I was messing around with some free weights scattered around the front yard. I put the barbell down and walked out to greet her. I was quite shocked she was here; she'd never been to our house.

"How you doing Mrs. Maples I said as she got out of her green Chevrolet?"

"Hello Michael, she answered, are your folks here, I was hoping I could have a word with them?"

"Yes ma'am, they're here, let me get them for you". I bound up the front steps and went inside to get my mother. Both her and her husband turned white as a sheet, I know they were thinking I'd told someone about the beatings he was subjecting me to. My mother also stood with the stupidest look on her face and stepped towards the front door. Mother came down the steps and shook hands with this white lady who she'd never met. Mother never attended any of my activities so none of the other parents knew her.

"Hello Mrs. Reeves, greeted Pat Maples, I'm Paul Maples mother, he and your son played pee-wee football together last year and Mike helps out with our program for the mentally challenged kids."

"What can I do for you Mrs. Maples, asked my mother awkwardly?"

"Paul invited Mike to go camping with us at Garner State Park in a few days, he said he would have to okay it with you first. We haven't heard back from him yet, so I thought I'd swing by on my way home from work to check with you, we're leaving Friday morning."

By now the stepfather is out on the front porch after hearing the visit was not about his abuse.

"He's never mentioned nothing about no camping trip to us, he said."

This is my husband Willie; said mother.

"How long is this camping trip? asked the man. this boy has work to do that can't be ignored."

"We've seen him on the truck with you all summer, don't y'all think the kid could use a little break before school starts? responded Mrs. Maples."

Caught off guard by her knowing who he was, all my stepfather could say was, "if it's okay with his mother, I guess he can miss a few days of work."

That six days at Garner State Park were, up to that point in my existence on this planet, were the greatest, most blessed days of my life. Me and the Maples kids celebrated life in a way I never knew existed. I was taught how to water ski by Paul and his brothers, we hiked the Hill Country trails, it was a world I never knew existed. I sat on an inner-tube floating down the river looking up at the beautiful Texas sky thinking, so this is what being a family is supposed be like. From that week onward, I swore to my soul that I would love these people the rest of my life. I'd gone to some camp outs in the boy scouts, but it was nothing like this. Louis and Pat Maples treated me like one of their own, and I loved them for opening my world up and allowing me to be a kid.

The summer came to an end, and I headed off to Junior High school with a joyous heart. After the first day of classes, I went straight to the field house with the rest of the kids who'd signed up to play sports. The hell with it, I thought, I'll just have to suffer the consequences, but no way was I going to let this evil man and my mother stop me from living my dreams. I took the beatings for not coming home after school to work on the garbage truck, even though my mother demanded that I do so. I told my stepfather I'd be happy to help him on the weekends, and once football season came to an end. The beatings eventually came to an end, I guess they grew tired of fighting a losing battle. I spent every minute I could at the Maples house just to avoid my own and dealing with two people I'd grown to despise. As I look back, I am thinking Paul's parents knew what was going on and their way of helping me was to never tell me to take my ass home. The first year of junior high was fun, other than my hassles at home, me and Paul got as close as two blood brothers. He played middle linebacker and I played defensive end. I grew two inches in height and added fifteen pounds of muscle to my frame, finally, I thought, I'm turning into a man. The stepfather and I hardly spoke a word to each other when I was at home. I worked as his helper on weekends, but our conversations never went beyond work talk. The man knew I hated his guts, I didn't completely shun my mother because like I said from the start, a boy wants the love of a mother, no matter how little or much.

Paul's parents, despite having five children of their own, seemed to possess enough affection to shower me with as much love as their own and I loved them back. There were periods when I would spend two or three days a week at the Maples house. One day I showed up at the trailer to my mother in a pissy mood, I think she caught her husband cheating again, but I just didn't care how she felt. I lay across my bed and started reading through a Boy's Life magazine. I could hear them at the other end of the trailer arguing, so I focused on blocking them out by turning on the radio. Suddenly, my bedroom door crashed open, it was my stepfather demanding that I get outside and wash his new pick-up truck. I guess I wasn't moving fast enough for him, so he grabbed me by the shirt and shoved me towards the door. I turned on him like a cornered bobcat and smashed him in the face with the most vicious overhand right I could muster. He recovered quickly and went on the attack, which I expected so I braced myself for what was coming next. The added muscle and height was a big help when it came time to absorb the attack, but still he out weighed me by fifty pounds, and was a more experienced fighter. This was the first time though, that afterwards it wasn't such a one-sided battle. My clothing was not just covered in my blood, but mostly from the busted nose I had given him. And whose aide did my mother go to? Her man, while she berated me for fighting back and busting his nose. While she tended his wounds, I changed my shirt, and headed out the door. Still in a fit of rage, I pulled out my Swiss Army knife and slashed two tires on his new truck as I left our driveway. It was as if Pat Maples could feel my pain as I entered her garage, where she was busy doing laundry. All she did was, without speaking a word, took me to the bathroom and tended to my injuries. She gave me two aspirins and I slept for the rest of the day. Two days later, I returned to the trailer to find a letter from my mother on the coffee table informing me that her husband was no longer going to put up with my disobedience, and that they'd moved to Baytown. Someone will be here in a week to take the trailer away, she added. I didn't see my mother again for five years, and of all places, at my high school graduation. I didn't leave the trailer for two days, I was so confused, not knowing at all what I was going to do. After not seeing me in school for two days, Paul showed up at the trailer looking for me. I showed him the letter from my mother and watched him read it with a confused look on his face.

"I'll be back Mike", he told me, I'm going to get Mom; she'll know what to do."

He jumped on his bike and peddled in the direction of Meadowview Lane. Forty-five minutes later, Pat Maples' green Chevy pulled into the drive, I pushed open the front door to greet her, Paul and her oldest daughter Martha.

"Paul and Martha are going to help you put your things in the car. You can live with us until your mother comes to her senses." She was the kind of woman who could not possibly conceive of a mother abandoning her child for her man the way mine had. I had known this woman for a little under three years, and she was more of a mother to me than my own had ever been.

CHAPTER
TWO

ME AND PAUL went on to have stellar high school football careers with all district and all-state honors, the college recruiters flooded the Maples home by the dozens. Paul went off to Southwest Texas State, in the city of San Marcos, Texas, I chose to follow a girl I was dating to a historically black college called Prairie View A&M in a Texas town of the same name. Me and Paul and another pal from Angleton, had over the years grown an affection for a band called The Grateful Dead. The pal, a guy named Frank Hargis, kept up with the tour schedule of the band, so during the summer break, we'd get together and follow the band around the country for a couple of months on our motorcycles. It was the seventies and it seemed that life in America could not have been more excellent for three free spirited knuckleheads like us.

Me and Paul would have to leave around the middle of July to return to our schools to begin training for the upcoming football season. The second year at Prairie View, I broke my collarbone during two a day workouts, along with that bad turn, the girl I followed to the school, met somebody new during the summer and dropped me like a bad habit, things were not going well for me. Feeling down on myself, and my shoulder not healing fast enough, I decided I should take a break from school and take off to the city.

Another pal from high school had taken a scholarship to the University of Houston, J. D. had wanted me to go to U of H with him and he ragged me endlessly for following the chick to tiny Prairie View. That didn't spoil me and J. D.'s friendship though, he saw my injury as a sign from above and suggested I move to Houston to live with him in his apartment off campus paid for by his parents.

"My dad thinks you should have come here in the first place J. D. told me, he says you and I was the most prefect guard – tackle combination in the state and he thinks we should have stayed in tandem. You get a piece of a job somewhere close to campus to tide you over while you rehabilitate that shoulder and it will be easy for you to walk-on at U of H next season, they don't got a defensive tackle as good as you here, it'll be a cake walk he said."

I did manage to get a job as a bartender at a little pub near campus where J. D.'s girlfriend was a waitress and he cleared it with the strength coach for me to use the football facilities to rehab my shoulder. J. D. was right, I walked on to the team and was right where I was in high school, next to J. D. on the Cougar defensive line cracking heads. I kept that bartending job though, there was just something about it that I liked, and I took every shift I could manage to fit into playing ball. The strength coach at U of H also became one of the positive driving forces in my life. Jeff Madden went on to head two other prominent strength training programs in the college ranks. His contributions to the program at the University of Colorado under Coach Gill McCarthy led to that school winning a couple of national championships in the eighties. From there Jeff, who his peers called "Mad Dog" joined the staff at the University of Texas Longhorns, the most prestigious school in the state, also resulted in several successful seasons and an eventual national championship. The man definitely knew his stuff and to this day, I consider Mad Dog Madden my greatest mentor and a good friend. Over the years after my playing days were over, our paths would occasionally cross in a nightclub or some weight lifting or bodybuilding event. Despite Jeff's expertise at rebuilding my shoulder from the injury, my college football career was short lived. My collarbone never healed correctly and after two surgeries, I was done with football. My life in the nightclub business though was just beginning to hit its stride. I took a course at a city bartending school and afterwards submerged myself into the bar business. My initial plan was to end up in a place like the bar on the television show "Cheers". I'd always loved that show and I thought the ensemble cast was great, but I quickly learned that the real money in the bar business was not in the "good ole" neighborhood spots, but in the night clubs. The eighties were an excellent time to be a part of the club scene in Houston and if your plan was to make a living tending bar, the clubs are where a person had to be pouring whiskey. By the luck of the draw I hit the ground running, I made my way across town to the Richmond strip where the club business was really happening. A couple of football players I knew from our days in high school who'd gone pro, lived and trained in Houston during the off-season and had decided to invest some of their earnings in a night club on Richmond Avenue. Chris Cravens and Joe Koonce were the stars of the U of H football team the year I showed up on campus. They were regulars at the campus pub me and J. D.'s girlfriend Cindy worked at. Cindy was friends with a girl from school that Cravens was living with, that's how I was connected to them. The two guys played on teams in other parts of the country, so they thought it a good deal to have somebody they knew and trusted on sight to help keep an eye on their investment. I hired on as bar manager and head bartender. A former teammate of Joe's who'd blown his knee out and washed out of the league was manager of operations, he and I made a great team. He loved to talk, and I didn't mind taking care of the whole club. I wanted to be successful in this business and if taking on a ton of responsibilities was what it took, then that I thought was the price I had to pay. I thought Joe's friend drank too much, but what the hell, the guy was a personal friend of one of the owners just like me, so why the hell should I care, as long as his drinking didn't interfere with operations. The city of Houston had two professional football teams during the early eighties, a bunch of rich cats had taken it upon themselves to challenge the superiority of the NFL over its dominance of money generated by pro football. The foolish mistake made by that group of men may have backfired in their faces, but for anyone owning a popular night spot, having two competing teams in the same city was a gold mine, and we drained it for everything it was worth. I don't know who to be more grateful to, the National Football League, or the new United States Football League, in retrospect, I guess I owe them both. Our club was called The World Champion, and it was owned by two professional athletes, so it was easy to have a cornucopia of pro athlete types lined up at the bar doing shots on any night of the week, we were also the place to be seen. On any given night, standing right in front of me could be the great Dan Pastorini, quarterback for the Houston Oilers, and his entire offensive line, or the next night it might be hall of famer Jim Kelly, the poster boy of the United States Football League, and his teammates who were the toast of the town due to their winning record.

We reaped the benefits of all these peoples' notoriety, and I had the okay from Chris and Joe to let popular athletes drink all they could consume. I assured the fellows that we could make quadruple the cost of the liquor off our exorbitant entry fees. Most people would give their souls to rub shoulders with the cream of the sports world. Once the owners saw that I knew what I was doing, all decisions concerning club operations went through me. It was easy for me then, to dispatch of the drunk ass operations manager. Friend of the owners or not, his drinking problem had become a big disability. I convinced the guys to let me hire J D's girl, Cindy to be operations manager. One hand washes the other, Cindy had helped me get to where I was, and the hell if I wasn't going to remember that. She was already managing the campus pub we'd both worked in and she was a hotel restaurant management major, so it wasn't like I had to train her much. The only thing I had to teach Cindy was how to manage the enormous amounts of cash money coming through the front entrance and get the owners to okay me a small budget to upgrade her wardrobe. I made it very clear to her that me and her were in the big time now and every woman coming through that door had to compete with her in the looks department. Cindy took to the role like a duck to water, she and I soon both bought Corvettes and, in a sense, became local celebrities ourselves. Eventually she and I became lovers. Certainly, she and J D's relationship was long over, I'd never stab a friend in the back like that.

Two years later, the Houston Rockets won their first World Championship, the United States Football League folded, a bunch of the more popular Houston Oilers retired or moved on and the fame of the World Champions died down. We shut the building down and went in search of the next project. Chris and Joe were hooked on the business and on me and were waiting for me to point the way. They'd foolishly let on to some of their pro athlete friends the amount of money they made off the club investment, and a hoard of pro players were now wanting in on the business. Everyone wanted to open a club on Richmond Avenue now, soon every square inch of Richmond, for three miles was a club restaurant or bar. Me and Cindy, now a team, realized this was the right time, so we made the decision to do something out of the norm. We sought out a building a few streets over that was just as popular as Richmond Avenue, only it was famous for its swanky department stores. Westheimer Road was nationally known for its enormous Galleria Mall. With the backing of Chris and Joe, we opened our next club a half mile down the road from the world-famous Galleria. Cindy used her influence to convince every beautiful girl working at the campus pub to join our crew of bar people and from then on, we always had the hottest coeds from the University of Houston on staff. A lot of them dated or knew athletes who were nationally prominent players in football or basketball, giving us a customer base to consistently build upon. Things could not have been more glorious for a used to be good defensive tackle from a small town in Texas. The misfortunes of my childhood were distant memories, all easily put out of my conscience as long as I didn't let the thoughts occupy any of my psyche. I pretty much severed all ties with my blood relatives and now saw the Maples as my actual family. I celebrated the holidays with them and even referred to Paul and his siblings as my brothers and sisters, we did everything together just like a regular family. I felt that God was rewarding me for the trials I suffered as a child. Me, Paul, and Frank still took our summer jaunts to see "The Dead" when we could. We all three hung on to our love for taking trips on our bikes, only difference was we couldn't do it for weeks at a time. My success in life and business, to put it bluntly caused me to get a little reckless and lackadaisical at times. Cindy caught me cheating on her and dumped me, ergo, ruining what was a great relationship. At the time, I didn't allow our breakup to bother me because in the life I was living, the women were plentiful, but the time did come down the road, where I missed Cindy and the closeness she and I shared. Cindy, still emotional about me screwing over her, came into my office one evening, dropped her keys to the building on the desk in front of me, turned and walked out. I went after her once I snapped to what was happening but by the time I got to the parking lot, all I could see was the tail lights of her Vette pulling out onto Westheimer Road. I haven't seen nor heard from Cindy since that day. I heard through the grapevine, that she took a job working for the Hilton Hotel chain. I've not decided whether I was too selfish or just too stupid for not trying to find her. Chris and Joe were a bit peeved with me too, once the word got to them why Cindy had walked away from our perfect situation, finding someone with the qualifications and commitment of her was a distinct impossibility. Chris, Joe and I turned our venture into a real business, soon we had clubs in New Orleans, St. Louis and San Antonio, my days of working behind the bar every night came to an end. Someone had to monitor the several different managers we were going through, they all seemed to be thieves at their core, I learned that the site of great amounts of cash easily corrupted most. What I mean is our formula was working, every building we opened was like a new magic act being introduced to a hungry crowd who seemed to only crave more. I informed Chris and Joe that there was no need to include any more of their pro athlete friends in the business, they got it once I told them how they and I made money off the clubs. I told them to flip a coin to decide who picked first, each one of you gets a night where the entire door goes into an owner's bank account.

"So, that will be your salary from the club, you each pay me a percentage of that night's take and pay taxes on the rest, therefore keeping the federal government off your ass."

"Everything else we put directly back into the building such as paying staff, building upkeep, and the tax on liquor sales", to want anymore would be greed and nobody can make all the money I assured them. Things were good for a few years and we all prospered, most of the spots we opened could hold upwards of seven hundred people and that's not including the VIPs and celebrity entourages that got in for free. At 10 to 20 bucks a head the cash was rolling in, we seemed to be unstoppable, though envied by the other pro ballplayers Chris and Joe still got their support when they were in town.

CHAPTER
THREE

BY THE END of the 80s the drug scene had permeated all aspects of the night life, there was just no way to avoid being affected by it, everyone from the busboys to the owners was doing cocaine. There was just no controlling its infection, especially once we started booking live acts to perform in our clubs, the famous musicians were either snorting or smoking cocaine and everybody wanted to do what the stars were doing. I did my first line of coke with the lead singer of a very famous musical group when I walked into my office to do my nightly checkouts and the singer and my boss Chris must have had what was at least a kilo of the white stuff on my desk, life was never the same after that night. Chris and Joe seemed to lose their way, the pro ball careers were over and due to their partying, they were running through their money like sand in a fishnet, I casually tried to get them back on track but to no avail, the little glass penis called a shooter was controlling all their actions now, all I could do was stand back and watch the ship crash onto a rocky shore. Before too long the fellows were instructing the club managers to deposit more than one night of the door take into the owner accounts, that eventually breached any safeguards I had in place to prevent the managers from skimming money off the door deposits. Once it was clear to me that all the control factors were gone, I stopped flying to the other cities to keep the various managers in check. My routine had been to visit each club one day every two weeks to do my own liquor inventory and to go over the register receipts myself, doing this kept our managers in check to a point. These guys all knew enough about the business to know if they put their own person on the door register they could use any tape from the register they chose to, and a computer key is just like a pen, what you press is what the person checking will see. If the tape showed one hundred less people on a Friday than there was from the Friday before, all they had to tell me, or the owner was that it was a slow night due to some other event in town. Whatever the reason, once the managers saw the owners siphoning off the money, they just did the same thing. Chris and Joe both got caught up in the life of being celebrity club owners thinking they could afford all the drugs and women they could buy and thinking the train would never stop. No matter how many times I attempted to get them back on track, my attempts went moot, it was like they were in a competition to see who could screw up the worst.

I will never forget the last time I saw Joe in person, he'd called me at the club one night and instructed me to retrieve a package from the office safe and to drop it off at his condo after I finished my liquor inventory. Even though it was concealed in black wrapping paper, I was certain of what was inside, you know what they always say, if it walks like a duck and quacks like a duck then it must be a duck. I found myself personally delivering a package of cocaine to the home of the man who paid my salary, upon arriving at Joe's condo I was greeted at the door by a woman who I'd frequently seen at the club, she showed me in and told me Joe was upstairs in the bedroom waiting for me. I walked in to see Joe crawling around on the floor picking little white specks of debris out of the carpet, he looked up and saw me with a big shit eating grin on his face and said," damn Mike I'm glad you finally got here." I took the package from my briefcase and tossed it to him and turned to leave," hold on he said, don't you want to hang out and party with us for a little while?"

"Thanks, dude I said, but I got some shit to do, maybe next time Joe, see you," I glanced back one more time to see him measuring some of the powder into a beaker to rock it up for smoking, I had no way of knowing that would be the last time I saw Joe alive.

Every woman Joe and Chris got high with and had sex with instantly was on the free drink list, right along with anybody who might be partying with them. Between Chris and Joe's whores and the pro athletes, the bartenders were serving more free drinks than they were selling. Once I stopped traveling I got back behind the bar, my percentage from the owner's night got smaller and smaller as the clubs slowed down on attendance. When it got down to it I was still just a bartender and I was the best at it and I knew pouring whiskey would always keep my tip jars bulging. The only women getting free drinks at my bar was the one I was sleeping with at the time, with me once I was done with some chick who was just a fuck buddy, I made sure I was rid of them, if they became a problem, I'd just tell the door bouncer she was barred from the building. One by one the clubs in the other cities started to do so bad the fellows were forced to shut them down, and then those two idiots came up with this stupid idea to open another club in Houston. Now every pro athlete in town who dug the nightclub scene wanted to have their own club, copying our operating model they all jumped in feet first, most attempting to hire me away from Chris and Joe. I stayed with Chris and Joe until they had a falling out over how much money each was getting and eventually parted ways.

The drug dealers soon picked up the scent of the night club cash flow and now they wanted in too. Freddie Branch and Demetrius LaFluer walked up to my well one night, ordered two shots of cognac, tipped me a thousand dollars, and then Freddie looked me straight in my eyes which were I'm certain big as saucers at the site of the stack of hundred-dollar bills lying on my mixing mat.

"We've heard about you big man he said, we got us a building over on Richmond right behind the Galleria that's going to shut this place down. A little bird told us your bosses was fucking it all up, that same little bird said if we want to get it right, you the man we need, the address is fifty, fifty Richmond, meet us there at three tomorrow, that stack of cash is to let you know how real the offer is, it's yours whether you show or not, we'll leave the door open for you "Big Mike".

The two men turned up the brandy snifters to down their cognac's, turned and walked away. I didn't know these men personally, but I knew who they were by reputation, they were two of the most powerful gangsters on the street and I knew they were serious men.

I showed for our meeting the following afternoon and they were not lying, the building was enormous, and they spared no expense on the decor, the place looked like the Taj Mahal. Demetrius came over to shake my hand," does this mean you excepting our offer Mike, he asked with a slight grin on his face."

"Y'all made it kind of hard for me to not at least hear what else you got to offer, I answered, and this place looks fabulous I added."

"We pay you a grand a week to do the same job you doing for Joe and Chris and it's up to you if you want to stay behind the bar, people say you the best bartender in the city too."

"I grinned back at him, I don't brag about that but thanks for the compliment, when y'all need me to start?"

"Last week he responded, but Freddie wanted to get the room fixed up before we offered you the job, he wanted to make it easy for you to just step in and get your staff together." From across the room I noticed a beautiful woman who I already knew," is that Veronica I asked Demetrius?"

"Yeah, she's the person who put us on to you a few weeks ago, we had you checked out and she was right, them fellows you work for owe us a shit load of cash that they got to pay us in a couple of days, I don't think they going to be able to keep the doors open many more days, ain't no need for you to even show up there anymore."

I sold my Corvette the next day and bought a brand-new Honda one thousand Gold Wing motorcycle to streamline my life, from now on I'm just going to be a bartender/bar manager, no more, no less. Joe Koonce was a big man at 6 foot six and 350 pounds, the man had been a beast of a defensive end with two different professional football teams, it seemed as though nothing or no one could handle this mountain of a man. The story goes he chose not to pay my new employer's the money he owed them, the disc jockey of the club told me he dropped Joe off at his condo one night and as he drove away he heard two shotgun blasts, big Joe took those two blasts to his upper torso and his life was over six years after I'd first went to work for him. It seems he was more embedded in the world of cocaine than I thought, rest in peace big Joe.

Joe's death was more of an eye-opener to me than anything else, these were dangerous men I worked for now, I would soon come to witness acts that I dare not speak of, I took care of their club and kept my mouth shut, I didn't need to do much training of the staff, everyone from the other club was happy to come with me to 50-50 Richmond which was the name given the club by its owners. The beautiful girl I saw the first day was a waitress at Joe and Chris's club who'd quit a few months earlier, Chris was putting the full court press on trying to screw her, she tired of his bold advances and just walked out one night. Another warning I'd given he and Joe from the start, don't fuck the staff I'd warned them, it can only cause trouble but again my warnings were ignored by my coked-up bosses. They both seemed to think being the owners gave them license to sleep with the women who worked for them, their indiscretions cost us many a good server. Veronica and I had a good working relationship, I had even tried moving her into Cindy's job, but she was still in college at the time and didn't feel she'd be able to commit herself to the job one-hundred percent. I'd missed her after she moved on, now here she was working as a club manager anyway, she had graduated and gone into the healthcare industry only to end up working for a company that folded under a national overbilling scandal. While we were talking one evening, I asked Veronica why she quit working for Chris and Joe. She told me about her hassles with Chris and how he tried to force himself on her in his office one night, I didn't know about that.

"He wasn't my type she told me and furthermore I wasn't going to sleep with my boss, she added."

"I always thought you would ask me out Mike, but I guess I wasn't your type, right?"

"There were always so many women at your bar I could never figure out which one was your woman after Cindy left. I bumped into her one time in the mall later, she told me what you did to her, after hearing that, no way was I going out with you."

That hurt, and I felt the need to explain," I felt bad about that Veronica and still do, I apologized to Cindy, but she couldn't find it in her heart to forgive me, if you run into her again you can tell her I'm still sorry for hurting her."

Me showing an honest contrition must have touched Veronica's heart, because a few weeks later we did start dating and lived together for a couple of years before her mother in Washington DC had a heart attack and she moved there to care for her, we parted as loving friends.

Chris walked up to my bar one night looking very much like the fallen warrior, gone were the thousand-dollar suit and flashy bling, he had on something surely bought off the rack and obviously still carrying his cocaine habit.

"I heard you was running this place from a friend, he said, I wanted to look you in the eye and apologize to you Mike. You helped me, and Joe build something wonderful and we let our egos ruin it and look how things ended up for Joe."

"The men who own this place ended up with most of the money you helped us make, how crazy is that. I'm in rehab now trying to get it back together, if I can get back on top again maybe you and me can do it again."

"Sure, I said, and I won't ever forget the good times Chris, it's good to see you Chris, let's do a shot," we threw back a shot of bourbon and shook hands, the next time I saw Chris was five years later when I was pulling the girlfriend of a millionaire I was working for out of a crack house, but that's another tragic story for another time.

CHAPTER
FOUR

T O KEEP IN shape, I found myself over on Elm Street in Southwest Houston at a place called Hanks Gym, a gathering place for the local power lifters and a few ex-football stars like myself, big Joe had been the man who turned me on to the spot. The owner Hank Breaker, who himself was a former champion strongman made you feel at home there if you were a serious lifter and not just some pretender. Big Joe told me I'd fit right in because the place was a true gym and not just some fancy fitness center and he was right. I'd never seen a professional bodybuilder in the flesh before I walked into Hanks Gym one sunny day, the first person I saw working at the front desk was a female bodybuilder named Betty Herndon, Betty was a pretty girl sitting behind the counter but when she stood, she was all man. I'd seen female athletes with a good amount of muscle on their frame before, but Betty was mind blowing, she carried more muscle than I had ever seen on any man before, right away I assumed she was a gay man and stupid me addressed her as dude only to be hastily set straight by the beautiful blue-eyed blonde. I graciously apologized and put down my cash on a six-month membership, I soon found out that there were many other female bodybuilders training at Hanks, just not any as extreme as Bee, the name Betty's friends called her, over time she forgave me for my initial error and we got along okay.

The gyms competitive champion was a petite curly haired blonde named Dena Anderson, a national level competitor loved by all including me, I made a point in making myself at least a casual friend. I'd always considered myself a big strong man, but in this place though I was as typical as a fly on the wall and vowed to myself to catch up. I took on another persona away from the night club world, if I went home with a woman from the club, by the time the sun rose I was gone, being totally committed to turning my body into one like that of my peers at Hanks. Over the next three years I became that and much more, I took, or should I say my body took to the regular weight training like it was a drug. There came a time when I was stronger than every man in the room no matter where I was, I soaked up knowledge from the competitive lifters like a sponge in a bowl of water. I knew I would never get into the contest part of the sport because I still loved my life at night, having all the new muscle attracted a whole new group of women and I knocked them down like they were bowling pins. I began injecting liquid testosterone and taking 20 mg of Russian Dianabol every other day, the wind could blow between my legs and my pecker would get as hard as concrete, I felt invincible and I needed women to soothe the savage beast so to speak.

Being involved in the powerlifting-bodybuilding scene was even a boost for Fifty-Fifty Richmond, everyone at Hanks knew I tended bar there so when the lifters wanted to hit a club, the one where they knew the bartender is where they would all go. The club was on its third year of popularity, a long life for a night club, between the pro athletes who hung out and the cluster of competitive bodybuilders we looked like a room full of sports superstars. Word of the place spread across the country and even the famous people wanted to be seen there, Veronica and I were, I would always tell her, qausi celebrities due to the fact we managed the hottest club in town. The reigning heavyweight champion of the world Iron Mike Tyson and his enormous entourage would fly in on occasion to hang out, his most famous nemesis Evander Holyfield, the eventual world heavyweight champ, who became a casual friend, even trained and had a temporary resident in Houston was a regular. Heisman Trophy winner Mike Rozier from the University of Nebraska was now playing for the hometown Houston Oilers made 50-50 his home away from home, the stars were endless, to think a club owned by two notorious drug dealers was the hottest spot in the country. The success was contagious; bartenders and servers would be waiting at the entrance seeking employment when I or Veronica showed up to let the cleaning crew in and receive deliveries. I only wished we were a legitimate enterprise, I witnessed some enormous drug deals take place in the back rooms of the building, the owners used the business to clean a lot of cash therefore involving me in some creative bookkeeping that I was never comfortable with, but I wasn't about to rock the boat, I saw what happened to the last guy I knew who crossed them. I'd never really known any real gangsters but here I was in the midst of the criminal element I'd only ever seen in the news and in the movies. There was one guy named Jimmy Binder who terrified the hell out of me, his reputation was drenched in blood, I tried avoiding him, but the son-of-a-bitch knew I was the owner's guy who handled the money so he, being a silent partner of Demetrius and Freddie, felt I was his guy too. I tried staying behind the bar when JJ, his handle, was in the club but for some strange reason the guy would insist on me doing a shot with him and chatting for a few minutes when he saw me. The dude looked scary, he was built like a cage fighter, not big like me, but he was as hard as nails with deep black skin and a steely stare in his eye, JJ was obviously a man you did not want to fuck with. His own personal occupation was pimp and manager of female singing groups, the man traveled with a bevy of beautiful women who all looked like supermodels. JJ was not handsome by anyone's standards but the company he traveled with made him the best-looking guy in the room. The one thing I did like about him was his willingness to spend his cash, even though his connection to the owners allowed him to have an open tab, he showered the bar and wait staff with huge gratuities. One night while I was in the office preparing banks for the bar registers, Freddie, JJ and some guy I didn't know walked into the room, I moved to close the safe and Freddie said," hold on Mike I need you to lock something in there before you close it."

The stranger took an envelope from his jacket pocket and gave it to Freddie who promptly handed the envelope to me," count this for me big Mike he said."

I pulled the stack of hundreds from the envelope and gave a quick count, fourteen thousand I told Freddie. JJ immediately turned on the stranger, "I told you to bring us all our money didn't I Beaver, he told the man."

Before the guy uttered a word, JJ pulled out a pistol and shot him in the chest, the man bounced off the wall and fell face first onto the floor. I didn't react in any way because of the shock I guess, I put the money back in the envelope and tossed it into the safe and shut it, picked up my bank bags, stepped over the body lying on the floor and left the office, not a word was said by either man. I did not take a breath until I was in the corridor leading back to the front of the club, I couldn't believe what I had just seen, and I never ever said a word about it to Freddie or JJ. My silence and the way I reacted when it happened must have impressed Jimmy Binder, he started to treat me like a lifelong friend, he'd taken my reaction to the incident as some kind of tough guy move, in reality a month later I was still in shock. Now I was not only complicit in money laundering, let's add to my accomplishment murder, what the fuck had I gotten myself into.

A group of people showed up a couple of weeks later in a white stretch limo, Freddie seemed to be familiar with them and I was instructed to give them the royal treatment, Veronica seated the group in the VIP section and I had the bar backs pull a few cases of Dom Perigon champagne out of the storeroom. Veronica informed me that they were associates of JJs, the men were representatives and photographers for Hustler magazine and the women were all models. I wasn't into pornography, but I knew Hustler was a big-time magazine just like Playboy or Penthouse, it made sense that the group was a part of JJs circle of people, the man was the biggest pimp in town and I guess the people had something to do with their drug business also. I avoided the area where they sat, but after a long bout on the dance floor a group of models came over to the bar to do shots, they seemed like just another bunch of drunk chicks having a good time. Someone appeared with a box of magazines and the women began autographing the pages with their photos on them for our male customers and a few females. One of the models who was leaning on the bar in front of me signing her name abruptly stopped writing, looked up at me and announced," this one is for you, what's your name?"

Caught off-guard by the gesture, I stammered out my name, she signed her photo and passed me the magazine.

"You should give this to one of our customers, I said but thanks anyway, the girl was drop-dead gorgeous."

"I don't want to fuck any of your customers Mike, but you I could go a long way with, I already knew your name, the waitress told me, I been watching you from the booth up there, you're a good-looking man and I like guys with big arms and big thighs like you."

"There are lots of big guys in this club who would be glad to take a run at a good-looking woman like you, I said, and some of them fellows out there are rich men, I'm just the bartender honey."

"You a lot more than just the bartender baby, she replied, I can tell by how these women at this bar are keeping their eyes on you, I bet you already slept with most of them, haven't you?"

"I laughed and answered her, some of them, I opened the magazine to see her name, so is your real name Sandy or is that your stage name like the titty dancers."

"That's my name for real, she said with a tinge of anger in her voice, we have rooms at the Westin Galleria near here, won't you come over to see me when you get off tonight and I'll tell you more about myself."

"What about all them fellows you with, won't they have a problem with you inviting a man to your room?"

"Those men are doing their job, I share a suite with one of the other models, she wrote her room number down on a napkin and passed it to me, see you when you get off Big Mike", and she went back to her friends. I gave the magazine to the bar back and went back to work, no way was I taking it to the apartment I shared with Veronica. She was used to me staying at the club after closing on an extremely busy night to do inventory and call in orders for the next day, so it was easy to sneak away for a few hours. I left the suite at the Westin and went to the gym to get a workout in before going home, something I often did so Veronica was never the wiser. The Hustler model named Sandy was from Dallas so a couple of times a month either I flew there, or she flew to Houston, we had a relationship like that for almost a year. Sandy soon moved to Los Angeles to become a porno film star, I never did figure out why she chose me.

I was never comfortable working for the guys at 50-50 Richmond after the shooting of the guy right before my eyes and was always thinking of a way to give up the job without irritating my bosses. Though a mere coincidence, Veronica's mother had a heart attack and she took off for Washington DC, a month later she came back to retrieve her belongings and to let me know she'd be staying in DC to care for her mother. I feigned missing her and told my drug dealer, murderer bosses that I was going to DC to be with her, they understood, I wasn't the first guy to fall in love with a fantastic piece of ass like Veronica. I gave all my stuff away to the goodwill, jumped on my scooter and headed north to New York City, I'd always wanted to see the place and on top of that I wanted to get as far away from these damn gangsters as I could, adios Texas.

CHAPTER
FIVE

I RODE HARD for twenty-six straight hours, mostly because every time I pulled into a rest area to take a bathroom break I consumed some of the 3 grams of white powder in my satchel. I guess I was just high and tripping while I was standing on the shoulder of the freeway taking a stoner look at the Detroit Lions domed stadium, when my plans changed. The one thing in New York I'd ever really been in awe of was Niagara Falls, New York City was just another city I thought, hell I've been in plenty of cities before. I did spend a night in a little hotel outside of town to rest up and get a good meal in me, then I mounted up and headed to Buffalo, got me a hotel room in a place called Aurora and for a couple of weeks I was just a tourist. Niagara Falls I found out was also a town and the falls themselves was an experience I'll never forget long as I live, it was the same rush I got the first time I looked down into the Grand Canyon. I spent a day on the United States side and then went over to spend another day on the Canadian side, when the lights came on at night to color the water the first time, I found me a secluded spot along the walkway pulled out one of the joints in my shirt pocket and celebrated the moment. I was very fortunate to not be spotted by a cop while standing at the edge of Niagara Falls smoking a joint, I felt lucky, not many people can commit such a spontaneous act without being discovered. A few months back I had met a girl bodybuilder from a town named Syosset at a contest in Houston and promised her if I was ever in New York I'd stop and visit, she and her husband owned a gym in town that was like Hanks, all the bad boys trained there. Jan Francis was much like my friend Betty Herndon who worked at Hanks in Houston, a very beautiful woman carrying way too much muscle, so much that it detracted from her femininity, still Jan was a cool chick and her gym was awesome. I took a break and stayed to train in Syosset New York for a couple of weeks. Without saying any goodbyes, I checked out of my hotel one morning and hit the road, my next stop was South Dakota to see the historical landmark called Mount Rushmore with the sculptures of the American presidents on it. The great thing about traveling on a motorcycle was for twenty dollars a man could pretty much drive to anywhere in the country he pleased. Fortunately, I had close to thirty thousand dollars in the bank, I could travel all the way around the world if my Honda Gold Wing could swim or fly. I lost track of everyone I knew for a couple of years just bopping around the country experiencing things I was curious to see and do. I never saw myself as this overly attractive man, but it seemed every town I hit some beautiful woman took a shine to me, it pained me some to always have to leave them behind. When we had a building in St. Louis I was never in town enough days to actually get to be a tourist, so I missed the opportunity to visit the St. Louis arch, so I headed to Missouri, I called ahead to let an old lover know that I would be in town in a couple of days and if she would be free to show me around.

Janet Collins was a local beauty who worked as the front door person at the Club Elan in downtown St. Louis, we'd had some good times but they all seemed to have taken place in my hotel room, I wanted to or at least I felt that I owed her a decent experience with me. Janet spent every free day she had showing me the sights of the city; I took her to dinner at a different restaurant every night I was in town. The entertainment section downtown called the landing is where we spent most evenings, before going back to my hotel room or her place to do what brought us together in the first place. After two weeks, I felt the urge to move on, I kissed Janet goodbye and promised to stay in touch, jumped on my bike and hit the road, no real destination in mind, I would just ride until I got tired.

I was rolling through Branson Missouri and spotted a cluster of bright lights in the distance; out of curiosity I took the next off-ramp to investigate. The sign out front read appearing tonight the Molly Hatchet band, knowing of and liking the band I bought a ticket and went inside. The place was just a big circus tent with beer trucks backed up to it, the stage and the bars were makeshift structures but there must have been five thousand people in the place, all white, I stood out like a Nun in a whorehouse. What the hell I thought, if nobody fucks with me I'll just drink a few beers, enjoy the show and be on my merry way, no such luck though. Missouri may be in the Midwest, but the mentality of its white people was pure deep south, I leaned on the bar enjoying the show not really giving a damn about anything else until these two rednecks decided to ruin my night. The biggest one eased closer to me and sneered, what you doing in here, you see any more niggers in here? Taking my cue from his statement I put my fist right in the middle of his face, I figured why delay the inevitable, his pals made a move to come to his aid, so I pressed my back up against the bar and readied myself for the attack. I knew they would still be in shock from watching me destroy the nose of their biggest guy and hesitated some, so I was ready.

These fellows I'm sure were accustomed to watching the big guy laying on the floor with blood gushing from his face, beat the crap out of some little guy, were not quite sure what to do with the 275-pound real bad ass standing before them. From behind me I heard the bartender say to somebody, go up front and tell the cops we got a fight, it wasn't quite that yet but I'm sure it was going to be just as soon as these two other peckerwoods summoned up a little courage, and here they came, heads down screaming stupid obscenities at me. The music was so loud in the big tent, it's a certainty no one heard the ruckus but the people nearest us, I ducked the first punch and with the hardest uppercut I could bring caught the guy under his chin, from the feel of it I knew he was done, no matter how tough a man thinks he is, a good punch to the head region from a 275-pound weight lifter with 24-inch biceps is going to rattle the brain or possibly kill him. There is no telling how many people have lost their lives because they thought fights on television or the movies are how it really is, I learned early in life from the blows I'd gotten from my stepfather that you got to be real tough to take a shot to the head and not go down. He knocked me out the first couple of times we got into it, over time though I learned to move and block to survive the beatings, if not for being outweighed by him he would not have bested me in every fight we had.

The third guy caught me with one on the jaw, but he was a little guy and it hardly phased me, I was still turned on and I turned my rage on him, I grabbed his ass and slammed him down to the ground as hard as I could. Two Branson city cops broke through the crowd to subdue me, I didn't resist, I recognized the uniforms and badges and after all the fight was only me defending myself. To my good fortune the crowd overall were decent people and most of the witnesses told the truth, I could tell the two hillbilly cops wanted the scene to tell something else though. By the time the paramedics showed up, the two law dogs were taking off the cuffs and escorting me to my bike, my parting words to them was fuck Missouri, I fired up my scooter and roared off into the night headed west.

Missouri turned out to be the one sour note on my journey in more ways than one, Janet did get me over to the giant arch for the elevator ride to the top, the view was fantastic, the fight at the Molly Hatchet show and an episode at a rest area put a dark spot on my stop in the" show me state". Now, I am in no way homophobic, I wanted to take a rest and maybe smoke a joint and have a beer, so I stopped at a gas station slash convenience store and bought a couple of Budweiser singles, packed them in ice inside my saddlebag and pulled into the next rest area. I picked the picnic table the farthest away from the restrooms, took my two beers and a microwave sandwich I picked up and walked out to the picnic bench at the far back of the rest stop. I popped open one of the cold ones and sparked up a doobie, the wooded scenery behind the rest stop was a great shot of Missouri nature as I sat enjoying my buzz and my bud, suddenly I heard something behind me and turned to see two white dudes approaching. Talk about a buzz kill, I reached into my back pocket and pulled my buck knife out and snapped it open turning to face the two approaching men. They noticed my sudden defensive movement and came to a halt, their eyes wide and a confused look on their faces.

"What the fuck y'all want I barked?" I was in a full defensive stance waiting for the two to team rush me, but neither of them took another step in my direction. Finally, one of them held up his hands in a nonthreatening manner, "we're sorry the man said, we thought you were looking for some company".

"Why the hell would I be out here looking for company, I snapped at the feminine sounding man, hell no I ain't looking for no company, now get the hell away from me".

"The other man said, if you ain't looking to make a love connection, you shouldn't hang out at a park where the boys meet".

"What the hell you mean by that I barked?"

"This is a spot where the gay truckers meet to hang out and hook up answered the man". Now, I was the one with the confused look on his face, rebounding I said," look dude I ain't no truck driver and I'm damn sure not gay so y'all might as well move on". Not quite giving up yet, the first one said, "you sure you don't want to get your dick sucked, I'm really good, you ought to give it a try, you might like it".

I was too stumped to say another word, I closed my blade up, grabbed up my stuff and walked away, promising myself in my head to never come to Missouri again, how the hell could there be a rest area that doubled as a pickup spot for gay truckers?

The Grateful Dead were performing at the Sanger theater in New Orleans in a couple of weeks, so I called Frank and asked him to meet me in New Orleans the day before the show, he was going to be there but said, "I got a vacation week coming up, so I'll see you in New Orleans in two days big Mike". Paul was married to a home girl named Trudy Dawn now, who me and Frank both knew, and in no way, was she going to let his ass just up and go, she thought I was a bad influence on him. That however didn't stop me and Frank from tearing up the French quarter for a few days and enjoying an outstanding Grateful Dead show.

I'd been on the road for most of a year now and being so close to Texas made it easy for Frank to talk me into coming home to see all the folks who missed me and me likewise missing them.

"I already told my girlfriend Lori you was coming to stay with us for a while, said Frank, she's cool with it, she's a" dead head" too, the only reason she ain't with me is she couldn't swing the time off with her boss, so you ain't got no excuse not to ride home with me", insisted my lifelong friend.

"We got our ten-year class reunion coming up next month, I got an email from Starr Peterson the other day to remind me, she asked if I knew how to get a hold of your ass, so everybody will be blown away if you show up, you ain't been home in close to eight years". Before I could say no he added that, he'd already paid the hundred and fifty bucks everyone anted up to cover venue rentals and food. Frank's girl Lori was cool, and she welcomed me like a brother coming home from the war, leave it to Frank Hargis to end up with the perfect woman. I told Frank the story of what happened at the rest stop with the gay truckers offering to give me a free blow job, it took his ass ten minutes to stop laughing.

"Shit Mikey, sorry for laughing so hard, he said, I know that must have been embarrassing as hell to you, I'm surprised your crazy ass didn't take your buck knife out and cut they asses up anyway, hell I didn't even know truckers could be gay. Seems like there would be some unwritten rule against that shit, I mean the truckers are usually such hard asses, right".

Instead of staying at his place, me and Frank rented a beach house down in Surfside a little town on the coast a few miles from Angleton, it gave us a chance to get Paul away from his wife for a couple of hours a day. Even though we had been friends since we were eight years old, the woman would chew his ass off for hanging out with me, she was some kind of weird holy roller who thought I was the devil because I made my living in the nightclub industry. Her biggest complaint was, I had a different woman with me every time she saw me, she'd shit her pants if she knew about the time Paul got drunk and grabbed a hold of the tits of that Hustler magazine model I use to sleep with.

The Reunion went well, it was great to see the ten years of physical change in everyone, most people thought something was wrong with me when I informed them that I'd spent most of the previous year bumming around the country on my bike. I reunited with my high school sweetie who was fresh out of a recent divorce, she'd gotten married to a guy from home that was a casual friend when we were younger so sleeping with her was a little on the weird side.

A guy who was on the basketball team whose life I'd saved at a pool party showed up and embarrassed the hell out of me by hugging me for too long in front of everyone. Joe Powell who nobody knew at the time couldn't swim, got shoved into the deep end of the city pool one day, Joe who was six-foot seven was drowning in 10 feet of water with sixty people watching and afraid to go to his aid. The guy was the star of the high school basketball team so I for one was certain the guys on the basketball team would attempt to save their star. Like hell, all of them tall sons of bitches were standing there watching Joe drown, I dove in, swam up under him, grabbed him by the waste of his bathing suit and swam to the pools bank with his lanky frame, me being just five-foot ten, that must have been a site. I had run into Joe a few other times over the past few years in one nightclub or the other, and every time he mugged me with hugs of gratitude, always stating to anyone present how I'd saved his life when we were kids. It wasn't that big a deal to me because I'd saved other people from drowning before, but it seems the ordeal bonded me and Joe for life.

CHAPTER
SIX

I STAYED WITH Frank and Lori for a month before bidding my farewell and leaving for Mexico to lay up in the whorehouses and spend more time and money just being a lazy ass. I met a millionaire at my favorite joint in Juarez, this sleazy whorehouse just happened to be his favorite place too, come to find out this guy who called himself Wild Bill, was from Houston. Over a period of days wild Bill and I became casual friends, he learned some things about me and me some things about him, my conversations about the nightclub business intrigued him greatly. One night while sharing a bottle of Johnny Walker Black, Wild Bill came up with the notion to open his own topless bar in Houston. I'd shared some of the stories of me working the clubs up and down Richmond and Westheimer with him and somewhere along the way and the drinking, he made the decision to have his own place. Wild Bill was a degenerate lover of young women with big breast, so his plan was to use his money to open his very own topless bar, he asked for my advice but all I could say was I never worked those kinds of clubs, so I really couldn't help him.

"Can't be that much of a difference commented the serious sounding Bill, a club is a club" cept" the women got their titties out, what's the first thing you did when you started up a club for the people you use to work for, he asked?"

"First, I said, you got to find a building, so you got an address to put on your liquor license application and I'm certain you going to need some other kind of a license to have a club with women walking around topless, it ain't the same as hiring waitresses".

We drank some more, and talked some more, then we both got us a girl and went to our rooms. Bill banged on my door the next morning scaring me and the beautiful Margarita awake, "what do you want said the girl in Spanish", Bill said something back in Spanish and the beautiful Mexican hooker told me, "he wants you to meet him downstairs for breakfast, he says there's something very important he wants to speak with you about".

"Okay Bill I yelled towards the door, let me get a quick shower and I'll meet you downstairs, I don't want to eat my breakfast smelling like pussy".

At breakfast, Wild Bill laid out his plan to me, "I don't need to find no building Mike, I already own some property right up on the freeway just inside the Houston city limits on the south side of town and I got the money to construct my own building with my own construction company".

"I've been thinking on this shit all night Mike, them licenses you mentioned, I got enough contacts in law enforcement to work that out too, all I need is someone to walk me through the process who knows the club business, that's where you come in my large musclebound friend".

"Whoa, whoa, whoa, Bill ain't you moving a little fast, your plan sounds like a winner, everything except the part about me, I said I use to manage clubs, plus I'm having a great time down here banging all this young pussy and getting drunk every day". Bill who resembled the famous country singer Charlie Rich cleared his throat and then fixed me with a steely hard stare, "I've been down here hunting for three weeks and in that short period of time I've seen you in two fights with these Mexicans where you could have lost your life".

"If you wasn't so big and strong and mean as a snake you probably would have been by now, you can't chance the odds for too long a time, plus I'll pay you three grand a month to come home and help me put this thing together. Besides that, big man you make one hell of a drinking buddy and something just seems right about us meeting down here in Mexico doing the same thing".

I still had enough money to stay another year in Mexico, but the man made me an offer I truly couldn't refuse.

"Don't make up your mind just yet said Bill, I'll be away on a hunting trip for a few days, I'm going up into the hills to shoot me one of them big mountain goats, by the time I get back to the hotel you ought to have your mind made up".

By the time, he got back from his hunting trip I'd decided to take him up on his offer, Bill I said, "you and me have been having some good times down here so I feel like I can trust you to be a man of your word, I'll give you a year because I'm not quite certain I want to go back to working no sixty-hour weeks".

"Sounds good to me Mike and I appreciate you agreeing to help me out, we can load your motorcycle on my truck and you can ride back to Houston with me. I got a place out in Seabrook, you can bunk out with me and my boys till you get your own place, you'll like my boys, as we shook hands he said let's make this last night in Jaurez a good one".

I'd been spending my money on the same girl for the past two months, even though I could hardly understand a word she said it was hard to leave that beautiful thing behind.

Wild Bill wasn't lying, the man owned a prime piece of commercial property right on Interstate forty-five between Houston and Clearlake City, one of Houston's many suburbs. Two days after we got home he had me sit down with one of his contractors laying out a design for his new building. In six months, we opened the doors to the Chesapeake Bay gentlemen's club, Bill was a boating man, so the place was set up on a boating theme. I lived in his mansion with him and his sons for three weeks then got my own apartment, the guy had quite a spread right on Clearlake with a dock, a big cigarette boat and six wave runners tied up to it. I showed his sons how to water ski and dug my days living in a mansion on the lake, but I prefer my own space. While the interior designers were putting the final touches on the new place me and Bill used the time to hit the topless bars around the county to see how many beautiful dancers we could steal. I'd been wearing nothing but Levi's and shorts the past couple of years, so Bill did me a righteous by treating me to a shopping spree to buy me a new wardrobe of suits and nice shoes. I started riding across town to train at Hanks, so I was back to top form physically, the weight training along with all the waterskiing had gotten me into excellent condition.

Bill allowed me to do my thing with the promotions and advertising of the new club, by the time we opened there were thirty women of all flavors on our staff. I'd looked up some of my old bartending buddies to take care of the bar and when grand opening day came, we hit the ground at full stride, our opening feature was a famous porno actress named Devon Michaels. I quickly discovered this world was nothing like the regular dance and drink places and started to wonder if I was in over my head, but I wasn't a quitter, so I put my nose to the grind of selling sex and learned on the run. Wild Bill turned out to be my biggest problem, he wanted to bed every woman we hired, even the damn waitresses. While he and I sat having lunch together one afternoon, I broached the subject of him banging all the trade.

"Dude every time you screw one of the dancers or waitresses she becomes difficult to manage as an employee, these women think once they put your pecker in their mouth they no longer must be like the rest of the staff, in other words they get lazy because as long as they are satisfying you, along with you slipping them a few bucks on the side they think that makes them special. It's bad for business Bill, plus once you get tired of them and stop giving them money and attention they get pissed and quit, leaving me the chore of hiring and training somebody new".

My words fell on deaf ears, the man's brain functioned through his penis, pretty soon I was down to hiring any woman that came through the door. I started taking on girls who either had pimps or major drug problems, and chicks whose boyfriends or husbands were drug dealers and, in some cases, both. The quality of the clientele eventually went from decent well-dressed perverts down to flat out sexual degenerate scum, now I not only had dancers with drug or alcohol issues but also ones who dealt drugs to the rest of the staff. I began to plan my exit strategy, I told Wild Bill we should hire another floor manager because I was starting to feel like I was working too many hours and days and didn't want to burn myself out. He agreed and started making attempts at poaching a good manager from one of the upscale clubs in the city thinking that would result in a better class of dancers. We finally settled on a little shit named Robert Glass, or Bob as his friends called him, who did come in with a few new dancers and they were great on stage. A part of me was hoping the white trash and ghetto chicks would learn some class from these new girls but Bob's girls shunned them and clung to themselves as a group only agreeing to work the shifts when Bob was the manager. Wild Bill in the meantime was falling for a long-legged blonde named Tangy who I knew was a full-blown crack cocaine whore. For a few grams of crack Tangy would suck a golf ball through four feet of garden hose, and that made her a very dangerous person to be associated with. The drug dealer and pimp crowd had taken over the place and every night a fight of some sort broke out in the room, killing whatever business we may have had that night. To my own dumbness, I must admit, I'd had the hots for Tangy when she first came to work at the Chesapeake. One of the dealers told me in bragging how he'd done the wild thing with her just for a fifty-dollar tab she owed him for some crack he'd fronted her. Amazed to hear this I purchased a hundred pack from him with the intent to see if I could get some of that ass. I caught her in the dressing room later and showed her what I had, Tangie's eyes got big at the site of the ten white rocks in my hand and just like that she pressed her firm titts up against my chest.

"Can I have some she asked in a sultry, seductive voice?"

"Yeah, I said if you want to hang out after work, matter of fact it's all for you if you let me get some of this I said as I put my hand between her legs."

"I'll meet you at your car after we close tonight, and you better not be just fucking with me big Mike," she said. We spent the next three days together, riding to work together and leaving the club at closing together, the woman was outstanding in bed especially when there was a plentiful amount of crack on the bedside table. I really dug banging her, but I wasn't about to be saddled with a chick who would do anything for a free hit off that little glass dick. I gave her some stupid reason why I couldn't hang out with her anymore and went on to the next dancer. Now, my idiot boss was in love with her and to my surprise had moved Tangy into his house, the poor sap spent a good deal of his time trying to keep track of her whereabouts, being thirty some years her senior they didn't have shit in common. I just hope she didn't tell him about our three days together, I was so not ready for the awkwardness of that shit and didn't want him to know that I used the crack cocaine to get her. Bill was a friend and I would not want to hurt him like that, once she was living with him I stopped going out to his place. I felt sorry for Bill, all his pals were his wealthy business associates, and all her friends were a bunch of doped up dancers. The son-of-a-bitch even bought her a brand-new Mustang convertible, that bitch went wild, the only thing she came to the club for was to hang out with her whore pals and the crack dealers. Tangy would disappear for days at a time, spending them at the home of one drug dealer or another. The couple of dancers she ran with stuck to her like flies on shit, Bill's money was keeping them all high, if Tangy missed work, so did her road dogs, things at the club were getting worse and worse. Bob glass didn't give a shit; he was making his money and I was keeping the rougher gangsters in check, so he never complained to Bill. Bob did tell me one day though that he had something in the works for the not so far off future and he felt that I would be a good fit for his plan. He didn't mention it again for a long while, so the conversation slipped my mind. One night one of Tangies pal stumbled in and went straight to Bills table, she was telling him something in a very animated manner, I couldn't hear because of the loud music, but the way she was moving her arms I knew it was something serious. The girl eventually went to the dressing room to change and Wild Bill waved me over to his table and proceeded to repeat to me what the girl had told him, evidently Tangy and her pals had smoked up more rock than the cash they had to pay, the dealer and his boys were refusing to let her leave until they got paid. Bill pushed a hand full of hundreds over to me and said I'm going to need you to go get her for me in a pleading tone, "you know if I show up there them black guys would try to kill me." Teresa says she won't go back over there because she's afraid, I really need you to do this for me Mike."

"What if they try to kill me Bill, I asked?"

"What then?

"Teresa says you know these guys, she says they are customers here sometime and that you know how to handle them. I've seen you fight off a room full of drunk Mexicans with nothing but a pocketknife before Mike, whoever these guys are they ain't going to want to fuck with you, please Mike go get her for me he asked pleading with his eyes this time."

"Okay dude I said, but you owe me big time for this one."

I went to the dressing room to get Tangies location from the other dancer. The dealer just happened to be the same guy who told me the story that prompted me to fuck her in the first place, I got directions and apartment numbers from Teresa and slipped out the back door to my car. Twenty minutes later I was knocking at the door of a dangerous violent crack dealer, someone looked through the peephole and I heard them say to someone else, "it's big man from the club where the white girl works." The door swung open and I stepped inside, after the guys shut the door behind me, I said, "what's up Brian to the one person I knew in the room, I come to take care of what Tangy owes bro, how much."

"Seven hundred the guy answered, and another hundred for her wasting my time, she thinks that white pussy can pay for everything but we all tired of fucking the same white girl over and over." I counted out the bills and handed them over, "where is she I asked?"

"Give my boy a minute, he got her back there getting some of his money back, he be through with that freak in a little bit, sit down and have a shot of yak with me big man."

A few minutes later Tangy and a guy came into the room, "get your shit and let's go Tangy, I said, Bill sent me to get you."

"Okay she answered but let me get another hit before we leave."

All I could think was, Bill you poor stupid fuck. That skank didn't even come inside with me when we got back to the club.

"Drop me at my car she said, I told Teresa to leave the keys under the floor mat, just tell Bill I'll see him at home tonight, I'm tired I need to get some sleep I've been up for three days." As soon as I gave Bill his leftover money and her message he took off for home. Any respect I may have had left for Bill was slipping away like sand through a screen, this chicks pussy was not that good, but I guess to him it was.

I dragged the other dancer Teresa into my office, "why the hell did you let Tangie stay there long enough to owe them fucker's seven hundred dollars I barked at her?"

"I tried to get her to leave earlier today Mike, but I couldn't, once we started fucking Brian and his friends they was letting us smoke as much as we wanted, my mouth is sore from sucking so much dick." Get the fuck out of here is all I could say to that stupid ass bitch.

A couple of weeks later Bob told me to meet him in the office, he had something to discuss with me. Bob laid out his plan to me, evidently one of the larger companies who owned and managed sexually orientated businesses was expanding their operations in the Houston area. The company's owner, I found out from Bob was a personal friend of his, he told me he was sent in to act as a mole and to find out if a building in that part of Houston could make big money. The company owned by a guy named Derek Barham had secretly offered Bill a big chunk of money for the building and property, which he stupidly refused. Bill kept the offer from me, but it should have been an eye-opener for him to straighten up his act, I mean a company that size offering to buy you out is a good sign in the club game, a sign that your spot has potential. Bill's ego and his penis hampered his ability to make logical decisions where Chesapeake Bay was concerned, all he cared about was his personal access to all that young pussy. We started out right though, selectively hiring staff, bringing on a four-star chef and, having a serious enough dress code to keep the drug dealing rabble out. My warnings to him as an owner about you shouldn't be screwing every woman who accepted your cash favors were ignored, I'd also warned him of the danger caused by constant staff rollover, the worst things got, the worse he got. That's why Robert Glass just stood back and took his pay and reported back to Barham, he knew Bill was bringing on his own demise in this business. Glass felt safe in the building because of the force I was, in keeping the gangster element under control while sporting a silk suit and tie. Once the clientele turned all the way bad I bought a Glock nine-millimeter handgun and made sure the truly bad ones knew that I was strapped. The few times I may have had to put hands on another man, I made sure I beat him close enough to death that he and his posse got the message that fucking with me was going to lead to some consequences. The dealers didn't fear me, but they respected me, I gave them respect in return as long as they didn't fuck up in my club, we never hired bouncers because at 275 pounds even in a silk suit I was an intimidating figure. Robert admired the way I handled the staff and customers and had passed his sentiments on to his boss in his reports. They had someone hired to check out my background and were impressed with the things I'd accomplished in the entertainment business, and thought I'd be an asset to Barham's company. Bob went on to inform me that at some point Bill was going to end up taking on so much loss that he'd have to close the place, then Barham would be able to get it for a lot less than he was offering him.

"Listen up Mike, said Glass, Bill's got his head so far up that dancers' cunt, he can't tell up from down, if he didn't have somebody like you holding it together around here, this place would have gone under a long time ago. We got a place down the highway, closer into the city that my boss thinks you'd be perfect for, he's been in here a couple of times and he's impressed with the way you carry yourself."

"He was shocked to discover this is the first sexually orientated business you've managed, why is that he asked?"

"I started out in this business as a bartender and as I learned the business the people I worked for kept moving me into other jobs. One day I just had too much shit to do to stay behind the bar, the men I worked for made the same mistakes Bill is making, just in another world so one day I just walked away, got on my bike and took off for New York."

"I hopped around the country for a year or two until I ran into Bill in a whorehouse down in Mexico, he got the itch to own his own tittie bar one night while we was getting drunk, offered me a lot of money to help him open this place and here I am once again witnessing the owners burn down their own palace."

"Robert stopped me with a raised palm, we open in five weeks Mike, my boss wants a commitment from you at least by next week, he's putting together his crew of managers as we speak and wants to know if you're in.

"I can give you my answer right now Bob, Bill's a friend and I can feel his ship sinking, I'm going to let him know tomorrow that I'll be taking off for Mexico and that I'm done here at Chesapeake Bay. He'll understand, I told him from the start I couldn't make this a permanent gig, tell your man I accept his offer, I'll give you a call in three weeks Bob. Two days later I rolled into Juarez, tracked down Margarita and spent the next three weeks partying and fucking."

The Night the dancer Set Herself on Fire

The beautiful brunette girl sitting on the barstool in front of me and her boyfriend, my co-manager in this very luxurious men's club. She sprayed a small amount of the lighter fluid onto the palm of her hand, moving the liquid from palm to palm before picking up a disposable lighter and igniting the center of her palms, moving the little ball of fire from hand to hand a few times before patting it out.

"See Mike, what did I tell you said Jeff, the other manager who'd chosen to champion the dancers request to do a mini pyro exhibition onstage while wearing

nothing but stilettos and a G-string." I felt very uneasy with the whole idea of it, but the little demonstration in the dressing room did appear to be harmless enough, so I gave in to Jeff's pleading. Not to mention Jeff was also Wild Bill's oldest son, whom I was supposed to be mentoring. I couldn't teach the guy much because his penis and his love of young pussy, just like his father, twisted his reasoning horribly where women were concerned.

His most recent fuck toy left the stage for a moment after her first song to disrobe down to her G-string, for her second song. Upon her reappearance, the gorgeous young brunette was not just topless but was holding one of those nine-inch barbeque lighters in one hand and a bottle of the green Isopropyl alcohol in the other hand. Right there before God and a room full of people, the girl drenched her upper torso with the alcohol! Then I heard the click of the lighter and every nerve in my body went into crisis mode. The girl's entire upper body burst into a large blue flame! The only thing now stranger than that was the different color of the enflamed G-string, it burned in a bright gold glow. Why I noticed that troubles me to this day, I stood frozen and shocked right along with the rest of the room and then it was as though everyone in the room looked to me all at once. I looked to my right at the now ghost-faced Jeff, who was looking into my eyes like I could tell him what do next. When my view swung back to the burning girl on the stage it was because she was running towards me screaming my name and pleading for help. Not the guy standing frozen in his shoes next to me, who was sticking his pecker in her every night. Instead she was screaming my damned name, her eyes begging to be rescued from this idiotic error in judgement we'd all made. In a flash, I jerked the tablecloths from the two tables between me and the stage where the flaming girl was still screaming and running in my direction. I leapt on to the stage, threw her down, smothering the blue-flamed figure with my body and the tablecloths. At some point, I managed to put the girl out, while the room filled with customers and staff, stood shocked in horror at what they had just witnessed. I lifted myself up to find my clothing also burned up and ragged, but my concern now was what to do with this young girl lying before me with burnt flesh hanging from her upper torso. She stood up and left the stage as if her song had just ended and she was going to the dressing room to change. The odor of burnt flesh permeated the air of the room, a horde of dancers jumped from the laps of the tricks and all ran to the dressing room.

"Call an ambulance Jeff I said, as I followed the herd into the dressing room. I don't know what kind of drug your girl is on, but when it wears off that bitch is going to be in a lot of pain. Oh yeah, fuck you and your fire tricks Jeff!"

CHAPTER
SEVEN

GLASS FAILED TO mention one thing about his new place, it was going to operate as a totally nude cabaret, something reasonably new to the Houston area and the first of its type for Barham's company. Robert read my shock and reassured me that all I had to do was run things the same as we ran them in the topless business, he would be my immediate supervisor and guide me through my initiation into this new world. My second shock was where the hell did all these new women come from, the nude scene was something way different, way more connected to prostitution than the topless world. Many of these women were magazine model worthy and I was blown away by the fact that they performed totally nude on stage and during private table dances, I guess you could say I was naïve. These women earned three times the money a topless dancer made in a club, it wasn't long until I learned that the more successful ones had a clientele that followed them around like trained puppies and paid them enormous amounts of money for sex outside of the club. I found myself drawn to a performer named Abby who outside of this world was a principal dancer with the cities nationally famous ballet company. Abby's beauty was hypnotically captivating, and I could not resist her charm, I understood the spell she cast over very wealthy men, if I had the money I would pay for her attention too. And then there was Devon, a wife and mother of two gorgeous children a boy and a girl, flesh wise Devon had the most beautiful body I'd ever seen on a female, it amazed me that her husband and kids would drop her off at work just like she was going to the office. I guess for the money she made, the husband just went with it. The guy dropped her off and picked her up, always in a very nice and brand-new vehicle. I was also surprised that some of these women knew who I was, they'd known topless entertainers who'd worked with me and I had become known as a manager who watched over his girls with an iron fist. Some of the boyfriends and husbands would introduce themselves to me and tell me how safe they and their women felt with me in the building. I thought wow, I own a high degree of notoriety in the sex industry, soon women would hire me to drive them to appointments outside of the club and to chaperone them at private parties. I was fucking amazed at this new world I'd found myself entrenched in and the amount of sex was endless, women would sleep with me just because they felt safe with me. Even the beautiful

Abby slept with me because a friend had mentioned to her, how good I was in the sack, afterwards I chose to avoid sex with Abby, just her touch made me weak in the knees, I couldn't afford to be that vulnerable. She understood the spell she cast over me and the two of us managed to remain good friends without the sex, I can truly say I felt a weird kind of love for Abby. This world of sex and money was like sailing across a vast ocean and finding on the other side a Shangri-La of new adventures. Anyone with enough wealth could play in that land as long as they wanted, some of those of wealth were people I'd known for a great deal of my life, men and women. Yes, women, some from my very small hometown, they were the cream of the crop so to speak, had been raised well and lived like royalty, married men of wealth, lived in the grandest houses in town and yet here they sat in the VIP room of my nude club. Most times to indulge some dark fantasy of the husband, but lots of times to satiate their bisexual cravings away from the prying eyes of a small town. I've watched the homecoming queen on her knees in the private dance rooms performing an act of oral sex on one of the beauties working for us, while her husband sat on the chair opposite masturbating. The starting quarterback of my high school football team who was married to the daughter of the most prominent public official in Brazoria County loved using his finger to anally penetrate a woman on her knees facing away from him. The cameras in the private rooms were there for the safety of the women, but it was hard not to watch if the customer inside was someone you'd known your whole life. Those cameras had also saved the lives of women on a few occasions, there are times when that man with the fist full of dollars was also a brutal sadist, if not for us keeping watch, who's to know how bad the ordeal could have turned. The beating we put on some of those bastards was akin to criminal and we usually lost that customer but who the hell were they going to tell," yes officer I was just minding my own business violently beating this beautiful girl with my fist and this large black man came into the room and beat the shit out of me", yeah right". The violence I was capable of frightened some of the women, but it gave them a sense of security to know that if anything did get out of sorts big Mike would save them. Some of the other women though got some sick pleasure out of watching me beat a man to a pulp, it turned them on and they turned me on, there was a long period of time where I slept with a different beautiful girl four or five nights a week. I was never narcissistic about my looks, but I was spending a great deal of my free time in the gym, so I know I was big and strong, I just loved weight training as a recreation. Bob Glass sent for me one evening to inform me that he was hiring a security man, you're my manager Mike, he said and it's cool that you look out for the girls but it's more important that you focus on overall club operations. The next evening Glass introduces me to this guy who looked Arab, he was an inch shorter than me and 100 pounds lighter.

" MIKE, I WANT you to meet Samir, he's going to handle security for you guys, it's fine if y'all back him up but let him handle anything that comes up." Samir turned out to be all that and two bags of chips, the man was some kind of cage fighter bad ass, he just didn't look like it in street clothes, on his second week there, one of the girls' boyfriend who was hanging out with his pals made the bad choice to smack her around in our club, I made a move to go to her aid, Samir pressed his palm to my chest to stop me, I got it Mike, he said. Samir got between the man and the dancer and informed him and his pals that they were leaving. As they neared the exit foyer one of the guys took a swing at Samir, to this day I bet that arm still bothers him, his boys stepped to his aid and before either of us could intervene there were three bodies prone on the floor before us. Samir was some kind of Muie-Tie bad ass, hell even I felt safer with him on the scene.

Wild Bill had a shit fit when he discovered I was back in town and working for Robert Glass running the all nude XTC cabaret 5 miles up the highway from him. And just like pouring salt into an open wound the women from Chesapeake Bay who felt so safe working with Big Mike, all took the plunge, dumped the G- strings and bailed to XTC, I couldn't turn the good-looking ones away. Just like Barham predicted things only worsened for Bill, he must have expended enormous amounts of money, out of pride to keep the doors open. Once his attempt to rehire me failed, he hired Chris, the guy I use to work for, who when I last saw was a full-blown crackhead. I didn't judge though, maybe Chris had gotten his head right and was back on track with his life. I was wrong, he and Tangy knew each other, that was how he got the job. Within two months of his hire Bill walked in on him and Tangy getting high in the office at the club. He got rid of them both at the same time, finally I thought, he saw the light. Too little, too late though, the place had to shut down, a shoot-out in the parking lot and a vice squad raid and Wild Bill was done in the sex club business. Tangy came to me for a job, and despite the rampant drug use that bitch still looked good, I didn't refuse to hire her because she was a crack whore, I didn't like what she'd done to Bill, fuck her I told Glass who was still considering taking her on. I hung with Glass for another year before that restless creature inside of me began to rear its adventurous head, my time here was coming to its end, that next week I started to sell off my stuff. I had a thing or two that I would hate leaving behind, one and the most important of all was the friendship I'd formed with Abby the ballerina. The one night we'd spent together had indelibly been imprinted on my being, if what I felt for her was what love felt like, then I guess I loved her. The fact that she was a nude entertainer and a high dollar call girl were the reasons I walled in those emotions, but still the feelings were there, and they were real. I asked Abby what it costs a man for one night with her, whatever it was I needed one of those nights, and when she said two thousand dollars I took a roll of money from my pocket and counted the amount out to her. What's this for she questioned, a puzzled and curious look on her angelic face. "I'll be taking off in a couple of days, I said, I'm certain that I will miss you Abby, the one time we were together was probably the closest I've ever felt to a female, it's like you crawled under my skin and left a part of yourself there. I couldn't tell you these things then because of the lives we both lead, I'm telling you now because I feel we may never see each other again, and I'm certain that what I feel for you is what a wise man describes as love." Tears formed in her eyes and she smiled up at me, what you're saying is probably the most honest thing a man has ever said to me, "I'm going to miss our conversations Mike, in another time and another place ours could have been the greatest love affair of all time, I'm very sure of that." Abby handed me the money back, "you keep this, and I'll follow you to your place after work tonight, I'm telling Robert I won't be here for the next couple of days and so should you," she added. We went to Galveston the next morning and got a suite overlooking the bay at the Galvez Hotel, for two whole days she and I were like two star crossed lovers who had just discovered one another. We went for walks along the seawall holding hands, chatting and laughing the way lovers do when they are truly in love with each other and then it was over. Abby went back to her life and I went wherever, there was a bodybuilding contest held down on South Padre Island every summer and I had promised a friend I would come down and support her, so that is where I headed to first. Padre Island was cool, other than a few too many college kids it was the hippest place on the Texas-Mexico border with great bars and lots of single women, I got there a week before the contest, so I had plenty of time to play. I was pals with the shows promoter, a guy named Ruben Ramirez, so he and his wife spent a day showing me the sights, we hit a few bars and ate some good South Texas seafood, the rest of the time I just laid on the beach and girl watched. And then there she came, the new girl of my dreams, Rhonda Gerard, walking down the beach with a guy who had quadriceps the size of redwoods. I gave her and the dude with the big legs a yell as they got near me and we struck up a conversation about the upcoming show, Rhonda was in the contest, but the guy wasn't. He had some big ass legs but carried no thickness in his upper body, they were from the neighboring town of Corpus Christi and yes, they were a couple, I ended up hanging out with them that whole week leading up to the contest. I trained with them at Ruben's gym in the next town over, and I was right, big leg Lonnie could squat all day with you, but if you wanted to pound your chest into submission he chose to do lightweight with a lot of repetitions, I could tell that Rhonda was impressed with my brute strength, even though Lonnie had them big legs, his squat weight was a hundred pounds behind mine. At the Padre Island, Classic, Rhonda blew everyone in her weight class away and won the shows overall championship, I was glad to be in her corner. At dinner after the show they invited me to visit the club where they worked if I ever got to Corpus Christi, they told me about the gym they trained at, anybody in town can tell you where the Iron Horse Gym is in Corpus Christi. I hung around Padre Island for a couple more weeks, but I kept thinking about Rhonda Gerards thick curly blonde hair, her darkly tanned skin and all that finely tuned female muscle she was carrying. I had this thing for female bodybuilders since I first met Dena Anderson at Hanks, so one morning I woke up threw my stuff into my beige and black customized nineteen eighty-four 280Z and hauled ass across the causeway headed to Corpus Christi, Texas. A few short hours later I pulled onto the shoreline drive at downtown Corpus Christi and Rhonda was right, the first guy I stopped to ask for the Iron Horse Gym, gave me exact directions how to drive across town to the neighborhood where the gym was. I found a nice hotel a mile from where the gym was and moved in with a plan to hit the Iron Horse for some leg training later that evening.

Big leg Lonnie was there and immediately after I asked about Rhonda, he preceded to explain to me that he and Rhonda were together at the show, but he was cheating on the woman he lived with, with Rhonda. He didn't want me to accidentally give him away in front of his girlfriend who trained at the gym also. Awe my bleeding fucking heart I sarcastically thought, a huge load of guilt fell from my thoughts all at once. Okay Lonnie, thanks for the heads up, is Rhonda going to be training here tonight, I asked? She won't do any lifting tonight, but she teaches aerobic dance classes for three hours in a room next door, I'll let her know you're out here, she'll come by to say hello before you leave. Lonnie left the floor and was away for about ten minutes or so, when he reappeared, to my great surprise Rhonda was at his side. She rushed into my arms gave me a long hug, a peck on the cheek and told me welcome to town, I hope you're staying for more than one day she said. Yeah, I said, I'll be here for a few days checking out y'all's town, maybe we can all get together for dinner before I take off. Why not tonight, Rhonda suggested, we all have got to eat after we train, how about it Lonnie you and Stephanie up for dinner after we're done asked Rhonda? I got to check with Steph first said Lonnie, but I'll let y'all know before we finish with our workouts. What about it Mike, you up for dinner out to welcome you to town tonight the beautiful gray/ blue eyes turned to me and asked. Count on me being on my best behavior I answered, we bumped fist and she turned to go back to her class, looking back over her shoulder to yell, see you in an hour and fifteen minutes Mike. There was some beast in the Iron- Horse Gym, no one who could embarrass me but some bad boys yet. The owner Rodney Serpa was a former pro lineman in the NFL and was the king of the hill in his facility, his wife Judy a competitive bodybuilder too was a hell of a woman. There were a few other people I recognized from contest around the state, but within two weeks I broke the gym leg press record. My good fortune in having begun my training among the most knowledgeable lifters in the state was always to my advantage no matter where I was training.

Lonnie and Rhonda worked as bouncers at the hottest bar in town so there is where I usually ended up on the weekends. Rhonda and I became better friends and at a point began training together on some days and eventually our dinners together became dates. She had two adolescent sons at home, so we spent a lot of time in my hotel room when we were not working or training, we were good together in and out of the gym. One evening Lonnie asked me, if I'd be interested in helping him out as a bouncer at the bar they managed, there were two military bases in Corpus Christi so there were fights every night, but what the hell I thought, I'm in there on the weekends anyway waiting for Rhonda to get off, so why not get paid for it. There was no risk in taking the job, the place employed so many bouncers they ruled by the numbers, the few times I had to use my fist, I made sure to put my man down. The city cops were constantly giving me shit about some idiot who got into it with me in the bar wanting to file assault charges against me, I always had plenty of eyewitnesses on my side, so nothing ever came of the complaints. No words were ever spoken, but me and big leg Lonnie stopped paling around once things between Rhonda and me were obvious, I felt that she was my girl now, at least as long as I can handle living in tiny Corpus Christi. Corpus was like a feeding trough and I was like a wild hog at it where the women were concerned, the women in the gym were like panthers in heat, if they were certain Rhonda was not in the area they swarmed around me like gnats at a piece of fruit, under the guise of training alongside me they worked their female jelly. At the bar, it was the same, Lonnie must have had ten women on the side that he was hitting for quickies after we closed at night.

Rhonda worked two jobs, so it was not hard for me to juggle the women, there was a school teacher named Valerie I met in the gym who reminded me of Abby, I couldn't help myself I slept with her every chance I got. Valerie's boyfriend a big steroid taking bodybuilder was also a personal trainer at the Iron-Horse, they didn't live together but I felt he knew she and I had something going on.

He wouldn't dare challenge me, the word had gotten around town about how I dealt with shit in a fight, it had gotten to where some of the Army or Navy guys would come to our bar just to try me in an attempt to beef up their own reps. Those idiots never think about the fact that there were twenty bouncers in the room so why would I carelessly take them on alone.

The bouncing shit was getting crazier and crazier due to the constant challenges from the young military boys and quite frankly the constant brawling started to get old. I saw a sign in the window of a bar down the street called Doctor Rockets Blues Bar that read bartender needed so I went in applied for the job and was hired. Behind the bar is where I belonged anyway, slinging whiskey and not on the floor breaking heads was more my style anyway. Doctor Rockets was a hard-hitting smoking spot for a bartender, it was purely hard-core blues, a reasonably small place that booked some big-time acts and charged enormous amounts to get in. The whole time I worked there I never saw the place at max capacity, though the owners were, to put it bluntly stupid, they had a potential gold mine but were crapping it away with some unreal dreams of grandeur. The couple in their mid-50s thought if they got a big-name act on a fucked up tiny stage in a room so wrong for live acts, people would pay big money to get in and buy a lot of high priced drinks. The room was set up where one half of the room had no view of the stage at all, the stage was an 8-inch-high platform in the corner of the other side of the room. There wasn't even a dressing room for some of what I considered A-list blues acts, and these people, the owners, thought they knew it all, the money and crowds were steady enough to make some rent money. I'd never known the blues scene, so I was very shocked to find women on the blues scene, good-looking mature honeys, I went wild on this new discovery of females who were closer to my age anyway. It was a good gig until the head bartender had the owner fire me for sleeping with too many white women, his woman too, she and I were so careful so as not to let him know, I guess the guy just felt it. And then again, he may have just been another jealous and envious piece of crap, the kind of people the world can do without. I had never been fired from a bartending job before, the feeling was strange because by bartending standards I was an excellent man to have behind your bar. I would not be discouraged though; Corpus Christi was a silly little town with its racist Mexicans and redneck white boys, but I was having a good time training here and hanging out on the beach. To conserve money, I took a job tending bar at a Tex-Mex restaurant over on the freeway headed back towards South Padre Island. I was just this guy, not a care in the world hanging out in a coastal town in South Texas, I spent my days either on the beach or in the gym and my evenings making ten different kinds of margaritas at the restaurant. My plan was to get in the shape of my life and win my weight class at Ruben's show next summer. It was still summer, and all the college students were still in town working summer jobs in the local restaurants, the restaurants hostess Amanda was one of them, an English major at the University of Texas. I was an English major I said, even though I wasn't, I was a journalism major, I'd had to take a couple of advanced English courses to get a degree in journalism, so it wasn't a complete lie. Amanda and I started to exchange little poems we'd write when it was slow at work, one-night Amanda's poems became uncomfortably personal like the words were meant for me. I was thirty-seven years old and Amanda may have been twenty-one and was so very beautiful, she started to ask me questions about Rhonda and other white women who came by the restaurant bar to see me. She asked if I only dated white women and if I lived with either of the women, it was obvious this beautiful young girl had something on her mind. We became sex buddies; Amanda was cool, she knew we couldn't ever be more than what we were due to the difference in our ages. When she was at home we stayed in at my apartment and when I drove over to Austin to visit, we spent the whole time in a hotel suite somewhere in town.

That next summer came fast and I was right where I wanted to be physically, Amanda was back at her hostess job at the restaurant, but for some reason dear Amanda felt it okay to let the other women on staff know that I was hers. That started a firestorm, Amanda was the crown jewel of this place, the pretty girl who greets you when you walk in the door. And she's having sex with the bald head musclebound nearly 40-year-old black bartender, within two days of becoming aware of our connection the managers concocted some ridiculous reason to fire me. Damn idiots, Amanda quit the same day they fired me, and she and I took off for Padre Island together, Amanda got a job as hostess at a restaurant on the island and I took a job bouncing at a bar called Louie's Backyard the hottest bar on Padre. I didn't do well in the contest but me and Amanda's plan was to spend the summer together on South Padre Island and then she was going to head back to school, my plans were still up in the air. As strange as it may sound, thoughts of Rhonda and what she was doing always meandered around in the back of my mind no matter who I was with or where I was, I'd never experienced anything like that before and frankly it worried me. The summer ended, me and Amanda kissed goodbye and she took off back to school in Austin, I stayed on at Louie's. I had to drive to Brownsville a few miles away to train at Ruben's gym but other than that, life on Padre Island wasn't so bad, I even started to learn a little Spanish. Rhonda came down with her sons every couple of weekends to train and to hang out with me, she was now a national level competitor, her next big win could result in her gaining her pro card. She did just that at the Junior nationals in Houston a month later, the pro card changed her life and she started making plans to move out to California, where the bodybuilding world ruled, and it was easier to earn a living in the sport. Rhonda's suggestion that I go to Los Angeles with her and her sons made up my mind as to what adventure I would go on next. We put all her stuff in a U-Haul truck of which I drove, she and her sons followed in my car. The Los Angeles scene was everything and more than we could have imagined, Rhonda kept winning and soon she was one of the biggest stars in female bodybuilding. She became a world traveler entering contest all over the planet, we just kind of grew apart due to some long separations and one day I just took off for San Diego and stayed there.

I got me a little place down by the ocean in a little surfer village called Pacific Beach, it was a lot different than Los Angeles, there wasn't that many bodybuilders, but there was a shit load of surfers, men and women. I was having a hard time finding a job as a bartender so again I hired on as a head breaker, I didn't like bouncing but damn, every time I was in a crunch for money the work was available. I did my time as the doorman at an upscale gentlemen's club downtown in San Diego, and to my amazement even the topless dancers in this town were surfers, eventually I met enough people and was able to earn some money as a personal trainer. I worked the door at the Palace gentlemen's club only on Fridays and Saturdays, the money was too good to pass up and I loved being around all of them beautiful California girls. Thank the Lord for bodybuilding, I was forty-one years old and women in their early twenties still found me attractive.

I met Macy in the Wave Surf Shoppe on Hermosa Beach one beautiful summer afternoon while I was just hanging out down there girl watching and stopped at the surf shop to grab a pair of sunshades, Macy worked in the stores clothing section. She asked me about my Texas accent and our conversation bloomed from there into us having dinner together that night. She didn't much care for the fact I worked in a strip club on the weekends, but I explained to her about how tough it is to make it as a full-time personal trainer in Cali due to the very high volume of people in the personal training business and she understood why I needed the second job. Thank goodness, there was a couple of honeys working at the Palace I wasn't quite done dancing with yet.

Macy was a competitive surfer, hanging out with her opened up a whole new world to me, I was flying over to Hawaii and Tahiti on a regular basis while she hit the pro circuit, my training didn't suffer at all, come to find out the surfers hit the iron too and there was always a nice gym near the beach wherever we went. I met some of the most famous surfers in the world while I was Macy's boyfriend, she was a fantastic surfer and very popular with everyone on the tour, men and women. Me and Macy were a good fit, she wasn't a bodybuilder, but her athletic body certainly looked like we belonged together. At times, I couldn't miss work or training a well-paying client and wasn't able to travel with her which gave me time to play and not screw up what me and Macy had, like I was saying we were a good fit. I met these two Mexican weightlifters on Pacific Beach one morning and they were pretty much just like me, some big dudes who looked like they lifted a lot of weights, but these boys was at the top of the heap. They was for sure two very successful drug traffickers, only thing is the drugs they brought in were just the steroids they sold to the West Coast bodybuilders and power lifters and business out here was good.

Rudy and Lonnie Balboa were two very bad boys, the only thing we had in common was weight training and I was always cautious around them, I could tell that they was them kind of men who didn't fuck around and I was certain they were killers. They loved to talk about bodybuilding and so did I, Rudy and Lonnie on the other hand would disappear for days at a time, and then shazam they'd show up at the gym just like they never left. Eventually we became better friends, but I still kept my distance with them, every now and then I'd go across the border with them to train at their gym and do some drinking. One-day Rudy asked me, how much money I made working as a bouncer at the topless bar, and when I told him he burst into laughter.

"What's so funny Rudy I asked?"

"Dude you do that shit where on any unlucky night for you, some drunk son-of-a-bitch could end your life, and that's all they pay." After I explained to Rudy the principles of the bouncer never losing due to his superior numbers, I told him, "dude

I'm just hanging out here with my girl, soaking up some California sunshine, the money ain't the most important thing all the time."

"I get it big man he said, but me and Lonnie was talking about giving you a shot at making some real money, just think about it a couple of days and get back to me."

A month later after a couple of crazy brawls with some sailors and taking some bruises, I reconsidered Rudy and Lonnie's offer. I trekked across some barren area adjoining San Diego to the Mexican border on a quad runner along with Rudy and Lonnie all of us loaded down with packages we'd picked up from some other guys on quad runners. There was not more than ten words spoken between the men and us, the exchange of money for goods and we turned around and rode back across the sand and just like that I'd become an international drug smuggler. The ease at which we moved back and forth across the border astonished me, it was kind of cool too because whoever we were working for were a big enough organization that our routes were protected by some corrupt border patrol guys. We looked just like three dudes out playing in the dirt but strapped to the back of these quad runners was several thousand dollars' worth of illegal steroids. My life did change, I quit bouncing in bars, got me a nice used Corvette to drive and focused on the life of a full-time certified personal trainer, my runs out into the desert with Rudy and Lonnie was my other self. In the real-world Macy and me were doing great, I'd even stopped cheating on her, she was sort of famous now and I didn't want to do anything to screw it up for her. We were the real West Coast couple, big musclebound bodybuilder and lean, svelte, blond, and deeply tanned female surf champ cruising down Santa Monica Blvd. in a satin pearl white Corvette LS eight. Macy ragged on me forever for stopping at a music shop to pick up a tape of Sheryl Crow singing her Santa Monica Blvd. song.

"I've always dreamed of doing this Macy, I said, watch it'll be cool, I cranked it up and eased back out into the Boulevard stream of cruisers."

"Why don't we move up here Mike Macy asked, you like that Golds Gym down on Venice Beach and the surf here is decent?"

After a brief second of panic I rebounded, "no way baby I responded, I love San Diego and living on P B with you honeybunch, LA is a cool place to visit but I'd rather live in San Diego." Well said Macy, "it's good to know how you really feel about my hometown, I only suggested we move here so you could be closer to the bodybuilding scene."

"My scene is wherever I am with you Macy, I said with great relief, I did not want the deal with the Balboa Brothers to be over just yet."

Macy finally introduced me to her parents who had been against her being in an inter-racial relationship, Macy and I were on our second year together, so I assumed her folks changed their way of thinking, because one morning she just informed me that we would be dining at her parent's home on Saturday night. I'd never had a problem with Macy's parents because I didn't know them personally, why would

I give a shit about how they felt about me. I only knew they didn't approve of our relationship because Macy told me how they reacted when she told them she was dating some black man almost twenty years older than her. I meant no disrespect to this woman I cared deeply for but what her people thought of me was the furthest thing from my mind, but I knew it was important to Macy. I knew she'd taken the time to get us to this point because Macy knew who I was and if I was not shown respect I would not be giving any. Her father and I made it through the evening being cordial to each other, we even had a thing or two in common like he played linebacker and tackle as a football player just like me. The guy and his wife were both a year younger than me which meant they had Macy at a very young age but they both looked older than me. I think that's what had the mother so intrigued, all through the evening she would ask, "are you really forty-two years old?"

"Yes, ma'am I said in five months I'll be forty-three years old." And proceeded to explain to her the value of healthy living and lots of exercise, overall Macy was happy and that's all I cared about.

I was building up a big bank from my runs with the Balboa Brothers, I know that nothing lasts forever but while the ease and low risk of what I was doing were so much in my favor, why quit now I was thinking, the odds do eventually catch up with us all. The bundles sometime were larger than usual and a bit heavier but what was I going to do, question the Balboas, we hardly spoke on the trips, they'd become like these little missions we went on for two or three days every couple of weeks. We met at an airport hangar a little way from town, jumped on the all-terrain vehicles and hauled ass for hours of hard riding until we met up with the exchange guys. One-day Lonnie told me to learn to shoot this new Glock he handed me in a pretty box while we were dressing to leave the gym.

"What's this for Lonnie, I asked?"

"The past few trips we've been bringing in some other product too, you a smart man Mike, I'm sure you noticed our loads are bigger and heavier now."

"Wasn't my business to pry Lonnie, you pay me to ride hard and carry the load no matter what it is."

I appreciate that Mike but now I need you to carry this on our runs out into the dunes, the other product has drawn us some unwanted attention. Some people would love to have control of what we do, but we like keeping our operation small, you, me and Rudy is all we need. Just in case somebody tries to persuade us to do something we don't want to do you might need this to protect yourself, me and Rudy are always strapped but I don't want you to get in a fix where you might need one of these and don't have one." I nodded my head, closed the box up and zipped it into my gym bag. I'm driving home thinking, shit just like that I'm an armed international steroid and cocaine smuggler, I put some time in at the shooting range and Lonnie showed me how to take care of the weapon as far as maintenance and cleaning goes. I asked him one day, "how come you and Rudy chose me to offer this job to?"

"Rudy got good instincts, he knew you was a righteous dude plus for what we doing you got to look like you mean it to keep people from fucking with you, look at you Mike your arms are the thickness of the average person's leg, don't nobody want to fuck with you bro."

"Follow me over to the Shrimp House and I'll buy us lunch."

While we ate, he broke it all down to me, him and Rudy worked for one of the lesser-known cartel families down in Mexico, though respected by the larger outfits, envy and greed were tiptoeing into their world. The Balboas were the single link to the US for the Ortega's and the Ortega's fiercely protected them on both sides of the border. Lonnie told me that I was always safe when I was with them, "there are always shooters with high powered weapons watching over us everywhere we go, even now he said," causing me to take a quick glance around us.

"Oh, you'll never see them unless they want you to, their job is to make sure nobody fucks with me and Rudy. We mostly stay out of that big-time coke business, we do fine with the steroid business, have been for many years and them greedy folks have left us alone because we've left them alone. Lately though, Javier the oldest Ortega son has convinced his father to start moving a few keys with the other stuff, at first the old man was happy with the extra influx of cash, so he let Javier add just enough to stay under the radar but now them greedy gentlemen want a piece of that too. The Sinaloas and the others know the Ortega's won't back down even if it comes to killing so they haven't made any kind of a move yet."

"The Ortega family is a smaller organization, but they have many old and loyal friends in Mexico, they are protecting you too big Mike, the gun is for just in case something happens."

"Javier and his Papa think you're a mean -looking fucker, they even asked us if you ever killed anyone, I told them I didn't think so, have you he asked?"

"Yes and no I said, some years back I got into it in a tittie bar where I was bouncing, with this cracked up dude who didn't get his knife out fast enough. I beat him and stomped him until there were no more teeth in his head, he got out of the ambulance and refused, to let the EMTs help him, the guy climbed into his truck, drove through the first red light he got to, got T-boned and that is what killed him, not the ass whipping I gave him, them same paramedics ended up loading his ass up anyhow."

"They told their cop buddies about how badly beaten he was before he fought his way out of the ambulance and drove away."

"The cops knew a relative of the guy who just happen to be an FBI agent, what are the fucking chances, I thought. The guys FBI agent brother has me arrested because his family thinks I hold partial responsibility for his death."

"Fortunately, the rich Greek who owned the club kept a bad ass lawyer on retainer for just such situations, and the guy was good, he managed to introduce toxicology and alcoholic levels from the autopsy to the court, making the dead guy look like a drug crazed maniac, and the case against me was dismissed."

"That's a crazy fucking story said Lonnie, did you feel bad for the dead guy?"

"Hell no, the first time I hit him he was trying to stab me, the few people who testified in my favor said the same, hell no bro, I didn't feel nothing for that mother fucker. I got to go meet Macy at some starving artist show, see you at the gym tomorrow dude, thanks for lunch." I didn't pick up on it, but Lonnie Balboa had just given me a sample test to see how I would react to a violent situation, and even though he didn't let it show, he thought I was responsible for the guy in the bars death too. We made three more runs out into the dunes over the next two weeks, not because of the cocaine runs but because there was some new Russian dianabol out on the black market and it seemed that it was all in the hands of the Ortega's. Lonnie, Rudy and me all tried it stacked with some injectable American testosterone and the shit was like the magic pill. We never sold to anyone, but we always got some for us out of the loads before handing it over to the Ortega Distributors in San Diego. Rudy and Lonnie weren't big weightlifter's height wise, but they were built like five-foot-tall tanks, the little pink pills we were eating like skittles turned us all into super hump back beast. I got so strong I frightened myself with some of the humongous lifts I was making. Me and the Balboa Brothers was three of the baddest dudes on the beach, on any given day.

On our next run out to the dunes, we rode up on the guys we were supposed to be meeting in a heated gun battle with some men a couple hundred yards away from our rendezvous site. We came to a stop and Rudy said, "get off and keep down y'all, let's wait for the Calvary."

Ten minutes later I had to say something, "what we waiting on Rudy, shouldn't we be trying to help them dudes out?"

From behind his quad runner where he was lighting up a joint and opening a cold beer, "remember them Guardian Angels I told you would always be watching over us big Mike, asked Lonnie?"

"Yeah, I said in reply."

"Well they ought to be getting into position right about now, listen for the sound of the rifle, whoever is shooting at our friends, I hope they kissed their woman and kid's goodbye when they left home this morning."

"Here have a beer he said tossing me a cold one, and then another, pass this one to Rudy, if you want to hit this joint you going to have to roll your big ass over here my man." Suddenly Krakow, Krakow came two loud explosions in the distance, five minutes later two more of the tremendous blast rang through the air, in the next hour I heard three more of the loud double blast, I never heard of two snipers shooting in tandem before. Sometimes later I heard the growl of the approaching ATVs, the two cats riding them looked like they were hand-picked from the cover of Soldier of Fortune magazine.

"It's all clear they said, y'all go on and take care of your business said the big square jawed white boy with a flat top blonde hair cut, a big sniper rifle in a scabbard at his knee."

"How are our friends asked Lonnie?"

"They're okay, we had to throw a couple of rounds their way to let them know we was here to help and to stop shooting at us along with the four men that ambushed them. Something spooked the ambush guys and made them go to early, I'm sure they meant to wait until y'all got here. Me personally said the other guy, am glad they went early and warned us, I didn't need to ride into no ambush today, my daughter's sweet sixteen party is in two days, and I can't miss that."

"Hey Mike, said Lonnie, I want you to meet Steve Robbins, and Todd Forbes, when we're out working you can always count on them being around somewhere close."

These men I was sure of were of a different breed than me, this man was speaking of death and a sweet sixteen party in the same statement. The two dudes in desert camouflage turned their ATVs around and rode off, while we chugged down the rest of our beers and mounted up. The guys at the exchange were more talkative this time than they'd ever been, I guess looking at probable death makes a man appreciate the opportunity to communicate more. They told us the shooters were drinking and getting high while waiting for us, "we spotted them moving among the dunes from a distance, not much at setting an ambush, are they?"

"They won't get to fuck up ever again, them shooters told us they put all four of them down said Rudy, they said they left the guns if y'all want to ride over to pick them up."

"Thanks, said the contact guy, things are getting worse now, the Ortega's are going to be pissed when they hear someone was trying to jack our load."

"They already know said Lonnie, them two that just saved our asses work directly for Don Ortega, they carry satellite phones and I'm sure they've already reported in."

"We've never lost a load to the law or anybody else said Rudy, that's why they want Don Ortega's operation, nobody knows how we get things done without any violence or risk of being caught."

"Someone has betrayed the Ortega's; the only way those men knew that this is where we were meeting is if somebody close to the Ortega's tipped them off.

Back at the hangar, Rudy was in the back room on the phone with his boss for a long time, when he finally came out he told me, and Lonnie the Ortega's were having all the people on the payroll checked out again, "he's sure it's someone new brought in by Javier since they added cocaine to the loads."

The old gangster was right on the nose, one of the men Javier assumed was now his man, really wasn't, Javier had hired him away from one of the other families, only the man was a plant to find out how the Ortega's got their shipments over the border without incident. Once found out the mole was promptly eliminated and me and the Balboa Brothers were back at it on our regular schedule. Macy took off for a two-week excursion to Costa Rica, some guy was doing an endless summer remake only this time including some of the successful female surfers and she was chosen to participate. She was going to be away filming for a whole month, so I had a lot of free space to fill in, I told the Balboa Brothers I'd be out of touch for a couple of weeks and stuffed a few things into a duffel bag and hopped on a plane to Corpus Christi Texas to hang out with Rhonda. A female pro-bodybuilder named Debbie Muggli was promoting and staging a big show down at the shoreline, Rhonda had been on the pro circuit for a while now, so she was the local liaison for the promoters. I got the opportunity to rub shoulders with some great pro bodybuilders that week and me and Rhonda were as good together as ever, it pained her that I wasn't staying longer than a couple of weeks but I did have another life on the West Coast. I got a good job out West I told her, I'm not ready to give it up yet, being as cool as she always was she understood, and we made the most of our time together. Rhonda and her kids had had enough of the fast pace of living on the West Coast, Los Angeles in particular a year earlier and had moved back to Corpus Christi, she told me they also were missing their family.

CHAPTER
EIGHT

HOT ON THE SAND

W HEN MACY GOT home from Costa Rica she was excited and exhilarated at how things had gone with the making of the film, and how great it was to have spent all the time with her little tribe called the surfers. I was very happy for her, the way her life was working out just the way she always dreamed it would, more than once she told me of her wishes to become a famous pro surfer and now it appears her dreams were coming true. A month later out of nowhere she sat me down to tell me she was pregnant catching me completely off guard, we'd never discussed having a child and I'd never pictured myself as a father. Being so weirdly independent, the next thing out of her mouth was, "Mike this doesn't mean I got no kind of hold on you. I've been wanting a baby for a long time now and I'm glad you're the father but with or without you our baby will have a good life."

"You never mentioned wanting kids Macy, that's why I'm so surprised and I would never abandon you because you're having my child, after all this time you don't know me at all Macy." She started to cry realizing how much she'd wounded me with such crass words, putting her strong arms around my waist and squeezing me tight to her. In my ear, "Macy told me how sorry she was for hurting my feelings and that she loved me enough to want me to be the father of her first child." We made intense love the rest of the day and I asked Macy to marry me at sunrise the next morning while we smoked a joint out on the patio. She accepted and informed me that this will be the last joint we'll smoke together for a few months, and on that very morning we started to plan a wedding. She called her parents to tell them about the baby and the wedding we were planning, her mother was elated, I don't know how the father was taking it though. Macy always said, he'd come around, so I just took her word for it, a new baby coming into a family changes everything.

We had a kick- ass wedding right near the waves on Pacific Beach, the wedding party looked like a gathering of warriors, all the bridesmaids were girl surfers and all my groomsmen were bodybuilders or power lifters, it was awesome. We honeymooned in Tahiti, a place Macy had been to several times to surf, she couldn't have been more on point, Tahiti is the perfect getaway for lovers. When we got back to PB Macy and I gave up our little apartment on the beach and we used some of my funds from the drug trade I'd been involved in the past year to put a down payment on a little house near the Pacific Beach community. Macy had never hassled me about how I made my money, she knew I was doing something that could get me locked up for a long time if I was ever caught, but I'd lied and told her I was never in any danger, so she let me be. Now that we were married with a child on the way, Macy was seeing our lives together as something more than we had been. She didn't demand anything from me but, in a loving way suggested I find some legal means of making a living. Many times, in the past I'd considered breaking away from the Balboa boy's business but the fact that I was making such good money at a less than minimal risk made it easy to banish the thought. That ease of my decision to stay in the business would soon be a foregone thought. While I was away on my month-long honeymoon down in the Pacific, things along the Cali-Mexico border had boiled over into a full-blown turf battle between the Juarez cartel and another major player named EL-Chapo Guzman over transportation routes. The Ortega's were a small organization in comparison but the fight to control their transportation routes were a part of the battle. The Balboas made it clear to me that the Ortega's kept to themselves for this very reason alone, these big wars over territory and transport routes always drew much unwanted attention from the media in and outside of Mexico.

"Things are going to be a little tough big Mike, said Rudy, the Huertas and EL-Chapo are pressuring Don Ortega and Javier to pick a side. He knows to do so would make him an enemy of the other, so we won't be making any more coke runs until these fucker's stop killing each other. We do well enough just bringing in the juice, so Don Ortega has ordered Javier to stop buying keys of Coke from any of them, hopefully they will come to see we don't need to do business with them and leave us alone. They don't know about us or you Mike, that's why they tried to take our couriers a couple of months ago, to make them lead them to us, so don't come out without your piece until things have settled."

Me and Macy moved into our new place and based on my talks with the Balboas about the danger we might find ourselves in, I gave Macy access to all the money I had in the bank and what I kept in a safe deposit box. At first, she was suspicious, but I smartly quelled her suspicions by telling her she was my wife and it was the right thing for me to do in case I was in an auto accident or something. She was amazed at the amount of money we had and asked why we didn't just pay cash for our home.

"Macy honey, I'm a personal trainer and you're a pro surfer, those things make us look like any normal couple with a kid on the way, us paying cash for a hundred-thousand-dollar house in cash makes us look like something else. Plus, if I suddenly have to quit what I do, we'll need money to live on whether we own a home or not,

I don't want you to be working at the surf shoppe when you're farther along with our baby."

"Better yet baby, what you think it'll cost us to own the Wave Surf Shop? Have you ever considered being a business owner, that would go well with our life here in Pacific Beach California?"

"I've never thought about owning a business, Macy replied, but I'll ask Randy how he feels about selling us the shop while I'm at work today."

"We do something like that honey, and my life immediately goes in another direction, I'm getting too old to be bouncing in these bars and clubs and the personal training business is getting too crowded and cutthroat to make a decent living."

"Randy Underwood, the owner of the Wave Surf Shoppe surprisingly was wanting to sell his store, he told Macy he would talk it over with his wife and his banker and get back to her. He had once been a pro surfer himself and had opened the surf shop with his first year of big prize money, he and his wife had started a family and already had three kids. His wife wanted to move to Aspen Colorado to be closer to her family with the children, by the next week he'd given Macy a number and to my surprise it was much less than I thought it would have been, hell I had a hundred and forty grand in a shoebox in the closet. Two weeks later we were the proud owners of the Wave Surf Shoppe at Pacific Beach California and Randy and his family were off to the Colorado Rockies. I told the Balboa Brothers that after two more runs I was out and going to focus all my efforts on running the surf shop. I thought they would be pissed about my quitting, but Rudy and Lonnie both were cool with my choice to get out, if I had a wife with a kid on the way I'd be looking to get out of this shit myself, said Rudy," it's going to be tough replacing you but all the same we're happy for you and your woman."

On the next run the Guardian Angels had to pull our fats out of the fire again, the other bosses had decided against the Ortega's decision to remain neutral. A group had placed a tracking device on the ATV of one of our courier guys and tracked him right to our rendezvous out in the sand dunes. They wore desert camouflage just like our guardians, so by the time we spotted them they were throwing lead our way, one round caught Rudy in the thigh and another dropped one of the handoff guys before we all hit the dirt. I crawled over to Rudy and used a bungee cord to tourniquet his leg which was spurting blood badly. The shooting kept up for a few minutes with us returning as much fire as we could from cover with our hand guns. I kept listening for the crack of the big sniper rifles, and finally it came in rapid amounts, it sounded like more than two guys were shooting. After a while the shooting ceased, and I heard the low growl of the approaching quad runners, the sniper Steve Robbins tended to Rudy's wound while we waited, it was bad, and I knew if we didn't get him to a doctor in a hurry he could bleed to death out here in the sand dunes. While the shooters tended Rudy's, wound I could see that one of them was hit too, and the guy went about his business like it was nothing, with just a tourniquet stemming the blood coming from his shoulder.

"Them fuckers had some long-range shooters with them too and caught us by surprise said the wounded one, his shoulder covered in blood."

"How bad is Rudy hit, he asked his partner?"

"I think they caught an artery, I'm having a hard time stopping the bleeding he said."

"I need to get to a doctor quick myself, said the big soldier, can you sit up and ride he asked Rudy?"

"We can get to a doctor quicker on the other side, faster than if we tried to make it back to the states, get him on back of Steve's machine, we've got a doctor already meeting us with an ambulance, I'll call Don Ortega to let him know we need two."

"What about them other shooters I asked, won't they be out there waiting somewhere?"

"Only thing them boys going to be waiting for is an undertaker, they should not have ever fucked with us, Steve wrapped a strap around him and Rudy to keep Rudy from falling off and they headed towards the border." The other man took the box of money from Lonnie, lifted the body of their friend across the back of one of the quad runners and headed out in the same direction as Rudy and the other men. We ended up leaving two blood-soaked ATVs where they were with a plan to leave them for anybody who wanted them. The Ortega's had arranged for a doctor with his own ambulance to meet the injured men just over the Mexico border, I was glad for that, Rudy's wound was much more serious than we thought. He would have certainly bled to death if we'd tried to make the run back to San Diego and then find a hospital with an emergency room equipped to save him. And then again, the first thing they would do is call the cops, leaving us to try and explain how our friend got shot in the first place. At the hangar after the goods were broken down and handed off, me and Lonnie sat down drinking some beers waiting for news about Rudy.

"Don Ortega is going to be damned mad about Rudy and the soldier being shot, this thing with the other families is fixing to explode. Those shooters were not out there just to jack the load Mike, they was sent to kill us, if you going to walk away, now is the time, things are going to only get worse from here on."

Two days later the lead story on the local news was of the fifteen headless bodies hanging from the border fence at Juarez on the United States side. Against his father's wishes Javier and his shooters took it upon themselves to even the score. From the kitchen, Macy heard me say shit, louder than I meant to at seeing the horror on the television.

"What's wrong baby, asked Macy as she waddled into the den carrying two cups of coffee."

"I didn't want to worry you baby, that's why I hadn't said nothing, but something bad went down on the last run me and the Balboas made." She passed me one of the cups and sat down on the sofa next to me, "tell me what happened Mike and please don't lie to me she said." I proceeded to tell Macy everything that had gone down, and about Rudy and the guardian shooter being seriously wounded and about the war brewing amongst the Mexican gangs.

"That's it protested my beautiful pregnant wife, I've been silent about what you and the Balboas have been doing because you assured me that there was no real danger, but this shit changes everything Mike." I was quite shocked because Macy never used profanity of any type, but from the tone of her voice I knew my wife was serious as hell.

"We've got plenty of money in the bank, enough to last us for a good while, I don't care if you got to shovel shit to make a living Mike, you're done with the Balboas anyplace but the gym."

I never went on another dope run with Lonnie and Rudy, but we remained pals and supported each other as bodybuilders and at powerlifting meets. Rudy healed up from his gunshot wound but he had a limp that made him walk like John Wayne, he never tried to get me to work with them again, but he and Lonnie set me up as their go to guy for good Mexican anabolic steroids. I managed to make some decent money between my personal training clients and selling steroids to the local power lifters and bodybuilders. My life was for now in a good place, I had a nice chunk of money stashed away, I was in the greatest condition of my life, and in a couple of months I was going to be a father for the first time, my life was excellent, I thought what could go wrong.

CHAPTER
NINE

HEARD MY name over the gym public address system summoning me to come to the front desk for an urgent phone call, Macy had gone into labor and was already in route to the hospital. She and her mother were out shopping when her water broke so they left the mall and went straight to the hospital, her mother was phoning me from the car. I grabbed my stuff, told my client what was up and promised him a free session for having to cut this one short and took off for the hospital. I was greeted at the obstetrics waiting room by Macy's parents who directed me to where she was waiting for me to join her, "glad you made it on time Mister Dunn, your baby is ready to come out," announced the doctor. I gave my woman a tender kiss as she grabbed my hand to squeeze it tightly, "here we go baby we're about to be parents she said." We were in a birthing suite, so Macy's folks came in to join us for this momentous occasion, I held Macys hand while her mother fed her ice chips from the other side of the bed. At last the doctor told Macy to make the final push and out slid this beautiful little girl with golden blonde hair and to my complete surprise, bright blue eyes. I looked into Macy's eyes which are brown like mine and then at her parents who also had dark eyes and the baby's skin color was white like a full-blooded white baby is supposed to look. Macy and I met eyes again and she saw the confused look on my face, "what's wrong she asked, is there something wrong with our baby?"

"No, I said, the baby is perfect," the attending nurse cleaned some of the fluids from the baby's nose and mouth and then brought her around for Macy to hold. One look at the beautiful little girl and Macy knew why I stood frozen with a dumbfounded expression on my face. It was clear to everyone in that birthing room that this was not a biracial child and I certainly could not be the father. We'd known for weeks the baby was a girl from the ultrasounds and we had chosen the name Zoe Margola for her, but at this moment none of that mattered to me. The doctor and attending nurses went about their work but it was obvious to them how the mood in the room had turned to something else other than joy. Call it pride or shame or whatever, all I knew is I just wasn't there anymore, I took a step back from the bed, gave Macy what I knew was for sure the last time I'd ever look into her beautiful face, turned and left the room. Macy could see the hurt and pain on my face and even though I heard her call my name as I opened the door to leave, I did not stop or even bother to look back. I was standing at the elevator just staring at a spot on the wall when Macy's mother touched me on the shoulder, I didn't bother to turn around as the feeling of shame was starting to take me over, and all I said to her was, "I don't want to hear it," the elevator door opened, and I stepped in to join the three people inside. As the door was closing Macy's mother said, "she just wants the chance to explain," the door closed, and I was out of there. I stopped by the bank and emptied my safe deposit box of the one hundred and twenty-five grand inside, stopped at the house to get some stuff I didn't want to leave behind and hit the road headed nowhere in particular, I just wanted to deal with my hurt and pain in solitude. I didn't feel that I could face the guys at the gym who were all waiting on news of my new baby, so I didn't even bother with any goodbyes. My cell phone rang with a number I didn't recognize so I let it go to voicemail, over the next few hours the same number rang time and time again, I was just too broken to feel like talking to anybody. When I finally stopped to buy some beer, and smoke a joint I was at a truck stop in Arizona, I didn't even know what town I was in. I bought a six pack of Budweiser and a bag of ice for my travel cooler and found me a place to park at the outskirts of the truck stop so I could smoke my pot in peace. I took out my phone and hit voicemail, put it on speaker and laid it on the seat next to me, every message was from Macy and I could tell that she was crying. She used up all the space on my voicemail explaining to me how on her trip to Costa Rica last summer she and an old lover got together for dinner after the contest, got drunk and ended up in bed together, other than that one time she said she'd never been unfaithful to me. I probably could have easily forgiven her for that one indiscretion but the humiliation from the birthing room would not leave my thoughts and I knew things would never be right between she and I. I left her thirty thousand dollars in the bank and I could care less what she did with the house, or the surf shop, over the next couple of days the phone continually rang with Macy's mother and father leaving me messages to please return their call, finally I just tossed my cell phone into the Grand Canyon. The last time I drove through the Arizona desert it was at night, so I completely missed the sign indicating Red Rock, so I took the off-ramp and stopped at the first eating place I saw. To my utter surprise Red Rock really was a town, I'd seen the movies with the Cowboys talking about Red Rock, but I always thought it was a town made up in Hollywood. Yet here I was in Red Rock Arizona, a big giant red boulder right off the highway to indicate its location, the thing looked like a rock, but it was the size of a small mountain, I walked into the little café and went straight to the restroom to splash some water on my face to revive myself a little before I ate. At the urinal stood a big white dude with dirty brown long hair relieving himself, the guy looked over his shoulder at me and said, "we don't allow no niggers in here, didn't they tell you that at the door boy."

I stopped what I was doing, took a step back and planted my foot right square in the middle of that son-of-a-bitches back, slamming him against the urinal, the big white boy was taller than me and big, but I saw that he was just a fat bastard and his timing could not have been worse. I knew the dumb bastard would try to zip up before he turned to face me, so I took the time to snap open my buck knife and plunged it into his ass cheek and then his thigh while pushing him against the urinal with my other hand. I pulled my knife out of his leg and let go of him, watching his big ass gut sprawled on the floor screaming in pain, I took aim and kicked that piece of shit in the head a few times before giving him a solid stomp of my heel to his face, smashing the back of his head against the hard tile floor and knocking him out. I'd been in enough fights in my time to know once a confrontation is inevitable, it's smart to strike first and fast, I wasn't sure if the guy had friends outside, so I hurriedly washed his blood off my hand and my knife and left the little café. That fellows timing could not have been worse, I was looking for something to ease the pain I was in and a shit smelling redneck would do just fine. Five minutes later I was back on Interstate 10 headed east through the Arizona desert in my red Corvette thinking, I guess I won't be visiting Red Rock again no time soon. I got off the highway in New Mexico got a room and slept for a whole day, I'd had my heart broken three days ago, and still wasn't quite sure what I was going to do with my newfound freedom.

I hadn't talked to Paul or Frank in a few months, so before I left the hotel I took the time to give them both a call to get my ass reaming for being out of touch for so long, and to see how things were with them. After bitching me out for a couple of minutes Paul finally settled down to tell me that a close buddy of ours, Duke Blessing was killed in a motorcycle wreck. His funeral is in two days Paul said, can you make it back to Angleton in time, despite it being a sad occasion, everybody would be glad to see you, he added.

"Count on it I said, see you sometime tomorrow night, and tell your wife I'm coming, that should make her smile," we both laughed sarcastically and then hung up. I gave Frank a call and he was already in Angleton at his folk's house, I told him I was on the way home and would call him from Paul's house.

"Hell, no he said, don't go to Paul's, you know Trudi Dawn don't care much for your ass, come to my folk's house, both of my sisters are married and have moved out, so there's plenty of room there, plus my parents will be thrilled to see you."

The following morning, I had a good breakfast in the hotel restaurant and then hit the road, this time with a destination in mind. I didn't make any effort to make it to our twenty-year class reunion, but it seemed that Duke's funeral was just that, everyone I cared to see again came back to town for the funeral, Duke was one of them cats that everyone loved. After the funeral reception, we all ended the day with a plan to meet at a spot down on Bastrop Bayou where we spent most of our free time as kids waterskiing and drinking. Paul and Frank took time out to bitch me out again for being out of touch for so long, while I was on the West Coast. During my absence, Jerry Garcia, the main player in the Grateful Dead band, who was a God to us, had passed away, I was aware of his passing but didn't get to mourn his death with my two devoted friends. I felt bad about it but what was I going to do, call them and say sorry I've been out of touch brothers, but I'm busy running drugs from the Mexico border to the United States right now. My high school sweetheart managed to slip away from her husband for a day and we ended up in a hotel room together that night, it felt liberating to sleep with another woman and not feel like I was cheating on Macy. I found out many years later that she and I created a baby that night together, the boy was nine years old when she told him who his true father was, too bad we never got to know each other, due to her secrecy and my constant wondering.

I stayed in Angleton for two weeks, took a few days to visit some old pals like Stanley Montgomery, a guy we all called Sponge, I never knew how Stanley came about having that nickname. He, I and his brother Dennis used to spend hours on the San Bernard River fishing, drinking a lot of beer and just being carefree country boys. Sponge had done what every other dude back home did once reaching maturity, if you didn't go away to college you went to work in the local Dow Chemical refineries. Growing up I noticed that all the fathers of the town kids worked at the chemical plants and then the children reached adulthood and did the exact same thing. I recalled thinking at a very young age, ain't no way in the fucking world I'm going to get stuck spending my life as a numbered employee of the chemical manufacturers, I knew leaving here after graduation was a certainty. For old times sake, me and Sponge grabbed his fishing gear, loaded up his truck and headed to the river for some R and R, we left word with a few friends of our intentions and by the days end the fishing trip became a full-blown land party. For that one day, we were all once again children with not a care in the world but what was happening at that moment in time. By midnight everyone was skinny-dipping in the river and pairing off for clandestine sexual encounters, just like we did in high school. Trudi Dawn even loosened the reins on Paul, and they both hung out on the river with us well into the night. The sun came up, and all the goodbyes and farewells were said as all my childhood pals went back to their boring, mundane lives, as I saw it, I love this town and these people, but I felt it impossible to live here full-time. It had been a memorable two weeks, that I'll always cherish but the time came for me to move on, I tossed my duffel bag in the car, bid my farewell to Frank's family and struck out for the city, Houston that is.

I walked through the front entrance of Hanks Gym on a sunny afternoon to find lots of the old crowd still training there and a bunch of new faces too. Betty

Herndon had turned pro and moved on to Los Angeles, I'd seen many photos of her in the bodybuilding publications and was aware of how well she was doing in the sport. Hank came over to give me a warm greeting and to ask, "where the hell I'd been these past few years." I gave him a brief update on everything except my time as a drug smuggler, I had spent a few days in a little town outside St. Louis Missouri and trained at the gym of one of Hanks old friends. George Turner was one of the original bodybuilders from the fifty's and was a legend right up there with Steve Reeves, Reg Park and Mickey Harrgitay, all three legendary Hollywood musclemen. Mickey was once the husband to the actress Jane Russell a notorious Hollywood starlet, Steve and Reg were famous for playing Hercules on the big screen. George Turner and Hank were both a part of this golden age of bodybuilding, Hank was thrilled to hear how well George was doing and was elated that I'd spent some time training at his gym. He's still in great shape, I told Hank, the man was sixty-seven years old and had the muscle structure of a man half that age. His wife who had to be well into her sixties was also in great shape, she even taught the aerobics dance class at the facility, Hanks face was lit up with pride and joy at hearing how well his old friend was doing. "How long you going to be in town he asked me?"

"I don't really know Hank but here's a hundred and fifty bucks, I need a place to train while I'm in town, if I'm still here by the time this runs out, I'll pay for another few months." Hank signed me up for a six-month membership, gave me a hug and said, "now get to work, it's good to have one of the old-timers like you back in the place."

I was still emotionally screwed up over the Macy ordeal, so being around people I know, and love was good healing juice for a barbarian like myself. I was happy the first female bodybuilder, whom I fell in love with on-site, Dena Anderson still trained at Hanks and she was training her clients there also, therefore I got to see her every time I hit the gym, every so often she and I would work out together. I told her I'd been keeping track of her career in the muscle mags and how proud I was to tell people on the West Coast that she was a friend of mine.

"I wondered where you'd vanished to so suddenly, she said to me one day while we were squatting together, I asked some of the others what happened to you and Michael told me you were living out West in San Diego." I nearly dropped to my knees when Dena told me what Michael said to her, I'm thinking how the hell did a guy at Hanks gym in Houston Texas know I was living in San Diego? Michael and I were not close friends, but we knew each other from training at Hanks and if he was competing in a show he could count on my support and applause from the audience, I'd say our acquaintance was casual at the most. We'd never had a full conversation about anything personal, so I was flabbergasted that he knew where I'd been for the past four years. Michael worked at the front desk for Hank sometime, so the next time I saw him behind the front counter I took a break from my workout and went over to talk to him.

"What's been shaking Michael I said to start up a conversation?"

"Hey big Mike, Hank told me you was back in town, welcome home big man, how you been these days, he asked?"

"Just great Michael, I was talking with Dena the other day and she said you were the person who told her I was living out in San Diego, how would you know that bro.?"

"Aw" shit dude, he said, I bet that did freak you out when she told you," my name is Miguel Ortega big Mike, does that ring any bells for you." I stood there completely stumped, "the only Ortega's I knew, I don't really know personally, and they live in Mexico, I said.

"You mean my Tio Victor and my cousin Javier, he asked." I was speechless and after me not saying anything for twenty seconds, Michael said, "the Balboa Brothers like you and once they told my uncle they wanted to get you to work with them in the family business, he wouldn't give them the okay until they had you checked out."

"Mexicans don't really do business with Blacks, so Javier was sure to do a full vetting of you before they put you to work, they knew you were a bodybuilder from Houston so I'm the first-person Javier called, I told them you was good people dude." You could have knocked me over with a feather at hearing this, all I could think of was, what a small world we live in. You know everything, I asked?"

"Dude I know you treated Rudy's wound out in the sand dunes that day them fuckers tried to take y'all out, the Balboas love you like family man, them two mean mothers don't just trust anybody, so consider yourself lucky. It's too bad shit's going crazy down there, it's even screwing up my business here in Houston, half of the stuff y'all was bringing over came here to me, we was doing just fine until Javier started adding "yayo "to the loads." You got out right when things was starting to get tragic, Javier told me you got married and settled down, did you bring your wife to Houston with you?" With a sad thought, I said, "that marriage is history man, it's a long story, I'll tell you about it sometime when it don't hurt so much," to change the subject I asked him how are Lonnie and Rudy doing?

"Them two knuckleheads are okay, I'll be sure to tell them you asked about them next time we talk, they been working for our family since they learned to talk. I knew who they was talking about the second Javier gave me a physical description of you, the minute he mentioned them big ass arms of yours and them hoop earrings you wear I knew it was big Mike the baddest squatter I know, if you need to make some dough, just let me know, don't fuck with anybody else dude, you family now."

Soon I was back in the game, Michael turned me on to people I could sell juice to on a regular basis in the small towns in the Houston area, high school coaches, college football stars, pro football players, competitive weightlifters, you name it the customers were endless. Michael and I didn't become best friends or anything like that, but I was someone he knew he could trust, I was making plenty of money just moving product around the area. I was very surprised to find out that a man younger than me who happened to be the strongest man in the world was one of Michael's main customers. I'd known Tony Clarke for a great deal of his life as a powerlifter, Tony was one of the young lions who at one time looked up to me like I was the king. In one weekend, I watched that young lion tie or break every lifting record in the world against lifters many years his senior. Over the next two competition seasons the guy became the King, his face was brandished on the cover of every bodybuilding and powerlifting publication in the nation. As a sign of humor, I used to say to big Tony who now weighed close to 400 pounds, "anabolic steroids changed the world big guy." The pro football players and the track stars were setting new records by leaps and bounds, and we were the key purveyors of the magic elixir that made men in to kings. I've got to say the Balboas paved the way for me to become a quasi-wealthy man. I felt some degree of uneasiness though, the Ortega's were paying for my success with their blood, the war between the cartels was going into its second year and was showing no sign of letting up. I got a phone call from Lonnie and Rudy every couple of months just to see how I was doing, I was quite disappointed to hear from Rudy that Lonnie had become a cocaine addict. Rudy said the Ortega's were on the verge of excluding Lonnie from the business, there is nothing more dangerous than a drug dealer on a high level with an addiction problem. The bosses were always concerned that if arrested a man with a drug problem might fold under intense interrogation and say something he shouldn't. To them it was more practical to just get rid of the problem altogether, that meant if Lonnie didn't clean up his act he could be silenced permanently, he was sort of a pal, and I didn't want to see that happen. Michael had made a subtle comment about Lonnie's drug problem to me one day, that's how I knew it was getting to a critical stage, I mean why would Michael give a shit what I thought about Lonnie having a cocaine habit. My own life was starting to get back on track, by that I mean my broken heart was mending itself with time, I'd taken on the training of a couple of promising competitive bodybuilders who'd done well in their first couple of contest. I'd even gone on a couple of dinner dates with Dena Anderson, a woman I'd always admired and come to find out we had some more things in common other than bodybuilding. Dena was making my efforts to forget about Macy a lot easier, Lonnie told me in a phone call one-day Macy had been showing up at Powerhouse Gym a couple times a week asking if they knew where to contact me. Once I told them what went down with us, they understood fully why I wanted nothing to do with Macy and were more than happy to lie to her about not knowing how to contact me.

I went to Vegas with Dena to compete in a show in which she won her weight class but lost the over-all award to who else but big Betty Herndon our home girl. The same Betty Herndon I'd mistaken for a man the first day I trained at Hanks, she was 3 inches taller than Dena and 30 pounds heavier, there were some men she could have easily beaten that night, it was cool though to see the show dominated by the Texas girls.

Michael Ortega and I stayed under the laws radar because we never sold juice to individuals, everyone we dealt with bought quantities from us and dispersed the chemicals to whom they pleased. Michael was at the front desk when I walked in to do my work out one morning, and he asked me if I had a few minutes to talk before my workout. "Sure Michael, what's on your mind brother, I answered?"

"Give me a minute to get somebody on the front counter, we need to have this talk in private," a few minutes later we were out in the parking lot in the cab of Michael's Chevy pickup. Michael sparked up a doobie, took a couple of tokes and then passed it over to me, after I took a good hit and passed it back, Michael said, "Rudy told me you use to be quite a bad ass head breaker in some rough bars out west, is that true?"

"I don't know how much of a bad ass I was Michael, but I have been able to handle myself in some tough spots, why do you ask?"

"Technically big Mike he said, you still one of my Tios boys, you know that right."

"Damn right, I said, I've been living a good life every sense Lonnie and Rudy took me on, you can tell your uncle how much I appreciate him bringing me on board."

"I'm glad you feel that way dude, Tio Victor wants you to go down to Corpus Christi with me for a couple of days and watch my back while I find this fucker that's into us for quite a large sum of money, except he's acting like he don't got to pay until he feels like it. Javier fronted him a few keys sometime back when y'all was bringing them in, after we got out of that market and this idiot started getting product from one of the other families, he felt like he didn't have to pay us what he owed, I'm going down there to remind him that he does."

"Not a problem Michael, be glad to help, do I need to be strapped I added?"

"Nah", don't worry about that, if there's going to be trouble, we got a couple people in Port Aransas who can come over to give us a hand, Tio Vic just wants someone from the family present. This dumb ass thinks all the Ortega's are living down across the border, he lives in Robstown, you know where that is right, and he thinks he can avoid us by staying out there."

"I been to Robstown a few times, I said, it's a nice little town, wouldn't want to live there though."

I asked Dena to take care of a couple of my clients whom I wouldn't be able to reschedule because I wasn't too sure how long I would be down in South East Texas, she agreed and in three days after he asked for my help Michael and I were headed to Corpus Christi. Robstown was maybe 10 miles from Corpus Christi but there were no gyms there, so we got hotel rooms near the Ironhorse Gym owned by my friends Rodney Serpa and his wife Judy. To be honest with myself I really didn't want to get involved in this strong-arm part of the Ortega's business, but I knew better than to get on the bad side of these very dangerous men. Me and Michael stepped into the gym on a beautiful sunny South Texas afternoon, I introduced Michael all around to everyone I knew and laughingly suffered through all the, two guys named Mike traveling together jokes, then me and Michael hit the iron for a chest workout.

While we were training Michael laid out our plan for the evening, the two guys from Port Aransas were going to meet us at a seafood restaurant in Robstown owned by Doug Pederson, the man we were looking for. With luck, he would be there, and this would be a short trip, Rhonda got word I was in the gym and came over to see me after teaching her dance class next door, she wanted to get together for dinner that night, but I told her I'd be busy for the next couple of days. I promised her I'd make some time to get together with her before we left town. On the way to Robstown that night Michael asked me, "big Mike what's the deal with you and these blonde haired white women, you don't like black women or what?"

"I love black women brother but when it comes to a relationship I prefer white women, they tend to understand what kind of a man I am more than black women do."

"I don't understand what you mean dude, he said."

"Well for one, the kind of music I like, black women don't care for, and I like female bodybuilders, bodybuilding ain't that popular a sport with a great deal of the sister's dude."

"That's it, Michael asked in an astonished tone, it's got to be more to it than that."

"Oh yeah, I love fucking white women a lot more than black women or Mexican women or any other flavor of woman." All he could say was, "you a strange man big Mike."

"Let me tell you a story about my life Michael, I growed up in this little town about 40 miles south of Houston, when I was in the third grade all the schools in Texas were suddenly integrated. Until that happened I hardly ever saw a white person, the powers that be immediately let the black dudes know that the white girls were off limits, to touch one of them could result in expulsion or something worse like death."

"By the time, I got to high school the biggest football stars in town were the black kids and the white girls couldn't keep they hands or lips off us. One year the football team went to the state championship, and all bets were off, if we were winning football games the white people looked the other way if we had a white girlfriend, because you know in Texas nothing is more important than high school football. In the beginning, I was banging the white chicks just because I knew how much it pissed the rednecks off, but as I got older I was used to having a white girlfriend around and that's it bro."

"So, what about that music thing you mentioned, Michael asked?"

"I got turned on to this band called the Grateful Dead when I was in high school by this dude on the football team named Frank Hargis. Whenever the band came near enough for us to drive and see them live, nobody liked them enough to go except me, Frank and the hippie chicks in town who all just happen to be white."

"That's some crazy shit man, I expected your story to be something a lot more complicated than what you just told me though."

Michael's cell phone rang, it was the two guys Javier sent to assist us, they were already at the restaurant in Robstown and so was Doug Pederson with some of his pals. We pulled into the parking lot of the Roadhouse Seafood Restaurant, and Michael parked next to a black Hummer, he got out and had a brief conversation with the two men inside the Hummer, afterwards he and I went inside and took seats at the bar. I ordered a draft beer and two dozen oysters on the half shell, Michael got a shot of Patron tequila, we ate our oysters and waited to get Pederson's attention. The man walked past us on the way to the kitchen and Michael said, "excuse me Mister Pederson, my name is Michael Ortega and I was hoping to have a minute of your time for a private word." I could tell by the look on the guys' face, he knew who Michael represented and why he was there, "this is my associate Bob," said Michael as he made a gesture in my direction.

"Why don't you fellows come back to my office, it's quiet back there so we can talk better in private."

I closed the door behind me as we followed the guy into a room at the rear of the kitchen, Michael immediately said, "you know why I'm here Doug and Javier instructed me not to leave without the money you owe the Ortega's."

"Does Javier think I just keep a hundred and fifty grand lying around this restaurant and besides that the Huertas told me not to worry about that money because y'all don't work with them anymore."

"You might be getting your product from the Huertas now, but you still owe Javier for the load he fronted you, and I don't care where you get the money from, said Michael."

"So, what said the guy, if I don't give you a hundred and fifty grand right now, what you going to do sick this big- ass nigger on me?"

"Before you do anything stupid Michael, the guy said defensively, you might want to know that those men at my table are both Nueces County Sheriff's, and they saw you two come in here with me."

"First off Doug, you are wrong for directing that racial insult at my friend here and second, if you don't pay up all I'm going to do is call my Tio Victor and let him know you refused to pay what you owe him, goodbye Doug", said Michael, he turned to me and said, "let's go Bob." Once we paid our bar tab and went back to the parking lot, Michael said "wait for me in the truck big Mike, I'll be back in a minute." A couple of minutes later after his talk with the men in the Hummer he got back into his truck cranked it up and we left the parking lot, "what now I asked Mike?"

"We go back to our hotel and wait for a phone call, and then go from there, won't you call that fine ass girl bodybuilder from the gym and see if she's got a friend, see if they want to go out for drinks tonight."

Me and Michael met Rhonda and her friend Skye, another beautiful bodybuilder at the Corpus Christi Surf Club a swanky little bar downtown on Chaparral Street the main drag for the night life in Corpus Christi. Skye was a gorgeous little brunette who I did recognize from seeing her in the light weight lineup at some national physique committee contest, she and Michael hit it off right away. We got a good table out on the patio where the bar featured live music, on stage was the band Storyville, one of the best bands in Texas featuring a guitar player named Jimmy Vaughn, the brother of famed Texas bluesman Stevie Ray Vaughn. Half- way through the Storyville set Michael's cell phone chimed, he excused himself and left the table to find a quiet spot to take the call. A minute later he came back to the table with a fresh round of tequila shots, followed by a waitress with a platter of freshly shucked oysters.

"It's crazy how much you like these nasty things big Mike, hey guys that was a business call I just got, something I've got to deal with right away."

"Here's my truck keys Mike, someone will be here to pick me up in a few minutes, ladies let's finish this evening off tomorrow if y'all are free and I'm so sorry I got to leave but this is something urgent I need to deal with tonight."

"You sure you won't need my help in any way Michael, I asked?"

"No way am I going to ruin these two-beautiful ladies' night by cutting it short, I got this Mike, but thanks for offering to help." Ten minutes later the big black Hummer pulled to the front of the bar, Michael passed me a couple of hundreds and said I'll see you at the hotel later tonight, he then gave Skye and Rhonda pecks on the cheek, apologized again, promised to make it up to them tomorrow and left to get into the back seat of the big Hummer. Who could have guessed, hogtied in the rear cargo area of the big Hummer, was none other than Doug Pederson himself.

"I like him said Skye, how much longer are you guys going to be in town?"

"I'm not sure Skye, we only came down to hang out for a few days on the beach, Michael's uncle has some business interests down here, he asked him to check on while we were in South Texas. If Michael's done with his family stuff by tomorrow, we still got a few days before we've got to be back in Houston, I'll know more when I talk to him in the morning, give me your number and I'll have him call you in the morning."

"Okay said Rhonda, I've been holding this in all evening, what's this I hear about you and Dena Anderson paired up at the Las Vegas classic last month, word is y'all two are a couple, is that true?"

"You are a big enough girl Rhonda my dear to not believe every bit of gossip that comes your way, Dena and me both train at the same gym and we both work our clients out at the same place, why wouldn't we be friends? You and I did the same thing when I used to live down here."

"Yes, we did Mister Mike Dunn, only difference is you and I have been sleeping together on and off for about five years now.

"Rhonda, you of all people know that the only women I'm attracted to are bodybuilders, so yes, Dena and me are spending a lot of time together but that don't mean you don't still hold this special place in my heart, you'll always be the love of my life darling," and in my heart, that was the truth.

CHAPTER
TEN

MICHAEL WASN'T IN his room when I woke up the next morning, so Rhonda and I showered and went to Denny's to have breakfast before she went to work. I called his cell and got his voicemail two times, so I stopped calling, assuming he must be busy and decided to just wait until I heard from him. I talked to Skye at the Ironhorse and we ended up training back and biceps together while she pressed me for information on Michael's relationship status. There wasn't much I could tell her other than us training at Hanks and him working there, anything else was too sensitive to share.

The following morning Rhonda and I were snuggling in bed watching the local news when the screen was suddenly filled with the image of Michael's face followed by the faces of two other Hispanic men.

"Oh shit, that's Michael," I grabbed the remote to turn up the volume. The scene then switched to images of a metal toolbox buried in a hole with a garden hose sticking out of it, the reporter said they were at a secluded farm out in Flower Mound, Texas just east of Corpus Christi.

"The body of local businessman Doug Pederson was found lifeless in the buried toolbox, dead from carbon monoxide poisoning. A lone citizen out doing some late-night rabbit hunting heard a man's screams from behind the barn and called law enforcement".

Michael and the two Mexican dudes were caught red handed by County Sheriff's standing at the hole, a garden hose taped to the Hummers tailpipe and stuck through the dirt into the underground toolbox.

"Oh, my God", I heard Rhonda say as she lay on the bed behind me staring at the television screen in severe shock at what she was hearing from the reporter's ghastly description of the crime scene.

"The victim had been severely beaten about the face before being placed in the underground tomb and suffocated," is what the reporter was saying. The report went on to say what an upstanding citizen Pederson was and how he was the front runner for the next mayors position in Robstown and what a great tragedy this was for his family and the entire Robstown community. Strange I thought, "they left out the part about him being one of the largest distributors of cocaine in Nueces County, I said under my breath," but Rhonda heard me.

"That man was a drug dealer Mike, she asked, an inquisitive tone in her voice?"

"Yes, honey and much more, I gotta get out of here, two County cops saw me and Michael having a meeting with that guy at his restaurant over in Robstown yesterday."

"What's going on Mike, asked Rhonda, a serious overly concerned tone in her voice, are you in some kind of danger?"

"Well I said, yes and no, yes if them cops remember me being with Michael and he decides to tell them where to find me, which I don't think he will. And no if I get the hell out of Corpus just in case I'm wrong." I stood for a minute looking down at Rhonda's beautifully tanned body stretched out before me on the bed, I was not ready to be torn away from her again like this, but I had to get the hell out of Dodge.

"I'm leaving town right now babe, not because I want to, but I've got to and I wish you would come with me, I pleaded." She looked into my more than serious face, and knew I meant every word coming out of my mouth, and then she started to cry. Once before, some years prior I'd asked her the same question, the last time I left Corpus Christi I'd asked her the same question, at the time she was on the cusp of earning her pro card and her two sons were in junior high school. To uproot them from family and friends just to run off with a man she was in love with, who her sons hardly knew was just wrong in so many ways.

"Cody graduated this year, and David is just beginning his senior year, if you let me get my last boy through his senior year, I promise I'll come to you wherever you are. She placed her hand against my cheek, and said now is just not the time, just like the last time you put me on the spot like this, you know how much I love you Mike, but our stars somehow are never in alignment with each other. Now get your ass back in this bed and make love to me before you blaze out of my life once again, God only knows when I'll see your muscle head ass again." We didn't just fuck, me and Rhonda made mad passion filled love to each other like it was our first time together, afterwards we showered together, I stuffed my belongings into my duffel, gave the love of my life a long last kiss, hopped into Michael Ortega's truck and boogied back to Houston. My plan was to put his truck in a storage facility until someone in his family could come to Houston and take possession of it.

I stopped at a truck stop in Victoria to call Rudy and let him know what happened, I also explained to him how if Michael hadn't insisted that I stay behind to see to his date getting home I would have been right there with him. I did not want the Ortega's to think for a minute that I bailed on their relative in any way. Rudy called me back two days later,

"big Mike, Don Ortega wants to thank you for going to watch his nephews back, the lawyer he's hired for Michael informed him that, Michael says you did not abandon him, it was just bad timing for that hunter to stumble upon them. Michael also sent you a message, tell Skye it was great meeting her and that he's sorry things turned out the way they did, oh yeah, he wants you to keep the truck, it's of no use to him now, and he's got no relatives that need it, I'll send you the title to it in a couple of weeks."

"Hey brother there's one other thing, that pretty white girl is getting kinda frantic in her search for your black ass, you sure you don't want to talk to her?"

"I'm sure Rue, that ship done sailed and I've moved on bro., If she don't stop bothering y'all, you got my permission to be mean to her if that's what it takes to keep her away."

"I understand big fella, she just don't get how much what she done to you can hurt a man where you can't see the wound, she's lucky you ain't Mexican, something like that could get her dead." I felt a cold chill crawl up my spine when Rudy said that and felt fortunate to have never gotten on his bad side, "appreciate everything Rudy and give a yell to your brother for me, talk to you later dude," and I clicked off. It's wild, since I'd been with Rhonda I don't think any other woman had entered my thoughts for days. I hadn't even driven a truck of my own since high school, now I owned a brand-new nineteen ninety-eight Chevy king cab, only thing I could do was use it as a second vehicle or sell it. Then I had this crazy thought, I'd give it to Rhonda as a gift to really commit her to coming to me when her son graduated from high school. She was shocked as hell when I showed up at the Ironhorse gym one evening and invited her to dinner after work and even more surprised when I handed her the keys to Michael's big black truck.

"I'll be expecting you to show up in Houston in about six months with all your girl stuff in the back of this truck and Cody and David too if they want to come, hopefully your sons like me enough."

"Even if you change your mind about me, the truck is yours honey bunny, Michael gave it to me, I'm gifting it to someone I love very much.

"At first, I wasn't sure about us Mike, because our lives were constantly moving in opposite directions, but somehow, we kept ending up together for brief periods of time."

"Rhonda honey, I even foolishly married a woman out in California a couple of years ago, within six months of marriage she did something that completely destroyed that relationship and I ended up right back here in Texas in your arms. I'm taking that as a sign that we belong together, and I'm more than certain that I've always been in love with you, forgive me for sounding overly presumptuous but I think that you love me too.

"With her strong lithe arms Rhonda took a hold of me, pulled me to her body and buried her face in my chest, I felt her tears begin to soak my shirt, being a man, I stood there holding her wondering how I respond to this. After what seemed like an hour but was in actuality about sixty seconds Rhonda released me from the tight hug she had on me and took a step back to lock her tear-filled eyes on me, "why couldn't you have said things like this to me four years ago?"

"Four years ago, honey I wasn't even sure about myself, let alone how deeply my love for you has always been, I always felt that there was something different and special between us, but I couldn't quite figure it out."

Rhonda placed her index finger to my lips to shut me up, "do you remember the last time we were at the Bahia Mar hotel, we'd gone down to Padre for Rubens show."

"Yes, I remember that weekend, why do you ask?"

"I knew that weekend that I was in love with you, I didn't say anything because I didn't want to ruin what we had by doing the clingy chick thing, you and that bunch of guys you trained with were like a little wolf pack. A pack of good-looking bodybuilders working the bars as bouncers and bartenders, any guy would love to do what y'all were doing, I wasn't going to try and take that away from you."

"If you had said things like this to me back then, sure I would have poured my heart out to you, but I understand what you mean baby, I responded.

"I've felt this way for years Mike, God means for us to be together and it's happening on his time not ours, why don't you stay in Corpus Christi with me for a while, David will be graduating in a few months?"

"I don't want to sound like I think there is something bad about your hometown, but I just don't like living in Corpus Christi baby. I've experienced more racism here than any place I've ever lived, and I've lived in a lot of places. We can live anywhere you want to live, but not this town, I'm sorry honey."

"Well she said, we've got about six months to decide where we're going to live, promise me though baby, we alternate weekends coming to see each other and when you can, will you travel with me to my shows."

"Deal I said, I'd love to travel with you like a groupie, you look so beautiful up on that stage, flexing all that sexy female muscle. The pride I feel when you're on stage is akin to the love I feel for you in my heart, I feel so blessed to have us to have finally come together as one."

We stuck to our deal like a religion, Rhonda was doing well in all her contest, and was making some money on the pro circuit, it seemed that us being in love made her train harder and shine brighter on stage, and she looked so sexy driving that big ass truck. Maybe it's just me, but beautiful Texas girls look so sexy when they drive big trucks. The couple of amateur bodybuilders I was training at Hanks benefited greatly from me and Rhonda's relationship, I often took them along to her shows with us as part of Rhonda's support team, they got to rub shoulders with lots of the best in our sport. I was starting to feel good about life again after my ordeal with Macy, I was with just one woman, it was easy to stop seeing Dena.

Dena's star was shining so brightly, she was winning in the IFBB professional shows over in Europe and everywhere else in the world, women's bodybuilding had grown right along with the men's. Her international travels kept her away from

Hanks and Houston for long periods of time, she just like Betty Herndon were now California pros.

Then one day I got the call from Rudy, "dude Don Ortega wants to know if you will take over Michael's end of the business in Houston, Michael told him that you are the only person he would trust to do things right. Of course, he says you will be well compensated for your time and efforts, it's a good offer big Mike, you'll be doing basically the same thing you, me and Lonnie have always been doing, only difference is you will have one big pickup and one drop off, one of which will be a money pickup that you hold, until someone contacts you to tell you where to leave it."

Now, I know that no matter how much I don't want to do this, I know better than to refuse, "be glad to Rudy, tell Don Ortega it will be an honor to help."

"Good deal said Rudy, someone will be calling you to give you all the particulars you need."

So, that's what giving me that damn truck was all about, the Ortega's were softening me up for the big "please do me this favor caper".

I was amazed at the amounts of cash I was picking up, sometimes a quarter of a million dollars in a gym bag that I was instructed to leave at a house right around the corner from Hanks. The steroid business was booming, lots of guys in the Houston area were getting into powerlifting and bodybuilding, the customers were plentiful, due to a boom in the fitness industry. Personally, I was raking in the dough as the months ticked by until my girl was joining me full time. Rhonda was already starting to dig the Houston life just from her bi-weekly stays with me, the bodybuilding scene was big in Houston and she fit right in, she became the resident female pro-at Hanks to replace the absence of Dena Anderson. I managed to keep my work for the Ortega's a secret from her, the thing with Michael and all, I didn't want her to worry, I had enough money put away for both of us to be personal trainers, on the surface we looked just like any fitness couple living a normal bodybuilders life. It was no damn bodies business that Mike Dunn was a part of the biggest steroid distribution ring in the state.

Rhonda only knew that I could always get her the finest cutting drugs from Europe for her contest preparation. The violence down on the border got worse and worse, the Ortega's managed to stay out of the whole shebang since their product had nothing to do with the sale of weed, cocaine, heroin or meth. Once it was clear they would not share transport routes with the big families, the larger cartel leaders found other ways to move their goods. The unsavory characters in the get high dope game was never a part of what we did, the punishment for peddling steroids was just as severe as for anything else, it's just that the feds focused a lot less effort on the juice business. Everybody I ever dealt with were people involved in the fitness industry in one way or another and nobody carried firearms. I even met a few professional football players who made large purchases from people we supplied, every now and then someone would get busted and you never heard of them selling out any of their suppliers. The outside world rarely heard anything about steroids until a few high-profile idiots started killing themselves by abusing the use of anabolics. These drugs have been around for eons of time, it's just that one has to regulate the use of them just like any other drug.

Rhonda and I decided to live at the beach in Galveston, fifty miles south of Houston, we bought a beach house right off the seawall at West Beach, the commute to Houston was only a forty-five-minute drive. Her sons were not ready to leave their friends and family in Corpus, so they stayed behind living with their father, me and Rhonda's sons were cool, so I made sure they knew our door was always open to them. Cody and David had grown up in the sport and they both were decent amateur bodybuilders, they just weren't as committed as their beautiful mother, my woman. We didn't give a shit about the critics who whispered nasty things behind our backs about our muscles and steroids, just as many people admired us and would regularly approach us for fitness advice. We walked down the shoreline hand in hand like we owned it, West Beach was now our home.

Pro-bodybuilder Lee Lambright promoted an amateur contest in Galveston every summer and Rhonda and I were aware that there was no decent gym on the seawall for the competitors to train, so we set out to open our own facility right smack dab in the middle of the Galveston Beach tourist scene. I had to do something with all the money I was making, we made a deal to buy a building next to a Kroger grocery store, which gave us ample gym parking. By the next summer the Island Gym was ground zero for all the competitors in town for Lambright's show, we even converted the upper level of the two-story building we were housed in and turned it into a dance studio for Rhonda to conduct her aerobics exercise classes in. We only hired people involved in the fitness industry as competitors in either women's fitness, bodybuilding or power lifting. Therefore, the entire staff looked like they belonged, just like in Los Angeles. That was our goal, to bring that LA bodybuilding atmosphere to Galveston Island and we were achieving our goal, our first celebrity appearance was non- other than the now internationally famous Dena Anderson.

I managed to have my marriage to Macy annulled without ever having to see her or let Rhonda know that I was doing it, then one day I placed a big rock on her hand and asked her to marry me. Again, after one of her long silent bearlike embraces, she said yes, with tears in her eyes, this time drawing water from me. I loved seeing her happy like this, this is where I belonged I knew it.

CHAPTER
ELEVEN

LIFE WAS GOOD for big Mike Dunn, the fitness craze swept over the island like an out of control wildfire, we were to a point of which we were forced to cut off gym memberships at six-hundred people. The overcrowding made it hard for people to get a good workout in, I jokingly mentioned to Rhonda that I was going to take over her dance studio and put weight training equipment up there, I'll never tell that joke again, she threatened me with castration. Being in love and successful in business at the same time was like an aphrodisiac for us, every chance we got, during the day we slipped away home for a love making session or used the sofa in our office to celebrate our love for each other. Paul and Frank happy as hell to have me settled enough to see me on a regular basis spent as much time on the island as they could. I never made it off Paul's wife's shit list, but Frank and his girl Lori were our number one couple to spend personal time with. I didn't need anyone else but my woman and my two best friends. Cody and David eventually decided that living on the island with us was the best life for them too, they moved in with us, and eventually got their own place in Galveston. Cody registered at the University of Houston and David took courses at the College of the Mainland in the neighboring town of LaMarque a few miles from the island, just over the causeway. Rhonda's and mines dreams were slowly coming to fruition, a local businessman named Dillion Fertita was grabbing up abandoned properties around the city and converting them into worthy businesses like restaurants and entertainment complexes. Fertita fed them and fattened them up and us at the Island Gym did what we could to work off the calories. Rudy and Lonnie would occasionally fly to Texas to train and hang out for a few days, even these two West Coast boys agreed that the bodybuilding lifestyle so popular in Los Angeles was just as prominent here on the Texas Gulf Coast. Me and the love of my life were integral parts of this sudden craze, bodybuilders and power lifters from all over the country were coming to Galveston Island to vacation and train at the now infamous Island Gym. One night me, Lonnie and Rudy were out on our deck smoking a joint and having a beer, Rhonda and her friend Skye, who was in town to spend a few days with her homegirl, were in the kitchen, whipping up a pan of Rhonda's made from scratch lasagna, of which I loved. Not only could my bride give me the physical loving that kept me happy, but the woman also cooked like a master chef. She and Skye's relationship went all the way back to their days in grade school so Skyes being here was like a visit from family. Skye was now engaged to a man named Carlos who was to join us a few days later.

"Stop bogarting the joint big Mike said Lonnie, reaching to snag the burning doobie from my hand. Don't make me tell that sweet ass little surfer girl you left behind how to find you, he said jokingly."

"Don't tell me she's still hassling y'all about where I am bro, I asked?"

"Yes, she is added Rudy, she threatened me one day, she said, if I don't find out where you live, she was going to tell the cops that we sell drugs. I laughed it off because she don't really know anything about us that she can tell anyone, even the cops. After three years, you'd think that chick would have moved on with the real father of her baby, but Mike that chick has got it bad for you, it's a good thing she don't know how to find your ass."

That conversation went in one ear and out of the other because I hadn't even considered one thought about Macy for some years now, in my heart I'd already forgiven her for breaking my heart. The happiness I felt in my life now, with Rhonda for me meant Macy and I were never meant to be married in the first place, the lawyer who handled the dissolvement of our marriage for me had told me how resistant she was about signing off on the annulment.

Lee Lambright's muscle beach extravaganza was on the near calendar three weeks away and I made the Balboa Brothers promise to come back for that weekend, not even thinking nothing bad could come of it. Macy was now a member of Powerhouse gym at Pacific Beach and was a regular workout person there, one would not have ever thought the cute little surfer girl was angling towards a hidden agenda. Macy was a very intelligent woman and even though I'd kept me and the Balboas true business from her, she was still aware that we had something going that wasn't quite aboveboard. She took a particular interest in the women at the gym who gave a lot of attention to Lonnie and Rudy, the Balboas would never discuss their business with some chick they were just having sex with, but if they were going to fly off to Texas for a few days to hang out with a bud that used to live in Pacific Beach, that information could come up in a casual conversation. Lots of people at Powerhouse knew who I was, so it would be easy for one of them to casually mention, Lonnie and Rudy are flying out to Galveston Island in Texas to hang out with "Big Mike" and think nothing of it. Macy kept collecting little bits of conversations from the Balboas women and friends and finally ascertained my whereabouts in Texas, I personally would have never taken Macy to be a psycho, but like a wise man once said," you never really one- hundred percent know a person no matter how intimate the relationship. Somewhere along the way she'd gone off the deep end of sanity and was intent on some face to face confrontation with me that she was certain would bring us back together. She'd completely relinquished custody of that beautiful baby girl with ocean blue eyes to the child's father, some surfer dude she once had a thing with in Honolulu, Hawaii. I'd just assumed she would tell the guy about the child and the two of them would get back together. Macy had some surfer friends on the island, and after a few phone calls it wasn't hard to find out if the guy running the most popular fitness facility in town was a big bald musclebound black dude named Mike. Under the guise of visiting a friend, Macy showed up on the island one warm sunny day, walked right into the gym and bought a membership just like anyone else. I wasn't going to be a dick head and not acknowledge her, the first day one of the trainers told me a cute little blonde was asking if I was in the gym, I went out to the floor to give her a hug and welcome her to the island. She was working out with some surfers who'd been members since we opened the place, that was not strange, this just could be a chance happening. These damn surfers are like a rare tribe anyway, it ain't strange that she's got friends on the island.

After all, she's the one who fucked us up, no way she's holding some sort of weird grudge. Well my logical thinking was crapped on immediately, I called Rhonda who I'd never told the entire Macy ordeal to, out of shame, over to introduce her as my wife and co-owner of the Island Gym. The first thing out of Macy's mouth was, "you have my man and I'm here to take him back." No handshake, no fist pump, no nothing, so I burst into laughter thinking she's just making a joke. Rhonda is looking at me, not thinking this is funny at all, then she just turns and walks away.

"Why the fuck did you say that to my wife Macy, I said in as threatening a voice as I could use out on the gym floor," even her friends had shocked looks on their faces.

"Because I meant it, she barked, you belong to me and you know it."

I turned and walked away, Rhonda was waiting for me in our office.

"What was that all about, she asked? Is there something you need to tell me?" At the moment in my head I was somewhere else, I was having flashbacks to an incident that happened in LA a few years earlier. This guy on the pro circuit named Ray McNeill, had a wife who was also a pro-bodybuilder who'd refused to let him go and one day she put six bullets into his body, ending his life and getting herself life in prison. Why I was thinking about that shit I don't know, but it took my beautiful muscular wife smacking me across the pecs hard to snap me out of the trance. There was no need to hold back now, I gave Rhonda the full rundown of mine and Macy's brief history, every detail even the ego crushing part about her having an affair and having another man's baby.

"How did you know you weren't the father, asked Rhonda?"

"The baby had ocean blue eyes and blond hair honey, how do you think, I walked out of the hospital went home to get some of my stuff and I haven't seen or talked to her until she showed up at the gym today." An image of Sally McNeill firing a gun at her husband Ray popped into my head again, I did not know how fucked -up Macy was in the head, but I prayed she wasn't violent. I'd always admired Ray and Sally when I saw them together at shows. And it was cool to witness how they supported each other's competitive careers, but behind closed doors something in the relationship must have been all wrong.

"Rhonda, I swear I don't know how she found out where I was, Lonnie and Rudy would never have told her, I know that for fact, if she causes us any trouble I'll go right down town and file for a restraining order."

"Well I can tell you right now my love, said Rhonda, that woman is going to be trouble. I could tell by the look in her eye when she was talking to me, I hope I don't have to kill, that bitch to keep her away from us." I on a whim had invested some of my steroid profits in a little winery out in Napa Valley, and maybe it was time I took my wife to meet our new business partners. I took my wife and we rented us a house on the property adjoining the large vineyard we owned a part of. My intention was to spend a couple of months away from the island and just maybe, Macy would go back to San Diego. Rhonda and I lost ourselves in each other for the first three weeks, we were like two high school kids in love, and then we got the call, it was Cody who was our gym manager. He was calling to tell us that our beautiful home on the shoreline had burned down the night before. After Rhonda hung up we both sat there in shocked silence, not wanting it to be so, but in our hearts, knowing this had to have something to do with Macy. We finally agreed to wait for the fire marshal's findings on the reason or cause of the fire, we were phoned with the results a week later, it was arson, gasoline as an accelerant. I phoned the Galveston police and informed them of our suspicions and my feelings about Macy's involvement, all they said was they would look into it.

"All your guns were in the house said Rhonda, but as soon as we get home, we're buying new ones, I'm not taking any chances with this girl."

We hit the ground at Houston's Hobby Airport the following Thursday, we got us an apartment in Houston and told no one our address but Cody and David. We became commuters to our own home and gym, every chance she got to engage me in conversation Macy hopped on it, repeatedly asking me to have dinner with her or let's take a drive together the way we use to. She showed no sign of understanding me when I'd say, no fucking way Macy, you fucked me over, remember, so won't you go back out west and leave me be.

"We still could have made us work Mike, Ricky didn't want me or the baby, we just got stoned together one night and I screwed up that one time. The kid lives with his parents, over in Hawaii and he doesn't even take care of her."

"What about you Macy, you ain't taking care of her either."

"You should have stayed, and we could have raised her together, I know you screwed other women before we got married, but I didn't let it end what we had."

"Macy, people would have clearly seen that the child wasn't mine, so I saved us both from going through a shit load of public embarrassment by just dropping off the scene."

"No, no, I don't accept that Mike, you leave here and go back to San Diego with me and we start over or I stay here and ruin your life."

"Macy your membership is revoked, the balance of the money you paid will be returned to you. If you are seen on this property again, I'll instruct the staff to call the police."

"You can't do that, she barked."

"Yes, I can Macy now get your things and get out or I'll call the cops right now."

As she stormed away towards the exit she turned and said to me, "you'll be sorry." I was shocked by the irrational way Macy was acting, this had always been the coolest chick in the room to me, the ultimate cool little surfer girl, and now she's acting like the chick from the Michael Douglas, Glenn Close movie. Rhonda just wanted to walk up to her and beat the crap out of her, but I knew that would only make things worse, by revoking her membership, at least that keeps her away from us while we're at work.

The last psycho woman I had was back in my days as a bartender, that one was always doing shit to my car, so I leased a regular Chevy and made a point of always parking near the front door.

Skye and her fiancé Carlos came to spend a couple of days with us, they knew about my stalker ex and understood our reasons for commuting from Houston to Galveston every day. The complex we lived in was gated and well secured. So, we felt safe at home, we had not seen Macy for a couple of weeks now, her friends who still trained at the gym said she was still living and working on the island. These surfers were just as shocked as me at her behavior, they like me had always seen Macy as the cool at the top of the mountain. They said they all still surfed together but other than seeing her out on the waves they hardly ever saw her. One of them said when she does run into her, all she does is bitch about you big Mike. One of the girls who sounded more worried than the others, told me also that one of the surf magazines wants them all to be in Costa Rica for an all-female contest, "we'll be there for three weeks, maybe she'll get over whatever's making her act like this."

That was good news to hear, the time away could be a good thing, one of them surfer dudes should put the moves on her and put her out of my misery. The insurance company gave us a check that same week and we set out to rebuild our dream house on the same spot, the cops investigated Macy as best they could, but found nothing to warrant arresting her for the arson of our home. One of the detectives thought it may have been some racist, upset with seeing me and Rhonda together, what an idiot.

"Listen dude I said, there's mixed race couples all over this island, why would the racist single us out on this stretch of beach houses?"

Rhonda loved the old house so much that what we ended up with, after a two-hour session with the contractor, was the same house with larger bathrooms, a bigger deck and a wine cellar type room next to the carport. Skye and Carlos joined us at the apartment in Houston to get ready for a show Skye was going to be in at the University of Houston. The show was hosted by local men's pro Jack Herman who'd done well in the past Mister Olympia in New York. This show was also the annual gathering of all the local muscle heads, the night was already a memorable one for the local bodybuilding, powerlifting community. Skye won her weight class, so we had good reason to party, we took the party to a hot club in southwest Houston called Club Oasis. The place was all turquoise and gleaming, we danced, drank a lot and partied hard, I turned around in one of my silly dance moves and was face to face with Macy. She was dancing with a big dude with red hair, but staring me straight in the eye, "strange seeing you here," she said. Rhonda stopped dancing and leaned around me to see what was wrong, "what are you doing following us bitch, she stated in a rough voice?"

"Just because we're at the same nightclub doesn't mean I've got to be following you, last time I checked this was a free country," responded Macy. I knew for a fact Macy didn't like bodybuilding contest, the whole time we were together she might have gone to two shows with me, she saw them as vanity contest and didn't care for them. Her eyes were locked on Rhonda's, "I came to watch you with my man, you man stealer," on that Rhonda attacked, I grabbed her and the guy dancing with Macy took her by the shoulders, restraining her.

"I told you to stay away from us lady screamed my wife, and I know you're the person who burned our house down. The cops are on to you, you psycho, Rhonda was enraged."

"Oh, sneered Macy, your house got burned up, what a shame." This woman who I once cared an awful lot for was right now scaring the shit out of me. I put my arm around Rhonda restraining her and we left the club, I gave Skye and Carlos the let's get out of here nod and they met us at the exit.

Once we were all in the car, Skye asked, "what happened in there and who was that girl?" The now fuming Rhonda spoke first, "that is my wonderful husband's stalker ex Skye, we thought she would be away surfing in Costa Rica, but I guess following us around was more important."

"She looks like such a nice girl said Carlos."

I could feel that fucker's eyes on me when he said it, I'm sure he was thinking what I had done to this beautiful girl that had her acting this way. But I was not about to repeat the embarrassing story about the baby not being mine.

"First thing we do is file a restraining order, she is acting really strange now and too much of this shit can't be just coincidence, we already know she's dangerous.

I had an old friend from my days as a bouncer named Gator McPeters, Gator like me was no longer bouncing but he'd gotten the training and weapons certifications to work as an armed bodyguard. He trained at our gym on the island and at Hanks in the city, so I saw him on a regular basis. I hired Gator to keep an eye on Macy to see if she was following me or Rhonda around, within two days he reported to me.

"Dude you in a world of shit, he said, if that little broad ain't at her job, she's following you or your old lady around. I mean Houston and Galveston man, it's like she don't have a life bro. What's with her man, did you do something bad to her?"

"No, Gator, she did something bad to me, she just can't let it go for some insane reason."

"What you want me to do now bro. asked my large friend?"

"Just stick close to Rhonda, I don't want her getting hurt, we've already filed a restraining order, so keep records of her movements."

I wasn't quite sure how dangerous Macy might be, so I wanted to have Gator keep an eye on my woman just in case. The last psycho bitch I'd been involved with followed me around and kept slashing the tires on my car, I eventually left town to get away from her. Things were different now, I couldn't just up and move somewhere, leaving my home and business behind, I had to do something to get Macy off my back. We were certain she was the culprit who'd set fire to our home, the cops and fire Marshal just never found a way to prove it, I'd have to do something about her myself. That night at dinner I informed Rhonda that Gator was going to stay close to her when she was in Galveston, she spent more time at the gym than I did, and she was keeping tabs on the contractor who was rebuilding our beach house. In Houston, we were reasonably safe due to the fact our complex was gated with armed security on the premises. It hurt my heart that I had to do all this shit to protect me and my woman from a woman I once loved, so I made the decision to try and talk things out with Macy one more time. I went by the surf shop where she worked on a beautiful sunny day and asked her if she could have dinner with me that evening after she got off work. Macy accepted my invite and we agreed to meet at the Happy Buddha Asian grill on 61st. street a popular cozy spot for couples on the island. I was sure she'd taken my invite the wrong way immediately upon her arrival, she came dressed to the nines in a silk camisole blouse, matching skirt and heels that showed off her tight toned legs. Her hair and makeup were perfect, and she smelled like a field of jasmine, my favorite fragrance and she knew it. She was attempting to take me back to a time when we were just two people in love. She'd touched a nerve and for a while it felt good to be sitting and talking with this beautiful person I used to love, we talked about everything except the shit she'd been doing to Rhonda and me the past few months. I asked if she still competed on the pro surf circuit, knowing she'd skipped on the contest in Costa Rica last month.

"I'm still surfing Mike, my career is just on hold until you and I get back together, I can't focus on surfing without you in my life. You can't tell me what we had together wasn't a good thing Mike and the way you just walked away was just wrong, you didn't even give me a chance to explain, you just left me there in the hospital like I meant nothing to you."

"On top of that, those two Mexican dudes you're in business with refused to tell me anything about where you were."

I stopped her by raising my hand because she was getting a little loud, "Macy, I forgive you for what you did to us, you say you got stoned and drunk and made a mistake and I believe you, shit happens, but your mistake resulted in you getting pregnant with another man's baby. You say that man didn't want to be with you so just like that you want you and me to be together."

"Would you be here if the surfer dude would have wanted you and the baby Macy?"

"I think at some point I would have realized how much we belong together. And yes, I would be here trying to get you to see the same. If those Balboas would have told me two years ago, how to contact you I might have found you before you married that musclebound bitch, she's got a tight body and curly blonde hair just like me. Is that what you were doing, getting with somebody who reminded you of me."

"No, I wasn't Macy, I knew Rhonda many years before you and I ever met and as far as her having a tight body and blond hair, I've always been attracted to women with those features."

"We're married Macy and we've made a good life together here in Galveston, why is that so hard for you to accept?" Her face turned hard and vicious looking, "that bitch stole you from me while your heart was hurting, and you weren't thinking clearly and what's tonight all about, if we're not getting back together."

"I wanted us to be friends again Macy, we had some great times together, times I'll always cherish but we can't hold on to the past forever." She stood and threw her napkin on her plate, "if you don't come back to me I'm going to tell the cops what you and those Mexicans are up to and I'll kill that bitch," then she turned and walked out. What she'd just said could get the both of us killed, I had to do something fast, I handed the server a couple of hundreds and dashed out the door after Macy. I caught up with her at her car, "okay Macy, I said, what is it you want me to do?" She pulled me to her and kissed me passionately on the mouth.

"Come back to my apartment with me and we can talk it over," she said in her most sultry voice. I needed to buy some time to disarm her, so I agreed, and the next thing I knew we were in bed having at each other just like we'd never been a part. I was feeling a ton of guilt about cheating on Rhonda with a woman who'd been our tormentor these past couple of months, but I needed to buy time to figure out what my next move would be. Macy didn't know exactly what me and the Balboa brothers did, but she wasn't stupid, she knew whatever it was, was illegal. I turned my cell phone off, cause the last thing I needed now was for Rhonda to call, which she usually did if she hadn't talked to me for more than a few hours. As bad as I felt for being here in Macy's bed, I had to admit to myself, damn she was a real firecracker in the sack. I'd forgotten about this part of her in my haste to get her out of my life.

After a night of lovemaking, I'd come up with a plan to at least temporarily get her away from Galveston.

"Okay Macy, I've got to walk away from Rhonda the same way I walked away from you, so what you got to do is get off the island and go back to Pacific Beach. In a month or two I'll be out to join you, can you at least do that for me, I'd like to make it as easy on Rhonda as I can. We own a lot of stuff together and I do need to get my affairs in order before I split, after all, I am about to betray her." She agreed to leave the island, and, in a week, she was gone, before she left, Macy gave me a warning.

"If I don't see you in San Diego in two months, Mike, I'm going straight to the cops and tell them about you and your Mexican drug dealer friends." Damn it I thought, I've got two months to cool this woman out, or me and the Balboas are going to have the law all up in our shit.

I didn't want to, but I had to give Lonnie and Rudy a heads up just in case she put the law on to us. Lonnie was pissed, "Mike, he said, the only reason we let that bitch slide the first time she threatened us is because she was your girl, she ain't your girl anymore big man, and if she opens her big mouth about our business, she's a dead woman, you hear."

I knew he meant what he said, Macy did not understand what kind of people she was threatening, I had to come up with some way to make her understand how much danger, she could put us both in. The Ortega's were so secretive about what they did that anyone outside of Mexico never heard anything about them, they never got themselves caught up in anything on either side of the border. Even though Macy knew factually nothing, they would never be certain of how much I'd said to her about the business, so their choice would be to eliminate the problem altogether.

Me, I would just be a loose end, no matter how much Lonnie and Rudy liked me. Macy didn't give me two months, three weeks after she split she was back on the island, back working at the same surf shop. She told me she didn't believe I would do what I said I would do, so she was going to stick around Galveston to get her point across, what she meant by that I had no way of knowing.

CHAPTER
TWELVE

THE FIRST SIGN of trouble hit me like a ton of bricks, two Galveston County Sheriff's walked into the gym one morning and asked to speak with me, the floor manager Calishia came out onto the floor to interrupt an intense chest workout me and Gator were into.

"Mike, there are two cops at the front door asking to speak with you," Calishia said in a nervous voice. I could see the serious look on the faces of the two cops as I approached them, morning officers, what can I do for y'all," I attempted to shake hands and they both refused.

"We got an anonymous tip that you might be running some kind of drug operation out of this place and this is a warrant authorizing us to have a look around," one of them announced," handing me the folded document.

"I don't understand officer, I said, why would someone tell you guys something like that?"

"We did some checking, we are serving the warrant here because it seems your home here in town was recently burned to the ground under some suspicious circumstances. Could that have anything to do with some turf war or somebody trying to send you a message," one of the sheriffs boldly asked?

"I got no idea what the hell you talking about cop and as far as that fire is concerned, I'm certain it was the doing of this insane stalker chick who followed me hear from out west, if you checked me out, you know that my wife and I already registered our complaint and filed a restraining order against the woman. You should be harassing that bitch, but go ahead, have a look around. You can start with my office, show them the way, please Calishia, I got to finish up my training, come on Gator." The two cops went through every inch of me and Rhonda's office and Calishias and the area used by the personal trainers to store their stuff. Afterwards Calishia came for me again, "they say they've got more questions for you and they want to get in the safe in my office, I'll only give them the combination if you say so Mike. I know this is a bunch of bull- shit instigated by that psycho surfer bitch."

"Go ahead open the safe for them, we don't keep nothing but money in there and some vendor contracts."

They wanted to know where we lived since we had no physical address on the island, but the gym.

"We live in a gated, armed security property near the Astrodome in Houston because we don't feel safe here since that woman, burned down our home and the law refused to do anything about it, you want to search my home in Houston now?" The two Sheriff's left, but I knew they wasn't done yet, Macy's mouth had fucked my shit all up.

I had two pickups to make for the Ortega's and a shit load of product sitting in a warehouse down in Edna, Texas that needed to be moved to some guys in Fort Worth, the upside was once I left town no one knew where I went or how to contact me, not even my wife. I hated being on the cop's radar and I prayed that they hadn't brought the Houston laws in on this. I called Rudy and Lonnie and told them what was going down, they immediately went ballistic.

"Dammit Mike, that bitch is too big a problem to ignore now, we'll be in Galveston in two days, get that chicks address for us and you and your old lady take a vacation for a couple of weeks." It took me three days to square away the Ortega's business and then I took my woman and left for the Napa Valley in California to hang out at the winery. I phoned Skye and secretly invited her and her new husband to join us as a surprise for Rhonda, I told her the trip was on me, because my wife loved hanging out with her homegirl. The cost of the airfare and lodging was very minor in comparison to sticking around to find out what the two brothers had in store for Macy. I had to get Macy out of my life, I tried in vain to warn her off, even cheated on my wife in the process, there was nothing more I could do to save her from an inevitable fate. The only way I could have helped Macy was to sacrifice my own life for hers, something I wasn't prepared to do. She was the cause of everything that was wrong with her life and now she was on a mission to ruin mine and Rhonda's, fuck her.

Rhonda and Skye were in the neighboring town picking up groceries and checking out the local shops for new clothes, while Carlos who just happen to be a wine connoisseur and I hit the tasting room. Carlos loved the idea of having a friend in the business, so he insisted on the girls going on their own, so he could spend his day impressing me with his endless knowledge of wines. Carlos to my utter surprise knew as much about the winemaking process as my business partners Jimmy and Dale, he was the wine guy I wish that I could be. While Carlos and I were making sandwiches for lunch my cell chimed, it was the local hospital, something had happened to Rhonda and Skye, they'd been in some sort of automobile accident and were both injured. They were still being worked on when me and Carlos got to the emergency room, so we had to wait a few minutes to see them. When I finally got to Rhonda's bedside, the first thing out of her mouth was, "it was that woman, Mike."

85

"What woman I asked, seriously surprised."

"Your ex-wife Mike, that's who, how did that psycho know where we were, if you didn't tell her, she's doing a damn good job of following us around. Me and Skye were walking across the street to the car and out of nowhere comes this white car right at us, if she wouldn't have clipped the tail of another car, we might not have looked over to see her coming at us." She still hit us, just not so fast, she knocked me and Skye both about 20 feet, the doctor says I've got a broken leg and some serious bruises, I don't know how bad Skye is yet, won't you go and check on her for me." I walked over to the room next door to find Carlos holding his wife's hand and doing what he could to comfort her, she had one arm in a cast of bandages and a dressed wrapping on her head.

"I was talking to the doctor who'd treated them later, and he was highly intrigued with us all.

"I admire what you people do for sport he said, to me and Carlos, if those women of yours were not such phenomenal physical specimens, I'm certain they would be in a lot worse shape. I need to hold them for a couple more days, just to be certain there are no internal injuries we didn't find today, but other than that they are both doing well. There are some policemen in the waiting room wanting to talk to you, Mister Dunn, your wife seems to know who it was that ran them down."

The two officers were having a coffee and chatting up the pretty nurses when I walked up and told them who I was, they repeated what Rhonda had told them about recognizing the person who'd run over her and Skye. Though I was certain of my wife, I had a twinge of doubt about the driver being Macy, I mean how the hell could she be here, I just seen her in Galveston, Texas three days ago. No one knew we were coming here, but the staff at the gym and Rhonda's sons Cody and David. "The woman has been a nightmare" to us these past few months I told the cops, she even burned our home down, but the authorities didn't have enough evidence to arrest her. If it was her, she's got to be the most proficient stalker on earth, to find us way out here.

Nobody got the license number of the car but every description of it were all the same, once the cops were done with me, I found a secluded spot and called Rudy.

"How's your vacation going big fella, he asked me?"

"Not as well as I would like it to be, how are things on your end?"

"Lonnie and me been here for four days and we ain't found that chick yet, she ain't even been at her work, but we not going home until we find her and deal with her."

"In reality, my vacation ain't going worth a shit Rudy, I think Macy just tried to kill my wife and her best friend with a car."

"What the fuck screamed Rudy, how the hell did she find out where y'all was, is your wife hurt bad, he added?"

"She's got a broken leg and some bad bumps and bruises, her friends injuries are little bit worse, but the doctor says they'll recover fine, he says if they weren't bodybuilders it could have been a lot worse." Rhonda says she's certain the person behind the wheel was my ex, but if you see her on the island somewhere please give me a call brother, the cops out here are looking for her."

Macy was on the freeway hauling ass to San Diego in a rental car she rented from the same agency where we rented our car. She'd been following me around Galveston the day before we left, and when I left for Houston she stayed on my tail all the way to where we lived. Evidently, she had slept in her car all night watching the exit gate of our complex, watching for us to drive out. She'd followed us the next morning all the way to Intercontinental Airport and somehow figured out what our destination was. I didn't know these details and was thinking or rather hoping Rhonda was the victim of a knock on the head from the car ordeal and seeing Macy behind the wheel was a symptom of it. A detective phoned to inform us that they'd had no luck in locating Macy but promised us they would keep up the search for who had rundown Rhonda and Skye. Skye was overly upset and swore an oath to kick Macy's ass the next time she laid eyes on her. She had a national level show coming up in a few weeks and her injuries assured, she wouldn't be able to compete, she'd have to wait six months for another Pro qualifier. The guilt I felt was overwhelming, being a bodybuilder myself. I knew how important missing three to four weeks of training was to a competitive bodybuilder. Rhonda and I paid all her medical expenses and Skye had to make me stop repeatedly apologizing to she and Carlos. Once she and Rhonda felt better, we hopped a flight back to Texas, Macy in the meantime was back in San Diego surfing and hanging out with her friends, thinking she'd done more damage to my tough- ass ole lady. Whoever on the island was feeding her information about us must have gotten word to her that other than a broken leg, Rhonda was okay and back working at the gym training her clients. Three weeks after we got home Macy was back on the island, Gator spotted her on the seawall across the street from the gym watching the building like she was waiting for it to explode, he said.

"Just stay close to my woman I told Gator, that shit in Napa was too close a call for me to ever underestimate her tenacity again." I didn't see much of Rudy and Lonnie, but I knew they were still on the island and I could feel the cops watching me, so I was glad not to be seen with them in lue of what they were in Galveston to do. I eventually got a call from Rudy informing me that they were back in Pacific Beach and, "your problems with your ex are done with."

"We can get back to business now," and nothing else was ever spoken about her. Gator told me he hadn't seen her in a couple of weeks, so I paid him off and told him

I guess she went back to P.B. and decided to leave us be. I tried not to think about what may have happened to Macy, but I'd done all I could to shut her up and didn't feel at all at fault for what happened to her, after all she'd attempted to murder my wife and her best friend. One of her surfer friends stopped me on the floor one day and asked me if I'd seen her around anywhere, they knew what she had been doing to me and Rhonda.

"No not lately, why do you ask, you know how she's been fucking my shit up lately."

"Her folks have been calling looking for her, but nobodies seen her in over a month, not here or at Pacific Beach, they told me to ask you."

"Tell them I'm sorry but it's been a while since we seen her, we thought she'd given up and gone home."

The work on our house was coming along well and it seemed that we were days from being able to move in, I was so glad, the hundred miles a day commute was becoming a drag and besides, I loved waking to the sound of the sea outside my door. Just when it seemed, life was getting back to normal, two detectives walked into the gym and approached me with questions about Macy.

It seems her parents had some idea that I would know something about her whereabouts.

"I don't know why they would be thinking that I said to the detectives, my wife and I have a restraining order filed against the woman, she burned our house down and tried to murder my wife and her best friend. You can check with the cops out in Napa, California on that."

"We heard from them a while back Mister Dunn, they were wanting to locate her for questioning about a hit and run incident, and we're aware of your restraining order against her." Still, we had to follow up on her parent's concerns, the woman's not been seen for two months, her folks wouldn't say, so you tell us, what's the deal with you and their daughter?"

"I don't think that's any of your business pal and like I said, I haven't seen her for some time now, is there anything else."

"Yes, there is Mister Dunn, Miss Allen told one of our officers that you were involved in some sort of illegal drug business, what do you have to say about that."

"Not a damn thing pal, she is just a woman I no longer wanted anything to do with trying to make trouble for me, just like any other crazy bitch. You should be helping the fire marshal find out who burned my home down."

"That's another matter Mister Dunn, right now those people are concerned that something may have happened to their daughter and felt that you may have knowledge of some information that could help find her, after all they say she came to Galveston to find you."

"Those same people also know why I chose not to be a part of their daughter's life and you can tell them for me, how I really resent them pointing you people in my direction. Macy's interference in my life has put quite a strain on my marriage. She's out west somewhere, my wife isn't the only witness that gave her description to the cops after she tried to murder her and her friend.

"What's this thing Miss Allen tells us about you and some drug selling activity, her parents also say she had some information that would incriminate you and some people out in San Diego.

"That's just some more shit she made up to make trouble for me, I got no idea what the hell that psycho could be talking about. Furthermore, I haven't lived in San Diego for over four years now." The detectives left and me and Gator went back to our work out, these fuckers had me on their radar now, so I had to be extra cautious in every move I made from here on. "That chick is really slick Mike, said Gator, it's like she knew I was tailing your wife because she never went near her when I was around, and it surprises the hell out of me that she showed up in California."

The work was complete on our house and Rhonda jumped right in on furnishing the place and doing all she could to make it look the same as it did before. She was so happy to have our lives back to normal, I was even being affected by her good spirits, we made love two or three times every day. Being back to normal in our home was like some sort of stimulant to us. I kept the apartment in Houston sort of like my hide- out, I didn't know how close the cops were watching me and I wasn't taking any unnecessary risk. I always stayed at the apartment in Houston the day before I made a business run, I got a second car to leave at the apartment, a resto-moded nine-teen eighty-two Nissan two eighty-zee. If the cops followed my vette to Houston, they had no way of knowing I was in the zee when I pulled out in the middle of the night.

After two months, I started to relax some, surely the Galveston Police Department didn't have the resources to do twenty- four seven surveillance on someone they had no concrete evidence against for an extended period of time, but still I took no unnecessary risk. The Ortega's wired my payments to an offshore account I had set up out in Barbados, so we had no big bank balance to draw attention to us. Rhonda and I were both very successful personal trainers, and when she placed in the top five of a show she received a nice chunk of prize money. There was nothing out of sorts about our life to make people suspicious of us, Rhonda cherished Michael's big Chevy truck I'd given her as a gift and she was still driving it, mainly because I found her so sexy in that big truck. We looked just like any other bodybuilding couple who owned their own gym, which was doing very well, we had a waiting list for memberships. Rhonda's aerobic dance exercise classes were a big hit with all the ladies on the island, things could not have been better. I felt that I was in love with Rhonda when I'd first met her many years ago, but the erratic way I lived back then made it hard to be sure if it was love or lust. Now I was certain, this woman was everything I'd ever wanted in a mate, she was beautiful, smart, funny and very athletic, all the things I required my special woman to be. Most important of all, she loved me back unconditionally, she knew I had some shit going on that I couldn't tell her about and she never pressured me in any way to tell her about my other business, oh yeah, she was the complete sex machine.

Her sons were good guys too, they had no qualms whatsoever about their mother being married to a black man, we made a very cool bi-racial Galveston Island family. The island was gradually becoming a popular destination for tourists due mainly to the spending of the local billionaire developers, such as this guy named Dillion Fertita. Men like him, and the Hogg family, who were among the original settlers of Texas. Not too long ago the tradition of Mardi Gras was reinvigorated by the new influx of money to the island. Galveston pride was so strong the original residents were wearing t-shirts declaring their island heritage with the letters" B.O, I. ". emblazoned across the front, which meant (born on the island), which was now the moniker of the locals. I got a little jealous because I wasn't a part of the group but being successful members of the business community was just as rewarding. I'd never before now been completely happy in my life and now it seemed that life could not be any better, all the bad shit in my past was now just that and it was all slowly being put out of my mind. I took Rhonda and her sons along with their girlfriends out to Barbados, where we now owned a nice condo right on the beach, the turquoise blue water welcomed us like an old friend, the surf there was a lot better than in Galveston, so Cody and David were in surfer dude heaven. I had a short meeting with the bankers there to discuss ways to invest some of our money in the islands of Barbados, we agreed that rental property catering to the tourist trade was the most logical option. I told my love enough to let her know that we would always be okay financially and if anything, ever happened to me, this is where our wealth was and how to get at it.

I got a call from Gator, who was now my regular training partner and a part of the Island Gym management crew.

"Mike, he said, there are four sunburned surfer guys on the island who come by the gym every day looking for you, any idea why bro?"

"No not really Gator, I know a lot of surfers from the time I spent with Macy, all her friends were surfers, but I don't think they know I live in Galveston."

"These boys seem mighty determined to talk to you Mike, is there anything you want me to tell them."

"I don't know if there is anything you can say to them Gator, seeing as I don't got any idea who they are, we won't be back for a couple more weeks, see if you can find out what they want and give me a call." I told Rhonda about the strange call from Gator and the first thing out of her mouth was, "I'll bet it's got something to do with that stalker ex of yours."

I was a little wounded, "please don't say it like that honey, I've told you the whole story with her and me and even you said you'd have done the same thing that I did, if betrayed, like the way she did me."

"I'm sorry baby, she responded, it just pisses me off that, that chick is still interfering in our lives, we shouldn't have to pay someone to watch our home while we're away because we're afraid she might burn it down again, that's just not fair to us."

"I know baby and if these guys have anything to do with Macy, we go directly to the police, I'm just as tired of her interference in our lives as you are."

The call from Gator drifted from my thoughts because we were too busy with our time together, just two people in love digging being with each other in the tropics. Our last week in Barbados we flew Skye and Carlos out as a makeup for the Napa Valley ordeal, Skyes injuries were healed and she was as good as new and back training for a shot at her pro card. We would go days, never wearing anything but our bathing suits even when we went out for dinner at night, fortunately" the no shoes, no shirt, no problem" rule was in full effect in Barbados.

Our first day home was like a mini celebration for our staff and the gym members, we'd never been away for a whole month before, Raheema, the female bodybuilder who was leading Rhonda's exercise classes was okay with the members, but Rhonda was an islander now and the locals missed her dearly. I asked Gator about the guys who were looking for me and he said he hadn't heard from them in a few days, someone must have told them I was home because two days after our return, this group of guys showed up at the gym asking for me. Gator was very uneasy about these long-haired sunburned fellows, so he followed me over to the front counter, Gator is as big as a side-by-side refrigerator so if there was going to be trouble, I had the right man at my side.

"I'm Mike Dunn fella's, what is it you cats so anxious to talk to me about, I asked the group?" A short stocky guy stepped forward like he was the leader of the group, not to shake hands, but the little fellow stuck out his chest and said, "my name is Ricky Slater."

"I'm the father of Macy's little girl, I'm sure you've heard of me buddy."

"Oh yeah, I answered, you the fucker that got my chick pregnant and destroyed me and Macy's marriage, can't say I'm glad to meet you boy."

"It's been six months since my little girl has seen her Mama and we come here to find out if you know why, Macy's folks say she came to Texas to take care of some unfinished business with you."

"I don't know why they would tell you that, all Macy did here was cause me trouble, once I found out the baby was yours I walked out of her life for good. You should be glad dude, she's all yours now, after all you are the baby's father." The guy showed a brief expression of shame on his face, then he rallied his thoughts and asked me, "when was the last time you talked to Macy or seen her?"

"I don't remember the last time we talked, but my wife saw her behind the wheel of a car that was trying to murder her and a friend out in Southern California last year, we just assumed she was still out there. Oh yeah, did her parents tell you she burned our house down, I'm sure they left that tiny bit of info out."

"The last time she talked to her mom she said you and her had spent the night together, and that y'all was getting back together, why would she say something like that if you wasn't talking to her."

"I don't know why Macy would tell the lady something like that, but I can tell you this, she was acting real crazy."

Her friends in town do say she was doing some crazy shit trying to get back with you, but we think you know more than what you telling us."

"You know what little dude, I don't give a shit what you think or what her parents think, now get the hell out of my gym before I call the cops." The group of men all at once took a glance at Gator standing behind me, turned and walked out. I turned to look up at the enormous man behind me, "sorry you had to listen to all that crap Gator, thanks for getting my back brother."

"No problem Mikey, he answered, but I don't think you seen the last of them white boys, you better watch your back man." I had to put mine and Gators concerns about Macy's boyfriend and his pals on the back burner for a while, I had some work to put in on the iron, that shit wasn't going to ruin a good leg session.

The Ortega's were sending me some product that me and only me knew where to pick up and drop off, along with a large sum of money to be returned to a house in Houston.

Some linebacker at the University of Oklahoma had tested positive for Anadrol and high levels of testosterone, who stupidly revealed his supplier to the authorities, so the Ortega family had streamlined business on this side of the border. The only people touching money and product on this side were the Balboa Brothers myself and the money man. The strict precautions taken by the Ortega's protected everyone in the organization from doing some serious jail time. You could have knocked me over with a feather when I opened the door to the storage shed in Huntsville, I'd never seen so much money at one time in my whole life. if you've ever wondered how many duffel bags it takes to hold twelve million dollars, the answer is seven, very large ones. I'm glad I started using the 280z to work, I had to lay the backseat down flat to fit all seven in the car, I'd added a black rear window louver to match the zee's custom paint job, thankfully, it was hard to notice the load of big black duffels in the rear of the car. On top of that, Javier had given me the address to a ranch in Hockley Texas as a new drop site, Hockley was a little town 30 miles west on the other side of Houston. Nothing ever happened in this little farming community, wouldn't that be some story in the local newspaper, a twelve million dollar find. I drove like Grandma Moses the entire trip, never allowing myself to go faster than sixty-five miles per. It was the same two men at the drop as always, two Mexican cats, who rarely spoke a word to me in the two years since I'd taken over for Michael. This time after I dropped the bags on the carport floor one of the guys asked if I'd like a beer in clear and articulate english, I didn't even think these guys spoke english. "Sure, I said to be polite," and now a little curious as to why the sudden gratuity from this man who in two years had barely said ten words to me. "Come on in big man" the guy said as his partner began loading the bags into a shiny blue Ford two fifty with a custom camper on back. To my surprise the inside of the modest ranch house was furnished just like any normal family lived there, I could even hear children playing somewhere in the house. Have a seat my friend, the man said, as he opened the fridge and passed me an ice-cold Bud Light. We sat silently for a long minute before the man said, Don Ortega has never had us work with a negrito before, you know that. Yeah, I've been told by some friends who first hired me, I said, not wanting to say too much. Lonnie and Rudy Balboa, I know them well the man said, they value your friendship greatly, that is why I wanted you to have a beer with me to try and see what it is they see in you. Some of the gringos up north have been talking to the law about our business so Javier is checking everybody out, he knows how tight you and the Balboas are, but still I am a very cautious man. This business that we are in does not normally draw a lot of attention from the law but all it takes is one gutless man to bring us all down. This is my ranchero, my wife and children live here with me, I've been a part of this community for eight years now, I value greatly my life here, to lose it would break my heart. I tell you these things out of respect for the Balboas and my friend Michael who you were also friends with, he sends his best to you, I went to visit him yesterday. You can take this any way you please my friend, it's only business, if you do or say anything to jeopardize what I have here I will destroy everything you love in this world before I kill you, that is not a threat, but a fact. I get your point brother, I said, I turned the bottle up and drank the rest of my beer in three big gulps, "thanks for the beer dude I better hit the road now," I said as I got up to leave. One more thing, he went to the kitchen drawer and pulled out an envelope and handed it to me, inside were photos of Rhonda, Cody, David, Gator, Skye and Carlos and even one of Macy which threw me off, more than seeing the others. The man could see the shock on my face, we don't take what we do lightly, I'm sure you already knew that. That pretty little gringa became a problem for you and us, so now she's out there somewhere fertilizing the watermelons.

Now I generally don't scare easy and I got a steely nerve, but this mother fucker with the photos had just spooked the shit out of me. "I get the point man, I said as I dropped the photos on the table and headed for the door, in the carport I was surprised to see the other truck gone.

"Drive carefully my friend, and from now on you can just bring the bags here, said the guy to me as I climbed into my car and drove away. As I jumped on highway fifty-nine headed towards Houston my thoughts were all over the place, was Macy's body really buried out in the watermelon patch on this guy's ranch or was he just trying to make a point. Whatever it was I wasn't about to say shit about what we did to anybody, not even my woman who I trusted more than anyone in the world. Man, was I missing the "good ole days "when me, Paul and Frank didn't have a worry in the world except where the next Grateful Dead show was and how long it was going to take us to ride to it. You'd think the anabolic steroid business could not possibly be so big and complicated and dangerous but here I was neck deep in the drug trade, to the point of having the lives of my loved ones being threatened. I jumped from fifty-nine on to the six- ten loop in Houston, I had to switch cars before heading back to the island, but I still had the complexities of my secret life on my mind. The more I thought about it, the madder I got about that damn Mexican threatening not only me but the people I loved most in this world, that's when I decided not to take that shit. I had more than proven myself in my loyalties to the Ortega's, there was no call for that guy to threaten my family so fuck him, and I made up my mind what I was going to do about it right then.

When I got to the apartment I went inside stuck my Glock into my waistband, picked up the keys to my vette and drove straight back to Hockley. I found a spot on the road leading to the house where I could back my car in out of the way and wait for the man who threatened my family. After a two hour wait, he drove past the spot where I was waiting, I allowed him time to get a couple hundred yards past me before I pulled out to follow him, he drove south on highway 59 for five miles, then turned off down a dirt road and was going somewhere deep into the woods, which was fine with me. As luck, would have it, that son-of-a-bitch was stopping to take a piss on this dark, out-of-the-way road, as I approached, I saw him in my headlights behind his truck, relieving himself. I slowed down as I got to where he was standing and pressed the button to lower my passenger-side window, when I got to where he was standing, he turned to see who it was. I pulled the trigger, killing his ass with his dick in his hand. How dare this piece of shit threaten my love ones, I got out of the car and put two more rounds in him, turned around and headed back to the main road, not thinking twice about what I had just done. His death was of no concern to me, I'd already seen how easy it was for the Ortega's to replace people they lost, it only took them a little over a month to put me into Michaels spot.

I didn't have to go back to the apartment this time, so I stayed north on Highway fifty-nine until I got to Highway forty-five and headed south to Galveston, to the waiting arms of the woman I love.

The drugs I dealt in couldn't get you high, but they damn sure made you feel like Superman, I remember when I was in high school before the popularity of anabolic's was so prevalent, only the rich kids could afford them, us guys who couldn't afford them or just didn't know about the stuff had to just live with what bad asses the users were. The only place I could hang with the users was on the field where only true talent counted, but in the weight room the users were exhaustless beast. Paul's dad was a weight lifter and he got us on the iron before we were teenagers, I took to lifting heavy weights like a duck to water, even on drugs the users got strong competition from me and Paul in the weight room, thanks to his dad. On the field those same guys were like something from hell. By the time, I got to college, all the bigger programs had jars filled with size and strength pills on the shelf in the trainer's room. I showed up on campus weighing two hundred and twenty-five pounds, by spring break, I was up to two sixty and a ball breaker from hell. Two-hundred milligrams a week of dianabol, fifteen ccs of sustenon and another fifty ccs of liquid test did the trick, I destroyed anything in a different colored jersey that got anywhere near me. Now everyone was doing the stuff, from Junior high to the pros, thing was the NCAA was getting fed up and beginning to implement testing programs. The National Football League was looking the other way, so business was great on that level, the ballplayers were doing more drugs than the power lifters and bodybuilders, some of the pro ballplayers were abusing the stuff so much they were killing themselves. That didn't stop the younger kids from wanting to take a ride on the train, only thing was when they failed a drug test the bastards chose to take everybody down with them.

When I got home I made love to my wife like she was new money, I'd survived a whole lot of shit to be where I was now and the last thing I wanted was to risk losing it.

My conscience bothered me some about Macy and it always would, but her actions were putting the lives of a lot of people in great danger and a part of me felt that she'd caused her own demise with her threats and the fact that she did put the law on to me and the Balboa's. I hoped like hell, the surfer boy and his pals had left town. When I got to the gym the following morning Gator said they hadn't been back, after our workout that evening, he invited me to go to a party one of the female members had invited him to. Me and Gator always went drinking together so there was nothing out of the ordinary about me hanging out with him, I told Rhonda I'd be home later.

"I like this mood, you've been in since you got home yesterday, so don't even come home too drunk to perform big boy," she added for a laugh.

The party was at the Holiday Inn down by West Beach in two adjoining suites on the third floor, there were two sixteen-gallon kegs in the middle of the room and a shit load of tequila on the counter. The two rooms were full of people in bathing suits like everyone had just come in from the beach, I recognized some of the people from the gym. Gator and I were some of the larger people in the room, so we got us a beer and a couple of shots of tequila and went out on the balcony where there was more space to move around. Gator though big as a house was a handsome dude and beautiful women gathered around him like bees to honey, it was cool observing him in action, it reminded me of my youth. Just when my buzz was kicking in from the joint we were sharing with some women from the gym, a loud voice from inside screamed "what's that mother fucker doing here?" It was Macy's boyfriend and his buddies, from the look of them I could tell they were already drunk or stoned on something and looking for a fight, so I readied myself. I gently moved the women away from me and tossed my drink.

Though there were four of them and just me and Gator, these boys was about to find out, the myth about being real drunk making you 10 feet tall and bullet proof was only a fantasy.

These California boys was fixing to get a real Texas beat down, courtesy of two former bad ass bouncers on Galveston Island. They rushed us all together, two at Gator and two at me. Gator was laughing as he grabbed the two guys by their throats and slammed them against the patio doors, taking the big glass door out of its track. I drove my fist into the face of one of the guys, but Macy's boyfriend wrapped his short ass arms, which were remarkably strong around my torso in an attempt to shove me over the balcony railing and he pulled the maneuver off. I grabbed a hand full of his hair and one of his arms and drug that little short son of a bitch over with me, we fell the two floors together, but by the time we reached the ground, his body was in between mine and the cement ground below. I woke up two days later in the hospital feeling like I'd been hit by a bus, Rhonda's head was laid against my side, and even though she was asleep, she was squeezing my hand. I squeezed her hand back and my beautiful wife opened her gorgeous blue/ gray eyes and gave me that smile that always melted me like a scoop of Blue Bell ice cream, in the summer sun.

"Welcome back baby she whispered softly, she picked up the call device to summon the nurses, they told me to call if you woke up, how do you feel?"

"Not too good baby, how long have I been out I asked?"

"A little over two days, the doctors weren't sure how bad your head injury was, so they shot you up with something to keep you under." You've had two CAT scans to check for damage, they didn't find anything, but your brain was shaken very badly."

"What happened to me baby?"

"You fell two stories off a balcony, you and that girl's boyfriend were fighting, he fell with you, but he's never going to be the same again, they say."

"Why didn't you tell me about those men Mike, Gator says they've been on the island for a few weeks now looking for your ex, that psycho bitch."

"I didn't want you to worry honey, you've been so happy lately, I didn't want to be the one to ruin that glimmer in your eyes."

"How's Gator, he didn't get hurt too, did he?"

"No, he's fine, he feels bad about letting that guy push you over the rail, he feels like he shouldn't have let the man get to you because he's the person who took you to that party."

"I don't remember much from that night, but if that little shit tossed me over the side, it was my own fault for letting him." The doctor and a nurse came in and put me through a battery of tests to finally say to us, "your body withstood the fall because it's covered with all this muscle, and the other man's body cushioned you from the impact of the fall."

"Your brain received quite a jolt, there will be some memory loss, it takes time to find out how bad."

"When can I take him home Doctor, asked Rhonda?"

"Not for a couple of days Mrs. Dunn, I need to keep him under observation for two more days, these head traumas can be tricky sometime."

When I woke up the next morning my wife was still at my bedside, I gently scolded her for not going home to sleep in her own bed instead of the uncomfortable hospital fold out cot. With a determined scowl on her beautiful face, my woman looked me in the eye and said, "my bed at home is empty without you being in it with me, end of conversation." God, that made me feel good despite my pain, how could I have gone all these years never having felt this kind of love from a woman. I was closing in on my forty-seventh birthday and it felt as though I'd been waiting my entire life for this feeling. I'd never felt any sort of love from my mother, so I guess something inside me, must have been shut down. My head was starting to clear some and I could remember that little mother fucker lifting me up over the edge of the railing and thinking, how strong he was for his size. I guess all that swimming builds good strong muscle, I'm sure I outweighed that guy by at least eighty pounds, he did know about leverage, because he was bent over with his arms locked around my waist. I remember grabbing a hand full of his long hair and twisting my fist into it as I went over the side. Gator walked in and a smile spread across his face when he saw me sitting up talking, "good to see you back in the world my dog," the staff will be glad to know you still with us."

"Hi Gator, said Rhonda," as the big man smothered my hand with his in a brotherly shake.

"While you got some company, I'm going out for some tacos, I've had my fill of hospital food, want me to sneak you something in baby?"

"Yeah, how about a couple of burritos with beef, you want something Gator."

"No thanks I already had lunch, I'm on my lunch break now, I've got a client to train in two hours, I just wanted to swing by and check on you."

"The doctor says I should be okay in a few weeks, if I take it easy and give myself a chance to heal."

"Man, that really freaked me out Mikey, when I saw you go over the side, they rushed us so fast that by the time I turned to help you all I saw was you and that guy flipping over the rail." You did have a fistful of that little shit's hair and a grip on his arm, I bet he never expected you to pull his ass over with you."

"When y'all hit the ground, you were right on top of him, thank God, he broke your fall, and his ass is all fucked up. He's in a room a floor down in the ICU, I ran into two of his pals on the elevator ride up, they was as quiet as church mice in the rain, I'll bet they can't wait to get back to California or wherever the hell they came from. It's a good thing we was blessed to be weightlifters, an ordinary man don't fall two floors and live to talk about it."

"You sound like Doctor Haung brother, he says my muscle frame is what saved me from being hurt worse."

"I ain't trying to be no smart- ass Mike, but what is it about that chick you used to be married to, is that pussy that good, these boys been on the island for a month looking for her and for some reason they think you know where she is. You ain't as big as me, but it's obvious you ain't the kind of dude that'll take any shit off anybody, them surfer boys got big nuts to come at two cats as big as us. And that one that you fell with done probably rode his last wave, the EMTs were surprised he was still alive after falling from that distance, and then a guy your size landing on top of him. I just hope that woman is worth it."

"It was her parents that put them on to me, they couldn't get the cops to do anything to me, so I guess them four turds was they second option. The last I heard anything about that chick was her running over Rhonda and her best friend out in California, I don't know why they in Texas looking for her."

I was released to go home three days later with orders to get at least three weeks' bed rest before resuming any of my regular activity, Rhonda was dead serious with compliance, she chewed my head off every time I got out of bed to do anything but use the bathroom. My body did hurt, but I missed my training, you never know how much you like doing something until you can't do it at all. Rhonda took off from her own training and work to look after me, our love for each other grew by leaps and bounds while I healed. I called Rudy to let him know what happened to me, he relayed the information to the Ortega's and then he flew to Texas to fill in for me while I healed. After a month and a half. I was back on my feet and back in the gym, Rudy was staying in the apartment in Houston and was chomping at the bit to get back to his life in Pacific Beach, so he too was happy I'd recovered. The new guy at the ranch house in Hockley was not as standoffish as the guy he'd replaced, if anything, he was the complete opposite. He was fascinated by my physical condition after hearing that I'd fallen two stories and lived.

"My friend Rodolfo tells me you fell from over 20 feet to the ground and didn't break anything.

"Yeah, I said, I guess you could say I was lucky, the man who pushed me over was between me and the impact of the ground, he didn't come out too well.

"You mean he's still alive too, both of you are very fortunate men, the Virgin mother watches over you."

"He lived I said, but somebody will be hand feeding him for the rest of his life, I'm not one hundred percent yet, most of what's wrong with me is on the inside, my body still hurts. "What the hell man, you still one tough bastard,"

I think I'm going to do like you and Rudy and start working out with the weights, by the way, my name is Joe John Serbantez and yours is Mike Dunn, right." This was crazy, this dude who I had just met was suddenly talking to me like we was long time pals, I wondered just what Rudy said to him that made him so cool with me.

"Come on in for a beer before you take off, my woman is out shopping, and I've got some good weed, you smoke, right?"

"Sure, my brother I answered," we tossed the bags of cash into the back of the other guy's truck and he got in and drove off. He was right about the weed, it was some bad shit, before too long we were jamming to some Led Zeppelin and I was on my fourth Corona. Me and Joe John were sitting in his den getting fucked up just like two old friends. On the drive home, I noticed that Rudy had gotten the windows on my Zee tinted, damn shame I had to be stoned as hell before I noticed. I took out my cell and called him, "hey Rudy appreciate the tint job brother. It looks real nice, what do I owe you for it."

"Not a thing Big Mike, I'm glad you like it man, I don't like to wear sunglasses all the time when I drive, so it's nice to have tinted windows."

"Hey dude, what did you say to Joe John about me, he was extremely cool to me today, the other guy hardly spoke to me at all.

"I just let him know that I'd trust you with my life, like a brother, if he's treating you good Mike, that means he likes you for real, consider it a compliment."

"Okay see you later Rue, I'm driving, and my new pal Joe John got me high as shit on some monster bud, later bro." After my conversation with Rudy, I cranked up the radio, it was Prince his royal badness, one of my favorite guitar players and performers jamming his song little red Corvette, my favorite haul ass song. After the song ended, the disc jockey announced the beginning of ticket sales for an upcoming show at the Compact Center, instead of bypassing all the malls I stopped at the Ticketmaster outlet in Meyerland mall and purchased fifteen tickets for me and Rhonda with the intent of inviting Skye and Carlos and the gym staff to go with us to see Prince. He is a phenomenal entertainer and is probably the only guy in the world Rhonda would dump me for, she adored him. My honey was over the moon when I handed her the envelope full of front- row seats to see her favorite musician live, right in the middle of the gym while she was training a client, she laid a deep, long, passionate kiss on her man. After her session, she escorted me to her office and ravaged me, afterwards, Rhonda went back out onto the floor to announce to the staff that they would be going to the concert with us. Even big ass Gator came across the room to hug her enveloping my girl in his massive arms, he told me later that he was as big a Prince fan as my wife, and then the big fucker even gave me a hug. A month later we announced to the members that we would be closing early on the day of the show and we all got dressed to the nines and hit the Compaq Center in style. Gator managed to wrangle two white stretch limos from the company he worked security for, so we were able to party the night away unrestricted, the night was perfect.

The following day the entire staff was still floating on cloud nine from the great night out we'd had out as a group, they even had the members humming and wording Prince songs, the buzz was contagious. Then, in walks the damn Galveston police detectives to ruin our great mood with more questions about Macy and the thing with her now totally messed up boyfriend. Her parents say you and she were still sleeping together when she came up missing, is there any truth to that?" I was so glad Rhonda wasn't present to hear that, "listen man I said in my most offended sounding tone, your talking nasty rumors like that could make trouble for my marriage, which is excellent by the way."

"We have no intention of causing you any trouble sir, we're just following up on what the woman's parents are telling us, so were you and Miss Dunn still intimate?"

"My wife, who's the only woman with the last name Dunn, I'm fucking cop, is in her studio upstairs teaching a class." Macy and I have been divorced for almost five years now and her last name isn't Dunn anymore." The cop could tell that I was getting pissed, "no need for profanity sir, he said, you didn't know she was still using your last name."

"Why the hell would I bro., like I said, we've been divorced for a long time and I hadn't seen her or heard from her in a long time until she showed up on the island, and no I was not fucking her dude." And fuck anything you got to say about that son-of-a-bitch in ICU over in John Sealy. I know you got plenty of witnesses that say he was the one that pushed me over the edge of that railing. Or maybe you cops have decided to blame that shit on me too, I think I'll have my lawyer interview every one of them witnesses just in case y'all try to screw me over. I'm done talking to y'all about this woman who burned my home down and attempted to murder my wife and her friend," I walked away, leaving the two detectives standing there. I was kicking myself in the ass mentally for sleeping with Macy that night, I never thought she would call her folks and tell them about it. My only intent was to get her out of town and not go blabbing to the law about me and the Balboas. Her parents were relentless, which got me to wondering what else Macy had said to them about us and drug dealing.

CHAPTER
THIRTEEN

UNBEKNOWNST TO ME, the law in San Diego had taken Macy's vanishing as something else completely, the fact that she disappeared right when she started reporting to them things about drug dealing and the Balboa brothers set them off. They actually were the ones who put Galveston PD on to me because the San Diego cops had Rudy and Lonnie under tight surveillance after Macy vanished. They just assumed we were into something like cocaine or heroin since the Balboas exhibited no means of working for the fine cars they drove or the nice house they lived in, it was easy to peg them as drug dealers who would commit murder, to cover up some nefarious activity. Rudy and Lonnie, I'm sure after all these years of anonymity had to be millionaires, they didn't show it but still, they lived extravagantly. The Ortega's were very smart business people, they stayed in their lane never looking to get into the transport of weed, cocaine or heroin across the border. Other than that, one-time Javier Ortega ventured into the cocaine trade, mainly from a greed standpoint, that eventually got Rudy and one of the guardian soldiers shot. The elder Ortega had to step in to straighten his wayward son out to get his organization back on track, the chemist in Mexico were very good at what they did. The labs were clean and sanitary, the packaging of the chemicals was as proficient as any labs in the states. The use of anabolic steroids in high school, college and professional sports was huge and if one could corner a big enough share of the market, you could make tons of cash under the radar. Out of sheer luck and Michael's misfortune I was making a nice piece of that cash with a minimum amount of risk, the only time I made physical contact with the drugs was when I had the Balboas fixing up an order for my personal use. Rudy would FedEx mine to me, so it was never a part of what was shipped to the American distributors. Rhonda was like me, a genetically gifted athlete so she only used drugs for cutting up for a contest and I forbade her to sell to anyone else, which she was cool with, she understood that I had my reason why. Skye only competed in the natural federations, so needing anabolics was never a part of her training regimen, and Skye was one bad-ass natural bodybuilder.

I never did cycles anymore because I'd stopped competing years ago, and there was no need for me to seek perfection, Rhonda's friend Skye only competed in the natural federations so a trail of drugs to us was nonexistent. We only hired competitive bodybuilders to work at the gym, if any of them was in the market, I'd set them up with someone from Houston who handled our stuff and wouldn't cheat them. As an organization, we were so secretive no attention was ever drawn to us, if Macy had not implied anything to the San Diego cops and then vanished. I don't think they would ever have started watching Rudy and Lonnie. If the Galveston cops were watching me I didn't notice, after all I wasn't doing shit, but running my gym and at the time, allowing my body to heal from the fall. I wasn't rich with money, but in life I was a millionaire, I'd never been so in love with a person in my life as I was with my beautiful wife, our relationship was always like brand-new to me. We did everything together like going for long walks on the beach holding hands and making plans about our future together. The physical image of a bodybuilder is always much different than that of the average person, I was closing in on forty-six and looked like a man ten years younger, my wife was thirty-eight and had the body of a twenty-two-year-old. We were even talking about having a child together. I'd never been a father before other than what I'd gone through with Macy, it broke Rhonda's heart to know what she'd done to me and something in her maternal makeup wanted to patch up that hurt. I couldn't help but feel a twinge of guilt about Macy's daughter, who had lost a mother who rejected her and now a father who would never be capable of doing much for her. I hoped that one or both sets of grandparents would step up and do the right thing by the child. I'd never found any value in looking back on something unpleasant, but I did wish for good where the little girl was concerned.

CHAPTER
FOURTEEN

THE SAN DIEGO cops had taken it upon themselves to connect Macy's disappearance to what she was reporting to them about us. They were thinking it was something more along the lines of cocaine, heroin or marijuana smuggling, the fact that the anabolic steroid market had gone global never occurred to them. The San Diego PD had enlisted the aid of the Feds who now had the Balboa brothers under constant surveillance, they relied on the Galveston cops to keep an eye on me. It was clear they had nothing connecting me to Macy's disappearance other than my report of her burning my house down and attempting to kill Rhonda and Skye, none of which they could prove so they let my complaints slide away. I was more than careful in my movements, especially when I was moving product and cash around the state. Rhonda was the only person who knew when I was gone on a run and I never spoke to anybody but Joe John. The DEA though, were all up the Balboas ass, them not showing any clear means of support made them seem even more suspect. The Guardian Angels had even been spotted as they tailed Lonnie and Rudy out into the dunes to do their biweekly exchange, the feds were using satellite surveillance techniques along with helicopters. Macy's parents had put pressure on some congressman, who took their case to the entities higher up in the search for their daughter. None of us knew how much the search for Macy had been cranked up so I'm certain the Balboas weren't taking the same precautions as I was. The Mexican cops, a hotbed of corruption refused to aid the DEA in its pursuit of the Balboas, they knew who the Balboas worked for, and weren't about to interfere. The feds intercepted Lonnie and Rudy as they rolled out of the desert back onto United States territory, both ATVs loaded with boxes of drugs from Europe, Russia and Mexico, a few million dollars' worth. The new Russian dianabol was the latest thing for enormous size and strength gains, you could stack it with liquid American testosterone and anadrol and turn yourself into the Incredible Hulk without taking human growth hormones. They missed the guardians who were using night vision goggles and spotted the takedown of the Balboas just before they crossed the border, they turned around and headed back to Mexican territory.

I got the call at three in the morning from Joe John, we were ceasing all operations until it was found out how the feds got on to Rudy and Lonnie. It never occurred to the Balboas that they were being followed around twenty- four seven. The first thing the feds questioned them about was the location of Macy Dunn, which caught the boys completely off guard. What they felt was the elimination of a nagging problem had turned into their downfall, the discovery that they were smuggling anabolic steroids and not drugs to get high on was a total surprise to federal agents, suddenly there was something new to deal with. The guardians made a call to Javier immediately and by the time the Balboa brothers were booked, the best drug defender in the state was at the DEA booking center. The boys wouldn't give up any information no matter what the threat, the lawyer was there only to arrange bail, if allowed, the guys would soon afterward vanish into the Mexican landscape. The lawyer was shocked to find out that this was all about the search for Macys whereabouts, so bail was set very high, thinking whoever the boys worked for would refuse to pay it. Therefore, giving the feds more time to pressure the Balboas about Macy, they couldn't have been more wrong.

The Ortega's paid the two million dollars to free their loyal employees and two months later I got a letter from Rudy, they now lived in a little fishing town way down in southern Mexico and just like that, my relationship with the Balboa brothers was over. They would take on new identities and as far as I knew never come back to America. The only two people who could connect me to Macy's disappearance had just dropped off the face of the earth themselves. Months passed, and I heard nothing from anyone in the Ortega organization. I settled into my life as gym owner slash personal trainer and a husband to Rhonda with no secrets between us. Rhonda seemed to be becoming more beautiful every day to me, not an hour passed where I didn't for long moments meditate on her and the love I was filled with for her. She was my peach and I was her tree, if I were taking my last breath, I'd want her at my side. I told her about the money I had snaked away out in Barbados and how to get hold of it if anything were to happen to me. She'd always known we had other money stashed away and accredited it to my side job. However, she was taken aback to learn we had close to three million dollars to do with whatever we wanted. Owning our own successful fitness center allowed no suspicion as to why we lived so well, not like rich people, but certainly like folks who made money. There was a waiting list fifty people long for the six- hundred memberships we never went over, we treated our members like royalty and the popularity of our gym was like that of a hot new nightclub. We weren't Venice Beach, but everything we had going for us was just as exciting, all the fittest people hung- out on the section of Galveston Beach that ran right across the front of the Island Gym, every dime we made in profit we sank right back into the facility, our way of maintaining an atmosphere of success. My beautiful wife even had me set up a workout spot out on the sand, just like the legendary pit on Venice Beach, with Gators help we outdid the pit in California and the tourist loved it.

CHAPTER
FIFTEEN

"**I**'M PREGNANT WAS all she said," Rhonda was spotting me on a set of incline dumbbell presses and right in the middle of my sixth rep she made the announcement. I thought she was just joking so I never stopped the set or responded to her comment, after I was done I racked my dumbbells and waited for her to do her set.

"Let's go baby, it's your set, I barked, I looked at her and she was eyeing me down with a real serious glare.

"Did you hear what I said Mike?"

"Yeah, I heard you honey but I thought you was just joking with me, are you serious, you're really pregnant."

"Yes, I am Mike, does that scare you?" Before Rhonda spoke another word, I had her in my arms with my mouth, pressed tightly against hers in full view of everyone in the gym. Rhonda was going to turn thirty-nine in two months and I was already forty-seven, so I was surprised to hear we were going to have a baby, not unhappy but surprised. The last time I had heard those words was Macy telling me the same thing and I remember being happy but not this happy. I felt a tap on my shoulder, it was Gator," hey you two are drawing quite an audience, what's going on guys, and why is Rhonda crying?"

At the top of my voice I yelled," we're having a baby," that's what's going on Gator, my gorgeous wife just told me like she was saying your set, the only thing I could think of to do was kiss her." While the members near us applauded, Gator said congratulations as he wrapped his tree trunk sized arms around us, squeezing us both in a bear hug.

"Then he said dinners on me tonight, this calls for a celebration, how about that Happy Buddha place you like so much Mike, the place where they cook your meal right in front of you."

"That sounds like a winner to me Gator, that fine with you honey, I asked Rhonda?" She barely heard me, the female members and staff were swarming her with hugs and kisses. The staff drew straws to determine who stayed to close the gym down that night, everyone else and several members joined us for our celebration at the Happy Buddha. In my mind and my heart, I kept thanking God for all the good that was happening in my life these days. All the crap from my childhood and the hurt from Macy's betrayal were all drifting away into an emotional void I never visited. The one thing I still felt some remorse about was not being able to tell Macy's folks what really happened to her, I took some solace in the fact that I did everything in my power to stop her interference. To the point of even cheating on my woman and still she persisted in pushing the envelope that doomed her. I decided that night to anonymously send them a letter explaining what happened to her, I badly wanted to give them some closure and not end up in prison for the rest of my life. Those people deserved to know that their daughter was gone and not coming back, but I felt in no way at fault.

Just like the fates were reading my thoughts, the Allen's complaints to the San Diego cops led to them pressuring the Galveston PD to push me harder for information about Macy. This time they showed up at our home very unexpectedly, immediately turning me into a man being wrongly persecuted by the cops. It was one of the same jackass cops from the day at the gym, it was also obvious the guy had some issues with our inter-racial relationship, a typical Texas redneck with a badge.

"Mister Dunn, we need you to accompany us to our office for some further questions about your ex-wife, the redneck detective stated, a request from our superiors."

"There ain't nothing I can tell you there that I haven't already told you the last time we spoke about her."

"Two men, you've been associated with in San Diego were recently arrested in connection with her disappearance, replied the cop, those same two men after posting a very large bond to be released have suddenly disappeared themselves."

"Am I under arrest cop, if I am I'll have my lawyer meet me at the station house and you and your superiors can question me about anything you want while she's in the room?" The lawyer I'd hired, a woman named Nancy Revilett had told me to call her immediately if the cops harassed me again, so I did before agreeing to go with the detectives. They stuck me away in a dull cold room with nothing in it but a table and three banquet chairs to wait on my lawyer, who was driving down from Houston. They left me alone to wait for Nancy, after I repeatedly answered with the word" lawyer", loudly every time they tried talking to me. I'd already brought my lawyer up to speed on what they were attempting to jam me up on, so even after Nancy arrived I refused to speak with them. After an hour of silence from me and the reading of the riot act from my lawyer I was allowed to leave. The only thing they were going on were accusations made by Macy's folks, and that fucked up white dude still recovering in an assisted care facility, and none of what they were saying, I knew could be proven. I knew the one redneck detective was pissed, we locked eyes as my lawyer and I left the room. I knew he was thinking to intimidate me and I wasn't about to let him think he was. I never broke eye contact and as I cleared the door I said, "goodbye cop" just to piss him off. The lawyer took me by the shoulder with her tiny hand, "please don't antagonize these people Mike, for some reason they've got their sites on you and it doesn't seem like they'll be letting up anytime soon."

"The woman they are looking for used to be my wife when I lived on the west coast. I didn't even know she was still using my name until that detective made me aware of it. We've been divorced for close to five years and I hadn't seen her for a long time before she showed up here on the island demanding, I leave my wife to get back together with her, she'd turned into a certified stalker. I've already filled you in on some of the evil shit she's done to my wife and me. Those cops refused to do anything about it, and now they want to blame me for her disappearance. You just don't let them railroad me on some false allegations made by Macy's parents. And that shit about some guys I use to lift weights with out in San Diego sounds like the San Diego cops are just making it up as they go."

My lawyer told me not to answer any more questions without her being present and to not be concerned about anything but a boatload of speculation on the cops' part, so I went back to living my life, which for the first time seemed complete. Rhonda and I went on with our plans of converting one of the spare bedrooms into a nursery. Galveston police detective Johnny Vasut, Galveston police officers Ollie Falks and Mike Gee though had no intentions of leaving me be. The three sat around the table in a conference room at the city law installation north of town brainstorming on what their next move would be. Vasut took the lead, "I know that "big ole" black boy knows what happened to that girl, her folks are positive she was on the island trying to get back with him when she went missing."

Falks chimed in, "why these damn women can't stick to their own kind just drives me crazy. Look at this woman, as he held up a photo of Macy to the other two, any white man would be honored to have a beautiful woman like this. Yet she chooses to waste her time chasing after some colored bastard who chose to use her and just throw her away like trash. I know that big fucker knows what happened to her and if it's the last thing I do, I'm going to prove it."

"We got all we can from that fellow over in John Sealy, said Vasut the one that fell over the edge of the balcony when he was fighting with Dunn. He's positive the girl was over here chasing after Dunn, he says him, and the girl got a child together and that's what caused Dunn to end his marriage to the woman. He says she refused to let it go and came to Galveston as soon as she found out he was living here. The guy is as certain as her parents are that she was here in Galveston when she vanished, and Dunn and his two Mexican buddies got to know what happened to her."

"Every time we try to put the screws to him, he's going to lawyer up and the DEA can't find hide nor hair of them two Mexicans since they made bail. After looking further into them two their investigation found a connection between them and the

Ortega family across the border, said officer Gee. When Dunn lived in San Diego the three of them was as tight as three tics on a cow. If we can keep a soft tail on Dunn for a couple of months, I'll bet we can catch him up to something."

"How in the hell he just shows up here on the island with a pocket full of money and open that big ass gym on the seawall? The only way we going to get something on him is to dig deeper into his past and I'll bet we find out more about him and his buddies, we get enough evidence together and the DA will have to let us arrest his ass."

"Hold on now Ollie said Vasut, my command ain't going to okay the manpower for a full- time surveillance on just my hunch and I'm not sure yours will either."

"What if we all pitch in some of our off- duty time, just for a couple of months to see if we can catch Dunn at something."

Thankfully, the Ortega's didn't have any assignments that required my inclusion at this time, the restructuring of their operations on this side of the border were as such to not include me. All those cops got to see was an old gym rat living the bodybuilder lifestyle and hanging out with his pregnant wife. I did have that odd feeling at times that someone was watching me, but I was never bothered by it due to the fact that for once there really wasn't a secret life running parallel to my true one. Then one day while Rhonda and I were having lunch at the Landry's seafood restaurant on the seawall, my phone rang, and on the other end was Javier Ortega. I excused myself and walked out to the parking lot to get some privacy,"

"how's it going Javier, been a long while since I heard from you, Rudy told me things would be quiet for a while."

"The arrest of the Balboas greatly upset my father, so he felt it important to slow everything down and once again look at everyone working for us. On top of that one of our associates in a little town called Hockley was found dead with three bullet holes in his back. As far as we can find out that "gringa" you use to be married to is how they got on to Rudy and Lonnie." "Our source inside the San Diego Police Department tells us the girls intent was to make trouble for you. Thankfully you are a wise enough man to keep certain things away from even the woman that you are sleeping with. The cops thought you and the Balboas were into something much different than what we actually do. They were quite surprised to find that our business had nothing to do with cocaine, heroin or weed, never the less, my friend, they now know of our existence in the other market."

"My father was right to pull me from my involvement in the other side of the drug business after the bad deal you and the Balboas ran into at the exchange that day. Hopefully you have taken the same precautions with the woman you are with now, because my families secrecy is what has kept us off the DEA's radar for so long."

"This ain't my first rodeo Javier, I know that men who live in the world we live in can't risk sharing everything, even with his woman. I apologize for Macy making trouble for the Balboas, those guys are two of my best friends and I do miss them," I added.

"Rudy and Lonnie both have always spoken very highly of you, that is why I'm phoning you today, the trouble started by the girl is still a problem. Joe John informs me that she will never be a problem to us again. You may not have noticed, but the Galveston cops have you under surveillance almost every day, that is why we haven't had work for you these past months.

"Damn Javier I said, I get this itch on the back of my neck sometime that somebody is watching me, but I blow it off as me just being paranoid, how did you find out?"

"I told you my father is very thorough when it comes to his business, we had to check everybody on that side of the border out down to the finest detail. The girls' disappearance has drawn much attention to you from some of the Galveston cops, but our sources tell us their superiors have tired of wasting resources following you around, so we expect them to eventually leave you alone. Your cover Mike, is perfect for what we do, your business is fully legitimate so there is really no reason for the law to suspect you of any wrongdoing. Everything was going well until the" gringa "started stalking you and making trouble for you and the Balboas. My father feels he can trust you and we need to get back to business as soon as we can, once we are certain the cops have left you alone I will contact you again," vaya con dios" my friend," he said and hung up. The conversation with Javier really threw me, not that the Galveston law was still suspicious of, and watching me, but so were the Ortega's. Not the suspicion but the fact that they were also keeping their eyes on me. I agreed with him on one thing, how much longer could the detectives justify following me around without gathering any evidence against me. It also seemed the Ortega's had a means of acquiring Intel from inside law enforcement that was surely creditable, that I was certain of.

CHAPTER
SIXTEEN

GATOR AND I decided during our training one day to meet at a bar slash club down on the Strand that recently opened called Yagas. The Strand was the downtown social gathering area for the island. The city fathers took measures to convert all the historic old buildings into usable properties by transforming and remodeling the insides into trendy clubs and restaurants. All along the strand were quaint little gift shops, bars, and there was even a hip little gym called Sergeant Rocks that was used mostly by the folks who lived in the converted lofts and apartments downtown. The small gym was stocked with state of the art equipment and enough free weights to get a good workout in. Our plan was to meet there for an arm training and abdominal session, then afterwards hit Club Yaga for some grub and a few drinks. Rhonda now six months into our pregnancy chose not to join us, so she and her sons Cody and David drove into Houston with the girlfriends of the boys to do some shopping at the famed Galleria Mall. She knew how I hated long shopping excursions, especially in giant malls, so it was easy to not include me. To me and Gators utter surprise, the crew at our gym caught wind of our plan for the evening. When we got to Yagas most of the staff was already there drinking and dancing. I promised the wife to keep my cell phone with me, so she could talk to me during the evening. We didn't really like being apart for long periods of time but when we were, we made regular calls to each other, at least my wife did. The phone vibrated in my pocket, so I excused myself from the group and went out on the bars patio to take Rhonda's call. In a frustrated voice my wife told me of the billboard up on the freeway with Macy's picture on it.

"It's one of those missing person announcements honey, if she's hiding out somewhere just to make trouble for you, maybe someone will spot her and tell where she is. I'll be so glad when that woman is out of our lives for good."

"Me too baby I said, me and Gator are down on the Strand and so are most of the staff, who were here when we got here. We're in one of the new bars and I swear with our bunch in here, the place looks like a bodybuilder convention, you guys made it to Houston yet?"

"We're just passing through Clearlake and I already miss you baby, I guess it's cause I'm pregnant that's making me so emotional these days, I'd forgotten about that part."

"You're my best pal woman and every minute that I'm away from you is a minute where I miss you too, okay. I should be home by the time y'all get back to the island, I'll wait for you to get home before I go to bed. By the way honey, since you're at that big mall, if you see some cross trainers that you think will look good on your man, buy them for me, I could use some new workout shoes."

I knew the law dogs was watching me, but I didn't think they'd approach me with anymore of their unsubstantiated allegations, until I was pulled over one afternoon. I was cruising across the causeway that attached the island to the mainland going to visit friends in La Marque the next town over.

"Out of the vehicle, commanded the Galveston County deputy," so I casually got out of my car as the travelers on the causeway sped past, "license and registration said the cop." Without speaking a word, I pulled out my wallet to hand him my license then reached back into the car to get the registration from the console and passed it to the cop. The guy didn't say a word, he just turned and walked back to his cruiser, got in and sat there like he was waiting on something. Even though he was wearing dark aviator shades I could feel his eyes on me. After ten minutes or so he climbed out of his car handed me back my stuff and said, "you're free to go and slow it down some." I knew that was an empty warning because I was in the far-right lane just taking it easy due to the fact my exit ramp was the first one off the causeway, I couldn't have been traveling much faster than fifty- five. So, this is how it's going to be I thought, they're going to just hassle me as much as they can within the restraints of the law, what for I couldn't figure. The detective Johnny Vasut had made up his mind that he'd connect me to Macys disappearance anyway he could, and I guess the use of the county sheriffs was a part of that process. He'd be shooting in the dark because I never did any of the Ortega's business in or anywhere near Galveston, I kept the apartment and second vehicle in Houston for my other life, not even my wife knew about them. Vasut kept up the harassment, at least once a week my vette was pulled over by a city or county law dog. They so badly wanted me to do something to escalate the encounter, but every time I remained unruffled and quiet through the entire ordeal.

Javier called again a few weeks later to let me know he knew of the constant surveillance and that it was all credited to one dogged detective named Johnny Vasut. He also wanted to know if there was any way I could evade the cops for a couple of days. There were some critical assignments they needed taken care of and only someone they could depend on could be trusted to do it.

"Sure Javier, I can avoid any tail they have on me easily, I never do any of our business in Galveston, so let's get to it bro." Something had gone down with the Ortega's moneyman in Dallas, Javier told me to go strapped because he wasn't sure if the guy was making a move against his family, or if the trouble was something going on with the interworking of his own organization. For some reason money that should have already been moved to the safe house in Huntsville was not there and the guy could not clearly explain to him why. Javier in response informed him that he was sending his own man to retrieve the money and "when he arrives in Dallas, you better have our money, he told the guy." The last time I heard a drug dealer say those words to a man, I watched the man die, because he didn't have all the money. I was to meet him at his gym that was more in Fort Worth than Dallas, so I got off highway forty- five on to highway twenty going west toward Fort Worth. I purposely told the guy I'd be arriving late because I didn't want to arrive at a gym full of people working out. If I had to pull out my little three eighty to protect myself, I didn't want to do it with a bunch of people on the other side of the door. To my surprise there was maybe twenty people still in the gym training when I arrived at the facility. The gym named Metroflex was in a little business park just off the main drag in a busy section of the community that straddled the dividing line between the city of Dallas and the small town of Fort Worth. There was one guy and his training partner, both as big as upright freezers, outside in the parking lot doing lunges with a bar loaded with two hundred and seventy pounds. A group of others stood off to the side watching the two behemoths train, it was clear these two were the largest benefactors of our product. I walked into the gym and asked the guy at the front door if he could tell Jeff Burke who was the owner, that Mike Dunn was here to see him. The guy picked up the phone pressed a couple of buttons and turned away from me to speak to whoever picked up on the other end, after a few seconds he turned and told me Jeff would be out in a minute to talk to me. My "danger Will Robinson" alarm inside my head immediately went off, this dude was supposed to hand off a package to me and send me on my way. Something wasn't right I thought, was this guy stupid enough to pull some shit on the Ortega's, wasn't this fucker aware of who he was dealing with? I knew firsthand what could happen to people who attempted to cross sabres with this family. Macy was only a minimal threat to their organization and just that cost her, her life. Now this mother fucker is screwing around with their money, so this is why Javier told me to come strapped, he knew this guy was up to something not cool. Eventually a white guy with flaming red hair, a big chest and some real skinny legs came out of a side office walking in my direction. I had to stifle a laugh, I'd known guys like this in the past, they loved what steroids did for them but were too much of a pussy to train the lower part of the body. These fuckers would train chest and arms three times a week and never do any leg work. Which made their physique look more like a bomb popsicle with a stick in it, guys like this were always a joke to me. Burke acknowledged me with a handshake and said, "I'll be with you in a minute as he stepped to the front door and beckoned for the two monsters in the parking lot to join him." Once the two were inside he said to me, "let's go back to my office" which was the same room he emerged from, I followed him trailed by the two men from the parking lot. I made a point of keeping my back to a wall once the larger of the two guys closed the door behind us. I wanted some room to move just in case I had to reach under my shirt for my weapon.

"I'm here to pick up a package for the Ortega's, I said, is there a problem dude?" Burke responded by telling me who the two bodybuilders were and what contest titles they held, one of them I knew of, he'd just placed in the top five at the most recent Arnold Classic the biggest show of the year.

"Pleasure to meet you fellows but, me and this man got business to get on with, then maybe we can go somewhere to have a few brews and talk about the sport we all love."

"Hate to send you away empty handed, said Burke, but we've been told we don't have to pay the Ortega's by our new supplier."

"You having another supplier has got nothing to do with what you owe Don Ortega dude, so I suggest you give me what I came for, and then you can consider your business with them over with."

Burke stood with a now serious sneer on his face, "these men here are my business associates in this gym and in everything else, and we all agreed not to pay, the Ortega's. Our new suppliers said, we've already made the Ortega's plenty of money distributing their goods over the past few years, so what's owed should be waived as a gesture of gratitude for all we've done for them. If the Ortega's don't like it, they can take it up with our new associates the Huerta family, I'm sure you've heard of them." The Huertas I thought, the same son of a bitches that set up the ambush on me and the Balboa Brothers out in the dunes six years ago, I wasn't surprised. They'd wanted to get in on the anabolic steroid game for a long time and now I guess they had. I found out later they'd hooked up a European connection of their own and were now muscling in on the Ortega American distribution chain.

"Now, said the red-faced white boy, I suggest you get out of our gym while you still in one piece and tell that hot head Javier not to send nobody else here." This idiot had just threatened me like I was some kind of a pussy and that pissed me off enough to make me reach under my sweatshirt and pull my pistol, aiming it at the face of Burke.

"Who the hell you think you fucking with you skinny leg piece of shit, you think this is some kind of a game, you two move over there next to your buddy," I said to his boys. The two big bodybuilders slowly eased over behind the desk with Burke, a weary look on their faces, they didn't know if they were about to die or what. Burkes face, which was bright red a few seconds ago, was now ghost white, and he was shaking like a little bitch.

"If you shit heads was smart, you would have just given the Ortega's what you owe them and been done with it. You can buy your product from whoever the hell you want to, but don't think for a minute this shit's over." With my pistol still aimed at Burke face, I stepped to the door and left with the gun under my shirt so as not to draw any stares from the people in the gym. I stopped at a service station took out my cell phone and called Javier to fill him in on what just went down.

"You should have killed those "putahs" right there, Mike he barked, what makes them think they can stick it to us like that and get away with it."

"There was too many witnesses man, I would have never made it back to the highway before the cops was on to me."

"I know, I know my friend, I'm just pissed, those faggots will be getting a visit from my Guardian Angels." Just hearing Javier say that sent a cold chill down my spine, I remembered how deadly them two white dudes were and was thankful my brief interaction with them was as an ally. As a last-ditch effort to retrieve his money Javier asked, if I'd spend the night somewhere close, he was going to get with the Huertas to try and get what Burke owed them, before setting the guardians loose on their asses. Since the Ortega family refused to cut them in on the steroid game, the Huertas dug up their own supplier and decided to steal U.S. distributors from the competition by undercutting the cost to them. The thing with them instructing the guy not to pay Javier was a stupid move on the part of the Huertas. Burke and his friends could lose their lives and then neither side would have him as a distributor on the U.S. side. I found a LaQuinta up on the highway and checked in to wait for further instructions. I spent the rest of my evening on the phone with Rhonda, our little boy was due sometime in the next couple of weeks, so we were both anxious.

"When will you be home she asked, in a tone sounding way more worried then I wanted to hear?

"My business here should be done before noon tomorrow baby, so I should be back on the island before the sun goes down. Now get some sleep and think of me in your dreams, I love you very much." It felt great to have a woman like Rhonda at home waiting for my return. I was awakened at eight the following morning by my cell phone ringing, it was Javier Ortega, "Mike, those ass holes have made a side deal with the Huertas and think that gives them the balls to not pay me, thanks for staying the extra day. There will be a little bonus in your Cayman account, we got it from here, see you amigo." I couldn't believe those dudes would risk pissing off the Ortega's, no matter who they were in bed with, I'm sure Burke and his boys time in this world would shortly come to an end.

Rhonda was the typical emotional pregnant woman, upon my arrival home she greeted me like I'd been away for weeks and not just a couple of days. She smothered me in kisses at the front door and despite her pregnancy, she made mad passionate love to me for hours. The next morning, I made her what I knew to be her favorite breakfast, a casserole I learned to make from Paul Maples mother, she used to make it for us on the weekends. It was made of grits, bacon, sausage, eggs and American cheese layered in a dish like lasagna. I never made it as well as Pat Maples, but my wife loved it and I loved making her happy.

CHAPTER
SEVENTEEN

THE MUSCLE BEACH Extravaganza bodybuilding contest was coming up so activity at the Island Gym was electric, competitors from all over the southeast region of the country had invaded the island. The city fathers had to take another look at this thing called bodybuilding and what this annual event brought to the city of Galveston. The city already had its Dickens on the Strand festival at Christmas time and the Mardi Gras celebration a couple of weeks before the religious-based week of Lent. Now they've got this event centered around the fitness industry that drew thousands of visitors to the island for a full week of activity, that injected a large amount of revenue into the veins of the islands economy. For one full week of a hot Texas summer, Galveston Texas mimicked the historic Muscle Beach of Venice, California to a T, from West Beach, all the way down to East Beach the seawall and the shoreline were covered with male and female bodybuilders and fitness competitors. The tourist ate it up just the way they did at Venice Beach and our gym was Ground Zero, we sold so many temporary memberships that Rhonda made me cut it off, she said I was being greedy, which I was. There is no way in the world for us to accommodate the large amount of people you're allowing the staff to sign up, what if all these people show up to work out on the same day at the same time, Mike? The facility is not large enough she told me, and my wife was right. I even had to instruct Gator, who was now the manager to only allow people who were competing in the extravaganza access to the gym and to apologize to the members for the overcrowding. That was the magic of what became known as Muscle Beach week, its popularity even drew professional bodybuilders who showed up just to be a part of the event. The contest itself was held at the Moody Gardens convention center less than a mile down the seawall from our gym, making it easy for the competitors to use our gym for preparation.

The Monday right after muscle beach week Rhonda's water broke while we were walking down the shoreline, my woman is such a bad ass. We were a hundred yards from home and she made the walk back to the car, rather than wait on an ambulance to come down for her. She was still chattering about the timing as she climbed into the car and telling me to go inside and get her bag of stuff that she was taking with her. What a woman, I was thinking all full of pride. Her obstetrician worked out of the women's center in Clearlake City, about a thirty-five-minute drive from the island, though a few miles away from the island, it was the best place to have a baby. Rhonda's doctor used the women's center for all her births, we'd gone through our Lamaze training there and the center used these great birthing rooms that were more like hotel suites than the cold surgical rooms. We thought that was really cool and made our son's birth that much more special. At midnight, the baby still had not arrived and the doctors were starting to worry due to Rhonda being fully dilated, so the conversation turned to cesarean section. At two thirty the decision was made to proceed with the c- section, we were told because our little boy was too big to come down the birth canal naturally.

Blaise Michael Dunn arrived into this world, weighing in at a stout 11 lbs. 6 oz., with his father's brown eyes and the face of his beautiful mother. That night I made up my mind to clean up my life, to make a clean break from the drug running and money pickups. The last thing I wanted was to end up in jail away from this woman I love so much and this new person she just gave to me giving me someone else to love unconditionally. The feelings coursing through me right now is what I'd been seeking my entire life, the shitty mother with her abusive men were suddenly meaningless forgotten memories. I wanted nothing other than to be with this woman and this child, to be in our own world of joy and happiness. The attending nurses teased me about the baby being destined to be a bodybuilder just like his parents, "look at him," said Peggy one of the surgical aids.

"He's got shoulders just like his daddy, that's why he couldn't fit through the birth canal." Even Rhonda still being stitched up had to join in the laughter that filled the room, thank God for the epidural drugs. We moved from the O.R. back to the birthing room to find Skye and Carlos along with most of the gyms staff waiting anxiously to see Rhonda and to get a look at Blaise.

Nurse Peggy used the scene for more humor, "my goodness, even this little mans extended family has muscles. I think we just delivered the next Superman to the world" she teased, as she shooed some of the people out of the way to roll Rhonda in. This was great I thought, most of the people I love in the same room with the two people I love most. Paul, his sister Martha and mother Pat had phoned to say they'd be here in a few hours, I had trouble keeping my feet on the ground because I was so high on happiness.

A NEW BEGINNING

Skye stayed with us for a couple of weeks to help Rhonda with Blaise while she healed from the C-section, as strong as she was even my superwoman had to relinquish her will to the soreness. The gym was doing well so I was free to spend as much time at home as I wanted with my wife and new baby. To my surprise nurse Peggy was now a part of the Island Gym family, she and Gator had connected the night Blaise was born and were now a couple. She didn't lift weights like us, but she came in three times a week to do the dance exercise classes and some circuit training on the machines with Gator as her true personal trainer. After her workouts, she and Gator would cruise down to our house for her to check on Rhonda, making sure she was healing okay from the surgery. Gator is 6 foot five and weighs in at a strapping 320 pounds in contest shape, which was where he was right now. He was fresh out of the Muscle Beach Extravaganza of which he took his weight class and the overall title. Nurse Peggy looked like she might weigh one fifty and was maybe five foot six, talk about opposites attracting, they seemed to be really into each other, I was happy for Gator. Our lovely friend Skye was training for a show in the All-Natural Federation and her conditioning was looking spot on, it was cool to have her hanging out and training at the Island Gym.

I dug having the competitive lifters in our facility, it was like having celebrities around to me, they also kept the gyms atmosphere electric and exciting. The regular gym rats were okay and that's how we made our money, but there was something extra special about having pros like Rhonda, Skye and Gator, who'd earned his pro card at the Muscle Beach show on the scene. The other members of our staff were also competitors, but the three pros in the house were royalty. We were successful as a group and I wasn't going to be mad about that. The city fathers had even taken note and begun including us in their events calendar for things taking place on the island.

THE ORTEGAS AND HUERTAS

I was used to hearing about the drug wars down on the border over the cocaine, marijuana and meth business but a war over the anabolic steroid trade was way out of the ordinary and I wanted nothing to do with it. Who knows what could have gone down with Burke and his boys up in Dallas if I hadn't been strapped, my exit strategy was in full effect. I put in a call to Javier once I saw on the news about a shootout in Nuevo- Laredo between his guys and the Huertas.

"Dude I said, the cops are all over me about the disappearance of the girl from San Diego, maybe you guys should keep me out of the loop until they let up," I asked him.

"Not at this time Mike, with these fucker's trying to move in on us, we are limited to who we can trust, and you are of great value to my family right now, you just must be extra careful with the cops. Joe John is a very cautious man, he feels very comfortable working with you and I trust his instincts."

"This detective Javier, the one named Vasut, the man is like a pit-bull holding on to a bone. I'm just concerned that he's going to luck up and catch me doing something. I don't want to do anything that could lead back to y'all dude, that son-of-a-bitch is watching me twenty-four seven. At least once a week he confronts me with questions *about that chick I use to be married to, you'd think by now, his department would be done with that shit."*

"Like I said Mike, you just need to be extra careful when you move around, them assholes in Dallas have been dealt with, our new associates in Dallas won't be any hassle to deal with. You just do the pickups and leave them with Joe John, like I told you before, we only have a few people in the states, who we can trust and you my friend are one of them, he said, I'll talk to you in a few days," and he hung up.

Damn, I guess I'm still in the game, the money was great, but I just wanted to be a father to my new son and a husband to my wife and not worry about getting murdered or ending up in prison.

CHAPTER
EIGHTEEN

THE IDIOTS FROM Metroflex did get more attention for their efforts at stealing from the Ortega organization. The guy Burke, other than being a popular gym owner was also a major promoter of NPC (national physique committee) contest. His sudden absence and that of his champion protégé, Miles Branch, the big guy doing the lunges out in the parking lot. The two were just gone, the vanishing of the men was not a big story to the public, but in the world of bodybuilding and powerlifting it was huge. Burke was a prominent figure among the amateur show promoters, Branch was the talk of being the next big thing. The writers of Muscle Mag, Flex and Iron Man the three leading muscle head publications were all over the story. We subscribed to all of them at our gym, so the story enjoyed a constant flow among the staff who were all competitive bodybuilders or power lifters at some level. The rumors in the magazines were all over the place, one writer even made mention of the two possibly being gay lovers who took off to Denmark to be together. The day Raheema the aerobics instructor handed me a muscle mag open to the page with that story, it took me five minutes to stop laughing. After a few months, the rumor and hearsay, died down and the world of bodybuilding moved on, thanks to the ever-changing landscape of the fitness industry. The disappearance of the two got lost in the jumble of deaths of athletes connected to multiple years of use of anabolic steroids. These drugs had been around for eons of time, every single one of the deaths could be easily connected to the abuse of them. Too much of anything in life, it's been proven, to not be totally good for anybody. The idiots with the over- blown egos were the principal abusers of anabolic steroids. The proper use of the drugs always resulted in the user becoming as close to being Superman or Superwoman as one could get without the cape and the ability to fly. The negatives at first were not that public, but once the football players, baseball stars and track and field stars discovered the magic of the drug, all the abuse followed. The power lifters and bodybuilders knew and learned to regulate the cycles from physicians they trusted. The public topic of abuse was not prevalent until the popular pro athletes started dropping dead from overuse. One of the most popular players in the National Football League, died at a reasonably young age, leaving his family dumbfounded as to why. After an extensive autopsy was conducted on his body, it was determined the man had destroyed his inner organs with anabolic drugs. Before his demise the man went on television several times revealing to the world how for most of his adult life and all through his professional career, he'd been on steroids. He told the world that he could not accept not being the baddest dudes in the room or on the football field, so he never gave his body time to recover from the use of drugs. Once this very popular player came out about his abuse of steroids, the dam broke and everybody started talking. Suddenly steroids were right up there with the negative connotations connected to heroin, cocaine and methamphetamine, therefore connecting every athlete's death to the use of anabolic's. A person could die of hepatitis and the press would automatically connect it to steroids just to sensationalize the story. Society chose to blame it on the bodybuilders and power lifters who were mostly knowledgeable enough about the drugs to know when to cut it off. The desire to be great as an athlete didn't go away though, the wealthy players used high-priced doctors to administer and monitor their use of the super chemicals. Testing for the drugs wasn't yet extensive enough to determine everyone who was on something so records continued to be broken and crushed by athletes at the high school, college and professional levels. Some of the baseball players started to resemble mini- versions of the Incredible Hulk. The high-priced physicians continually devised ways to skirt the testing. One female track and field star became the darling of the Olympics setting or breaking several records and never testing positive for anything suspect. The doctors doing the testing were in no way the equal of the ones who administered and masked the chemicals in their patients.

Javier Ortega was true to his word; my assignments were relegated to me just moving bags of money from place to place. I started to look forward to my visits out to Hockley to drop off to Joe John. His girlfriend would cook a big dinner when she knew I would be making a stop at their house, Joe John would insist that I stay for dinner. His woman Irene was one hell of a cook and not just Mexican food, Irene was a whiz at anything culinary. Joe John loved hearing me talk about weight training, he and his girl joined the local gym and over the next few months under my tutelage, they both worked themselves into excellent condition. The little gym in Hockley was sparsely equipped in comparison to our place and the other larger facilities around the county. Once Joe John and Irene spent a weekend on the island and training at our gym, the tiny Hockley place would never do for the enthusiastic young couple.

I showed up at Joe John's place for a drop one evening and he literally dragged me out of my car, in his haste to get business out of the way. Joe hurriedly took the duffels of cash from my vehicle, tossed them into another vehicle and yelled "hasta la wago" to the guy behind the wheel then told me to get into his truck. Irene was already in the truck and she was as giddy as her man, "we have a big surprise to show you Mike," Irene stated. We cruised through Hockley's small business district and

Joe John stopped at a building that looked like it was once a drugstore, something like a Walgreens.

"Mike, I already told the owner of the gym where we train that I would be opening my own place here in town. He knows something this size will put him out of business, so he's selling us his equipment and shutting the place down. Don Ortega and Javier have already agreed to finance anything I need, if you agree to consult me and Irene on how to get it together." "They really admire how you and your wife have a business that is legitimate in the eyes of the law. No one can question your prosperity or the way you live. Rodolfo and Lonnie also tell me, if I listen to what you say everything will go well, we would greatly appreciate your help Mike."

In my mind, I'm thinking the Ortega's are backing the opening of a gym for this guy, he must be way up there on the list of people they care for.

"I'll be glad to help y'all Joe John, but keep in mind bro, running a gym is a full-time job. Me and my wife spend a lot of time at our facility, we're lucky to have a winning staff to keep us from being overwhelmed."

"You just tell us which way to go and what to do Mike, said Joe John, the Balboas tell us you won't steer us wrong, those two-fucker's love you man."

"Them are my boys bro and I miss having them around, I still get to talk to them on the phone every so often."

Over the next few months we turned the empty shell of a building into the Island Gym West, not the name given the place but it's working name, while Joe and Irene brainstormed on what to name their fitness facility. They wanted every piece of equipment we had on the islands floor in their place also, and it seemed the Ortega's had given them carte blanche. The place was an immediate success, it was as though the citizens of this area were waiting for a place to gather and work-out together. The Ortega family were thankful to have a legitimate foot on the ground in the US and they rewarded me for helping Joe John and Irene set things up. The extra fifty grand in my Cayman account rocked me a bit, so I phoned to let them know of some error they'd made, only to hear, "Mike, my father appreciates all you've done to ensure the success of our investment."

"Joe John has been instructed to seek your counsel on any business decisions regarding the facility,"

Joe John and Irene committed their all to running the place, it didn't take much effort on my part. Whatever promo we did in our place, was repeated at the City Gym, the name we all agreed sounded good. Rhonda, Skye, Gator, and anyone at the Island Gym who were known competitors conducted regular seminars at Joe John's place. Joe had the okay from the Ortega's to pay them whatever I said was fair. Baby Blaise, Rhonda and I did everything together, my happiness was spilling out all over me. Yes, I was involved with a criminal organization and sure there was no way out, so I remained cautious and kept on making the money.

After a year of breaking my balls about Macy, Vasuts superiors ordered him to cease and desist with his vendetta against me. The fucked-up surfer and his pals went back to California and so did the problems they came with.

Cody and David loved their baby brother so much, it bordered on ridiculous. I don't think we ever needed a babysitter for the first years of Blaise's life, his big brothers trusted no one with him. Poor kid was destined to become either a surfer like his big brothers or a bodybuilder like his parents, maybe both. Rhonda and I at times had to insist that the boys let us spend time with our own baby.

By the time he was four his brothers had taught him to swim and to stand up on a surfboard. All I could think was, what a beautiful amazing son we had. My wife's beauty seemed to be trapped in a time warp, she was as gorgeous now as the day I first met her years ago, on the beach at South Padre Island. Our love seemed to grow stronger everyday, sometimes we would finish each other's sentences. I walked into the kitchen one evening and Rhonda was crying, when I asked what was wrong?

She turned to face me, tears streaming down her cheek, she said "these are my happy tears baby, I'm so happy with our lives that it makes me cry, you are the man I've known I wanted to be with since the first day we met on the beach, something just clicked inside of me that day. I would see you in my dreams and wonder how long it would take you to feel the same way." I asked God many times to make you see me in your dreams and then one day you were at the Iron Horse Gym, and in my heart, I knew you were there for me, for us."

With her strong arms, she pulled me close and kissed me like it was our first one together, our love went to another level that day. Something I can't explain, but it was powerful, when we made love that night, it felt as though my woman had crawled under my skin and it felt wonderful. After we'd finally stopped our lovemaking like two teenagers I asked, "where is our son baby?"

"The boys begged me to let them take him to Port Aransas with them, I got tired of fighting with them and Blaise and gave in. Something about a storm bringing in some righteous waves, at five years old your son understands surfer lingo, is that strange or what. That child looks like you, but he acts like his big brothers, we made such a beautiful child."

"I feel very blessed that his brothers love him so much honey, but what do their girlfriends feel about them always having a little kid with them?

"Those girls love Blaise more than they love the boys, Cody and David say their girlfriends have spoiled him rotten, always letting him get his way."

"I've never known a brother's love like that, I said, guess that's why it seems strange to me baby."

CHAPTER
NINETEEN

MY SYMBIOTIC RELATIONSHIP with Joe John and his woman made our dealings with the Ortega's, the very thing they sought as an organization. The men in the northern part of the state were their own company, so to speak, and so were Joe John and me. We knew nothing about them, and they knew nothing about us, the exchanges between us were most times completely wordless. I didn't want to know these people, the amounts of money and drugs we dealt with could sometimes make people take stupid risk.

The guy Burke and his pals who I can only guess what became of, foolishly attempted to take advantage of the Ortega's. Just because they were in another country the men felt they'd gotten away with something just because they were white Americans. Drugs and money are power and any attempt at robbing or stealing from those who possess either will always incur some consequences. I'd learned that years ago, from my association with the drug dealer nightclub owners.

Witnessing JJ murder the man named Beaver just for shorting him on a payment opened my eyes, drugs, money and friendship could never exist cohesively. I kept my mouth shut, followed instructions and made the most of an inescapable situation. Keeping my family and friends completely in the dark about my second life and in the process snagging twenty thousand dollars a month, which was being added to my account in the Caribbean.

The only time it had gotten personal for me, was when the first guy at the Hockley Ranch flat out threatened my family and friends for no reason at all. I felt no remorse whatsoever at having made his ass into worm dirt. Even after Michael Ortega and the Balboas vouched for me, that son-of-a-bitch chose to intimidate me with a threat. I sensed that he didn't like me from the moment he made that remark about my race and the Ortega's not regularly associating with black people. I was certain he would eventually concoct some scheme to discredit my character with this clearly dangerous organization. May that piece of shit rot in hell.

Joe John listened to my advice and kept all Ortega business away from his facility and the tiny hamlet of Hockley. He eventually discovered the benefit of using anabolic's to enhance muscularity and gain strength. I couldn't tell him everything, but I knew enough to keep him from abusing the chemicals we sold. Joe John competed in his first contest, a year after he and I first met, and he was hooked on bodybuilding and being up on that stage, showing his muscles. His woman, Irene excelled as a fitness competitor and was on her way to superstardom in the sport. They admired Rhonda and I and how we ran our gym and took care of the people in the sport, they mimicked our every move.

Like us, they only hired people involved in our sport as either a bodybuilder, power lifter or fitness competitor, City Gym was a carbon copy of the Island Gym. The Ortega's were pleased with the way me and Joe John were handling ourselves as regular businessmen and not drug dealers, every now and then we were rewarded with nice sized bonuses.

Me, Rhonda and Blaise were living in a familial bliss, my entire existence was one of love, my son was growing by leaps and bounds, and my woman was growing more beautiful every day. Her competition days were over, so we trained her sons Cody and David on their quest for bodybuilding stardom. They were more surfer than bodybuilder but having grown up with a mother in the sport, the two men had been affected long ago with the muscle building bug.

They'd turned their baby brother into the most popular kid surfer on the island, by the age of eight the kid was one of the most known surfers in the state. Under the tutelage of his big brothers, Blaise was doing things on the waves kids twice his age couldn't accomplish. Film the boys made of him and put on the Internet quickly went viral and the surf magazines came calling.

Blaise was bigger than his age, though strongly regulated by Rhonda and me he'd been weight training since he was six years old. If his big brothers were doing it, he wanted to do the same, they all worked out together and they all surfed together. Cody and David knew we were serious about not letting their little brother overdo it on the lifting, so they were good dudes and followed our instructions. Blaise was old enough now to when he was curious about something, he would ask questions.

Rhonda and I were lying in bed one night and she said to me, "your son asked me this morning, where you go when you're away for two or three days at a time?"

A bit alarmed I responded with my own question, "well what did you tell him honey, just in case he asks me too?"

"There wasn't much I could tell him, because I really don't know myself. I'm sure you've had your reasons for not letting me in on what you do when you're away, and you tell me that there's no danger in what you do so I've let you be all these years. I told Blaise, we have a stake in the gym run by Joe John and Irene and sometimes you have to spend time in Hockley working with them. It's the best I could come up with and not flat out lie to him."

"That was quick and smart thinking honey, technically it's the truth, and if he asks me, I can respond to him and not lie, I love you Rhonda Dunn."

"Show me how much my woman said," as she placed her hand on my head and pulled me to her breast, that at forty-six were as firm as a woman half her age. The one great thing about us was, our love was always like brand-new, we made love every day if I wasn't away or she wasn't in Corpus Christi visiting her family and her pal Skye. If we were apart for any extended length of time, we talked to each other on the phone at least twice a day. Our reunions were always celebrated with long bouts of lovemaking, as long as we'd known each other we'd never argued about anything. She'd scolded me a couple of times during our ordeal with Macy, but other than that there had never been a cross word between us.

Cody, David and Blaise would all three at times admonish us for the way we acted like teenagers in love, no matter where we were. The boys all knew how much in love we were, and their teasing was just that, they all relished the fact their parents were so in love with each other. We had no unhappy days with the boys or with each other, and then one day, a private- eye shows up on the island wanting to ask me questions about Macy and the Balboas.

The guy's name was Phil McDisi, a former pro football player and competitive power lifter, his thighs were thicker than big leg Lonnie's, our friend from Corpus Christi. Up until now Gator was the biggest white dude I'd ever known, McDisi towered over Gator by 3 inches and I'm sure outweighed him by at least eighty pounds. I agreed to speak with him, but not at our gym, of which he was immediately in awe of, and that conclusion was only from what he could observe from the front desk. I told the giant private-eye to meet me at the Subway shop down at the end of the walkway,

"I'll be breaking for lunch in twenty minutes, if you got time to wait I told the giant behemoth.

The giant man insisted on paying for lunch, we both ordered turkey subs on wheat with drinks and chips, both typical meals for fitness buffs.

"My bad brother he said, for showing up at your gym like this, the Allen's didn't have a number for me to contact you by phone."

I couldn't resist asking him before we went any further, "man how much do you weigh", you the biggest fucker I've ever seen and what made you choose private investigator as a profession?"

"Okay, since you're a fellow muscle head, I weigh four-hundred and six pounds and make a point of never going much above that number. The private-eye thing stems from my love of television P. I.'s like Magnum P.I. and Simon and Simon. I always thought it would be great to be in that line of work, and as it turns out, I'm very good at it all, except when I got to follow someone around. It's kind of tough to be discreet when you're my size.?

"Okay brother, I hear you, a man should always follow his dreams."

"It's been close to ten years Mister Dunn and the Allen's are still waiting for their daughter to come home, they strongly feel the search for her starts with you."

"You could have just gone to San Diego PD, everything I know about Macy's vanishing is on record with them and with the detectives here in Galveston."

"I know all that, I've looked at everything they both have, including your suspicions that she may have burned your home down and attempted to murder your wife and another woman by running them down with a car."

"All that shit really happened big man, she was just so slick with it, the cops could never find anything on her."

"I've spoken with some of Macy's friends in Pacific Beach Mister Dunn, they all tell me she never got over the split up of you and her marriage. They say she was acting very erratic, and ignoring, even taking care of her child, who happens to be a beautiful little girl, have you ever met her?"

"I was at Macy's side, when the little girl came into this world, she was my wife at the time, does the girl look bi- racial to you? Mr. McDisi. Macy had fucked some old boyfriend of hers while she and I were married, when the baby came out with blue eyes and blond hair, I knew I'd been betrayed. To make things easier for us both, I chose to walk away from the whole humiliating scene. As a man, I was destroyed emotionally by her betrayal and her parents knew it, why they keep pointing the finger at me, I don't get. I left her a good sum of money and full ownership of a business we purchased together, did they tell you that?

"I didn't know about the little girl Mike; can I call you Mike the giant man asked me?

"Sure brother, like you say we're brother muscle heads."

"I'm sure the thing with the child must have been very tough for you and I can get why you chose to walk away. The Allen's felt you'd be more open with me because of the brotherhood of iron we share, so please Mike, don't leave any little thing out. The Allen's say you and their daughter were still sleeping together here in Galveston and just before she vanished, she'd come home saying you and she were getting back together."

"That's not at all true man, Macy is a very beautiful woman and despite the betrayal I still cared about her as a person until she torched my home and attempted to murder my wife. I will tell you this much, when I lived in Pacific Beach, I trained with these two brothers who we all bought steroids from. The last time I spoke with them, they said Macy approached them with questions about where I'd moved to. They said she threatened to go to the cops and tell them about the two brothers selling steroids. She showed up here threatening me with the same thing, so I guess the brothers must have informed her on where to find me. I warned her about the danger in making threats to the Balboas, who are not the sort of men who take kindly to being reported to law enforcement."

"She was playing a dangerous game Phil and I more than one time told her so, her last threat to me was if I didn't leave my wife and move back to Pacific Beach with her, I'd be sorry. That was the last time I'd seen or talked to her, other than my wife telling me she was behind the wheel of the car that hit her and her friend. By the way, we were out in California when that happened, so you should probably be searching for her out there bro."

"It appears Ms. Allen had become something of a stalker Mike and I agree with you about the risk she was taking in a threatening the drug dealers."

The private dick closed his notepad, reached his tree branch size arm across the table to shake my hand and said, "I really appreciate you taking the time out to talk to me Mike."

"Your gym looks like the real deal, how much for a two-day pass, this is my first visit to Texas so I'm going to stick around and do the tourist thing for a few days."

"I'll leave you a one-week pass at the front desk, I told the giant, don't worry, whoever is at the counter will know who you are once I describe you to the staff."

"Thank you, Mike, I hate missing my training days because of travel."

I went back to the gym with a clear conscience, after all this time I felt I'd given the private-eye enough information to conclude that Macy was gone forever. Not by my doing, but from stupid shit she'd done to draw danger to herself. The private-eye was no slouch in the gym, I'd seen many strongmen in my life, but none the likes of this giant of a human being. Folks in the gym could not help but notice him, he towered over everyone in the room, even Gator was amazed at his size and strength. He'd asked Gator to spot him on a couple of heavy squat sets, we all stood in awe watching big Phil McDisi do four repetitions with eight hundred pounds on the bar, the man was amazingly strong. Gator was chatting with him after the two heavy squat sets, to me it didn't seem like they were talking about weight training. I thought it better to stay away from him, I wasn't up to fielding anymore questions about Macy.

Later that evening Gator mentioned the guy did ask him a few questions about her.

"I told him what a nightmare she became to you and Rhonda Bro. I even told him about that boyfriend of hers that flipped you over the balcony at the Holiday Inn. He knew who I was talking about, he said he interviewed the guy before he came to Galveston. Big Phil says the guy is in a wheelchair and must be cared for twenty-four hours a day."

"Better him than me Gator, whatever bad fortune that "ole boy" come to, he brought on his self for coming out here in the first place."

"Phil says the woman's parents and the surfer dude all say you know something about her disappearance that you ain't saying."

"You and me both know they're wrong about that Gator, so let them go on spreading falsehoods about me, I'll get over it. I'm just glad she ain't been around here trying to kill me and Rhonda anymore."

"He mentioned anything to you about what he's planning to do next?"

"There are a few of Macy's friends here that he needs to interview and then he's going home to let the chicks' folks know what he learned over here in Galveston. I told him how she was acting like some psycho stalker, how I followed her around while she followed you and Rhonda all over the place. He was surprised when I mentioned you hired me to shadow your wife because of Macy's threats."

The private detective hung around the island and amazed us with his feats of strength for three more days and then he was gone, just like he showed up.

CHAPTER
TWENTY

THE VIOLENCE AT the border was worse than the American public could stomach, dozens of headless bodies were showing up on both sides of the fence. The media was having a field day reporting stories of the wars going on between the different cartels. I rarely heard from Javier Ortega anymore, any information for me came through Joe John, he told me the Ortega family were forced to choose a side in the battle for transport routes. The corrupt politicians would appear on the television news, declaring all they were doing to stem the flow of illegal drugs into the U. S. and to eradicate the violence. Rudy and Lonnie told me long ago, how the rich powerbrokers put on airs like they opposed the drug cartels, but in reality, financed and mostly benefited from the drug trade. There was always a front man to keep the eyes off the true bosses, the rich landowners would help some poor farmer get started.

Once the guy's name and face became too notorious, it was easy to give the DEA enough information to bury the front man. Old Victor Ortega knew of the web of secrecy the wealthy cast over themselves and how they couldn't be trusted. That is why he'd made a point to not associate he and his family with the true benefactors of the international drug trade. Cuidad-Juarez my old hang- out grounds, the town where I'd been befriended by the millionaire called Wild Bill, was now a bloody battlefield. The news reports depicting mass graves and blood covered body's right on the street were being aired all over the world. The Ortega's had sided with one of the families whose patriarch was a lifelong friend of Don Ortega, whom out of loyalty he had thrown his support to. Joe John informed me that work for us would all but come to a halt, until things were not so volatile in Mexico, which was fine with me. Our off- shore account was in a place I never dreamed it would be, the gym was doing spectacularly, and Rhonda and I were pulling in a great deal from our personal training business. I was so in love with Rhonda and our beautiful son all at the same time, could life be any better for a muscle head like me. If my work for the Ortega's came to a halt, so be it, I've had a good ride.

I stayed in contact with Joe John by phone, and over the next six months we only saw each other twice to transfer money from Dallas to the Hockley change off. Life was good as I went about my real existence on the island, no cops hassling me and no angry parents delving into my past, searching for a daughter who was gone for good. I walked through the front door of the Houston apartment one evening and noticed the piece of thread I'd lightly taped connecting the door to the frame around it not there. I did this to alert me to anyone having been inside of the place during my absence. The piece of thread lay on the floor just inside the door, so it was obvious the apartment had been entered. I took out my cell phone and called the leasing manager to find out if they'd been inside to do some sort of maintenance.

"No sir Mister Dunn, there has been nothing scheduled to be repaired in your apartment, is there a problem the woman questioned?"

"No ma'am" it just seems as though someone has been inside while I was away."

"Well, have a look around sir, and please call me back if you discover anything missing, we value the security of our tenants greatly."

I kept two guns in the closet, so I went there first and to my surprise, both were missing. Not only were the pistols missing but so was the ammo I kept on the same shelf.

The bathroom door was jerked open and out stepped the giant private detective Phil McDisi, with my own forty- four Glock aimed at my head. I stared into his eyes which were cold and emotionless, so I froze to await his next move.

"Didn't think anybody knew about this secret apartment you keep here in Houston, did you Mike?" I said nothing in reply, so the giant kept talking,

"listen to me clearly mother fucker, I didn't come here just to ask you a few questions and just take what lie you feed me back to the Allen's. I'm not just a private investigator "old sport", I handle punishment for crimes committed that the cops can't because of legal restraints."

"Let me guess I said, the Allen's hired themselves a hitter and you took the contract."

"Not entirely true, the girl's mother is too good a person to order your death, the father on the other hand, wants you to burn in hell. The man is certain you know what happened to his kid and he wants her body back, so he and his wife can mourn their loss without all the fucking mystery. The Galveston cops think you're guilty of her vanishing too, they're just too gutless to put the screws to you. Me on the other hand, suffer from no such restraints."

"You tell me where the girl is, and I promise you a swift death, don't and I promise your last breath you take will be in screaming agony."

My mind was racing at a frantic pace, I had to have more time to get myself out of this fix. This son-of-a-bitch may have me in a tight lurch now, but I ain't telling him shit he could take back to the law.

"Lower the gun Phil and I'll talk, I'm a little nervous with having my own weapon aimed at my head by a giant."

He lowered the weapon, "now talk mother fucker and don't even think of trying to rush me, I promise you ain't gonna make it."

"I can't tell you where Macy is big man, I'll have to show you and we'll have to leave this apartment for that to happen."

"All right black boy let's go, we take my vehicle, both your cars only got two seats and I don't fit into either. I don't get why a guy your size likes them little sports cars, and your woman drives that big truck. She's a gorgeous woman, maybe after I'm done with you, I'll come back to Texas to console her, let's go."

McDisi's car was a big Lincoln town sedan, the seat was so far back my legs couldn't reach the pedals. McDisi insisted I drive so he could keep the gun aimed at me.

"Where we headed Dunn, asked the giant man?"

"A town a few miles outside of the city out in the country to a place only me and one other person knows of, he helped me hide her body. I need to phone ahead to let him know I'm coming, and that I got somebody with me so that we don't get shot, if that's okay with you, big Phil."

"Go ahead, but don't try to sneak some kind of warning word in, I'll be listening."

Joe John knew what was going on the minute I said I'd be at his place in forty-five minutes, we never talked on the phone on days I was bringing him cash. On work days, we both did our part, so there was no need for unnecessary phone calls. The minute I said I got a friend riding with me, Joe John knew I was in trouble.

I turned off onto the road leading to the little ranchero in Hockley, this was a workday for us, but I was five hours early and in a foreign vehicle along with another person. The place looked deserted, even the truck we transferred the money into was gone. I stopped outside of the garage and turned the car off, "let's go Phil I said."

"Where's your friend asked big Phil, shouldn't he be coming out to meet us?"

"He's inside, he knows I'm coming so the door will be unlocked, won't you put the weapon away, so we don't spook him right off, I'm going to take you to her body bro.

As soon as the giant man's head cleared the door jamb blood and brain matter splashed all over the top and the hood of the white Lincoln. His large body flopped over into the space between the open door and the front fender. From the brush across the road behind me came Joe John and the Guardian shooter Steve Robbins holding his long- range rifle.

It had been a few years since I'd last laid eyes on him and I could not have been happier to see the clean-cut white dude.

"What did I tell you Steve, Mike would never bring anyone here, so I knew he was in trouble and look at this big ass car, Mike only drives cars with two seats set low to the ground?"

I shook hands with Robbins and thanked him for saving my life a second time, then I walked around to the large body and took my pistol from his waistband.

"This cocksucker was going to kill me with my own gun."

"Who is he Mike, asked Joe John?"

"He works for that woman's parents; the one I use to be married to that caused all that trouble for the Balboas. Her father sent him here to find the girl's body and to kill me, he would have if you hadn't understood my call."

Robbins pulled a twenty-dollar bill from his pocket and handed it to Joe John, "you called it brother, you got good instincts."

"Not good instincts, I know Mike Dunn like a brother, he would never bring danger to our family.

I took a wallet from the pocket of the giant, "this guy told me he was a private investigator sent here to look for Macy, I just want to see if that was the truth, or if he came here just to put a bullet in my head."

After examining the contents of the dead man's wallet, I discovered he was really a private eye but also in the wallet was other ID stating he was FBI. I guess working as a hitman was his night job.

"This ass hole has been bird dogging my every move for a month, he used his skills as a burglar to gain entry to an apartment I keep in Houston. He was inside waiting for me when I got there today, and he told me, Macy's father hired him to kill me, but to force me to show him where her body was before he did it."

"I can say one thing about him for sure, said Robbins, he is a big mother fucker. I had to make it a headshot, anywhere else may not even have brought him down with just one round, what a strange profession for a guy this size."

We put the Giants body in the backseat of the Lincoln rental, after dark Robbins followed me to the Colorado River where I rolled the vehicle with the engine still running into the muddy fast flowing water. Robbins offered to drive me back to my car in Houston, "listen Mike he said, you can't be certain this is the only shooter the girl's father will send at you. Keep your head on a swivel and keep your weapon handy just in case." He passed me a card from his shirt pocket, if you need me, call me."

"Me and Todd live in Texas now, it'll take me a few hours to get to Galveston from where I live, but if you in a fix, call."

"I certainly will and thanks for looking out for me Steve."

"Don't mention it blood, it's part of the job, the Ortega's pay us to protect their people."

"How did you manage to be in Hockley today, I had to ask?"

"Me and Joe John go back some years, it's deer season, I came in yesterday, me and Joe are going out hunting in the morning. I'll leave you some venison in Joe's freezer, you can pick it up next time you out there. Joe John is as good a shot as me and Todd are, even if I hadn't been here today, Joe John could have made the shot. I shot that fucker cause Joe was too busy tripping out on the size of that guy."

Joe John phoned later that night to let me know, he'd called Javier to explain to him what happened and, in a day, or two we'd be back on schedule. I broke the lease on the apartment, complaining to the manager that someone had gotten in and stolen my guns and other items. The lady agreed to not put it on my credit record and that she would give me a clear reference on my new rental. My next hideout was in a fifteen-story apartment building on Sage Street, four blocks from the Galleria Mall and across the road from the building at fifty- fifty Richmond, my last job for the gangsters I once worked for. The place was now, of all things, a tittie bar, high class, but still a tittie bar. The parking lot was in the underground of the building, the only surface entry was a large, well-lit lobby with a security desk before gaining access to the elevators.

I didn't tell Rhonda about the giant trying to kill me, but I did tell her about the new apartment, I had to show her how nice it was, mine was on the fourteenth level with a balcony. The view of the city was great, and I wanted to share it with my woman. The big boys took Blaise mostly everywhere they went, so we always had time to be alone, just us, we missed Blaise, but brothers will be brothers, so we never insisted they leave their baby brother behind. They all three were surf junkies and like I've always said, the damn surfers are like a strangely bonded tribe. The kid was sixteen years younger than his older brothers, yet they were one in the same so Rhonda and I never interfered with that bond. Blaise understood that during the school term he had to knuckle down and be a regular kid, good grades and all, plus give Rhonda her mommy time. He excelled at both, being a perfect child for his loving mother and an excellent student. Cody and David were still working towards their degrees, so they were going to school part time and setting a fine example for baby brother Blaise. When summer hit the brothers all three turned into something else, Rhonda and I were extremely proud of all of them.

Johnny Vasut and Ollie Falks showed up at the gym the next day, me and Gator saw them at the counter and we both started laughing at the same time.

"Okay Mikey stated Gator, who did you kill this time?"

"Let's go over and see what they up to this time Gator, I answered."

"Mister Dunn, you may not remember us, but we talked about another case a few years ago, started Vasut."

"I remember you guys, and it's been close to nine years since the last time y'all tried to railroad me on something. What do you cops want now, I asked in as mean a tone as I could?" Falks, who was the larger of the two men stepped forward, "here's the deal Mister Dunn, were you contacted by a private investigator around this same time last month?"

"Yeah, I know, a big fucking giant, he hung around here training some and asking the same questions y'all ask and then he left. Why do you ask deputy, did you lose a four- hundred-pound man somewhere?" Gator and the two female staffers behind the counter got a laugh out of my off-color joke, causing the burly deputy to turn a crimson red. Big Phil McDisi had missed his last call in for the investigative firm, he worked at. And they were searching for their very large private-eye slash hitman.

"This gym said Vasut, is the last place he was seen while he was on the island and you were observed having lunch with him at the subway shop down the sidewalk."

"And that means what, you think we got a man that size locked away somewhere in this building," I couldn't help myself.

"Mister Dunn, this is the second time someone has come to this island specifically to talk with you and then afterwards vanish from site." I stepped over behind the counter, went into my little junk drawer, took one of Nancy Revilets cards out and handed it to Vasut.

"Don't come here again, you cops are bad for business, if you do need to speak with me again, call this lady first."

Gator was still cracking up, "now Galveston PD is accusing you of making a man that big disappear, they really want to stick you with something."

It was funny them coming to me, that big fucking white dude kept a low enough profile to follow me around town for close to three weeks. Hitman or not the big guy was good at what he did, he just couldn't anticipate the tight ship the Ortega's ran. An image of McDisi's headless corpse slumped over dead flashed into my thoughts for a brief moment.

CHAPTER
TWENTY-ONE

LOCAL PROFESSIONAL BODYBUILDER Jack Herman fresh off a top five placing at this year's Mister Olympia was promoting his own amateur contest in the Astrodome city. The five feet six, two-hundred-pound statue of Herman under stage lights looked as big as men twice his size. The contest he promoted came out of the gate as a national qualifier and to win your weight class in this show could change your competitive bodybuilding career. Jack got a handful of his pro-level friends to show up for some added flavor and all the muscle heads gathered together at the Cullen Auditorium on the University of Houston campus. Dena Anderson was retired but she served as the master of ceremony at the nighttime finals, local Texas stars like she and Rhonda were royalty. Lots of the old gang from Hanks were in attendance along with muscle heads from gyms all over the state, I got to swap stories about the early days of the sport with some people I hadn't seen for several years. All the pros, past and present were recruited by the muscle publications to sign autographs and to take photos with the fans, something that was good for the sport. I had to relinquish the wife to the fans for a couple of hours, giving me the time to talk our facility up to anyone wanting to swap life's happenings. Most folks in this part of the country already knew of the Island Gym from its connection to the other big show of the year the Muscle Beach Extravaganza on Galveston Island. The show in Houston became from here on the annual gathering of the Houston area muscle heads, the female athletes would dress to kill making it a glamorous occasion. Rhonda and I painted the perfect picture of the bodybuilding family, Cody, David and eight-year-old Blaise were all bodybuilders, just like their parents. The three surfer brothers were the picture of pride to us, Cody and David so darkly tanned, they were the same color as their mixed-race baby brother. They all had long black hair, the only thing separating them was size, Blaise looked just like me, but was a mini- version of his big brothers. Rhonda was perfect, she knew how much I loved her in Levi's and high-heeled boots, and she nailed it. Us and our kids, I must say, looked good. Jack Herman promoted a great show and me and my brood never missed it in the years to come.

The detective and the deputy made a stop at the office of their friend Mike Gee who'd been elected to the office of police chief after years of service to the department. Gee along with Vasut and Falk's never stopped suspecting my involvement in Macy's disappearance, for all these years they'd hoped for another chance at implicating me and with the vanishing of big Phil McDisi felt they had.

Gee took the lead, we have got to be more than thorough this time men, we all agree that something just ain't proper about that "olé boy". I ain't going to never think he didn't do something to that pretty little girl, his two Mexican buddies might have gotten away, but we ain't going to just let him get away with this crap twice. That private eye left me copies of every interview San Diego PD had with the girl before she vanished. Everything in this transcript implicates Dunn, and them two Mexicans, she knew enough to warrant the DEA to electronically track the two Mexicans out into the desert where they were apprehended along with a ton of illegal steroids. Them drugs and all this weight lifting, and bodybuilding crap go hand in hand, there is enough money involved to get someone killed. I think that little girl wasn't aware of the danger involved, and that's what may have caused her vanishing. Now the next person attempting to connect Dunn to the drug dealing Mexicans has suffered the same fate. Dunn and some of them big musclebound fellows, he works with could get a big boy like that private-eye under control. We need to get somebody from that gym to talk, Ollie you can take a couple of men to help put some pressure on some of them others. Start with that big one that Dunn pals around with, if anybody knows something, he does.

Gator didn't live on the island, he was a home owner in a suburb outside of Houston called Sienna Plantation, a neighborhood popular with present and former professional athletes. He would take Highway Six, which started at the north end of the causeway and ran all the way to the Missouri city suburbs where he lived. Gator got off the causeway at Tiki Island, that's where Falks staked himself out to stop Gators big red Dodge Ramcharger truck. Without requesting license and registration, the deputy ordered Gator out of his vehicle, and keep your hands where I can see them. His vehicle was searched, and he was detained at the side of the road for almost an hour before being allowed to leave without any explanation as to why he was stopped. This harassment of Island Gym staff went on for weeks, what the Galveston County cops expected to gain from the stops was unknown to any of us.

We're getting nothing chief, I know you expected one of them to fold under the pressure and give us something to use against Dunn but ain't a one of them talking. The only ones who had any contact with the giant private- eye were Dunn, and that big fella they call Gator said Falks.

Vasut spoke, "what if he didn't have nothing to do with either case chief, could we be going in the wrong direction with our investigation?"

"You know what Johnny, answered the chief, my gut is telling me the same as it did nine years ago, and that is that son-of-a-bitch is as guilty as sin. He's made a mistake somewhere, we just need to find it. I had his life examined as far back as the past twenty years, other than sometimes he seemed to just have dropped off the planet for long periods of time. Everything he's been involved in was connected to men involved in the drug trade, always through some nightclub."

"Many years ago, he was connected to a man named Jimmy Binder, Binders in prison now, but before his conviction he was connected in some way to at least twelve killings. At one-point Binder was the biggest drug dealer in the state and he was suspected of running the largest sex trafficking operation in this part of the country. This Dunn has a history of working with these kinds of people and I for one don't think a tiger ever changes his stripes."

Falks broke in and spoke, "I've questioned several local people connected to some business ventures with him and his wife, their reputation on the island is impeccable chief, I tend to agree with Johnny, maybe the guy is on the up and up and we could have been wrong about him all these years."

"The hell we are Ollie, why wouldn't he have a good cover to hide what he's really up to. First that little gal and now that private investigator, just gone man, that ain't no coincidence. "The last person they both came here to see is that big "ole colored boy," Ain't no chance of the two not being connected somehow, that girl's parents call here a couple times a month to see if we made any progress in trying to find out what happened to their daughter. They are certain she was with Dunn at some point the last time they talked to her, and remember she told them her and Dunn were getting back together. The woman has a daughter that hasn't seen her mama in nearly ten years, I'm pretty sure the woman's dead boys. We owe it to that little girl to find out what became of her mama."

"Hey Javier, what's up bro?" A call from Javier late one evening was a surprise because I hadn't heard from him directly for a few months.

"Mike, my source at San Diego PD say they are looking into your connection to Rudy and Lonnie again so I'm certain the DEA is now involved. I've already spoken to Joe John; my father thinks it would be wise for you two to stay out of each other's company for a while. If they are going to be watching you, we don't want the DEA connecting him to you, you've done an excellent job with the gym. Joe and Irene should be able to handle things on their own for a while. Robbins told me about the private investigator, smart thinking on calling ahead to warn Joe John."

"Yeah, the guy was dead set on making me tell where that chick's body was, he didn't believe that I didn't know, he was sent here to kill me anyway, by her parents."

"How are you so sure of that Mike, Javier asked?"

"Because he told me so, her father hired him to take my life even if he found the girl. I'm lucky he was careless enough to let me make a call to Joe John."

"Did the soldier give you a way to contact him?"

"Yeah, it was cool of him to offer his assistance."

"If you suspect the father has sent someone again, call the soldier immediately, his service to us now is to back you and Joe up."

"The cops are still looking for the private-eye so for the time being, stay away from any new strangers that try to approach you. You should also arm yourself, I'll talk to you when the time is right, goodbye Mike."

The giant had both my guns on him, all I had to do was clean, his blood and brains off my Glock, he had my three eighty along with all my ammo in the trunk of his car. Finally, the Ortega's felt it better to avoid contact with me for a while. I'm going to focus on being a good husband to my woman and a father to my son.

CHAPTER
TWENTY-TWO

BLAISE WAS DOWN on East Beach with his brothers, so I had the house and my woman all to myself on a Sunday afternoon and I was in the best of moods since my conversation with Javier the day before. Rhonda was becoming more a part of me every day, she was busily preparing Sunday dinner for us, the boys and their girlfriends. We made it a steadfast rule in our family to always have a big Sunday dinner together, it made Rhonda so happy to fix dinner for her family.

She wore cut- off Levi's that showed off the great feminine muscularity and symmetry of her legs, and a lavender color sleeveless T-Michael sweatshirt that I loved her in. I sat at the dining room table where I had a clear view of her while we chatted, my wife was so beautiful, I could watch her all day. At forty-six her hair was still golden blonde, and I don't remember her skin ever not being the color of cinnamon. I lit up a joint, took a good hit then went over to give some to Rhonda, she told me to hold the doobie to her lips because she was busy kneading bread dough. After she took a big drag off the joint I stepped back to lean on the counter to just watch the beauty of this woman who'd told me years ago, that she knew we belonged together. She said she'd loved me from the moment we first met, and how she'd asked God to bring me to her.

She felt my eyes all over her body and asked, "why are you standing in my kitchen staring at me," without even turning around.

"How do you know I'm staring at you woman, I said defensively?"

"Because I can feel your eyes on me honey, anytime you're near me baby I can feel you, when you're away from me, I spend every minute anxiously waiting for you to get home. I thank God, every day for our life babe, I don't need anything else but us. I never trouble you about what you do or where you go when you're away for days at a time."

"That was your life when I met you, God had given you to me and I wasn't about to blow it by trying to change you. You're my man and the father of our child, even my sons love you like you're their father, my life could not be more perfect."

"I take that last part back, when you go away I don't sleep a wink until you return."

"I stopped her, I won't be going away for days anymore for a while honey, I'm taking steps to break away from that life." All the time she'd been talking Rhonda kept kneading the dough, she dropped the glob of bread dough and turned to face me.

"Are you serious Mike, she asked with a serious glare?"

"Yes baby, the men I work with are taking measures to replace me, for now I'm out."

With her wrist and forearms covered in flour and tears in her eyes she grabbed my head and pulled my lips to hers. My cinnamon girl and I made love to each other in our kitchen, even managing to burn ourselves on the hot oven a few times, my most memorable Sunday dinner to date.

The months passed, and I still hadn't heard from Javier, so I assume Vasut and his boys were still monitoring my movements. I'll bet it burned them white cops up to see me and Rhonda walking together down the shoreline, stopping occasionally to embrace and kiss in the setting evening sun. We both still loved training, so we were never out of shape, our competition days were behind us, but our love for the great sport of bodybuilding never wavered. People sunning themselves on West Beach often commented to us on how in love we looked, and when Blaise was with us we made the perfect picture.

Falks and Vasut sat in a cruiser parked on the seawall observing us with binoculars,

"I can't believe that beautiful woman is with that black bastard Ollie. Chief Gee is right, we've got to find a way to bring that uppity son-of-a-bitch down."

"Why don't we do like the old days, said Vasut, take some of the drugs from the evidence locker and set his ass up."

"The chief says we got to get him on some of the shit he's really done, that lawyer of his has already filed a complaint with the County D.A. about our constant surveillance. She's a smart one, we need something solid to bring his black- ass down."

CHAPTER
TWENTY-THREE

JUST LIKE THE surfer boys came to the island looking for Macy, two private investigators showed up at the gym one day asking questions about the giant. I refused to talk to them, but Gator let them know about McDisi hanging out at the gym for a few days and then leaving. They must have had a description of me, because one of them tried talking to me anyway,

"go fuck yourself I told him as I picked up the phone to call the cops."

"That was the law mother fucker, if you boys are still here when they arrive, I'm filing trespassing charges against you both."

Ollie Falks responded to the call, we watched through the glass as he and the two men stood talking in the parking lot. They looked like three friends just chatting, so I assume Galveston PD knew they were coming here to try and question me about their dead giant friend. I couldn't help myself, these fuckers had pissed me off, I walked out the front entrance trailed by Gator and walked over to the three men.

"Officer, I said, maybe you should clip a tracking device to these two fuckers', so you don't lose them too," me and Gator burst into laughter.

The two private eyes rushed us screaming some stupid obscenities, I caught the first guy and used his forward momentum to take him up over my head and slammed him as hard as I could on to the asphalt parking lot surface. Gator hit the other guy in the middle of his face with a left jab from his Python -sized arm, I heard the bone and gristle crush in the man's face, and knew he was done. Falks drew his firearm and trained it on me and Gator yelling the command to freeze. We both raised our hands in a surrender gesture, we were done anyway, both of our assailants lay motionless at our feet. Falks glanced up to the front glass of the gym to see every member observing us with shocked looks on their faces and then holstered his weapon. The other male staff were standing in unison behind Gator and me, they'd all come to our aid at the first sign of trouble. The adrenaline was coursing through my veins as I barked,

"you was going to shoot me and my friend for defending ourselves deputy." Gator stepped closer to him, his large presence, towering over Falks, "it's a good thing there are a hundred-people watching deputy, he said." Gator was so mad his tan had a red tent to it, I'd never seen him mad before, he stood over Falks with a death glare in his eyes. Right about that time, Nurse Peggy and Rhonda squeezed through the jumble of people, Peggy taking Gator by the arm and pulling him away and Rhonda doing the same to me. Falks stood looking down at the two men on the ground for a few seconds before stepping to his cruiser and calling the E. M. T's. Those men must have been very confident in their skills as fighters to attack two men who together outweighed them by at least two- hundred pounds. For whatever reason, they'd both strongly regret the choice they'd made by morning. Falks, even though he was present had nothing to offer in the men's defense, it was clearly obvious to anyone witnessing the incident that Gator and I were defending ourselves.

The two private-eyes lay on hospital beds in the same room, one with a fully bandaged head and a plastic brace over his nose, that was obliterated by Gators punch. The other still unconscious from my having slammed him so hard on to the asphalt surface. The one with the smashed in face was telling Falks and Vasut how their friend and partner had been reporting in every other day, and then just like that he stopped reporting.

"His last conversation he informed us that he'd tailed Dunn to an apartment complex in Houston. Evidently Dunn switched cars and he missed him leaving the apartment, he didn't get eyes on Dunn until three days later back in Galveston. The man obviously has something to hide, why does he have an apartment and a second vehicle in town 50 miles from his home. "Our friend was on to something, he's the best investigator in our firm, and he would never go this long without reporting in. Dunn knows something, and you fellows should be putting the pressure on him to find out what happened to Phil.

"Can't charge him with nothing said Vasut, you and your friend here attacked the man under the eye sight of over a hundred witnesses. Consider yourselves lucky, the last fellow from San Diego that attacked Dunn left this island taking his meals through a straw. Both of them men are built like tanks, y'all are mighty brave, thinking you could take them on.

"We're just mad as hell detective, I know something terrible has happened to our man, it's not in us to just let this go, Dunns' got to pay."

Chief Mike Gee listened closely to Vasut and Falks version of the events in the gym parking lot and the words spoken by the hospitalized private investigators, before speaking.

"That big fellow assured us he was only here to talk with Dunn, and we can't allow them other two to be on the island acting like some damn vigilantes. As soon as the two of them are cleared to leave John Sealy, y'all put them on a plane out of here. Johnny see what you can get out of that Dunn fellow about him having some secret apartment in Houston and check with DMV about another car."

The moment Vasut walked through the front door of the gym, I waved him away, I was in the middle of a training session with a client preparing for the nationals. Raheema was walking towards the front so I beckoned her over,

"Raheema, would you please tell that cop for me, if he has anything to say to me I've already given him my lawyers card."

"Sure Mike, be glad to, is that all you want me to tell him?"

"Yes, ma'am and thank you very much." I watched as a scowl formed on the detectives' face as he blushed from the embarrassment. Back in his car Vasut was fuming, how dare that big muscle head son-of-a-bitch dump on me like that in front of all those people, he said to himself. He pulled out his phone to call Chief Gee, "Chief, Dunn refused to talk to me, he referred me to his attorney."

"There's more than one way to skin a cat Johnny, check with the DMV, that second car might be registered to another address." To Vasuts surprise, my Zee was registered under the apartments address, so he immediately took off for Houston. At the security gates Vasut parked and got out of his car to speak with the guard on duty. He showed his badge, prompting the guard to let him into the little security office. Vasut explained to him the case he was working on followed with a description of Mike Dunn. The guard immediately knew the tenant he was asking about, "yeah, that big fellow and his wife have had an apartment here at the Lakes for a long time." Don't see the wife much, but the man is here a few times a month, he says they live in Galveston and only use the place when they got business in Houston. You should talk to the guy who relieves me in a couple of hours, he told me some FBI agent was here doing surveillance on the resident in unit 1403, the big man's apartment."

"An FBI agent, repeated the now stunned detective, did you ever get a good look at him?"

"No, he was only here in the evening, my shift ends at noon, the other guard said he let him through a few times, once he showed his badge."

"I'm going to grab something to eat, tell your relief, I'll be back."

Vasut returned to the complex two hours later to question the other security guard, the man was a little older than the first guard and was more authoritative acting, more like a cop than security guard. Discovering he could be of some assistance in two real investigations in as many months was exciting to the man.

"Can you fill me in on who and why the FBI agent was keeping under surveillance officer, Vasut felt treating him more like a fellow law man would help in the man's cooperation?" He said, "Mister Dunn, the tenant in 1403 was involved in some sort of theft and his assignment was to follow him in the hope he would lead him to the stolen property. "I let him through the gate three days in a row while he waited for the tenant to show. The day Mister Dunn showed up, thirty minutes after he arrived, the agent and the tenant passed through the exit side in the agents' car. Funny thing though, Mister Dunn was driving the agents' car, haven't seen either one of them since that day."

"Can you describe the FBI agent to me, sir, asked Vasut?"

"Biggest damn man I ever saw, said the wide-eyed rent a cop, guy must have been 7 feet tall."

"Would it be possible for you to let me take an unofficial peak into Dunns' apartment?"

"If you can clear it with the leasing management detective, I personally don't have a problem with it."

Vasut was running into one puzzle after another, the complex manager informed him that the Dunns' broke the lease and moved out a week ago,

"Mister Dunn was quite upset because someone had broken into the apartment and stolen some valuable items. I offered to cover any damages his insurer found viable, but Mister Dunn said he'd rather just move."

"Did he leave an address to where he moved to?"

"No, he didn't, a moving company came in one night and within two hours the place was empty, he didn't even bother to ask for his security deposit back. We would have gladly refunded it, because of the burglary, we were so sorry about that."

Vasut was very confused, had the giant private detective impersonated an FBI agent to gain entry to Dunns' apartment. Why would he and Dunn be riding in the same car and where could they have been going, this whole case was going ballistic. He phoned Chief Gee to bring him up to speed on what was becoming something of a labyrinth surrounding Mike Dunn. His next move was to find out what airline the private-eye flew in on and what car rental service he used. McDisi came in on Southwest Airlines out of Hobby Airport and his office was still paying for the rental which had not yet been returned. Vasut asked the Avis employee if they had GPS trackers on their rentals.

"Yes, we do, said the pretty young clerk, if you give me a minute detective I'll tell you exactly where that vehicle is. Oh, that's strange, declared the cute brunette, the cars tracking device seems to have stopped working somewhere near Sealy, Texas. I don't know what to tell you sir, we'll have to wait for the vehicle to be returned before I can tell you more." Holy shit thought Vasut, not only is the giant private-eye missing, but so is the car he was driving, what the hell is Dunn up to.

L. G. Henry, one of my protégé middleweight competitors had earned enough competition credits to qualify for the NPC nationals which were being held at the convention center in Dallas, Texas this year. The atmosphere in the gym was electric as the whole staff focused on his preparation for the amateur event of the year, L. G. was representing us all up on that stage. I rented a big RV bus that could accommodate a great deal of the staff and a few members up to Dallas to support L. G. If a competitor looked good enough to get into the top five, a vocal and enthusiastic support team in the audience could get him over the top. His condition was on point, Rhonda and Gator both gave him the thumbs up on his preparation for the nationals.

Joe John and Irene gathered the few bodybuilding aficionados training at their gym and came in a caravan of cars and trucks. Rhonda and I expressed the value in supporting the sport by attending a few bodybuilding shows a year and, in the process, promoting their own facility by sporting active- wear with the name and location of the place emblazoned across the front or back. Skye and Carlos flew in from Corpus Christi with two fitness competitors they were training, who'd also qualified for the nationals. The reigning Mr. Olympia was the contest guest poser, preparing to win his sixth Olympia, the man was in excellent condition. Joe John had never attended a contest of this magnitude, with so many professional bodybuilders and fitness athletes in the building, he was scrapping for autographs like a fat kid in a cake factory. Again, I had to stand back and let the wife do her thing, though she'd stopped competing years ago, fans of the sport still loved her.

One of the muscle- head publications, from somewhere came up with a stack of photos of her and away she went, her popularity in the sport was still huge. Me, Gator and Blaise took off to watch the pre-judging, which is the meat of a bodybuilding contest, Gator eventually was taken off by one of the magazine writers for an interview, leaving me and Blaise to see the sights alone. Cody and David were backstage with L. G. helping with his stage prep for the pre-judging. I ran into a few old friends from Hanks and some other guys I'd met at George Turner's gym up in Missouri. Sadly, they told me George had passed away recently. The staff and the group of members we brought along were scrambling all over the place snagging autographs taking pictures and bragging about our gym and how great it was to work for Rhonda. I insisted everyone from the island sport one of our T-Shirts at the pre-judging. Rhonda teased me later about it, "we have one of the most popular gyms in the state, and still you can't stop bragging". She loved getting on me when I was in overkill mode. I bumped into Dena Anderson, she like my wife was getting better with age, she fell in love with Blaise on the spot, it made me feel good to hear her say, "he's a little you Mike." My son would later say to me, "she's a fox dad", is that one of your girlfriends before you met Mom?"

"Boy, you ain't but nine years old, what you know about a fox, I stammered out."

"When Cody and David see a good-looking girl, that's what they say."

"I think your brothers are making you grow up too fast, don't let your mother hear you talking like that. Your mother took me away from that woman little dude, I fell in love with your mama the first time I met her, it just took me a couple of years to figure it out, your mama is the girl of my dreams."

"Most men go their whole life not having met the girl of their dreams, I'm a lucky man son, I hope the same thing happens to you someday."

L.G. made it to the night show finals but lost out on the overall title to a light-heavyweight entrant that stole the crowd and contest with perfect muscularity, symmetry and condition, along with some perfect posing. Still, the Island Gym was well represented as a cohesive threat to be dealt with in future contest.

CHAPTER
TWENTY-FOUR

VASUT WAS BACK at John Sealy hospital the following morning, he sat in a chair placed between the beds of McDisi's two colleagues from San Diego.

"Is there anything about that giant private-eye you fellows left out?"

Kyle Mankin and Shawn Heffernan were both still drugged up from the Demerol coursing through their system for pain relief. Both knew Vasut had discovered enough, something that unveiled the ruse they perpetrated as a private detective agency. For years, the three had doubled as hired hitters under the table, the men were responsible for several contract killings around the country. The bulk of the agency's money was generated from those killings, you had to know somebody who knew somebody to hire them.

"What are you accusing us of detective, questioned Mankin?"

"We came here in good faith to look for our associate, anything else you think has nothing to do with that." Vasut stood, his eyes going from one man to the other, "how and why was your guy flashing credentials that identified him as an FBI agent?" Seeing no reason to lie any further the men came clean, sounding like somebody with a nasal problem Heffernan spoke slowly.

"We sometimes use it as a tactic to gain access to people or places, we would ordinarily not have."

"How did you find out; did you find Phil? Asked Mankin.

"You boys ain't been completely honest with us so the chief says we done exchanging any pertinent information with y'all. Chief says soon as the doctor releases you two, to put you on a plane out of here. We'll find your colleague on our own and send him back to California too."

After Vasut left the hospital room, Mankin and Heffernan agreed to freely leave the island, "after we heal up Kyle, we going to come back here and deal with that Dunn fella on our own terms. I think Phil's dead and that fucker has got something to do with it, we're not going to just walk away from this, Phil wouldn't do it to us."

Back in San Diego, Heffernan and Mankin sat in the living room of George Allen, reporting to him on the disappearance of their colleague and how they'd gotten into a physical altercation with Dunn and lost.

"We're more certain if anything, the man is guilty of causing your daughter's vanishing Mister Allen. The same thing that happened to her has happened to our associate Phil McDisi. Dunn was the last person they both were in contact with prior to them, suddenly disappearing. He's managed to outsmart those hillbilly cops in Texas, I promise you that won't be the case with us. Phil evidently made some mistake and we're sure it cost him his life, even the car he rented has vanished."

"He and your daughter were not aware of how dangerous the man is. We won't stop searching for your girl, but that other thing you're paying us to do, are you still okay with that?" "You damn skippy, I still want the deed done, I'd like to have my kids body back, if you can't get that out of that bastard, so be it, I want the man to die. My wife is still suffering from a broken heart after all these years, my child's daughter looks more like her mother every day. My wife starts to cry sometimes just by looking at my grandbaby, finding Macy's remains and giving her, a Christian burial will at least give us some closure. Not knowing is like being tortured by our memories over and over even after all these years. It may not bring any relief to my wife but if you men take care of that heartless son-of-a-bitch, I personally will be able to sleep better. First, he breaks my girls heart and then he destroys my family, when you kill him, please see to it that he dies in pain, for me."

"That guy and his wife are hurting a lot Shawn, I guess losing a child and not knowing what happened to her is an emotional form of torture.

"I know Kyle, just listening to him made my heart feel for him, we got to do this thing for him, his wife and Phil. That fucker is smart Kyle, whatever he's into, the people on that island are oblivious to. I've always seen Phil as indestructible, it's hard for me to accept him being taken out by that piece of shit muscle-head."

"The doctor said I can take the dressing off my face in two weeks, he tells me I may need some cosmetic surgery later to make my nose look normal again. I've got a score to settle with that other big bastard Kyle, we're going back for Dunn, but that fucker is going to get it too. We're driving to Texas this time Shawn I'm taking my guns with me, that's probably how he got the drop on Phil, he didn't have his guns with him. I say we grab that wife of his and use her as bait to draw both of them big bastards into a trap.

"That sounds good, let Dunn watch us rape and kill his woman, before we put a bullet in his head. He ain't ever going to take us to the girl's body, hell, he probably doesn't know where it is his self, said Mankin, the old man will just have to accept the justice we issue to Dunn."

CHAPTER
TWENTY-FIVE

I TOOK JAVIER'S advice by not being too open to strangers and always keeping a weapon close at hand, I even kept my three eighty in my gym bag. That little voice in my head was annoying the hell out of me for some reason I couldn't figure out. Rhonda, Blaise and I went into Houston to spend the weekend at the new apartment in the high-rise and to shop for Rhonda a new truck. We'd traded Michael's in on a new Toyota four Runner a few years back, but Rhonda never stopped missing the big American gas hog. We were going to check out the Chevy dealerships to find something to make my beautiful female bodybuilder wife happy before returning to the island. Blaise insisted on choosing the color and like always the beautiful girl let the handsome prince get his way, I didn't mind, I loved hearing the two of them bicker over the issue. Now at our third dealership owned by stock-car legend, A. J. Foyt, the two of them finally agreed on a royal blue four-wheel-drive Chevy Silverado. My agreeing with them both made it unanimous, Rhonda with her darkly tanned skin, beautiful blue gray eyes and curly blonde hair looked just the right sexy to suit me. She said her farewell to the Toyota, hopped into the new Chevy and our little family headed back to the island. We went to the gym first to show Cody, David and the staff Rhonda's new toy.

The two private dicks from San Diego were still in Houston sitting on the signal of the tracking device they'd so slyly attached to Rhonda's Toyota. It was midnight by the time, they realized something just wasn't right, the truck hadn't moved in hours and the dealership was deserted before those idiots went back to the island. We had a very elaborate alarm system installed on the new truck due to the very expensive add-ons we included in the purchase. Mankin and Heffernans plan to snatch Rhonda to use as bait to get Gator and me was temporarily foiled by our decision to buy a new truck the day after they'd placed the device on her Toyota. The first time they attempted to attach a device on the new truck the alarm was set off at three o'clock in the morning. I grabbed my shotgun and went outside to see what was going on, I got to the bottom of the stairs just in time to see a man jumping into the passenger side of a dark-colored sedan as it sped away. We lived on the safest stretch of beach in the city, crime in our neighborhood was pretty much nonexistent. I instantly felt that this was something else, my little voice was now yelling in my ear, something wasn't right. I used the key bob to shut the alarm off just as lights in the surrounding homes began to pop on and went inside to calm my wife and son.

"What was it Dad questioned Blaise?"

"Somebody might have been trying to steal your mama's new truck, I saw some white dude jump in a car and haul ass out of here. Good thing we got that bad ass alarm system installed honey, you ain't had that new truck, but three days and already some ass hole is trying to steal it."

Javier's warning rang through my thoughts, I didn't want to worry my wife and son, so I remained silent about my suspicions. The next morning, I telephoned Steve Robbins, the guardian to let him know I needed his aid. I stayed close to Rhonda and Blaise until his arrival, after my discovery of Phil McDisi being a hired killer. I wasn't going to be so naïve as to think he was the only one. I checked every crack and crevice of Rhonda's truck and my car before either of us drove them every morning. George Allen still wished me dead and I wasn't going to make it easy for that fucker. As luck, would have it, Cody and David were going to Hawaii to surf for a month and their little brother did not want to be left behind. Rhonda had never been separated from either of the boys for such a long period of time, and certainly not Blaise who at the age of ten, she still considered her baby. The boys knew not to butt heads with their mother so little brother Blaise was on his own, he and Rhonda were at it for two days. He was clearly her son, they both contained the same strength of wills and determination, it was close to being comical listening to them, go at it. My reasoning for getting into the fray was purely self-servant, if Blaise and his brothers were off the island, that left only Rhonda for me to protect. Between me and Robbins, I could keep her protected twenty-four seven, I wish those fuckers would just come at me, now that I was aware of the killers, intentions, I stayed ready. The day before the boys were to leave for Hawaii, I sided with Blaise and the boys, drawing the full wrath of the beautiful woman who was my wife. She felt that her whole family had ganged up on her, she remained pissed at me for two days after the boys and their girlfriends along with little brother Blaise boarded a plane to the Hawaiian Islands. I'm sure we were quite a sight, walking through the terminal of George Bush Intercontinental, three long haired surfers all carrying surfboards. Their mixed-race parents trailing behind, the mother in tears and me happy as shit on the inside at having them all out of harms way. The love of my life never ceased to amaze me, she held all three of her boys in the grasp of her strong arms for the longest time.

"Honey, you gonna make them miss the plane if you don't let them get on board, they just made the final boarding call."

"Don't cry Mom said Blaise, we'll be back before you know it." She released her grip on the boys, looked up at Cody and David and said, "my baby better not have

151

one scratch on him, when y'all get back and I better get a phone call from you boys every day, I don't care what time it is."

"Okay Mom said David, we promise, now can we get on the plane?"

On the drive back to the island, Rhonda was quieter than usual, I just figured she was still steaming over me taking sides with the boys. To break the tension. I asked if she'd like to stop at Benihana's for dinner and a few drinks before going to the house. She accepted my offer but was still quiet, something was on her mind. By the time we got to Clearlake about half way home she finally opened up, "what's going on Mike, you're not fooling me, something has been going on with you since the alarm was set off on my truck the other night."

"You're my husband and I love you with all my heart, we've been together long enough for me to feel it when somethings on your mind. I saw you checking under my truck yesterday morning, what was that all about? I really love it when you hang out with me, I love every minute we spend together, Mike, you went shopping with me at the mall the other day. You hate going to the mall and you never get in it when I'm on your sons' ass, yesterday you practically insisted I let Blaise go with his big brothers on this trip. Start talking big boy, she said in her most determined voice."

I got off the freeway in Dickinson and pulled into an Exxon service station to park.

"Honey, remember the big man from California that was here looking for Macy a couple of months ago?"

"Yes, I remember, you and Gator had a fight with some of his friends in front of the gym one evening, right."

"That strong ass giant was sent to the island by Macy's father to kill me baby. He almost got away with it too, he was just too stupid to do the deed, I led him into a trap and he was killed by the people I work with in my other job. Before he died, he was bragging about Macy's father hiring him to take me out, and them two fellows me and Gator fucked up are back on the island to finish the job. I haven't seen them but I'm sure they're on the island, I think that was who set the alarm off on your truck. What you saw me doing yesterday morning was checking for an explosive device, or maybe some sort of tracking device. I've been sticking close to you to protect you, Blaise is always with his brothers, so I don't have to watch him so closely. The people I work for are sending a man I know from San Diego, who's better at this shit than those two ass- holes are. He'll be on the island tomorrow, you won't see him, but once he gets here them two fuckers are dead."

For a long minute my loving wife sat silently just watching the cars pass, then said, "and you haven't said anything about this to me because."

"I didn't want you to worry baby, you being happy, and the boys' safety are my number one priorities. It would be much easier for me to deal with this if I could convince you to go and hang out in Corpus for a few days honey."

"Not on your life buddy, my beautiful wife responded and this better be the last time you keep something this serious from me, I mean that Mike."

"I'm sorry baby, I was just doing everything I could to protect you and the boys."

"You are not protecting me by sending me to Corpus Christi, so I can spend every minute worrying about you. Why have you been taking me to the shooting range with you all these years teaching me to handle a firearm? Now is when all that practice will come in handy to protect us and the kids, do you have a weapon with you now?"

"Yes, honey, I said, as I reached under the seat and handed her my Glock."

"Then I should have one too, since we're in this danger, do you have an extra clip?"

"Look in the glove compartment." She popped open the glove box and took out the extra clip and dropped it and the pistol into her purse.

"This one's mine since you decided to stash it in my new truck without telling me, I'm sure there is already one in your vette."

"The people you do your other work for, do they know all about this?"

"Yes baby, the man who's coming to help works for them and they don't go for nobody fucking with their people."

"Do the Galveston cops know anything about this Mike, my wife asked, inquisitively?"

"Sure, but they think the men are only here looking for their huge friend.

"Crap, honey, ten years and your psycho ex is still interfering in our lives."

Steve Robbins, the guardian phoned to let me know he was on the island and had already spotted the two men.

"Whatever they've got planned, has something to do with your woman, they don't seem concerned with you at all. That's how gutless Shit-heads like this operate, they get some kind of a sick ass high from hurting what you love to hurt you. You are armed, aren't you Mike?"

"Never leave home without it, my wife is packing too and she's a better shot than me."

"They'll never get anywhere near your wife brother, if they make a move on her, they'll be dead before they know what hit them. Those two fuckers are at the Taco Bell on 61st St. eating right now, they're driving a black Chrysler that's in bad need of a wash job. Don't worry brother, I don't think these two cats are gonna make it back to the West Coast alive, talk to you later Mike."

Two days later Robbins called again, "something just came to me dude, the night the alarm went off on your wife's truck, I don't think it had nothing to do with a bomb or nothing like that."

"What else could it have been then Steve?"

"It's obvious these boys ain't the smartest dogs in the pack or you wouldn't have caught them tampering with your vehicle. I'm certain they were trying to plant some sort of tracking device on your woman's truck. The one thing they're good at is patience, they haven't scrapped the plan on the tracking device, they're just waiting for the opportune time to plant it." "They aren't concerned with you just yet, they know the Galveston cops have a soft tail on you and the plan they got involves your wife. Mike, we're going to give these idiots a little help and then I got'em. Get your wife to leave the windows down the next time she goes to the grocery store, they'll see it as the opportunity to plant the device. Once it's done I'll call you with the rest of the plan."

I relayed the plan to Rhonda and assured her she was in no danger. The next day, she and Raheema. the other exercise class instructor left the gym and drove over to the Galvez Mall, she did as instructed, intentionally parking her truck a good distance from the mall entrance. She told Raheema to leave her window down because she hated getting into the hot truck, don't "worry, they've got great security out here, she assured Raheema.

"Here's our chance Shawn, she left the windows down, so the alarm can't be set, I'm going to take that spot next to her, stay low and attach the device under the rear fender." The men did the deed in under thirty seconds and left the mall parking lot.

Robbins sat in his truck laughing at how easy they fell for the trick and then phoned me.

"They took the bait Mike, like dogs to a steak, tomorrow use your wife's truck and call me once she's safe at work."

I called Steve the following morning after Rhonda left to do her eight AM exercise class, I kept her truck under the guise of needing to pick up a piece of equipment I was having repaired.

"Okay Mike, Robbins told me, they won't be so attentive now that the tracking device is on the vehicle, they'll just wake up and follow the signal to where the truck is. Where is the most out of the way place on the island, he asked?"

"It ain't exactly on the island, but out on the Bolivar Peninsula, you got to take the ferry to get over there, the only other way is to drive damn near to Beaumont where you've still got to take the ferry over from the other side. There ain't but a few people living out there this time of year, other than that, ain't nothing but sand and water."

"Sounds perfect, drive over to the ferry and stay in the truck until I call to let you know they are there. Once you go across take them as far down the beach as you can, they're going to get anxious thinking the opportunity to grab your wife has fallen into their lap.

"Don't worry I'm better at trailing someone than them two idiots are, you never spotted me and Todd shadowing you and the Balboa brothers, did you?"

"No, not until I heard the sound of them big rifles you dudes use."

Where I was parked, I could watch the road, so I saw the dirty black Chrysler coming, I cranked the truck up and got in line to load the ferry for the next crossing. The guardian must have seen me because he didn't call until I was on the ferry.

"They're about six cars behind you Mike, I'll be across on the next ferry, stay in the truck so they don't spot you." Once I was off-loaded on the peninsula side I drove very slowly down the shoreline headed towards a part of the Bolivar Peninsula called Key Lago where there was only a few beach houses. No one really liked living on this end because the county didn't spend anything on maintenance this far down. The only people who ever came down here were the fisherman or people looking for a secluded place to have sex. Robbins called to let me know he was on the other side and headed my way, "go ahead and park somewhere and stay in the truck." I eased up close to the waterline and turned the truck off, I could see the black car stopped about a hundred yards from where I was. I guess they were getting the plan together on how to snatch my wife, I still didn't see the Guardian, but I knew he was near. I kept my eyes on the black car, waiting for the two private- eyes slash hired killers to make a move on me, safety off on my pistol and ready.

"What do you think she's doing way out here?" Shawn, asked his pal.

"Your guess is as good as mine, let's give her a few minutes, maybe she's waiting on somebody."

"Here comes a car maybe that's who she's meeting, could be a secret boyfriend or something, wouldn't that be a hoot."

Suddenly the oncoming car turned in behind the black Chrysler and rammed it hard enough to shove the vehicle into the water. Robbins jumped out of the car with his pistol out barking some command at the two men in the black car.

"Let me see your hands fucker's both of you the Guardian commanded. Out of the vehicle hands in the air, do anything but that and you will get a bullet, I promise you. You on the passenger side, get around here with your buddy." Heffernan came around the front of the car splashing through the knee-deep surf.

"Who the hell are you mister he questioned as he stood beside his partner, both men, with hands still raised over head."

"None of your damn business answered Robbins, what I want to know is why are you boys following that blue truck?"

"You must be mistaken man, we weren't following that truck."

"Bull shit, barked the big white dude with the military buzz cut, flat on the top, y'all been following that truck all over Galveston for two weeks now. I know that because I've been following y'all, now talk, I hope you two wasn't planning on doing something unchristian to the woman who drives that truck, were y'all?"

Mankin picked up on the critical fix he and his partner were in, the man knew what they were doing so he attempted to talk his way out of the predicament.

155

"We seem to be in the same business brother, what say we work something out, the man who's paying us will pay you double what the woman's nigger husband is paying you. We don't intend to hurt the woman, we were just going to use her to get some information out of her husband. We know for a fact he had something to do with the disappearance of a beautiful girl and a friend of ours who came out here to look for her."

"You wrong on both accounts the Guardian replied, Dunn don't know shit about either. The girl made threats against people she should have never screwed around with, and it cost her a life that she could have lived if she'd just minded her own beeswax. That friend of yours you speak of, I deep-sixed that big giant fucker myself, if I had the time, I'd show you where I buried them both. He should have never brought his big ass to Texas, unfortunately, neither should you two idiots have come here either."

The soldier raised his hand and signaled for me to come over. I drove down the beach and parked next to the soldier's car and got out, the shocked look on both men faces was priceless. "Now do you boys want to say that, shit to this man's face, Robbins stated to the men."

"I thought you might want a front row seat to the show Mike, these boys say they were going to use your woman as bait to get their hands on you and then just let her go, do you believe that?"

"Not for one damn minute brother."

"You two strip down to your skivvies ordered Robbins and be quick about it."

Once the two were standing in front of us in just drawers Robbins ordered them to turn around and face the incoming tide.

"You fella's see that oil rig out there with the flashing light, if you make it that far you get to live past today, now start swimming," he commanded.

"That rigs got to be at least a mile offshore mister, you don't expect us to swim that far, do you?"

"If you ain't in that water after the next ten seconds I'll just shoot you and leave your body here on the beach, least out there you got some kind of a chance."

I stood next to the soldier as we watched the men wade out past the first sandbar into chest deep water and start swimming. After about fifteen minutes, the two black dots on the deep aqua colored surf vanished from sight. On the evening news, the next day the lead story was of the two bodies found by fishermen floating in Galveston Bay, possibly a double suicide.

"I'm headed back to Waco in the morning Mike, I don't think the girls father will be stupid enough to send anybody else, if you notice anything strange, don't hesitate to call me brother." We stopped at Joe's crab shack for a big meal on me before Robbins took off, as a small thank you to him, afterwards we shook hands and just like that the crisis was over.

CHAPTER
TWENTY-SIX

"**Y**OU GOT TO be shitting me, screamed the red-faced Galveston police chief at Falks and Vasut standing in front of his desk."

"It's the truth chief, the two bodies them fishermen pulled out of the bay yesterday morning were identified as Kyle Mankin and Shawn Heffernan, two private detectives from San Diego, California." A car registered to their office and some clothing with their identifications in the pockets were found on the beach at Bolivar Peninsula, way down on Key Lago."

"I'm sure I told you to put them on a plane out of here, didn't I."

"I watched them get on the plane at Hobby myself Chief, said Vasut. There were some expensive firearms found in the car, I guess that's why they drove back to the island."

"What do y'all think, is this shit connected to that "big-olé" weight lifting colored fella too?"

"Got to be chief exclaimed Falks, they was already pissed at Dunn about that missing partner of theirs, and then him and that big one they call Gator put a pretty good whipping on them." They was talking a lot of trash about making Dunn pay before they left."

"This shit can't be happening to us three times, but I know it ain't all a coincidence, expressed Gee under his breath. I'm going to the DA one more time men, this Dunn guy is piling up bodies too damn fast for me, I'll get back to y'all later, and don't say nothing to the County people that can connect them two drowning victims to us."

The secretary who manned the phones at the Moonlight Private Detective Agency was shocked and adrift on the open sea of confusion. All three of her employers had taken trips to a town named Galveston Texas, and neither one had returned to San Diego alive. The only thing she was certain of was they were all three working on a case for Mister and Mrs. George Allen. That was all she could tell the police detective from Galveston who'd phoned to tell her of the men's death. Mary Davis was still wiring money to the Avis car rental hub at Houston's Hobby Airport for the car, Phil McDisi had not yet returned. Neither of her bosses had any immediate family that she knew of to contact so the woman took it upon herself to arrange the transport of Mankin and Heffernan's bodies back to the West Coast. She used up half a work day going through the men's Rolodex searching for some relative to send their remains to. In the end, all she could do was have a local funeral home receive the bodies of Mankin and Heffernan to prepare the men for burial. The firm had plenty of money in an operating account she was authorized to write, and sign checks on. Until a relative came forward or McDisi showed up she was the company, so the girl ran an ad in the paper looking for licensed private investigators to take over for her deceased bosses. George Allen had phoned a few times for an update on his case before Mary finally told him what happened to her bosses. Allen was fuming at hearing this terrible news, he'd paid the Moonlight firm every dime, they'd gotten from the sale of Macy's surf shop, and still no justice. The man had gone off the deep end mentally, all he could see in his own mind were visions of Mike Dunn, a black man having sex with his white daughter, and then dumping her body on a trash heap. His daughters' betrayal of the man was of no significance to him, the only outcome to satiate Allen's bloodlust was the death of Mike Dunn.

Galveston County district attorney Red Richmond sat stoically taking in the amazing turn of events connecting Mike Dunn to possibly four murderers.

"I'm sure what you are saying is the truth chief, but everything you're telling me will instantly be taken as speculation and hearsay by any defense attorney in this country."

"Everything you said will be taken as hearsay in court, you and your men cannot expect me to order an arrest warrant based on some gut instincts the Galveston PD has. I'll loan you a couple of County detectives for a month, see if they can come up with something to substantiate your suspicions of Mister Dunn."

Galveston County District Attorney Red Richmond was true to his word, two plainclothes officers from County were assigned as a task force to observe and document the movement and actions of Michael T. Dunn. Richmond and Chief Gee had known each other since childhood, though not possessing any factual evidence against Dunn, Richmond trusted the instincts of his old Galveston O' Connel high school classmate. The two undercover cops started out by attempting to sign up for memberships at the Island Gym. To their utter surprise, there were none available, during the month before muscle Beach, the only people allowed to sign up were competitors entered in the contest. The show was now a national qualifier so bodybuilders and fitness competitors from all over the Southwest region of the country were flocking to the island weeks prior to the show. The two under covers were relegated to old-fashioned surveillance of the subject from a hidden distance and a soft mobile observation.

"They wouldn't even sell us a membership to the damn gym Red, Hank Morrisey was complaining to his boss. Our plan was to get in with that fitness crowd to maybe get closer to Dunn and his wife. Them muscle heads are a tightknit group just like those damn surfers are, if you ain't with them you ain't getting in with them, added his partner," Detective Weldon Jones.

"We've been on him for two weeks now Red and he ain't even been across the causeway, if the guy is up to something he's not doing it on the island."

"You men just stick with it until I say otherwise, I trust Chief Gee of the city cops. He's never been wrong before and I've known the man my whole life."

"If you say so Red, there is some big contest coming up that they all are talking about maybe once that's over Dunn will do something out of the ordinary," added Morrisey.

Detective Weldon Jones was a secretly lascivious thinking man, "that little wife of his is a very beautiful woman, if she didn't have all them muscles I'd take a crack at her myself."

"Get your mind back on the task at hand Weldon, said Morrissey.

CHAPTER
TWENTY-SEVEN

"IT HAD BEEN nine months since I'd done any work for the Ortega family so the phone call from the Don himself, Victor Ortega was quite a surprise. It's an honor to finally talk to you in person Mister Ortega, I'm used to getting my instructions from Joe John or your son."

"The pleasure is all mine Mike, my nephew Michael and Joe John as well as the Balboas hold your friendship with them in high esteem."

"Mine towards them as well Mister Ortega, my relationship with them has also been mutually rewarding."

"Unfortunately, my friend, my son Javier was murdered by one of my adversaries some weeks ago. My days of mourning are now over, and I must get back to business, the friends of my son are all drug users, so I find it impossible to trust them. I have conferred with Lonnie, Rudy and my nephew Michael and to a man they all agree that you are the best man to handle some work for me on that side of the border."

"What can I do to help Mister Ortega, I asked, not wanting to sound so surprised at him choosing me to bring into the family circle?"

"These are matters we must speak of in person, Mike, would it be possible for you to meet with me at the home of Joe John on this Saturday coming?"

"Not a problem sir, what time would you like for me to be there, I asked?"

"Joe John's wife is an excellent cook, stated the old Don, if you are there by five in the evening we will be able to share a meal together before talking business. I look forward to enjoying a meal prepared by Irene, she is a master in the kitchen."

"I agree with you one-hundred percent Don Ortega, I've had many a meal prepared by her and each and every one was remarkable."

Once I was off the phone I sat back in my recliner to contemplate the conversation I'd just had and who I'd had it with and my mind was blown. This man who I'm sure was a multi-millionaire and who was the patriarch of one of the most powerful families in Mexico was coming to tiny Hockley, Texas specifically for a meeting with me. The following morning, I was putting on coffee and watching CNN when the story broke about two-hundred bodies being found in a mass grave outside Veracruz, Mexico. I was alarmed only because many times I'd heard Rudy and Lonnie talk about all the good times they'd had in a town called Veracruz. I knew I was in over my head as far as my involvement with the Ortega's was concerned but there seemed to be no way out. This visit from the man himself surely meant I was being drawn deeper into the family business. I wonder if this thing in Veracruz had anything to do with the death of Javier. The phone rang, snapping me out of the vision I was having of what two-hundred dead bodies looked like in a big hole. The call was from Joe John, "hey what's going on bro," I answered?

"Everything is cool on my end Mike, Irene say's hi and to let you know she'll be making the zucchini bread you like so much for dinner this weekend."

"Tell her she's my favorite cook in the world, and I'm looking forward to sitting at her table."

"That's why I'm calling Mike, Don Ortega will have his bodyguards with him, so I wanted to make sure you come in your Vette because I've already told them you'll be driving a white Corvette. There will be people watching the road leading to my ranchero, I don't want them to shoot you by accident. They are already tripping on the fact that you're a black man, we don't need them mistaking you for some stranger. You are the first negrito to work with us so anyone who doesn't know you will be suspicious. Michael is Don Ortega's favorite nephew and the Balboas are just like family to him so the word of those three are like gold to him."

"He's aware of how much I look up to and trust you also Mike, so be comforted in the fact that he wants to sit down and break bread with you, that's a good sign. Plus, Irene is his favorite as far as cooking goes, if she wasn't my woman I'm sure he'd have her as his personal chef in his home."

"He told me Javier was murdered, is that strange for him to share something like that with a stranger?"

"You're no stranger to our family big Mike, believe me, we wouldn't be talking if the Ortega's didn't know everything about you."

Hearing shit like that always made me think twice about my involvement in this business.

"The soldier named Robbins has told him about the Galveston cops having you under surveillance. There are two new ones now but they're lazy, they work for the county and our sources tell us the men think watching you is a waste of time."

"Give my love to your beautiful wife dude and I'll see you Saturday evening."

I was up before the sun Saturday morning and was crossing the causeway headed north just as the big golden ball was rising over the bay. Not many people going north on a Saturday this time of year, but the water hungry throng headed south to the island was already building. As a precaution to be sure I wasn't being followed. I took the Bay Area Boulevard off-ramp at Webster, Texas and went east to Red Bluff Road. At Red Bluff, I turned back North and let the six-hundred horses under the hood of my Corvette loose. Red Bluff was all farm road this far out for five miles, which meant no cops watching for speeders. If anyone was tailing me, they wouldn't be for long unless they were riding a stallion comparable to what I was driving. There was no one in my rearview when I crossed the Pasadena city limits sign just before Beltway eight where I turned back west headed towards Houston. I stopped at the HEB grocer to grab a few items for breakfast, we didn't have anything in the apartment fridge but beer, bottled water and some orange juice. I made me a breakfast of sausage, eggs and toast, ate and then laid down on the sofa to let the television watch me take a nap. Around two my phone rang, it was Blaise calling to ask if I'd be home in time to go to the movies with the family. Champion big wave rider Laird Hamilton was being featured in a new surf film called Riding Giants, part of our family tradition was to all go out for dinner and see a movie together twice a month. I had not forgotten, it was just this thing I had to do today took precedent over family obligation this one time.

"I don't think I can make it home in time son, I've got an important business meeting to attend at five this evening that I must attend. What do you say I take the whole gang to lunch tomorrow and then we can all visit the Space Center, how's that for a makeup dude?"

"That sounds great Dad, can I pick the restaurant?"

"It's cool with me bro. but see what your mom has to say, let me talk to her before we hang up, I love you pal?"

"Hello love of my life, I just smoothed things over with our son for missing family movie night so can you see if the big boys and their girls can join us for lunch and a trip to the space center tomorrow, on me?

"Yes, honey said Rhonda, I can do that if you promise to wake me up and make love to me in the morning like you did today before you left.

"Not a problem my love, oh yeah "Babe", I told your son he could pick the restaurant for lunch tomorrow if it was okay with you. You know if he does we'll be smelling like them stinky crawfish all day, why that boy likes them damn mud bugs so much is a mystery to me."

"Cody and David won't give a crap, but I know you're not a big fan of pinching and sucking on a big pile of crawdads, answered my beautiful bride.

"I need to get some arms and shoulders in tonight, so I'll be at the gym when y'all get out of the movie tonight.

"Alright baby, I'll wait up for you and be careful okay, see you tonight."

Joe John was right; the Dons security men were staged at several different locations along the road leading to and around his home. The man was better protected than the freaking president, I'm glad they were expecting me. Knowing who I was didn't stop the security men from giving me a full pat down before allowing me access to the big boss. Shockingly, the man came out to the garage with Joe John to greet me, Don Ortega looked like the guy from the" dos equis" beer commercials. He gave me a good look up and down before extending a hand to shake.

"Michael and the Balboas are right he said as we shook, you do look a lot bigger in person than you do in the photos. Your arms are as thick as my leg, I'd hate to get punched in the face by you, my friend, I'm sure not many men choose to get into an altercation with you."

"It's an honor to finally meet this black man from Texas all my nephews speak so highly of, they all speak of you with great affection." And I honor my relationship with them equally in the same regard sir. I turned to give Joe John a hug, I hadn't seen him for a few months, so visiting him and Irene was a treat.

"Come on inside big Mike, Irene has been preparing this meal for my Tio and you all day." I hadn't seen Irene in a while either, it must have been at least four months and she looked like a different woman. Her raven tinted hair was all blonde now and there could not be more than 10 or 12 pounds of female body fat on her lean and mean looking frame. We embraced in a hug as she greeted me, and the woman felt like my wife did, all feminine and strong. Irene was born to be a fitness competitor, she'd gotten the bug just like her man, and I knew she and Joe John would be tearing up the stage for a long time. The feast she'd prepared was fit for a king, prime rib, del monico potatoes, asparagus, and of course her outstanding zucchini bread. Don Ortega, Joe John and I talked mostly about bodybuilding and the gym business while we ate. After dinner, we three moved to the den to talk business while Irene busied herself tidying up the dining area.

"Mike, my son's death has placed me in a precarious position, I don't trust most of the men who worked for Javier because many of them are cocaine addicts and I don't trust them. I'm rebuilding my organization from the ground up, beginning with you and Joe John, there will be others bringing the product into the U.S. but only you two will be handling the money. From a warehouse in Edna where all the goods will be stored, I'll have people to pick them up for distribution. The distributors will hold the cash until you pick it up and bring it here to Joe John's Ranchero. There are only three pickups Mike, you and only you will know the three addresses, one in Huntsville, one in Dallas and another in Atlanta. I am going to furnish you with a custom built recreational vehicle so that you can travel in comfort. The vehicle cost one million dollars to build Mike, to anyone observing you, you will look just like any other person out seeing the sights. There is an auto repair business in Pasadena, Texas, where you'll pick up the vehicle and leave it after you have finished. The R.V. will always be in excellent mechanical condition, the only thing you will be doing is stopping for fuel a couple of times. The man at the shop will instruct you on how to gain entry to the hidden storage compartments.?"

"Why an R.V. Sir, I questioned?"

"Because Mike my friend, you will be picking up at least twelve of the large black duffel bags once a month and you can't do that in your sports car. No one knows this but you and Joe, not even the man who's storing and caring for the vehicle knows what it's for. Using the RV is an excellent cover for the task you'll be performing for me, Mike.

CHAPTER
TWENTY-EIGHT

I DIDN'T LET on about my suspicions to the old man or to Joe John, my little voice was screaming at the top of its lungs. The two or three duffels I usually moved from Dallas to the Ranchero contained maybe two or three million bucks at the most. Now suddenly, I'm moving six times as many bags and in a customized recreational vehicle. Did these Mexican cats think I would be so naïve as to believe that shit? The steroid black market was lucrative I know, but not twenty million dollars a month by one small organization. The truth of the matter was, to quell the tension between the Ortega's and one of the cocaine and marijuana distributing cartels, old Victor Ortega agreed to move all the cash back across the border. The Ortega transport routes had never been compromised or intercepted by the law and whoever they were now in bed with wanted to take advantage of that. I didn't know the details of Javier's death, but I'm certain it was the catalyst for the deed I was now responsible for.

The following morning while Rhonda and I lay in each other's arms chatting about our plans for the day, my phone chimed, but I let it go to voicemail. While Rhonda was showering, I took the time to check for who it was, the message was from the Guardian Steve Robbins to give him a call.

He answered on the second ring, "hey big Mike, just wanted to touch base with you, the Don forgot to tell you that Todd and me will be shadowing you on every run. Just call me when you pick up the RV and we'll catch you on the highway at Conroe. We got a picture and the description of the RV emailed to us already, I'll let your phone ring twice and then hang up, so you'll know that we got you."

"I feel better and safer already knowing you cats are watching my back Steve. From what Ortega tells me, I'll be moving a serious amount of moolah."

"Yeah brother, makes them little jaunts out into the sand dunes seem like a lifetime ago, don't it?"

"Yeah it does man, the old man says I'm one of the few people he trusts to do it, you think that's the truth?

"Got to be, if it was important enough for him to show up on US soil to offer you the job, it has to be. You okay driving something that big, I bet old man Ortega forgot to ask you that."

"I've driven a few big trucks in my time, so I should make out all right, I think I'll go over to that shop a couple times this week and take it out for a little practice anyway."

Ortega wasn't kidding about the RV. It was something akin to a luxury Learjet on wheels, the shop owner instructed me on how to access the hidden compartments. Afterwards I took the beautiful gray and black behemoth out for a test drive into Houston and around the highway six-ten loop. The forty-five-foot-long vehicle drove better than a lot of cars I'd driven, all I had to do was watch myself on the corner turns. After a couple of weeks of practice; driving the luxury RV was like driving a big car.

I knew what I was doing was something on another level, especially after Robbins notified me that he would be present on my trips. As serious as my situation was. I still heavily resented the Mexican Godfather thinking he was leaving me in the dark on the truth of what I was doing. My weapons were registered in my name, so I took my forty-five glock with me on my first run. I headed straight to Atlanta for the first pickup, the address was perfect for doing a clandestine loading. The people were waiting for me, I was waived into a large warehouse with overhead doors, once I was inside all I had to do was snap open the hidden area of the storage compartment. The entire task took all of five minutes and I was on my way back to Texas, twelve hours and the first stage was done. My plan was to do the whole run in two days and ease back onto the island in time to have dinner with my wife, who was never far from my thoughts. The Ortega's did have everything set up for smooth loading undercover in a big bus accessible structure. All three buildings were legitimate pipe making companies I'm sure owned by one of the Mexican cartels. I only made two stops for fuel before the last pickup in Houston, sixteen bags and all offloaded onto the three-camper covered pickup trucks at Joe John's ranch.

"We haven't seen Dunn for a couple of days Red", reported undercover detective Hank Morrissey, I know for a fact he's not on the island."

"Falks and Vasut have been keeping the gym covered and we've been sitting on his house for most of the day. Some kind of way we missed him leaving home two days ago, he must have left sometime during the night."

"Chief Gee tells me the man keeps a second car and an apartment somewhere in Houston, check with HPD, see if you can nail down that second resident. Don't let on too much about why you tracking Dunn, I've got a feeling there's a lot more going on with this guy, than what we see, and I don't want HPD stealing the case from us."

The Galveston County boys did find out where the new apartment was, but considering it was in a high-rise tower with underground parking. There wasn't a whole lot they could do without a warrant.

The Galveston police tried every trick in the book to get information about me, even recruiting gym members to subtlety ask questions about me from my staff. As close as we all were there was nothing to tell but what a great boss, Rhonda and I were. Only my wife knew when I was leaving, or when I was returning back to the island and my very protective wife would never discuss my personal life with the cops or anyone else. If the city or county law ever got too close, I'm certain the Ortega's would find out through their source of intelligence and let me know. I was only doing one run a month for the Ortega's, if the cops were attempting to surveil me every day their efforts were going to expend a lot of manpower for zero results. At some point, whoever counted the pennies was going to intervene. Eventually the two county detectives were reassigned and Falks and Vasut were ordered to move on to other solvable cases.

CHAPTER
TWENTY-NINE

GEORGE ALLEN HAD become a man obsessed with the driven urge for revenge, his daughter's disappearance was all he thought of. His wife though suffering from a broken heart, filled the space with caring for her now 13-year-old granddaughter. The little girl resembled her mother more and more as she grew, every time George Allen looked at his grandchild his hate of Mike Dunn was exacerbated. Over the years, he'd used Macy's house as rental property in the hope that one day she would return. The house had been on the market now for two months and the real estate agent was certain it would not take too long to sell due to its proximity to the Pacific Ocean. Feeling cheated by life, two times, one by the loss of his only child and again by the deaths of the people he'd paid to exact his revenge on the man he felt responsible for his daughters disappearance. His attempts to regain some of the money paid out to the moonlight private detective agency fell on deaf ears. The woman now running the company had no record of the money paid for the death of Mike Dunn. The money paid for contract killings to the firm was always in cash and kept off the books. On the very day, the sale of Macy's house was closed, Allen cashed the $85,000 check and went in search of someone to finished the deed of ending the life of one Mike Dunn.

George Allen started his search for another killer by flipping through the soldier of Fortune magazine in search of an armed security contractor. Attempting no caution whatsoever Allen told his first interviewee exactly what he was wanting to pay for. The man refused Allen's offer but agreed to connect him with a colleague who took on this type of work with no reservations. The call came two days later from a man who served as a mercenary and armed bodyguard for a price.

Dale Morris told Allen the job would cost him fifty thousand dollars plus expenses. Allen agreed to pay half the money up front and the rest after the job was done, he didn't want a replay of his last two efforts, where he'd lost all the money with zero results.

The two men met at a park in Allen's neighborhood to close the deal with info on the target and the initial down payment. To Morris, Alan spoke like a man possessed, he went through every detail of his daughters contact with Dunn, and how the last men he'd hired went to Texas to do the job and never returned. He spilled every detail except the one where his daughter had a baby with another man while being married to the man he wished dead. All Morris could conclude from the briefing was, Mike Dunn must be one bad mother fucker if he managed to take out three killers all by himself.

He wasn't taking any chances with Dunn; the hit would come from a distance without him ever having any contact with Dunn other than killing him. Morris began preparation for the assignment in Texas by spending the day at the shooting range, hitting targets up to a thousand yards out. His first twenty shots he used a rifle he custom-built, a .308 caliber rifle built on a Remington 700 platform placing eighteen of the rounds in the center circle. Twenty more shots he used his Lapua.338 caliber weapon with a suppressor attached. These were Morris favorite weapons, he'd taken down many targets in Afghanistan with these very rifles.

Crossing over the causeway into Galveston, Morris thought, shit if I have to escape and evade for some reason in a hurry I'll have only one way off this little island. The killer didn't anticipate having to escape in a hurry, now he was forced to come up with an alternative plan of execution. This was not going to be a cut and dry hit, and after seeing Dunn and his friend, he was glad he'd decided on a long-range shot. These are some big fucker's he thought as he stood on the seawall with binoculars watching Dunn and Gator doing flat dumbbell presses with one-hundred and thirty-pound weights in each hand. It was still the middle of the summer, so all the weight training equipment was still out on the sand. That guy could probably knock my head off with one good punch from one of them big ass arms. That big son of a bitch with him looks like he could empty a bar full of drunk Marines all by his self, he was thinking to himself. There are always hundreds of tourists out here, I better find out where Dunn lives, maybe I'll have better luck finding a spot to shoot from.

Morris waited outside the gym observing the surroundings from his mini-van, with his binoculars he could see people moving around the room working out. Every so often he would catch a glimpse of his prey through the big glass front of the building. At around eight o'clock Dunn walked out of the front door climbed into his car and left the parking lot, followed by Morris. Two miles down the seawall the pearl white Corvette made a left turn into a tiny cluster of beach homes built a hundred yards from the shoreline. Seeing no way to park and observe the house without being spotted on the street, he decided to call it a day and go back to his motel room.

"This hot ass Texas weather is draining the fucking energy out of me, Morris thought to himself, I'll catch a few hours sleep, maybe when I wake up I can come up with a way to get him at home, thought the killer."

Morris sat up wide awake after seven hours of sleep, in his dreams he'd seen himself, making the shot from a boat out on the water. He'd seen it done in a movie one time and at the time thinking how ridiculous it looked. On second thought, that shooter in the movie could not have been as good as me so it's worth a try. The man's always among lots of people every place he goes, and I need a secluded enough spot to wait for my chance at a kill shot. The one thing he'd learned working as an Army shooter was patience. Morris flipped through the Galveston Yellow Pages for a place where he could rent a good-sized boat for a day. He settled on a company over the causeway in another beach community called Tiki Island, the company rented him a forty-two-foot cabin cruiser for six-hundred dollars a day plus fuel. Morris paid the place for a four-day rental and loaded his gear on board to do a little fishing he'd told the man running the place. The man told him where he could purchase bait and chum from a little shop near his office. He motored out onto the bay looking for the Dunn beach home along the shore, once he spotted it he dropped anchor and spent the day observing the house through his high-powered rifle scope. He finally got what he wanted, Dunn would always go out on the balcony to smoke what looked like a joint. Sometimes with his wife, but mostly alone, he was thinking this big bastard does sure smokes a lot of weed. This'll be one of those times where smoking does kill, Morris thought with a laugh.

For the next three days, he saw no sign of Dunn, at the gym or at his home either, where the hell could he be thought the hired killer?

I was on my money run for the Ortega's, it took three days because the cash from the Dallas pickup had not all been accumulated yet, so it took one more day to complete the run.

Six months of motoring the big RV from Texas to Atlanta and back and not once being stopped by the law was a sobering thought. Twelve to sixteen large duffel bags stowed away in the secret compartment, one would think with all the millions of US dollars going into Mexico once a month, the dope dealers had more money than God. How in hell could there be so much poverty in that country, there had to be several billionaires in Mexico. The heavy influx of indigent people flowing into Texas, Arizona and California could surely be the blame of these greedy drug lords not investing their ill-gotten gains back into their own country. Old man Ortega and every one of his friends were covered in the sin of greed and avarice.

Morris stood at the stern of his rental watching the Dunn home through his high-powered binoculars, there you are, you mother fucker, where the hell have you been the past three days, he thought to himself? If I can get the windage right and time the pitch of the boat, I'll be able to score a hit from close to a half mile out. That should be some kind of record from an un-sturdy craft.

It was Sunday morning, Rhonda and I usually stayed in on Sundays, we spent the day making love and preparing a huge feast for our little family. The boys would surf all day and then show up at the house with their girls for dinner, they'd named the regular event, Mom's day and they never missed it. I went out on the balcony to burn one while my wife busied herself in the kitchen, basting some chickens she was slowly roasting. I stepped back inside to turn the stereo on and put on some Allman Brothers live at the Fillmore, my favorite album by the band. As I stepped back through the glass sliding doors out to the deck, I felt something burn my neck just as the glass doors behind me exploded into a thousand pieces. That little voice inside my head has been trying to tell me something all week but I couldn't think of any logical reason why. I hit the deck flat on my belly immediately and yelled for Rhonda to get down. Somebody had just taken a shot at me and I had the blood seeping from my neck to prove it. I crawled through the broken glass back into the house looking first towards the kitchen to be sure Rhonda was down on the floor and okay. Other than her eyes wide with fear locked on me, she seemed to be unharmed, so I made my way to the bedroom to get a weapon.

"Stay down honey I screamed, I don't know if whoever that is out there is gone yet, you got your cell phone?"

"Yes, she answered, you're bleeding Mike, Rhonda franticly screamed.

"Call 911 baby and tell them somebody out on the bay just shot at our house."

Shit, growled Morris at himself, I guess making the shot from a boat this far out was a tougher task than I imagined, I do think I might have grazed that big fucker though. The shooter stuck the big rifle back into its protective case and fired up the engine, hauling ass back to Tiki Island.

Once certain the shooting was over I went to my closet to get my binoculars, crouched behind my balcony railing I raised up to have a look out across the bay. The nearest craft to the shore must have been at least a mile away, there were plenty of boats on this section of the bay. A few sailboats and some motorized cruisers, the kind used by the plentiful deep-sea fishing operations on the island. None with anyone on deck aiming a rifle in the direction of our home, so I settled down to wait on the cops and ease the nerves of Rhonda. Within minutes two Galveston PD cruisers pulled into our drive and with weapons drawn, the two officers climbed the steps to our front door. While I was giving the two cops the rundown of what happened there was a knock at the door, Rhonda left my side to see who it was. It was the Galveston PD detective Johnny Vasut and another detective in a cheap looking unkempt suit. The two uniforms acknowledged them and passed us off to the detectives, telling them they were going out to question some of the neighbors. The crime scene unit should be here any minute now folks said Vasut, I heard the call to your address go out over the radio. The chief wanted me to respond just in case this had something to do with the case where your home was burned down a few years back. That was the stupidest thing this ass hole could have said, like they were still investigating the fire after all this time. Are you folks sure the shot came from out on the bay the idiot in the bad suit questioned? I was still pressing a towel to the wound on my neck, so Vasut called an EMT unit to the scene. You see all that broken glass don't you detective and I was standing out on the balcony looking out across the bay when this happened, where else could the shot have come from?

The crime scene unit dug the slug from a high-powered rifle out of the wall near the front door and clarified my reasoning to the detectives. Detective this is a bullet from a very large rifle, as he handed the evidence bag to Vasut, "this is a .338 caliber slug the tech said."

"The only people using a round this large are the military or someone who was in the military, and it's used only for long-range shooting."

All the neighbors were now outdoors, curious as to why our house was surrounded by police cars, a CSI van and an ambulance, the uniformed cops stood among them asking if anyone had seen or heard anything.

While the EMT was bandaging my neck wound and the cuts on my hands and knees the boys showed up, Blaise crashing through the front door first, tears in his eyes, a frantic expression on his face.

"Mom, Dad, he screamed," as he ran across the room to us, followed by his brothers and their girlfriends all with the same worried expressions. The detective tried to halt them, "don't touch them I yelled, those are our kid's." I stated in an angry tone.

"What happened Dad questioned Blaise at the same time as Cody and David embraced Rhonda, asking the same question?" We gave the boys a brief synopsis of all that had happened after the cops and medics were gone. I didn't know what was happening, but I was certain the shot at me wasn't just some random incident. I first had to secure the safety of my family, so I pulled Cody and David away from everyone else to have a talk with them.

"Listen closely fellas, I ain't sure what today was all about but I need some time to work it out and I can't get it done with you guys and your mother being put at any risk. Your mother ain't going to like my plan one bit, but I need you cats to take her, and your kid brother to Corpus for a few days so I can work some things out without y'all being in harm's way.

"What else can we do to help Mike," David asked with no reservations in his voice?

"First take your mama's truck to Home Depot and get me two sheets of three-quarter inch plywood, so I can board up the patio doors till I can get somebody over here to fix them. While y'all are gone. I'm going to do all I can to get my wife to see things my way, I just need you two to agree with me that it's the best thing to do."

"Okay Mike, we understand what you're saying, I'd do the same thing if I was in your shoes and my family was in danger," said Cody.

"By the time my two stepsons returned with the wood, Rhonda and I had finished our heated debate over why she and the boys should get off the island for a few days. In the end, I had to firmly insist that she do as I wished, whether she wanted to or not. She was afraid that something might happen to me and she wouldn't be here to help me, which warmed my heart to know.

An hour later, I stood in the driveway as my wife and her sons backed out and drove away leaving the island headed for Corpus Christi, a great deal of relief on my heart. My next move was to call the guardian angel Steve Robbins and fill him in on current events. Without one word of conversation he just said, "me and Todd will be at your place before daybreak in the morning", and he hung up. My next call was to Gator, "Mikey he answered, is your timing bad or what, me and Peggy were just climbing into the shower, together big dog."

"Sorry Gator, I'll be quick, I just need to tell you to bring your weapon with you tomorrow, somebody took a shot at me today and barely missed."

"What the fuck" he screamed, I'll be at your place in two hours Mikey."

"Hold on big fella, I'm okay for now, I just shipped Rhonda and the boys off to Corpus for a few days and I'm held up at the house with my weapon in hand. I pity the fool that comes through that door unannounced, I just need you to watch my back for a while, consider yourself hired for the next few days if that's okay with the pretty brunette standing next to you naked?"

"If you say you'll be safe until I get there in the morning, okay Mikey."

"Say Hi to Peggy for me Gator."

We were both laughing when we clicked off.

CHAPTER
THIRTY

"**I**T LOOKS LIKE somebody tried to kill Dunn yesterday Chief and just barely missed," Vasut was telling his boss the following morning.

"Dunn's got a flesh wound on his neck and the crime scene techs pulled this, as he took a plastic evidence bag from his jacket pocket, from the wall of his house. I thought you might want to have a look before I put it in the evidence locker."

"This is a pretty good-sized slug, Dunn's lucky the shooter missed, something this size would have blown his head off. Any sign of the shooter or where the shot was taken?"

"Dunn is positive the shot came from somewhere out on the bay. He was standing out on his balcony when he was hit, but the only boats out on the water must have been at least a half mile from shore. There was a piece of a marijuana cigarette on the deck, maybe the man was stoned and wasn't sure where the shot came from. I informed the Coast Guard to be on the lookout for anything suspicious, when they asked why, I told them there could be someone taking shots at the beach houses from a boat."

"This Dunn fellow is a barrel of mystery, ain't he Johnny, first people are saying he killed someone and now it looks like there's somebody trying to kill him."

"What next" huh" Chief, we don't know where to start with investigating this, none of his neighbors heard nor saw anything out of the ordinary."

The next morning before sun up Robbins big Ford duly pulled into our driveway, with him was the other angel. I hadn't seen either man in four months, all our contacts were by phone, making money runs for the Ortega's. The two men were all business, "where did the shot come from Mike? asked Forbes as soon as he cleared the door.

"I'm certain from out on the bay, I felt the bullet burn my neck just before the patio door exploded behind me. That's why the patio doors are boarded up and there's still glass all over the floor. I sent my family away and have been sitting here with my pistol since I talked to Steve last night. I don't think too much can be expected of the local law dogs, they seem to take it as some random act. They've still got the red ass with me about not being able to pin the disappearance of my stalker ex-wife on me."

"The same detective investigating her vanishing showed up here last night, asking the same kind of dumb ass questions. I'm sure some fucker out there on a boat tried to put a bullet in me yesterday."

"We believe you" said Steve, it can't be none of the Ortega's competitors because not a one of them know who you are or where you live." It's got to have something to do with your ex-wife's father, it took him some time to get the money together and to find another hitter, but it's got to be him." Robbins looked up at the hole in the wall where the crime scene tech had removed the slug, "how big was the slug they took out of the wall" he asked?

"It was pretty damn big" I answered, if it would have scored I'd be dead for sure."

A knock at the door and both men pulled pistols from under their shirts and turned to face the door, "whose there I beckoned?"

"It's me Mikey, Gator, don't shoot me bro."

"He's a friend, I told the two angels, prompting them to put their weapons away."

"Come on in Gator, I said towards the door." I introduced Gator to the Angels telling them he was going to be watching my back until things got worked out.

I hated leaving Gator in the dark, but not knowing exactly who Robbins and Forbes were was the safest route to take for now.

"Gator these men are private detectives I've hired to look into this bull- shit for me, Ted, Bob, this is my buddy and bodyguard Gator McPeters."

"Pleased to meet you fellas said Gator as he shook hands with the Angels."

Glancing at the wood covered patio door and then at the bandages on my neck, he added, "he shot at you through the patio doors Mike?"

"Naw" I was out on the balcony burning one when I felt a burn on my neck just as the glass behind me exploded into a thousand pieces. The crime scene people pulled a high-caliber round, out of the wall behind you, they say it's the kind only the military guys use. Grab your self something to drink Gator while I walk Ted and Bob out, then I'll take you to breakfast before we go to the gym."

Out in the driveway Forbes told me, "good call on keeping who we really are from your pal, he probably won't ever see us again anyhow. Remember how we work Mike, you won't see us, but we'll be right there, so just relax and go about your business."

"I feel safe anytime I know you two violent mother fuckers are near. We had a good laugh as the two angels got into the truck and drove away, stopping for a moment to admire Gators big red Dodge ram charger.

We took Gators truck because he hated squeezing his large frame into a two-seated vehicle, "where'd you find those two hard looking cats Mikey, they look like they've been in a few battles."

"A friend of one of the cops recommended them, I don't think Galveston PD is taking this seriously, that detective Vasut didn't believe me when I told him the shot came from out on the water. When I asked him where the fuck did it come from then, all he had to say was I don't know."

Feeling confident that no attention had been drawn to him by his failed attempt, Morris set out to extinguish the life of Big Mike Dunn, one more time. He got a glass cutter and made an eight inch in diameter circle in one of the side rear windows of his mini-van. His plan now was to kill his prey from a much shorter distance, he parked the dark blue dirty mini- van on the busy seawall boulevard and prepared to wait. Morris set up a tripod and mounted his Remington .308 caliber rifle to it and then attached a suppressor to the end. The Windows at the rear of the van were so darkly tinted, seeing through them from the outside was impossible.

In his head thoughts were, if that big bastard leaves that gym even for a minute he's dead and if that other big fucker gets in the way, his ass is worm food too. Morris was trained to show extreme patience for long periods of time during his deployments as a sniper in Falluja and Afghanistan. The two front windows were half way down, but it was still hot in the van, dammit Texas is hotter than fucking Afghanistan, he said to himself. He was stripped down to his undershorts and sweating like a fat man in a sauna, the twenty-four pack of bottled water in his cooler of ice was down to twelve.

In the last parking slot of the gyms lot was parked Robbins big silver Ford Dually, inside with the windows up and the air conditioner on high, sat the two angels watching everything in front of them.

"Hey Todd, check out that dirty ass blue mini -van about a hundred yards to our left down the seawall, you notice anything strange about it?"

Forbes took off his sunglasses and studied the dirty vehicle for a long minute through his binoculars before saying.

"If I didn't know better, I'd say there's a perfectly round hole in the side rear window."

"Exacta Mundo my brother and it's been parked there for as long as we've been parked here."

"Do me a favor, call Mike and tell him to step outside the front door for a few seconds and then back inside immediately."

Forbes made the call and I did as directed with the phone still to my ear, not a second after I stepped out of the glass door Forbes frantically yelled, "back inside quick."

"What's happening I asked, the phone still to my ear as I stepped back inside the gym doors."

"Now get away from the front entrance, he can still see you," said Robbins.

"This fucker has got a set of balls on him, don't he Steve, he's going to take the shot with these civilians all over the place, I'm sure I saw the tip of a silencer come out of that hole in the glass."

"Call Mike back and tell him not to leave the building until he hears from us, and then have a look with these binoculars Steve."

Dammit cursed Morris at himself, I should have filled the gas tank and left the engine running with the AC on, fucking sweat dripping into my eyes made me miss my opportunity. He crawled up to the front, rolled the windows up, started the engine and set the air conditioner on high then settled back in to wait some more. Two more hours passed and still no sight of the target, I'll try again tomorrow and start with a full tank of gas, knock on wood big boy, you get to breath for one more day.

"Come on Todd, let's see where he goes, it's almost dark, he's either going for food or to his hotel room to get a reprieve from this hot Texas humidity."

Morris made the right turn onto sixty-first street then another right into the Wendy's drive-through, from there to a flea bag motel up on the highway. While Morris was unloading his gear from the van to his motel room Forbes noticed something familiar about the man.

"Son of a bitch Steve, that's Dale Morris."

"No, it ain't dude, Morris is still over in Iraq working security for Black Bear."

"I'm telling you that guy is Dale Morris, I recognize the man who saved my ass in an ambush, we woulda" bought the farm for sure that day if he wouldn't have been on his job."

"Shit man, he's a brother, we can't ice him, it just wouldn't be a righteous thing to do man."

"I agree with you Todd, but we also can't let him take Dunn out, we're making damn good money, easy money watching Dunns' tail on Ortega's payroll. Not to mention, the extra bonus we're getting since Mike started moving cash for his cartel pals."

"We can't wait for him to make another move on Dunn, said Robbins, let's get the room number and call him right now."

The Angels and Morris were once contract militia working for the Black Bear private security firm. Morris as a sniper to cover ground forces protecting government dignitaries in and around Falluja, Iraq. Forbes and Robbins were hired by Ortega through a family member who also worked for the same agency. The money Ortega paid wasn't as much as the hired soldier money, but it was good enough and not in a war zone.

Morris was shocked when the phone in his room rang and even more shocked when the caller was Todd Forbes, a comrade from his soldier for higher days. He was sitting on the bed with pistol in hand when the phone rang, "how'd you find me Forbes, was that you tailing me in the pickup truck?"

"Good job making us brother, Steve Robbins is with me, we need to talk, can we come in?"

"Sure, but unarmed and no jackets, the doors unlocked."

Once all suspicions were alleviated the three men sat down to talk things out. Forbes chose to reveal their mission first,

"the guy you almost took out a couple of days ago works for the same man we work for Dale."

"What do you mean almost, I missed the shot?"

"Not quite my friend, he's got a nasty wound on his neck, what's strange is you never miss."

"Fucking waves bro, I took the shot from more than a half mile away, from a boat out on the bay. I got the windage right and thought I had the pitch of the boat timed, a weird gust of wind and my shot went wide." I saw that" big ole" black dude duck and just assumed I'd missed, just that guys' lucky day, I guess."

"Why you fellas care if he lives or dies anyhow?"

"He does a very important job for the man we work for and part of our job is to keep him alive. We can't let you kill the guy Dale," stated Robbins sternly.

"My client out in San Diego already paid me half the money up front and he's right now on the hook for another three grand in expenses. What y'all expect me to do, drive back to California and give him the cash back?"

"Besides, that guy told me the big black dude killed his daughter and they never found her body, don't y'all agree the man deserves some sort of justice?"

"That ain't quite the truth Dale, you see the guy's daughter use to be married to Dunn and while she was his wife she screwed some other white dude and had his baby."

"When Dunn discovered the betrayal, he called it quits with the girl, and moved to this island. The woman tracked him down here and came to town threatening to go to the cops and tell about a drug business Dunn was involved in if he didn't leave his wife and get back with her. Her daddy didn't tell you that did he Dale?"

"Dunn did all he could to warn the woman off, she was fucking with more than just Dunn by running her mouth, said Forbes."

"That's why she vanished, and Dunn had nothing to do with her disappearance, you got my word on that brother."

"Well shit Todd, what am I supposed to do about that, why she vanished ain't no business of mine, I got a job to do just like y'all."

"Listen mother fucker we spotted you before you spotted us, we" coulda" just blowed you away, but we owe you brother, that's what this face to face is all about."

"We just want to work this out some other way where we all win, said Robbins, can you at least give us another day to work something out. Do us this favor and we'll bring you in with us, the money is steady, and the work is easy, meaning there is no risk of ending up in prison."

"Okay brothers, y'all handle it, I trust y'all, but please make it quick, this Texas heat is fucking my shit all up." The men all gave each other brotherly embraces and Forbes and Robbins left to have a chat with Mike.

I was still waiting to hear from the Angels when Rhonda called, "hey baby, how's everybody in Corpus doing?"

"Everyone's fine honey, I'm calling because I'm worried about you."

"I'm still at the gym and I haven't heard a word from the cops, Gator picked me up this morning, he's watching my back, just in case George Allen is up to something."

"Do you think after all these years he's still got it in for you?"

"Who knows honey, you can never tell with people who refuse to accept reason and like the song goes," you can't argue with a sick mind".

"Mike, this doesn't have anything to do with your other work, does it?"

"Not a chance baby, believe me, nobody knows anything about that except me and the man I work for. To his competitors, I'm a ghost, this should be all worked out in a couple of days, maybe less. I love you honey and thanks for being such an understanding wife."

"Just hurry and get me back to you, you know I hate us being a part for too long a time.

"Where are the boys?"

"I'll give you three guesses and the first two don't count, they were up and gone to Port A. before the sun rose this morning. They didn't even bring clothes honey but they all three brought their favorite surfboards, go figure that. Mom was so upset, she was looking forward to making them a big breakfast this morning."

"Tell her to make a big dinner tonight, you know they eat like a pack of wolves after a day on the waves."

"I love you Mike and something in me says I should be with you right now."

"We are together my love, you're a part of my every being, I can still taste on my lips the last time you kissed me beautiful wife. The scent of you is always with me honey, I always smell Jasmine when I think of you, which is always."

"You know how it turns me on when you talk like this, so stop it before I get in mom's car and drive home tonight."

"You and Skye going to train together while you're in town?"

"Yes, I've already called to let her know I was in town, I'm meeting her at the Iron Horse to do legs in the morning." I've got to take this call honey, I've been waiting for it, I'll call you before I fall asleep tonight, see you babe." It was Steve Robbins calling to let me know something big had come up, we're on the way to pick you up, be there in five minutes.

Gator was on the floor training a client, so I left a note with the trainer at the front counter letting him know I took off to run an errand and that I'd see him in the morning. The Angels were waiting for me out in the parking lot, I climbed in next to Robbins, and we pulled out onto Seawall Boulevard.

"Mike, we found the guy who took the shot at you fast enough, he was parked out here on the seawall waiting for another crack at you.

"So, is the assassin dead, I asked?"

"We followed him back to a little cheap motel up on the highway just this side of the causeway, Mike, the man is a friend of ours, said Robbins. He was hired by the father of your ex, we found out after talking to him. He's agreed to back off the hit if we work something out to make it look like he got the job done."

Forbes broke in on the narrative, "the man saved our lives one time while we were over in Iraq working a job for the Black Bear security firm. You may have heard of them, if you watch CNN, him and some others guarding an Iraqi dignitary opened up on a car approaching the motorcade killing the family inside. The man driving the car didn't understand the english command to stop and drove right into a hail of gunfire, a tragic mistake. The scandal was enormous, Black Bear not wanting to lose the government contract fired the men on the detail, changed the company name and managed to stay in country."

Dale, that's his name, said Robbins, found himself a pariah and out of work, took up the occupation of a paid shooter to make a living. We've got a plan to make it look like he did the deed, so he can get the rest of his money from the chick's father and the guy can feel his daughter's death had been avenged. All you got to do Mike is play dead for a few minutes and your ex's father goes on with his life." Robbins handed me a bottle of red liquid, "this is fake blood we picked up at a costume shop, we're going to pour it all over you while you lay down for a picture."

"Dale's going to use his camera phone to do the same, then he's off the island back to the West Coast to get the rest of his pay and we all live happily ever after."

"That's fine with me" fellas" I just want to get back to my life and make sure my family is safe. Let's do this so I can call my wife and boys and tell them things are cool enough for them to return to Galveston."

Two days later my beautiful cinnamon girl was back where she belonged, back on the island right next to me. The boys were down on East Beach surfing, so we took the day off and went down to watch them, Rhonda was the best mother in the world to her three sons, and she as well as me took a prideful pleasure in watching them do their thing out on the waves. From out on the water they could see the big royal blue truck pull up next to David's Jeep Renegade and in unison the three of them all gave us a wave. Julie and Michelle the girlfriends of Cody and David sat in beach chairs in front of the Jeep with another girl who looked to be kind of young to be hanging out with them. Julie introduced us to Brandi the young woman who just happen to be Blaise's girlfriend. She had blonde curly hair and ocean blue eyes, to my surprise she resembled my own cinnamon girl.

"I'm so glad to finally meet you folks she said, Blaise and his brothers have told me so much about you guys. They told me their parents were bodybuilders, but I didn't expect y'all to be so beautiful, and you two look so wonderful together."

"Thank you, Brandi" was all I could say in response, Rhonda didn't say anything right away, like me she was shocked at hearing our eleven -year-old son had a girlfriend. Once she recovered from the surprise she gave the young girl a gracious hug and thanked her for the compliment.

"It's a pleasure to meet you too Brandi, Blaise never told us he had a girlfriend, and neither did these two she added, turning towards Julie and Michelle, who spend as much time with the boys as us." At the same time both young ladies said to us, "we thought Blaise had already told you guys about Brandi." I'd never thought of my son as anything other than a little boy who loved surfing and hanging out with his big brothers. My wife on the other hand still saw him as her baby, who she still felt she knew everything about.

By the time the boys came in from the water, Rhonda and Brandi were chatting each other up like two old buddies. Blaise had done good, he'd picked a girl that not only resembled his mother, but who was also a kindred spirit. Later my son made me even more proud to be married to his mother when he said, "isn't Brandi gorgeous just like Mom, Dad."

"I think she's a good-looking girl son, but she does look remarkably like your mother, did you choose her for that reason alone?"

"No Dad, it just worked out that way, we met when me and my brothers were down in Port A. surfing last summer. She surfs too Dad and she's almost as good as me, just wait till you see her out on the waves."

"Why haven't you ever mentioned her to us if you met her last summer?"

"I wasn't sure about us until this summer Pop, she lives in Houston, so we've kept in touch by phone, her folks own a beach house in Port A., so we saw each other a few times a year." "I guess it just happened like you and mom. I just had to finally figure out she was the right one, and ain't it cool she looks like Mom, even that cinnamon colored skin you say looks so good on Mom?" I never told her you were black dad, I wanted to see how she reacted when she finally met you, I'm proud that you're my father Pop, if anybody has got a problem with that, this family don't need them."

"Cody and David don't talk to their father too much because he said some nasty things about you and mom. You make their mother happy and that's what matters to my brothers, they love you Dad. They've learned a lot about life from you, I mean things like how to treat a woman and being responsible for the people you love. When we're around other people, they say you're their father, they are proud of you and Mom. I've even seen them whip the crap out of guys who use the word nigger around me, my brothers are bad- asses Dad."

My son was making me tear up saying all this cool shit about me and Rhonda, so I made a move to change the subject.

"Brandi seems to like something about bodybuilding, where did that come from?"

"She was a fan of the sport before we met, she feels lucky to be with somebody who's involved in bodybuilding like our family is." David waded in from the waist deep water and told us the women were hungry and wanted to go for dinner somewhere. At dinner, Brandi's sense of humor was infectious, she told us she just assumed Blaise was one of those people who held a good tan year-round and she felt some jealousy about it. This brought the entire table of us to raucous laughter; this girl was going to fit right in with us. She had an uncle and aunt living in Dickinson a few miles down the highway from the island who she was spending the summer with. After dinner, the boys spent ten minutes separating her and Rhonda to get her home before her uncle's curfew time.

On the way home Rhonda couldn't stop going on about what a darling little girl Brandi was.

"I agree honey, she looks like a mini- you, skin color and all, our kid chose well. I guess our baby isn't a baby anymore, he is growing up fast babe, next thing you know he'll be asking to borrow your truck."

"I think Blaise is more a sports car guy, I'm sure you'll get that question before I do. You do know his brothers have already taught him how to drive, don't you?"

"What, are you serious Rhonda?"

"Yes, I am, surprise, surprise my loving husband."

Jack Herman's bodybuilding contest was coming up and it was just our year, not only was my step- son David competing in the middle weight class, there were several members of the Island Gym taking the stage. Joe John had gotten huge and showed up the favorite to take the heavy weight class. He'd discovered the magic of human growth hormones and now stepped on stage at a whopping two-hundred and sixty pounds at ten percent body fat. His girl Irene was the queen of the show, her body and routine were so close to perfect, two competitors in her class refused to go on stage after her. The City Gym came in with six female competitors and four males, along with the fourteen entrants from the island, we dominated the cheering groups. Blaise and Brandi spent the whole time collecting autographs and taking photos of bodybuilders they'd seen in the muscle mags. Brandi was ecstatic at discovering how popular Rhonda and Gator were and was now my wife's biggest fan. Dena Anderson was now an NPC judge, so I took a minute to stop by the judges table to tell her my step- son David was in the middleweight line- up. Families like ours were good for the sport and I wanted to use every iota of influence I had to let the judges know. The weekend was dominated by our entourage, Irene took first in women's fitness and Joe John and David took the top spots in their respective classes. During it all, I invited any competitor doing the Muscle Beach show coming up in four months' free passes to train at the Island Gym that week.

CHAPTER
THIRTY-ONE

THE WEEKEND AFTER Jack Hermans show me and Joe John were back to the other business at hand, moving money for the Ortega family. Joe John was Victor Ortega's nephew, but his name wasn't Ortega, he was the illegitimate son of one of Victor's older brothers. Old man Ortega treated him better than the other people working for him, but not like blood. He was the bastard son of his brother, so he felt obligated to take care of him. Every now and then Joe John would say something that made me aware of the animosity he felt at being treated like the family shame. The only members who were aware of him were the men involved in the drug business and all were warned to never let the wife of Emilio Ortega find out about Joe John.

We'd been doing the money runs in the luxury RV for close to two years without a hitch, so I'd gotten comfortable with the ease of the task. Not once thinking anything could go wrong especially with my Guardian Angels watching over me. Without getting the okay from the Ortega's, Joe John had started his own mail order operation with two brothers in Florida. The Ortega's assumed he was using the product for himself and a few friends he was training at his gym, which technically was owned by the Ortega family. At the time, I didn't know how deeply Joe resented being seen in the same light as an employee. He was never allowed to attend any of the family functions held in Mexico due to his undeniable resemblance to Emilio Ortega. It was more than risky using the United States Postal Service to move the injectable steroids, moving that shit through the mail was a federal offense. If by chance a package was crushed, and the little glass vials were broken, the jig was up. The feds would be all over the sender and receiver of that package. I'm glad I knew nothing about Joe John's side business, relative or not I don't think the Ortega's would forgive him for attracting the feds to himself.

Rhonda and I drove out to Hockley one weekend to train at City Gym and go out for dinner and drinks with Irene and Joe. This was only a few weeks since Jack Herman's show and Joe John looked fifty pounds bigger, he was obviously overdoing the growth hormone thing. Not only was he changing physically, he was somewhere else mentally, we both were sticklers for proper gym etiquette. One of Rhonda and mines steadfast rules was, no mishandling or abuse of the gyms equipment or slamming dumbbells to the floor after a set. The rules were if you couldn't lower the weights properly and return them to the rack, you had no business picking them up in the first place. I'd adopted this rule while training at George Turner's gym in St. Louis and the man was right. Slamming a one-hundred and twenty-pound dumbbell to the floor would eventually warp the bar and made it impossible to tighten the collars safely. George Turner didn't care who you were, a pro-from St. Louis named Tony Pearson trained at Turner's place. One day Tony slammed a pair of one-hundred and fifty-pound dumbbells to the floor after a grueling set of presses. George stormed across the room to where Pearson was and reamed him out verbally, threatening to revoke his membership if he ever did it again. This to a guy who'd placed in the top five at the last Mister Olympia, Pearson never committed the transgression again. We were never as hard as George on the members, but we did give hard warnings to members who screwed up. While Rhonda and I were training back on the cable machines somebody over in the free weight area dropped a pair of dumbbells to the floor after a set. Within ten seconds of the act Joe John was all over the guy's ass, he was in the members face so close spittle was spraying into the man's face. That was when I realized my friend was surely abusing the drugs we peddled, he was so vicious, I'm certain the guy never came back to City Gym again. Later I asked Irene, how often does something like that happen? She informed us that he seemed to be getting worse and worse; as in meaner every day, the littlest things seem to make him upset.

"He doesn't realize that we've lost a few of our members because of his temper, could you please, Mike, say something to him about his temper, Irene pleaded. I tried talking to him about his temper and he turned on me like I was some random stranger."

Later that evening me and Joe were sitting in his garage smoking a joint and I cautiously broached the subject again, and it was as if he didn't hear a word I said.

"Big Mike, I think I'm going to ask my Tio to sell me the gym, my registration for citizenship was approved last week and I want to be my own boss without having to get his permission on every move I make. What if he gets killed or goes to prison, whoever in his family that takes over might not want me and Irene running the gym."

Joe John was talking crazy, he knew Ortega was using the gym to legitimize some of the cash they made on this side of the border. There were plenty of fabricated invoices for expensive pieces of equipment that weren't even in the building. Joe John was losing his way, he'd completely disregarded the fact that his gym was a cover for a criminal organization. When we first met, Joe weighed maybe a hundred and sixty pounds at best, now he was bigger than me. I weigh two-seventy and never allow my weight to go much above that. Joe John weighed at least three-hundred and he looked very intimidating at that weight. I casually questioned him on what he was cycling on at the time. This stuff from Germany called sustenon, I'm stacking it with some human growth shit and liquid test and the combination is kick ass. He went inside the house and returned with a box of preloaded syringes, see Mike, it comes already loaded, all you got to do is take off the cap and shoot it.

"Fuck Joe, I said, this is a twenty-gauge needle, you sticking this big ass thing in your ass?"

"It hurts like hell and leaves a big bruise, but the rewards far outweigh the pain." I'd cycled on sustenon in the past, that came in the same preloaded syringe that I'd open and draw out with a much smaller needle. The preloads were actually for injecting large animals, the stuff worked wonders as far as strength and size gains but mixing it with HGH could make you crazy if you overdid it. On top of that, why the hell was he talking about Ortega dying or going to prison, the old man traveled with an army of bodyguards.

I was quiet the whole drive back to the island and my woman who could literally read my thoughts waited until we were in bed and the only sound was the waves hitting the shore.

"What's wrong honey she questioned, as she tucked her cheek against my chest and snuggled up close to me."

"I'm sorry baby, I'm worried about Joe John, other than that crazy shit at his gym he was telling me things that could make life tough for him and Irene. He's stacking some powerful shit and it's got him saying and doing some very erratic things, things that could get him killed. I'll have to distance us from him and Irene socially honey, I can't allow Joe to drag us into some mistake I feel he's about to make. If they come to Galveston to visit us, cool but we won't be visiting Hockley again no time soon. Irene is doing so well in the sport and I plan on her having our continual support at competitions but no more hanging out with them for a while."

"You're my man and my place is at your side, whatever you feel is best for us and our family is fine with me, I love you Mikey." The next morning, I was awakened by Blaise banging his surfboard against the wall, getting ready to be picked up by his brothers. I went to make coffee and there was my son chowing down on a bowl of Cheerios while watching television. Morning bro, what you guys got planned for the day?"

"We're going to Dickinson to pick Brandi up and then to Surfside to do some surfing and hang out, you and Mom should come with us."

"I'd love to son, but your mother has got three classes to teach today and I've got a couple of clients to train this afternoon, thanks for the invite though son."

That little voice at the back of my conscience was constantly nagging the crap out of the peace of mind I should've been free to enjoy, since the dismantling of George Allen's most recent attempt to have me killed. That buddy of the Angels had phoned and confirmed with them the hoax had worked, Allen paid him off and thanked him for getting it done. I was glad for the guy, in his place I'd have done the same thing if I thought someone had harmed my only child. That urge I once harbored of anonymously notifying him to let him know his daughter was gone for good, I no longer had. The man had attempted to have my clock stopped three times in the past ten years. The only life I'd ever personally taken was that of the piece of shit that had Joe John's job at the Hockley Ranch before him. The man made it pointedly clear the first time we met that he didn't like working with a "Miyata" the word used by Mexicans to describe black people, which was fine with me, I didn't need to be his friend to do my job. If that fucker wouldn't have threatened my family and friends, he would still be alive today, I felt no remorse whatsoever at having put three rounds in his ass. He'd mentioned to me that Macy was fertilizing the watermelon patch on the ranch, I wondered if he was serious? Too bad we didn't know each other long enough for me to find out.

CHAPTER
THIRTY-TWO

FORBES OR ROBBINS, one or the other would give me a call the day before we went on a money run for Ortega, giving me ample time to prepare for our trip. The trips had become so uneventful and routine over the two years I'd been doing them that I was not making the effort to pack a firearm with my stuff. For some reason, my little voice told me to clean my .44 Glock and slide it into my travel bag, over the years, events had taught me to heed my little voices warnings. The guy who usually passed the keys off to me wasn't at the shop in Pasadena when I arrived to pick up the RV. One of the mechanics spotted me driving my vette around to the back of their shop and walked around to meet me. He spoke to me in Spanish pulled the keys from his pocket with a grease covered hand, tossed them to me and turned to unlock the gate to let me out. My little voice was smacking me on the back of my head, in the two years I'd been coming here I'd only been in contact with the one guy and we'd never had any words, not even to say hello or goodbye. The other guy would just toss me the keys and walk over to open the gate for me, allowing me to pull the big shiny RV out.

I got my regular call from the Angels as I crossed over into Montgomery County informing me that they'd picked me up. I never worried about anybody following me because I knew the Angels were back there, not once thinking someone could be following them.

I pulled into the warehouse in Atlanta at two in the morning, the pickups were now scheduled after the screw-up of the Dallas stop a few months back. The Angels and I had stopped at a roadside rest area outside of Atlanta and napped for three hours so we were all well rested. It took me ten minutes to down a protein shake and eat a tuna sandwich, by the time I was done the men outside were closing the storage compartment and raising the exit overhead door for me to leave. The stop in Dallas went just as smoothly as Atlanta, no delay in Huntsville and I'd be home in my baby's arms by dinner. The Angels gave me a call just outside Conroe, telling me to stop at the next Bucky's, Robbins had to take a dump. Robbins liked Bucky's Travel Stops because the restrooms were always immaculate, and he loved the varieties of beef jerky the stores offered. We all went inside the Bucky's, I used the stop to get from behind the wheel for a while, stretch my legs and grab a cup of coffee. My thing with Bucky's was they had the greatest coffee bars and I love good coffee. We were only away from our vehicles for fifteen minutes or so and never out of eyesight of them, so why worry about someone screwing around with them in such a highly-trafficked parking area.

The indiscriminate white van following the Angels had done a good job tailing them across two states without being noticed by the two trained soldiers. Maybe the Angels like me had become lackadaisical and comfortable over the ease of our work. An explosive device had been attached under the fender weld of Forbes silver Toyota Tundra and another near the right rear wheels of the luxury RV. As I crossed over the city limits sign into Willis, Texas, "boom" the explosion scared me so bad I lost control of the big RV for a hundred yards or so. By the time I regained control of the behemoth of a vehicle my cell phone was chiming, I pulled on to the shoulder and stopped before making any effort to answer it. By the time I stopped the call had gone to voicemail, I hit voicemail and it was Robbins letting me know, they'd had a blowout and for me to get off the highway and wait for them to change the tire. My little voice was screaming loud as shit now, what are the chances the Angels would have a blowout at the same time as me in the RV. I hit speed dial for Robbins, "dude, something's up", I frantically said, I just had a blowout on my right rear. How far back are you guys?"

"We can't see you, so at least a mile or more, don't leave the vehicle and please tell me you're strapped Mike."

"Locked and loaded brother I answered, what's the plan?

"This is certainly starting to look like a snatch and grab bro said Robbins, if anyone comes near that door you let them know that hell is waiting for them on the other side. Me and Todd will be there as quick as we can, you just hold them off as long as you can, keep in mind Mike, they have to kill you to pull this shit off."

I caught some movement in the driver side mirror as a white van pulled up behind the RV and three Spanish dudes climbed out. They were all dressed in coveralls like a mechanic would be wearing, one walked up to the driver side window and tapped on it with a ballpoint pen.

"Hey buddy, he yelled to be heard above the traffic roaring past, we're mechanics, do you need some help?"

"No thanks pal, I yelled back, I already called triple A, thanks anyway."

The RV was still running, so as the guy reached into his coveralls like he was going for his gun, I hit the gas. The other two who I could see attempting to pry the door open with a crowbar, jumped back, drew weapons and started firing shots through the door. I was only moving about twenty miles per hour, but still I was pulling away from the men running alongside the crippled RV firing into the side of the vehicle. The three men turned and ran back to the van and fell in behind the RV limping down the shoulder of the highway with two blown tires on the right rear. I'm certain they were contemplating their next move, the last thing these idiots expected was for me to make a run for it. After following the limping vehicle for a half mile or so down the shoulder of the highway, the van pulled around and hauled ass to get in front of me. The rear doors of the van flew open and the guy from the mechanic shop and another man unloaded a barrage of lead right through the RVs windshield. I hit the floor as the RV crashed over a mile marker and rolled off the shoulder onto the grass median. The men were still shooting through the glass as the RV came to a stop, so I pointed my weapon over the dashboard and gave them a few rounds in return. That got their attention because the shooting stopped, I sat on the floor waiting and listening for the next assault. Then I heard, "you men drop the weapons and down on the ground," a second later two more shots rang out and it was quiet again. A voice outside the RV yelled, "we just want the money buddy, let us have it and you can go on your way."

Yeah right, I thought, "fuck you cocksucker, the Ortega's are going to be dealing with you fucker's in due time."

"Old man Ortega is dead amigo, just like his son, and if you know what's good for you, you'll give us the money.

"Come and get it I yelled as I raised my pistol up and let go a few more rounds in the direction of the voice." Suddenly I heard a sound I clearly recognized, the sound made by the big rifles used by the Guardian Angels. Blam, Blam, Blam, Blam and then silence, I sat on the floor now with a full clip ready for what came next.

"Mike, Mike, you hit, I recognized Robbins voice?"

"No, I'm okay what's going on out there, is it okay to get up?" Robbins came around to the door and yelled for me to open up.

"Quick give me your weapon and do what you can to find the cartridge shells, these fucking Mexicans killed a state trooper." I'd fired eight shots and that's how many shell casings I picked up off the floor, I handed them to Robbins who stuck them into his pocket.

"Mike, I know your pistol is registered but the only bullets in them three bodies outside are our hours, all hell's going to break loose here in a few minutes. Just tell the cops you were waiting on Triple-A to come to fix your flat when these men and some others who ran off started shooting at each other. We got to get out of here, call us when the cops turn you loose, we'll be close by, they might want to hold the RV as evidence. This state trooper being killed changes everything Mike, we gotta go."

"One more thing Steve, one of them dead Mexes told me Victor Ortega was dead." With a stunned look on his face Robbins backed away, hopped in the truck with Forbes and they took off.

The Angels knew it would do no good if I went with them leaving the RV behind, my fingerprints were all over the thing. Knowing my background, the Ortega's had certainly informed Forbes and Robbins of the six-month stint I'd done in the Harris County Jail when I was younger. It wouldn't take long for my name to come out of the Codis international criminal search engine. I thought of phoning Joe John but thought it better to concentrate on my story for the cops, the Angels I'm certain will have already done so.

By the time the state troopers, the Willis and Conroe cops got to the scene. I had my story down, after all my cover was that of a lone traveler out seeing the sights. The blown tires were easy enough to explain, "I ran over an object on the road officer and lost temporary control of my vehicle, when the rear tires blew. By the time, I regained control I was on the shoulder, crashing into the mile marker I'd run down." Two vehicles were stopped at the roadside, where I eventually came to a halt, and that's when all the shooting started. The men in the van were in a gun battle with some other men in a dark colored SUV, I hit the floor as soon as the bullets started hitting my windshield. I didn't raise my head until I heard you guys." Incredible and strange turn of events, but believable and possible, I was hoping. Most of the concern was for the dead state trooper at the side of the road, his weapon was lying near his body, but he never got a shot off before he was gunned down by the three shooters. The trooper wasn't wearing Kevlar so every shot that hit him was fatal. The more focus the cops placed on the dead trooper and his three dead assailants, the more I looked like a victim of circumstance. The officers even had the paramedics look me over, other than a few glass cuts on my face and arms I was okay. When I requested permission to call a wrecker to tow my RV to the nearest auto glass repair shop, I was given the okay once the crime scene techs were finished retrieving slugs from the RVs inner walls. I left my contact information with the state troopers and then hitched a ride into Conroe with the wrecker driver. All three law enforcement departments were I'm certain, glad to be off the hook for the heavy-duty wrecker charge which cost me four-hundred bucks. The staff at the glass shop gave me the number for a truck tire shop who would come and repair the tires while the windshield was being replaced. I did end up spending the night at a motel in the town of Conroe due to the window shop closing down an hour after I was towed in. Forbes and Robbins grabbed a room at the same motel, which gave us a chance to finally take in what went down.

"Are you certain it was the same guy from the auto shop, questioned Forbes?

"I'd bet my life on it Todd, we've never talked much, but for the past year and a half, I've picked up and returned the RV keys to the same man. Plus, I recognized his voice when he was trying to talk me out of the RV, and he was the one telling me that Victor Ortega was dead, he even mentioned Javier's death. Y'all get any word on whether or not he was telling the truth about Ortega?"

"Can't get nobody on the phone, not even Joe John, there's some crazy shit going on and we seem to be right in the middle of it, added Robbins.

"Give me a couple minutes" fellas", I need to call my wife to let her know I'll be another day, she's expecting me home tonight."

Just like that, things went from bad to worse, "your ears must be on fire honey, Joe, John and I were just talking about you, I told him you should be showing up any time now."

I went straight into crisis mode, "what do you mean Joe John and you, is he on hold?"

"No baby, he's standing right here next to me, he came to the island to hang out at our training station out on the beach. He wanted to show off all the new muscle he's put on these past months to the girls. We're in the gym now on the treadmill, where are you?"

"That's why I'm calling baby, I blew a tire on the vehicle I was driving, the shop I'm at can't get a replacement tire until in the morning. I'm at a motel in Conroe, hey honey let me talk to Joe for a minute."

"Big Mike, how's it hanging brother he said, feigning a degree of deception for my wife."

"Get out of my gym and away from my wife Joe John, I barked into the phone, you got something to do with this bull shit, don't you?"

"I'll call you back on my cell phone in a few minutes Joe John said, I need to get that information from my glove compartment, here's Rhonda."

'You're only a couple of hours away honey, do you want me to come and spend the night with you?"

"No baby, as much as I'd like that, it would be better if I pick up the vehicle in the morning and finish my work before I come home, where's Joe John?"

"He went out to the parking lot, is something wrong, he seemed a little agitated when he handed me my phone back?

"Everything is fine honey, I'll see you in the morning, love you wife and I clicked off." Forbes and Robbins picked up on the change in my demeanor right away, "what the fuck is Joe John doing in Galveston Mike? Ain't he supposed to be waiting for you at his place in Hockley, stated Robbins?

"Hold on Steve, he's supposed to be calling me right back."

My ring tone was the song "One Way Out", my favorite Allman Brothers song, at the sound of Greg Allman's voice I immediately pressed the answer button.

"What the fuck is going on Joe, I guess you already know somebody tried to jack the load today, don't you?"

"The fact that I'm talking to you and haven't heard from my man, means things didn't go as we planned."

"You stupid mother fucker, your Tio Victor is going to cut your balls off and feed them to you."

"My Tio won't be cutting nothing off Mike, my business partners wiped out him and his whole security team this morning. The old man got rid of Javier's guys and thought they would just walk away from all the money they were making. Tio Victor was very wrong Mike, those men just went to work for his competitors, I picked up that word from bodybuilding; he added with a laugh."

"So, you and that cocksucker from the mechanic shop made a side deal and you betrayed your own blood Joe."

"Blood my ass, the only reason he had anything at all to do with me, is because his fucking brother got my whore mother pregnant."

"So, what you getting out of the deal Joe?"

"The gym will be all mine, and the money from this load, which I'll still get if you don't want anything to happen to that beautiful" gringa" of yours. My plan was to be with her when she got the call that you were dead, allowing me to be the friend to lean on, and console her. Eventually, Rhonda would come to see me as more than just a friend and then she becomes my woman and the rich owner of two gyms."

"What a stupid plan dude, what about Irene, and did you think the soldiers would let you get away with betraying their patron."

"I've already ended my relationship with Irene and sent her back to Mexico and the gringo soldiers work for a price. My money is just as green as Victor Ortega's, I don't think they will be a problem. Now where is my money Mike, please tell me I won't have to harm Rhonda and that little half-breed to let you know how serious I am. Since you ain't dead I assume you still have the RV and my money, just bring the RV here to your home and I'll take over from there."

"I'm going back inside to finish my work out, then I'm going to take your wife and son out for dinner, when can I expect to see you and my money?"

"The RV is at a shop having the tires repaired and getting the windshield, your pals shot out replaced. I should be home sometime before noon tomorrow, you harm my family and I'll kill you myself Joe John."

"My men were supposed to kill you today Mike but no matter I can do it myself," and then he hung up.

I turned to the Angels, "that son of a bitch Joe John made a side deal with Javier's former crew and somebody down in Mexico, Victor Ortega and all his men are dead," he said.

"I was really disappointed.to hear he's involved in all this, now I've got to get him away from my family before I kill him. You were right Steve; those men were ordered to kill me, take the cash and just leave the RV for the cops. He as much as labeled you men whores, who's only concern is getting paid, I guess he intended for me to let y'all know he'll be paying you" fellas" from now on."

"That piece of shit has got us all wrong Mike, said Robbins. Just like in the cowboy movies, we are loyal to the brand, we sign on with. Joe John betrayed the Ortega's, which means he betrayed me and Todd, what's your next plan of action Mike."

"He wants me to bring the RV to the island and trade it, and the money for my wife and son. I ain't about to reward that ass- hole for trying to kill me and threatening to harm my family. The next time I lay eyes on Joe John Serbantez, he's a dead man."

"Slow it down some Mike, don't forget he's holding your family hostage, even if they ain't aware of it. Where is he right now, asked Forbes?"

"At a restaurant, someplace in Galveston having dinner with my woman and kid."

Forbes opened his duffel bag, pulled my Glock from it and gave it to me, "it's still loaded, let's go we can come back for the RV anytime."

"Does your wife's phone ring or vibrate? Forbes questioned.

"If she's in a restaurant I'm sure she'll have it on vibrate, why?"

"I was hoping we could find a way to warn her and get her away from Joe before we get to Galveston. He's got to get the money for any of his betrayal to pay off. So, we still got some leverage on him. He won't hurt your family as long as there is still a chance for him to get the money.

"I forgot to tell y'all, a part of his plan is to be with my woman after I'm dead, so me being dead is still a part of his insane thinking."

"What about his woman chimed in Robbins on our conversation?"

"He says he already got rid of her and sent her back to Mexico."

"Damn said Robbins, seems like he's been planning this shit for a long time, we got to get word to your "olé lady" some kind of way Mike."

Forbes was hauling ass, weaving in and out of traffic going south on interstate forty-five. We were passing through downtown Houston when it came to me,

"I got it I said, I know how to get a message to my wife without letting on to Joe John. My stepsons live on the island, they will do anything if they think their mama is in trouble, I pressed speed dial for Cody, who answered on the third ring,"

"Cody, it's me Mike."

"Hey Mike, you still out of town?"

"Yeah Cody, but I'm on my way home, I don't have time to explain, but I need you to do something urgently important for me. "Anything Mike, just tell me what you need me to do."

"Rhonda and Blaise are in danger right now, they don't know it, but they are. Listen closely, my friend Joe John is not who he seems to be, right now he's somewhere on the island having dinner with your mama and little brother. Call her and tell her David was in a traffic accident and being rushed to John Seeley, keep David out of sight, but meet her and Blaise at the emergency entrance. I'm on my way but I need to get her and your brother away from Joe John, so do whatever you got to do to get that done. As soon as that's done call me back, I'll explain later but for now, I need you to do this for me buddy."

"Okay Mike, we're leaving now."

Rhonda's phone rang, she, Joe John and Blaise were at Joe's crab shack, Blaise with his usual heaping pile of mud bugs, Rhonda and Joe drinking frozen margaritas waiting on him to finish.

"It's my son, excuse me Joe, she said while answering her phone." Joe leaned in to listen, just in case it was me tipping my wife off. After a few seconds, Rhonda leapt to her feet, "David's been in a car wreck Blaise, come on we've got to get over to the hospital."

"Hold on, let me drive you said Joe John," his words fell on deaf ears, Rhonda and Blaise were through the door and in her truck in a flash. Joe hurriedly paid the dinner bill and went after them, by the time he reached the parking lot Rhonda's big blue Chevy Silverado was speeding down the boulevard. Unfortunate for Joe John he didn't know where John Sealy hospital was. By the time he got directions Rhonda was pulling into the John Sealy emergency entrance parking area. She and Blaise spotted Cody standing on the unloading dock and ran in his direction, Cody wrapped his arms around the two of them and hustled them through the emergency room doors. His mother in tears frantically asking the whereabouts of her middle son.

"He's fine mom, said Cody, he's waiting for us in his car out front. Mom, I need for you and Blaise to stop and take a breath, Mike called a while ago and said something not cool is going down with Joe John. This was the only way to get you guys away from him without letting him know Mike was on the way."

"What else did he say Cody, don't leave anything out? Rhonda demanded.

"He said Joe John is not who he seems to be and that he would explain everything later." They went out of the hospital's front entrance and got into David's car,

"now call Mike, mom, he told me to call as soon as you and Blaise were with us."

Joe John walked up to the nurse's station of the emergency ward and requested information on an automobile accident victim named David Fowler who was just brought in.

"We haven't had any auto accident victims in since last night sir," the nurse on duty informed him. He knew immediately he'd been had, now even his fucked-up plan-B had blown up in his face. Joe John's phone chimed, as he sat in his car fuming at how he'd been out done, he had no money nor hostages to bargain with.

He knew it was me, "Mike you fucking" nigger puta" I'm going to kill you and your whole family, I want my money."

"Dude you got as much chance of getting that cash as a snowballs chance in hell and we gonna see who gets killed first, you piece of Mexican shit."

I sent my wife and the boys to the apartment in Houston, the only thing I had to focus on now was finding Joe John and stopping his clock.

CHAPTER
THIRTY-TWO

THE FAMOUS FINAL SCENE

"**H**E'S ALL ALONE now Mike stated Robbins, once Joe made his side deal and conspired to kill his Patron, Victor Ortega, he can't even go back to Mexico. Without the money, every back- stabbing move that him and whoever he's crawled into bed with made, mean absolutely nothing. The Ortega's have friends in Mexico who will eventually learn of his betrayal, without the money he can't even run off and hide. The only thing he's got left is to find you and either hopefully persuade you to see things his way or torture you into turning over the cash to him. He ain't going to quit until he's accomplished one or the other Mike, the ball as they say, is in your court."

"His next thought will be to contact us to find out if we know where you and the money are, said Robbins, and if me and Todd will help him find you or your family. The only option you got, added Forbes, is to find Joe John and make his ass disappear."

"The way I look at it, his little group of bandits could have just as easily killed me and Steve out there, they didn't hesitate to take that state trooper out. Take my word for it, there is going to be hell to pay for that one, I'll lay you five to one the Texas Rangers are right now, all over that shop where you pick up the RV from. Once the law identifies them three dead Mexicans we iced out there saving your ass Mike, they will take them fellows lives apart piece by piece. The governor is going to want somebody's head to chop off for the death of that trooper, I suggest that you never go back to that shop again.

"My vette is still parked in the back I said, more sorrowful than complaining."

"You can get another vette big man said Steve, besides you get to keep the RV and all the cash stashed inside. I say we find Joe John, deep-six his back- stabbing traitor ass, and we split the money up and I'm out of this whole life."

"Y'all can have the RV for all I care Todd.

"Robbins said, turning to his friend, I think this bald headed black dude just laid out our retirement plan for us." While we all were having a good laugh Robbins phone rang, "speak of the devil boys."

"Joe, what the hell is going on man, Robbins screamed at the phone? Some men hit the RV, people died, and we don't know where the shit Dunn is, tell us what the hell is happening, we're on our way back to Waco now."

"There has been a change at the top my friend, but I still need your assistance, I will see to it that you get double for your help. Don Ortega and all his men are dead, I am now the boss, your first assignment is to find Mike or his family. It doesn't matter which is first but if possible, I prefer his woman."

"We'll give you a call when we get our hands-on Dunn, I'm shocked the cops just let him go out there. He must have given them some story, four dead bodies and one a state trooper, he's either the luckiest man in the world or he's setting you up for the law." We was on our way back to Waco when you called, Todd's turning around now, where you gonna be?"

"I know Mike has his family stashed away by now, I'm going back to my ranchero and wait until I hear from you." Once he was off the phone Robbins looked at me and Forbes, and said "what a dumb fucking Mexican, he's going back to his ranch. You'd think after all the people he's betrayed, that would be the last place he'd go."

"Steve said Forbes, you really think Joe believes we'll just forget about him setting us up today."

"Like Mike said, Joe John thinks we're just two poor white trash whores with no honor, who don't care about nothing but the money. Let's consider this our last official act as shooters for Don Victor Ortega, avenging his death by killing the man who betrayed him."

"In a way, Joe's got it right Steve, I said, you are doing it for the money, difference is you cats already have the money."

"I'll call that glass shop and let them know I'll be coming to pick the RV up in a couple of days, let's go to Hockley and make that piece of shit Joe John disappear."

The Angels were right about the extreme efforts the cops would make to get everybody involved in the death of that state trooper. The mechanic shop in Pasadena, Texas on Red Bluff Road was raided by the state troopers the following morning, backed up by a Swat squad and the Pasadena police. The three dead cop killers all had wallets with name and addresses on their driver's license in their pockets. Joe Johns ineptness was becoming more and more obvious, even the gang he recruited was stupid, all three were even employed at the same shop. The search of the property produced three kilos of cocaine and twenty kilos of marijuana, enabling the state troopers to seize everything on the property. Whether I wanted to or not, my satin pearl white ninety-eight Corvette was gone into the government's coffers. I was however able to reacquire my beloved vette by keeping track of the law enforcement state run auctions, I paid only half of what it was worth. The modified engine was worth way more than what I paid for it at the auction.

Just in case we guessed wrong about Joe John we devised a plan to at least get us close to him. The next day Robbins called him, "we got Dunn tied up in the truck Joe, what you want us to do with him?

"Did he tell you where my money is yet?"

"No, we just got him, we caught him at his house about an hour ago."

"Bring him here to my ranchero, I can get his woman later, I might just keep him alive until you find her for me. Let that "nigger puta" watch me fuck her in the ass before I cut her throat like I did to that other white bitch he was married to."

"We should be at your place in about two hours, see you Joe."

"That mother fucker is anxious to put a hurting on you big Mike, he says he's going to keep you alive until we can bring your woman to him. He says he's going to make you watch him fuck her before he kills her right in front of you."

"He's mine when we get there" fellas", he crossed the line fucking with my family Steve. I can tell y'all this now because it don't matter, that dude who was at the ranch before Joe made the mistake of threatening to harm my family. I closed the shop door on his ass the same day he made the threat to me."

Forbes burst into laughter, "Mike, you sly dog, Ortega was certain one of the other Mexican gangs killed Leal to send him a message."

"There's one other thing Joe said, Robbins was trying to stifle his laughter at the action I'd just admitted to them, he says he raped and killed your ex-wife."

"That other dude told me Macy was fertilizing the watermelons out there, you think he was telling the truth?"

"Could be dude, him and Joe love treating women rough, they're half-brothers you know."

"No, I didn't, how's that?"

"Victor's older brother loves fucking young whores, once they get pregnant, he just tosses them away, that old fart has probably got fifty kids running around down in Mexico."

"Get your legs up here on the seat so I can tie your ankles together, we got to make this look real until we get close enough to disarm him."

Robbins did the same to my wrist as we turned onto the gravel road leading to the ranch. I laid down on the rear seat and pretended to be in duress, Joe jerked the door open and with all the extra muscle easily pulled my two-hundred and seventy-pound frame out onto the driveway. Once I was out on the ground he gave me a hard kick in the ribs, that's when Todd pressed the barrel of his revolver to the back of Joe's neck.

"What's this all about Joe asked? as Forbes clamped his free hand on the back of his neck pushing him down to the ground next to me. Robbins bent down with his knife and cut the ropes from my hands and feet. I stood up, dusted myself off and politely kicked Joe John in the head as hard as I could, knocking him out.

When he woke up tied and trussed up like a freshly killed deer, we were out in the watermelon patch. Robbins and I were digging a hole next to him, he shook his head to clear the cobwebs and realized what was happening. The panicked look on his face was priceless,

"I told y'all I was the boss now he started to plead to any of us who was listening. You men work for me, why are you doing this he screamed?"

"We tried to find Macy's grave, so you wouldn't have to be alone Joe I said, no luck so this spot will have to do."

I had the angels drive me back to the island to get Rhonda's truck from the hospital parking lot, then we went to Conroe to get the RV. The tire guys had come over and replaced the two blowouts at the right rear. After paying off both businesses, I drove the RV down to the San Jacinto River and parked in a secluded spot. Forbes followed in his truck and Robbins in Rhonda's, they both parked in a way that prevented any prying eyes from seeing what we were doing. I crawled into the storage compartment and pulled one of the large black bags out and unzipped it.

"How much you think is in there Mike, asked Robbins?"

"I ain't got the slightest idea, and I don't care Steve, I count sixteen bags in all, I say we split them three ways and y'all can take the extra one, and here's the keys to the RV, I said tossing the keys to Forbes."

I passed five of the bags to Forbes and five to Robbins, who then tossed them onto the bed of my wife's truck. As I climbed out of the storage compartment Forbes bent over and crawled into the storage area to retrieve one more bag. He passed it to Robbins who casually tossed it over onto Rhonda's truck, "we insist you take the extra one Mike, giving us, the RV makes us all even brother."

The three of us gave each other brotherly handshakes and hugs, we chugga-lugged a beer together to seal the deal. I climbed into my wife's big blue truck, and it would be four years before I laid eyes on the angels again, now I really was free of the drug trade. I'd already sent my family home and promised to take everyone to dinner when I got home, and to explain the events of the past three days.

I told Rhonda to leave lunch open for me the following day, I took her by the hand and we left the gym together, she followed my directions to a self-storage unit on sixty-first street. She nearly fainted at the sight of all the cash.

THE END

Printed in the United States
By Bookmasters